THESE GIRLS JUST WA...
LOOK FOR THESE WONDER...
DOWNTOWN PRESS ...

Irish Girls About Town

PAINT THE TOWN GREEN WITH THIS INTERNATIONAL BESTSELLER

FEATURING STORIES FROM

MAEVE BINCHY ★ MARIAN KEYES ★ CATHY KELLY

AND THIRTEEN OTHER IRISH WOMEN WRITERS!

Irish Girls Are Back in Town

A HIGH-SPIRITED GATHERING OF ALL-NEW TALES FROM

CECELIA AHERN ★ PATRICIA SCANLAN

GEMMA O'CONNOR ★ SARAH WEBB

AND FIFTEEN OTHER IRISH WOMEN WRITERS!

Scottish Girls About Town

GET READY FOR A HIGHLAND FLING WITH THE STORIES OF

JENNY COLGAN ★ ISLA DEWAR ★ MURIEL GRAY

AND SIXTEEN OTHER SCOTTISH WOMEN WRITERS!

American Girls
A BOUT TOWN

down town press

New York   London   Toronto   Sydney

DOWNTOWN PRESS, published by Pocket Books
1230 Avenue of the Americas, New York, NY 10020

This book is a work of fiction. Names, characters, places and incidents are products of the authors' imagination or are used fictitiously. Any resemblance to actual events or locales or persons, living or dead, is entirely coincidental.

Compilation copyright © 2004 by Simon & Schuster Ltd.
"My Great Brit Book Tour" copyright © 2004 by Adriana Trigiani
"Five" copyright © 2004 by Julianna Baggott
"Leaving a Light On" copyright © 2004 by Claire LaZebnik
"Moving Day" copyright © 2004 by Cindy Chupack
"Yoga Babe" copyright © 2004 by Lauren Henderson
"The Truth About Nigel" copyright © 2004 by Jennifer Weiner
"Voodoo Dolls, C-Cups and Eminem" copyright © 2004 by Melissa Senate
"The Bamboo Confessions" copyright © 2004 by Lauren Weisberger
"Amore" copyright © 2004 by Laura Wolf
"Andromeda on the Street of Ducklings" copyright © 2004 by Judi Hendricks
"Bad Manners" copyright © 2004 by Chris Manby
"The Two-Month Itch" copyright © 2004 by Sarah Mlynowski
"I Know a Woman" copyright © 2004 by Quinn Dalton
"Just Visiting" copyright © 2004 by Nancy Sparling
"Forty Days" copyright © 2004 by Jill Smolinski
"The Uncertainty Principle" copyright © 2004 by Lynda Curnyn
"Small Worlds" copyright © 2004 by Gretchen Laskas

Originally published in Great Britain in 2004 by Pocket Books, an imprint of Simon & Schuster UK Ltd.
Published by arrangement with Simon & Schuster UK Ltd.

All rights reserved, including the right to reproduce this book or portions thereof in any form whatsoever. For information address Pocket Books, 1230 Avenue of the Americas, New York, NY 10020

ISBN-13: 978-1-4165-0731-4
ISBN-10:   1-4165-0731-0

First Downtown Press mass market edition August 2005

10 9 8 7 6 5 4 3 2 1

DOWNTOWN PRESS and colophon are trademarks of Simon & Schuster, Inc.

Cover illustration by Anne Keenan Higgins

Manufactured in the United States of America

For information regarding special discounts for bulk purchases, please contact Simon & Schuster Special Sales at 1-800-456-6798 or business@simonandschuster.com.

Contents

CONTENTS

Foreword

To raise money for charity, America's most popular women writers joined forces to create *American Girls About Town*, a spirited collection of all-new stories. Originally published in the United Kingdom and Ireland, a portion of the proceeds from each book sold were given to Barnardo's, the United Kingdom's largest children's charity, and Make-A-Wish Foundation® International, a nonprofit organization established to grant wishes to children outside the United States who are living with life-threatening medical conditions. Barnardo's, Make-A-Wish Foundation® International and Make-A-Wish Foundation® of America will each receive a donation in connection with the release of the U.S. edition of *American Girls About Town* as well.

The Make-A-Wish Foundation® began in the U.S. in 1980 and quickly spread to other countries. There are presently seventy-five chapters in the U.S. and twenty-seven international affiliates on five continents granting the wishes of children around the world. The Make-A-Wish Foundation® strives to provide wish children and their families with special memories of joy and laughter at a stressful time in their lives. Make-A-Wish Foundation® is the largest wish-granting organization in the world. More than 127,000 wishes have been fulfilled worldwide since 1980. From humble beginnings and fewer than 100 wishes granted in 1981, the Foundation has grown to grant more than 13,000 wishes per year around the world. For more information about the Make-A-Wish Foundation's work in the United States, please visit www.wish.org; and for its work outside the United States, visit www.worldwish.org.

Barnardo's is the largest children's charity in the United Kingdom, supporting over 100,000 children, young people, and families through more than 300 services. Their work with families covers a wide range of age groups and issues, including homelessness, abuse, poverty, and tackling the challenges of disability. For more information about Barnardo's, visit their website at www.barnardos.org.uk.

American Girls

ABOUT TOWN

A Day in the Life of
My Great Brit Book Tour

(plus a fabulous chocolate cake recipe)

ADRIANA TRIGIANI

I should have known that when a certain airline, which will go nameless (clue: one that carries the name of a Madonna pop hit), promises a bassinette for an overseas flight, they guarantee not a bassinette but a shoe box lined in the finest felt from the finest bottom of some poor soul's finest shoe; we were in Big Trouble. When my husband Jim put our daughter Esme into the bassinette, it was like watching a park ranger attempt to stuff a squirrel into a matchbox. The baby howled and wailed so loudly, she frightened the passengers in rows A through J, as the rest of the plane, K through M, just looked at us with hatred. Perhaps our ten-month-old American baby was just too tall, or maybe the bassinette was just too small, but whatever the issue, the baby was determined not to spend ten seconds in her plush (the airline's word, not mine) accommodations.

We had no recourse except to hold the sweet pea in our laps. That's when we learned our baby did not like to be held for longer than fifteen-minute intervals. We began to take volunteers for the hold-her-so-she-won't-cry shift at twenty American dollars per hour. We had three takers, one Texas granny who wouldn't take the money, an American teenager with pierced eyebrows who would, and a British nanny who wanted double. We paid the lovely Miss Havisham (name changed to protect the terse and crabby) her double.

When our daughter decided she was done exhausting her father, she snuggled into his shoulder and went to sleep. Soon my husband was snoring as was Miss Havisham and the bulk of passengers who were not glued to *Notting Hill* as it played on the turkey-platter-sized screen in the bulkhead. The screen was so small that it was a rare thing to see all of Julia Roberts's hair in one shot. Good thing the movie watchers were wearing headsets, as the communal snoring was so loud, you would have thought the flight was a charter on its way to a sleep apnea convention.

As a new mother is wont to do when she gets a free moment, she collapses. I began to weep quietly and wistfully at the way my life has turned out. I had dreamed of this book tour long before our daughter arrived, so thrilled at the thought of taking the UK by storm with my new mid-list hit novel *Honey If You're Leaving Me Take Your Mother With You.* They call it chick lit in my country, and I don't mind. In fact, I don't mind anything since I had the baby, not my deadlines, not the laundry and certainly not my personal appearance. I should have been flattered when an old friend who hadn't seen me since the baby was born complimented me on my uni-brow, thinking it was a homage to the freshly popular painter Frida Kahlo. I assured her it wasn't a homage to anyone, well maybe to a season, my own Ode to Spring, and the caterpillars that come with it. The truth is, I just can't find a spare five minutes to pluck my brows.

Even though I am swamped to the gills and committed up to my eyeballs, I could hardly wait to board the plane for one of my favorite countries. I love Great Britain because it is the setting of some of my favorite books. Imagine Jane Eyre in France or Cathy and Heathcliff in Portugal. Impossible! There's no place like England for hard rain, forbidden love, hot gossip and nannies running off with the man of the house while his wife dies slowly on a morphine drip.

I check my reflection in Esme's training spoon, not liking what I see. I'm already worn out like an old shoe, but I'm hoping this tour will be a grand success. Imagine days spent signing copious numbers of books in towns with "shire" at the end of their names, wearing glamorous clothes to the pubs in Scotland, clopping around Piccadilly Circus in high heels and taking tea every afternoon with attractive male journalists who flirt back and have the quiet intelligence and height of Colin Firth and the wicked sexuality of young Oliver Reed (OK, just my quirky romantic combo). I have a dreamscape for my UK book tour that rivals any sexual fantasies that Elizabeth Barrett ever had after a carriage ride down

Wimpole Street while tipping a bottle of Jamaican rum under a blanket with Robert Browning. I am determined to have a blast with my little family.

"Miss Martinelli! Over here! It's me, Nigel!"

As I push the caravan through customs, baby seat, stroller, and luggage stacked like the stones that formed the base of the Great Pyramids of Egypt, and hubby carries the baby, I look up to see Nigel Waxman who is waving a small British flag at us. We've chatted on the phone and been emailing for months, so Nigel looks exactly as I had hoped. He's chic and trim in all black (very beat poet), and his face is handsome, a real Celtic combo. Imagine if Ringo Starr and Pierce Brosnan had a baby.

"Kiss, kiss, come darling, we must get to the television studio. Here's a mint."

Nigel gives me a small mint, which I nearly choke on as I introduce my husband and baby. "I hate children generally, but your baby is adorable and I love her instantly!" he says as he coochie coochie coos Esme. It is love at first sight for her, too. "Now, we must run. The telly awaits us."

"What telly?"

"Oh, I got you a last-minute booking on a fabulous television show."

"But I look terrible."

Nigel raises an eyebrow and takes a closer look at me. "The makeup artists at this show are magicians."

"Can they make broken blood vessels around my nose from three hours of pushing out Esme during hard labor disappear?" I chomp down on Nigel's mint.

As I chew I realize it isn't the candy that has shattered into rocky rubble, but my back molar. I grab my jaw.

"What's wrong?" my husband asks instantly. I groan and point to my tooth. Jim looks into my mouth; his face goes from concern to worry. "You're right, it's your back tooth. It's missing a wall."

Nigel, who has plowed ahead, turns around impatiently. He sees us huddled in agony and runs to us. "Did you get robbed?" Jim explains what has happened. Esme listens to her father as though she understands every word. She has never seen me like this and is fascinated by her mother in pain. "Here is the plan," Nigel begins, "we stop at the pharmacy and get a temporary tooth kit."

"Temp . . ." I try to speak but when I do my tongue lashes against the broken tooth like a sea serpent being bludgeoned by a pirate in one of those old B movies.

"Don't speak," Jim instructs me.

"It is a kit, darling. It has paste, wax and tools. This very thing happened to me on holiday and I fixed it up and went along with my day. In fact it worked so well, I ate roast at dinner that night and met the love of my life over dessert, all with a temporary filling. You must remain calm." Suddenly Nigel sounds like Julie Andrews as Mary Poppins, but like all of weak faith (and those in pain), I am looking for someone to hang on to. I want to believe that he can fix this tooth. "Now let go of my arm, darling. After I spackle, and you become a UK television star, I'll take you to my dentist."

"Now open wide," Nigel instructs as he spackles my tooth. Esme opens her mouth wide too, as does Jim.

Nigel heats up a small ball of wax and stuffs it onto the side of the tooth. "How does that feel?"

"OK," I tell him but "OK" sounds like "Mokie."

I look in the mirror. My right jaw protrudes, reminding me of Marlon Brando in *The Godfather.*

"Honey, take Esme for a walk," I say to my husband. He has to process what I said for a moment, and then quickly he says, "Yes. Yes."

"Do I sound funny?" I ask.

"Only on 's' sounds," Nigel chirps.

I want to cry. Jim smiles at me sadly as he takes Esme out of the dressing room.

A tall, cool blond breezes in. "I'm Charlotte. I'm doing your makeup." I marvel at her strong jawline, which doesn't have an acorn-sized lump like mine. "You will love the host Jenny Barnett."

"Hellloooo." An alabaster brunette beauty in the English rose tradition of Elizabeth Taylor sticks her head in the door. "I'm Jenny. I love your book. Good fun! And the cake recipe!"

"Did it turn out all right?" I say slowly. Nigel explained in the car on the way over that this show makes recipes from books and then interviews the authors as the dish is prepared on television. "Did it turn out all right?" I ask Jenny again. Jenny's head bobs as she follows each of my over-annunciated words like she's watching a juggler's balls in midair at the circus.

"Darling, I heard about the tooth. You sound *fine,*" she says reassuringly, which tells me that I must sound horrible.

"I'll try," I promise. Of course, I sound like I said "I fry." Jenny pretends not to notice.

"We made your cake and thank goodness we made two, because one was completely gobbled by the crew. Can you take a look at this recipe to make sure we have it down correctly?" Jenny gives me a card with the Chocolate Coca-Cola Cake recipe.

CHOCOLATE COCA-COLA CAKE

CAKE
2 cups plain flour
2 cups sugar
A pinch of salt
2 sticks butter
3 tablespoons cocoa
1 cup Coca-Cola
1½ cups miniature marshmallows
½ cup buttermilk
2 eggs, well beaten
1 teaspoon vanilla

ICING
1 stick butter
3 tablespoons cocoa
6 tablespoons Coca-Cola
1 pound powdered sugar
1 teaspoon vanilla

1. For cake: Combine flour, sugar and salt in a saucepan, combine and heat butter, cocoa, Coca-Cola and marshmallows until it begins to boil (add marshmallows last) . . . remove from heat and stir to dissolve marshmallows.

Pour over sugar and flour, and blend well . . .
add remaining cake ingredients and blend
well. Pour into greased 9 x 13 pan and bake
at 350° for 30 to 40 minutes.

2. For icing: Combine butter, cocoa and Coca-
Cola in a saucepan and bring to a boil . . .
mix with powdered sugar and vanilla till it
makes a thin paste, then drizzle over the cake
while it's hot from the oven.

A haggard stage manager (no more haggard-looking
than me) bolts in. "Jen, you're on in five. Miss
Martini . . ." He looks at me.

"Martinelli."

"What?" he says impatiently.

"Martinelli," Nigel says quickly. He implores the
stage manager with a look that says, Isn't this one pathetic? Then looks at me sadly.

"You're up at the top of the show. The cake is a
smash." The stage manager goes. "See there? The crew
adores you already."

"Nigel, I can't *talk.*"

Nigel looks at me as though he is one of those
world leaders who wears a headset at the United Na-
tions and is on tape delay for the translation. Once he
figures out what I've actually said, he pipes up. "Oh,
right, right. Just nod and smile a lot, and let Jenny run
the show. You'll do fine."

Nigel leads me down a hallway and a set of metal
stairs to a door marked studio. He pulls the door open
and ushers me in first. Jenny is talking to the camera.
"The show is live," Nigel whispers.

"*Now* you tell me?"

Suddenly the crew convenes on the stage, a glamorous stage kitchen with a gorgeous cooking island in the center. A team of men commences moving chairs and cameras and tables reconfiguring the lot. Jenny stands in the midst of the fray reading off cards. The stage manager grabs me and puts me in the center on a bar stool next to the cooking island. Two absolutely stunning male models stand by.

"Do you like my bookends?" Jenny winks at the male models.

"They're cute," I tell her. She gives me the same look of confusion that Nigel does, except she is quicker to decipher my poor speech.

"Yes, yes, *cute*. That's a very American way of putting it." Jenny laughs.

A young woman steps behind the camera and counts back from five.

"We have a treat for you this morning." Jenny speaks directly to the camera. "Anna Martinelli joins us from New York City. How do you like the UK?"

"Smashing." I smile to the camera. Catching my reflection in the monitor, I quickly move the bad jaw upstage so as not to frighten the viewers at home.

"Say hello to Jeff and Dino."

Instead of speaking, I nod to the handsome models.

Jeff, or is it Dino, looks into the camera, while slicing huge hunks of Chocolate Coca-Cola Cake and shoving it onto delicate bone china dessert plates. As they arrange it artfully on the dish, they explain the ingredients.

"What a sweet treat!" Jenny takes a bite.

"It's as if cake and fudge had a baby," I offer.

Jenny looks confused, as do the male models. "Oh quite right. Fudge and Cake had a baby."

"Jeff?" I ask.

"No, I'm Dino, he is Jeff."

"Is this the first time you baked?" Jeff and Dino instantly look confused.

"Do you know who we are?" Dino asks.

"You're . . . I don't know."

"We're chefs. I'm at the four star Brigadoon restaurant . . ." Dino begins.

". . . And I own Winston's," Jeff adds.

"Oh," I say brightly. Suddenly everyone understands my speech it seems.

"Now, do you understand?" Jenny says gaily. "These are real chefs. They are also menopausal eye candy, but they do have talent too."

"Mr. Delicious," I point to Dino, ". . . and Mr. Scrumptious," I point to Jeff.

"Yes, yes! Now you've got it!" Jenny applauds. Then, in what I will remember on my deathbed as a mad blur, Jenny describes my novel to the viewers. I see peppy Nigel pacing off camera, but smiling. I look over to the studio door with the porthole window in it and see Esme's tongue licking the glass from the other side and her father pulling her away and winking at me.

"Jenny? May I say something?"

"Of course, darling."

I look into the camera. "Dear people of the United Kingdom . . . we had a terrible flight. The baby wouldn't sleep. And when we landed, Nigel, he's my publicist, gave me a mint and I bit it and then I broke a tooth. My cheek is usually not this swollen. And I'm usually in better shape. I'm normally quite thin, but I haven't been able to lose the twenty pounds, I don't know the translation in stones, but I put on the weight with Esme. Please don't judge me with this speech impediment and bad hair. I'm really quite funny . . ." Suddenly, it all is just too overwhelming and I begin to weep.

"Oh for God's sake, we're all working mothers, darling!" Jenny says graciously. "Jeff, Dino, give this American author a hug." Jeff and Dino embrace me. "That's it. A hug sandwich! Two hunks of burning love and a . . ."

"Slab of American cheese," I add.

"Hilarious! I love it!" Jenny thanks me, and the cameras pull away to another part of the set. "You were magnificent. You turned that rotten tooth into a comic monologue. I loved it! You're a genius!" The crew seems to agree with Jenny. Nigel runs over to me. "Tomorrow when you do the BBC breakfast show, I'm going to blacken your front tooth. You were marvelous! Marvelous!" Nigel practically jumps up and down.

"May we go to the dentist now?" I ask meekly.

"Of course! Though, I'd rather you keep the lump." Nigel holds my jaw tenderly. "The lump is golden!" I look over to my husband and Esme. Jim is holding up Esme's hand, giving me a thumbs-up.

As I follow Nigel out the studio door and through the catacombs back to our car, Esme reaches for me. I take her into my arms, and for a moment I forget the perfect picture I had of this book tour. I wanted to be funny, glamorous and smart on the telly. Instead, I looked and felt like every mommy that ever had a bad day, or should I say, disastrous day. It's our first day of the book tour and I have already learned a big lesson: let go. Let go of the perfect picture and embrace the moment because the moment is extraordinary.

"I hope you're going to shake this pensive mood," Nigel says as he takes Esme into his arms and hands her off to Jim. He helps me into the car. "And don't be afraid. My dentist is the best. See?" Nigel opens his mouth widely as the lion does in Esme's circus book. "They're quite straight and lovely, aren't they?" Nigel asks.

"Beautiful." Except when I say it with the temporary tooth it sounds like "Dutiful."

"I know that our reputation around the world is that our British teeth are a bit like tombstones—we can thank Charles Dickens for that—but the truth is, we have come a long way with our dentistry. I would put our choppers up against any in the industrialized world. Or Hollywood," Nigel says with a grin.

"You sold me," I promise Nigel.

As we careen through London, I hold my baby and my jaw, and rest against Jim, who looks fifty years older than he did the day I married him, eight years ago, when he was only twenty-seven. I have ruined this man with a crazy life.

"Are you happy?" I ask my husband, as I do whenever I feel a bit vulnerable.

Jim looks confused for a moment, and then quickly deciphers what I said. "You're never boring, Anna." He kisses me on the forehead. And that, on the first day of my very first UK book tour, is accurate.

———————————

ADRIANA TRIGIANI grew up in Big Stone Gap, Virginia, and now lives in New York City. As well as being the internationally bestselling author of *The Queen of the Big Time, Big Stone Gap, Big Cherry Holler, Milk Glass Moon,* and *Lucia, Lucia,* Adriana is an award-winning playwright, television writer, and documentary film-maker.

Five

JULIANNA BAGGOTT

"When we were kids, she wouldn't take the elevator at LeMar's department store if the doors opened as soon as she pushed the button. She said she didn't trust anything too willing to take her for a ride." I'm talking to my husband (soon to be ex) about Elysius, my sister. I'm her opposite; it's one of the ways I define myself. "I loved LeMar's elevators. I'd jump on them any chance I got, push buttons, glide from floor to floor with nowhere special to go."

Bobby and I live in a Memphis suburb where the men sit in saggy lawn chairs on Sunday afternoons, soaking their feet in metal tubs where their beer cans go from cool to piss warm, and the wives bitch over rusty fences about grass seed that won't root. In the bend of one elbow, I've got the strap of a plastic bag crammed full of last-minute bathroom stuff—lip liners, panty liners, a half-eaten roll of Tums. I'm already in my traveling clothes: a tank top, short shorts and go-go boots from high-school marching band, which were a bitch to zipper and now cut into my calves. Every once in a while Bobby sighs. He's my fourth husband. I'm twenty-seven. He knows I'm leaving, even my dog Fipps knows it. He's outside digging up backyard bones.

"I know. I didn't marry your sister," Bobby tells me. He's an environmental scientist who wants to lecture everybody about the corporate destruction of the planet, but doesn't. He holds back. It's his nature, which makes this whole scene easier.

I bend over to pluck aromatherapy candles from the tub's moldy corners. "If Elysius was in my shoes—and believe me my sister wouldn't be caught dead in my shoes—she'd stick this out. That's the right decision here." Elysius lives in California in a *très* modern house with her one and only husband, a hugely successful artist.

I don't make the right decisions. Bobby knew that going into the deal. Fourth husbands have to be both blindly optimistic and soberly realistic. I'm reminding him, though, that he was fairly warned; somehow that absolves me a bit.

When I was fourteen, I seduced a deli clerk, Chip. His hands smelled like pepperoni and honey ham and there were always bits of cheese in his hair from where it caught and spun out of the slicer. I convinced him that he should get himself out of Kernersville, North Carolina, and take me, a junior on the twirling squad,

with him. On the highway out of town, I did a backbend out the window and flashed truckers my tits with
the warm wind in my yellow hair and the road whipping below my head and the whole upside-down
world in front of me. He was my first husband and I
loved him. But he cried a lot because he missed his
buddies, which really meant his mother and everything familiar, and so after two weeks of wedded
sniveling bliss, I sent him home.

I loved all of my husbands for different reasons in
different ways—Chip, for the way he found a small
bird outside our little walk-up and cupped it in his
hand and fed it with a dropper; Pat, because of the
way he counted syllables to poems on my back when
he held me at night; Joe, because he was good with
numbers and could make things with his hands, step
ladders and boats in bottles; and Bobby, for reasons
yet to reveal themselves in their fullest proportions,
but right now for his patience.

Elysius doesn't believe that I've loved any of them.
"You only love yourself," she said when I called a few
weeks ago to tell her that I was getting itchy. "This
type of love-them-and-leave-them behavior gives you a
perverse kick."

She's wrong. The whole process—falling in love and
hoping and falling out of it and leaving—eases my
wanting. My father left us right before Elysius was off
to college, a scholarship to UNC. He was a flight in-
structor for a rinky-dink operation and one day he
scribbled a note on the back of a water bill and slid it
under a sweaty glass of sweet tea.

I don't think about him as much as I think about

what life was like minus him. My mother moved us in with his mother who lived in a one-bed one-bedroom house. I was a virgin tucked between two celibates, and we were all three wanting, wanting, wanting, the walls of the house seemed to breathe with all of our desires: my mother for her husband, my grandmother for her missing son, and me, at first for a father and then for a lover and soon I was gone.

I sent Elysius letters about how I was going crazy listening to Grandmother pick at Mother, "For God's sake get a pillow to sit on, you have no ass," and how Mother was a bundle of nerves, rattling teacups against saucers, staring up at the sky for Daddy to appear in his tiny airplane, a parachute flapping open at his back, floating him down to earth like Mary Poppins and her little umbrella. But Elysius told me not to write about those things, that if anyone found a letter like mine at college she'd have no friends. But I went on writing her—from Austin, Hoboken, Baltimore, Boston, and a million Lizard Lick towns in between. I still send her letters. I never stopped. Just last week, I sent her a postcard of a really old Elvis impersonator with chops painted onto his jowls. On the back I wrote that I was leaving Bobby and that she should be expecting me to show up any day. Then I said I was wanting again, so bad I felt like I was choking on it, like choking on a beer bong in back of the Tastee Freeze dumpsters in freshman year of high school.

Elysius hates when I bring up life in Kernersville, but even more she hates the idea that I might just show up. I pepper all of my letters to her with cherry lip gloss, Aquanet hair spray and tube tops—the kitsch that made up our hometown—and a lot of travel arrangements. But this time she knows I might just end up there. I usually do whenever I leave a husband.

I've got to go. If I don't, I can tell that one day soon Bobby will come home with a metal tub for beer and folding chair; he'll take root in the front lawn, and I'll take root at the fence, and we'll be stuck on our bald splotch of yard for the rest of our lives. There are those signs of excessive contentment. He's started patting my hands when he passes me in the kitchen. Long kisses have been replaced by these automated Santa type of cheek-pecks. Instead of a fiery argument, we may as well just press the Play button and go to bed. We've been together well over two years.

I unlock the door and open it to find him, staring at me wide-eyed. "These boots were made for walking," I say.

"I thought they were made for girls in high school who quit the twirling section of the marching band to get married." He looks sad.

"You get the picture though."

"I've seen this picture coming." He steps back to let me pass. I can see he's shaking and I think he's going to cry but then he laughs. "It's a relief," he says. "You haven't really been all here for a while. I should be good at missing you. I've had the practice."

I realize I love him because I don't ever think he really trusted me. He's known all along that I would bail out but was fine to go for a ride, for as long or short as it lasted. He was fine with the idea that one day—today, in fact—the bell on LeMar's elevator would ding and I'd get off on one of the floors without him. That's right, maybe that's what I love most, and I make a mental note of it.

I can't imagine driving across country in a palsied Toyota with Fipps itching beside me on the seat, all of those miles and miles of nothing. I prefer not to soul-search in the wide stretches between 7-Eleven Big Gulps and sleepless nights at Super 8s. So, I get a sour deal for my truck from a used car salesman who snaps his gum and calls me "little lady," even though I'm three inches taller than he is. I get a ride to the airport from a friend, Janet, who has already taken Bobby's side and fiddles with the radio, the sun visor, change in the ashtray, anything not to talk to me. I can't blame her. As I get out at the airport curb, she says, "He was too good for you. You know that?"

"That kind of thing doesn't really play into it," I tell her. "That's not really the point."

"You're a strange woman."

"I know."

She drives away as I'm waving.

I buy a plane ticket, one-way, and pack Fipps in one of those airport cages. I get an aisle seat next to a woman a little older than I am, an artist type with clay under her nails and a heavy metallic doodad on a long piece of shiny cord for a necklace. I look at her and can tell that being her is my worst fear, a possibility. In just one glance I know that she's one of those women who lists her dog on her answering machine like the oddly named lover she doesn't have . . . *Tippy and I can't come to the phone right now* . . . and she lives in an apartment building filled with women who list cats and parakeets on their answering machines, *Jacques and I can't come to the phone, Poppie and I can't come to the phone,* who shuffle the halls in thin sweaters, saying over and over, *My, it's terribly chilly.* I think of my mother after my father left and I look over at the artsy lady. She has poofy hair and a wide rump. I cry from the moment the seatbelt light dings till we land.

Elysius's husband thinks I'm a kick in the pants. I say, "How's it hanging, Alex?" And he whips away from his painting, takes off his glasses and blushes. He draws the glasses to his chest and folds up his chins like a little accordion. I'm the only one who treats him like he won't fall to bits if I tell him he's got a piece of spinach gummed up in his teeth. I come to his studio out back because if I ring the front door, Elysius won't let me in.

"Tilly," he says. "I hope you've come to stay for a while."

I'm surveying his new paintings. They're abstract, which means that you feel sad when you look at them but don't know why. Art snobs just eat them up. They're chaotic, but calming.

"What's this one supposed to be?" I ask him.

"A boat far off, with full sails," he says. "And loss."

I sit down on a stool and unzip my boots. My feet are swollen and tender. "You've got to cheer up," I tell him.

"My cheerleader has arrived."

"Twirler," I remind him. "I was good even with both ends lit on fire." I know that people don't respect twirlers much, but I was damn gifted. In my spangled leotard with its flared skirt and my go-go boots, I could throw that baton up into the sky, turning myself around, and I knew that it would land in my palm, spinning like crazy. I was a sight to see. The football crowds roared.

"The little dog, Fipps? And Bobby? Are they with you?"

"Bobby didn't make the final cut, if you know what I mean. The lady of the house at home?"

He nods solemnly and I drift outside.

Fipps is squatting his little territorial pee-pees all over the yard, and I walk up the back steps into the kitchen. I dump my purse on the table, eyeliners and lipsticks rolling to the floor, and rummage through a little pile of receipts folded with wads of gum, tampons that have shed their wrappings, fuzzy stray lifesavers, and find a neon lighter and one dented cigarette. I walk through the house, puff my cigarette, run my hands over little statues and bumpy canvases.

I'm amazed how Elysius has arranged this perfect life in a big house out in the Palisades by taking small steps in sensible heels with a matching handbag. If California broke off and fell into the ocean, Elysius would be absolutely prepared. She's probably growing gills this very minute for just such an emergency.

All the appliances are in black as if mourning the death of a fallen dishwasher or something, and so shiny I see myself all over the place in warped reflections. The living room furniture is so sleek I'm afraid I might slide off if I try to sit down. It's airy and high-ceilinged, almost echoey. Everything's perfect, a geometric wet dream, but still I feel like there's something about Elysius's house that's not right. I can't quite put my finger on it.

Soon enough, I hear Elysius's high heels clatter down the steps in a mad scurry for the kitchen. She pauses in the doorway. I'm staring out the back window at Fipps now curled in a sun spot near a tree. I'm feeling warmer too.

"Jesus, I thought something was on fire. Put that thing out."

I'm finished anyhow and hand the cigarette to her. She holds it under the faucet and then throws it in a garbage can hidden under the sink. "So I take it Bobby's been left behind?"

"You could say that." I change the subject quickly before she can start in on me. "You look smashing, darling," I say in an accent that probably doesn't make much sense.

"We're going to a dinner party. Isn't Alex in yet?"

"Oh, no, no, thank you, really it's sweet of you to invite me, but I haven't shit to wear."

"No kidding," she says, looking me over. I'm still in my short shorts and tank top. My go-go boots are unzipped and flapping open.

"You know Alex will ask me to come along. He'll say he wouldn't hear of me not going."

Elysius leans over the sink. She's beautiful, wearing white full-legged pants and a sleeveless suit top. She's that creamy color all over with dark dark hair, the beauty our mother was once a long time ago. She looks nothing like me, always yellow haired and tan.

"For God's sake," she sighs.

"Do you have anything shiny in a size eight, silvery or gold?"

Elysius sighs heavily and rolls her eyes. "Clean up that crap and come on."

I rake my stuff off her kitchen table into my purse, scoop up the things that fell on the floor, and follow Elysius upstairs. She doesn't fool me. She uses Alex, her total agreement with all of his wishes to protect his frail genius spirit, as an excuse. The truth is, I'm family. Mother died first. She had a rattling cough that turned to pneumonia and she refused to leave the house. The sun from the window warmed a square of light on her bed each afternoon and she had a view of the sky. Grandmother died a few months later, mainly I think because there was no one to pick on, to fight with, so she just quit. There is a handful of uncles and aunts all with their own oddball lives, but I'm the only family Elysius's got, really, and she knows it.

Her bedroom looks fluffed, colors picking up bits of themselves from curtains and blankets and paintings. She pulls out a black sleeveless dress, flowy and a little sheer but casual, and hands it to me. I hold it up, tightening it around my waist with one arm and peeking through the triangle of the hanger. I twist this way and that to see if the dress will flare out if I turn quickly.

"When are you going to settle down?" she asks.

I hold up one hand, palm wide open like I'm about to catch a baton, both ends lit on fire: number five.

Elysius laughs. "What makes you think number five will be any different than husbands one through four?"

"If you take out the ingredient of hope, the whole soup tastes like water." I'm not sure if I can convince myself with the hope talk this time around. I've been feeling a little weary. But the first step is convincing others. I kick off my shoes and shimmy out of my short shorts.

Elysius is sitting on the edge of the bed, legs crossed at the ankles. "You should settle down and have kids." Elysius knows that I've never had much interest in kids. I didn't really much care for them even when I was one. I know that if I had one now I couldn't leave it the way I do a husband, and so I'd end up wanting something else and resenting it for keeping me pinned down.

"Auntie Elysius, you're one to talk," I say. She's thirty-eight. In Kernersville she'd be the age of some grandmothers.

"Some people are meant only to be aunts and uncles," she says. "A few things, no matter how much money and science you throw at them, are still decided by God."

And that's when I realize what's wrong with the house. I recognize the wanting. I think of Alex's boat.

As I step into the black dress, I imagine Elysius staring at the white toilet bowl tinged red with blood month after month, trying to muster hope at the end of it, how it must have grown tougher each time until finally she just gave up. "Oh, sorry," I tell her. "I didn't know. I was just mouthing off."

She sighs and hands me a pair of low-heeled strappy shoes and stands next to me in the mirror. With the tilt of our heads, the slant of our hips, our small high breasts, and the weariness just around the eyes, for a second, anyone would guess we were sisters.

★   ★   ★

It's an outdoor party with colored lanterns strung up around the edges of a pink-and-white-striped tent. I drink too much wine and wander the edges of the party, at one point almost falling into a small pond catching the runoff from a lawn waterfall. Everyone is smily and coupled-up. It's the picture-perfect world that Elysius always dreamed of, the place she belongs, and I'm wondering if anyone can tell that I'm thinking about Bobby in Memphis, trying to figure out what he could be doing and then its opposite, because I never could figure him out. I imagine him lonely, wallowing in our bed covered with snapshots of the two of us, a bottle of Jack spilling on the bed sheets, and then I envision him rocking my single friend Janet's trailer, their bodies pressed against her mirrored closet doors. I'm pretty sure I'm the only one in this crowd thinking about my ex doing it in a double wide.

I hold up my hand, signaling number five to Elysius and Alex on the other side of the tent and look around desperately. Elysius laughs. Alex checks his watch like I'm talking about time and then Elysius leans in to explain it to him.

Someone asks me what I do and I muddle my way through a conversation about soil samples, Bobby's job. Later I say I'm an accountant like sensible Joe, but get stumped on a tax dodge question and pretend to choke on a crab puff. Next I say that I'm a poet, like Pat, and I tuck in my chin the way Alex does when he talks about his paintings, and I say that almost everything even laundry snapping on the line is really loss. Then I'm a deli clerk, complaining about how tough it is to get all the cheese out of my hair. Finally, I say,

"I'm a pilot." The woman I'm talking to raises her eyebrows as if she'd expected me to be a dental hygienist, the much too young date of someone rebounding from a nasty divorce. But as soon as it comes out of my mouth, I feel unsteady. "I'm not a pilot," I tell her.

I feel sick and rush off to the house to find a bathroom. I look at myself in the mirror, brush the hair from my eyes and run cool water over my wrists. I'm flushed and dizzy. I linger there—poking around in the medicine cabinet, spritz with hostess's perfumes— until I hear the chatter of a line forming. I open the door and shuffle past them.

I walk to the balcony overlooking the yard. A young man follows me. He's short and handsome despite his wide teeth. "Can I join you?" he asks.

"Sure," I say.

"So, how do you know the Wettsteins?"

"Is that who lives here?"

He nods a little, shaken, like he's not sure he pronounced it right.

"I'm a baton twirler from Kernersville, North Carolina. I wouldn't know a Wettstein if I'd fucked one." And it feels good to say it. I stare at him the way I used to look out over the football crowds after I'd spun around and caught the baton, its fiery ends ablaze. He takes a step backward and then hurries into the house. I wonder if there'll be a number five at all.

I stay there to watch the lanterns bob in the breeze and Elysius drift among her friends. The wind picks up. The guests trickle home. It starts to rain, lightly, and those still on the lawn rush inside as if they might melt, and it occurs to me that maybe they will.

I shut my eyes as each drop cools my arms and face. When I open them, I notice that Elysius and Alex are standing at the edge of the tent. They're looking out over the yard. Alex has wrapped his arms around her shoulders, standing behind her. His mouth is near her ear and she's smiling. And then the wind blows a white tablecloth up and it billows across the yard. Elysius and Alex and a few workers start after it, running downhill, to catch it before it flies off. Elysius is beautiful, running after the white cloth, something that's all wings. It's the most goddamn beautiful thing I've seen.

The borrowed dress clings to my skin. The gauze is a little rough and feels too tight across my shoulders. I feel like I've got to make a decision, like I just have to give a little nod to myself, some future me who seems to already know what I'm going to do. And that future me is not Elysius or my mother, not the sum of the men I've loved, a figure neatly printed beneath a line.

Elysius and Alex are folding the linen like kids playing house. Behind me, a dishwasher hums. It's comfortably quiet, and even though I'm alone it's like I'm standing with someone that I could spend hours with, never saying a word.

JULIANNA BAGGOTT is the acclaimed author of three bestselling novels, *Girl Talk*, *The Miss America Family*, and *The Madam*, as well as a book of poems, *This Country of Mothers*. Her work has appeared in dozens of publications, including *Glamour, Best American Poetry 2000,* and *Ms. Magazine,* and has been read on NPR's *Talk of the Nation.*

She lives in Newark, Delaware, with her husband and family.

Leaving a Light On

CLAIRE LaZEBNIK

*I*t was one of those glorious evenings in early fall when the light turns golden at around seven o'clock, and the way it glitters on certain leaves and windows and throws everything else into deep shadow makes your throat catch, and you think, from now on, I'm not going to be ordinary or do ordinary things. There is greatness in my future.

Kathy was going to a bar.

Technically, it was a restaurant, but she wasn't interested in the eating part. She was planning to sit down at the bar—written up not long ago in some magazine as one of the ten hottest nightspots in Los Angeles— get a big stiff drink, sip it slowly, and wait. And, at the end of the evening, she would not be leaving alone.

Kathy pulled her car up to the valet stand. As she

undid her seatbelt, she leaned forward to check her face one last time in the rearview mirror. She looked good. She had blown her wavy hair straight and rubbed a few drops of shine serum in it, so it fell long and sleek on her shoulders. She was wearing a lot of makeup, and, since most days she didn't wear any, she looked not like her regular self, and she liked that.

As she swung her feet out of the car, Kathy admired the new spike-heeled black mules she was wearing. Even if they made her lurch a bit, they were worth it. She stood up and tugged the short skirt of her dress back into place. It was a killer dress—black, like a sexy dress *should* be, with tiny little spaghetti straps and a neckline that dipped low.

As she took the ticket from the valet, it occurred to Kathy that she wouldn't mind running into an old boyfriend that evening. And Kathy only ever thought that when she knew she was looking pretty damn amazing.

Like the twilight outside, the restaurant flickered with a range of golden light and dark shadows. The dining room had white tablecloths and clean-looking blond-wood booths and was half empty. The bar, by contrast, had dark wine-colored leather stools and tiny black tables, most of them occupied. People were there in groups—twos, threes, fours, some crowded around small tables, some sitting at the bar, most standing. Kathy didn't see anyone who was there alone.

She wasn't worried. The night was throbbing in her veins, and she knew someone would come, if not now, then in a little while. She wasn't in any hurry and liked the idea of being by herself at first, surveying the territory, picking out the right spot to sit and wait.

She found a stool she liked near the end of the bar, with an empty seat on each side, and slid into it. The cute bartender, who was pouring martinis for an extremely young couple—God, they couldn't have actually been twenty-one, either of them, could they?—spotted her and winked, holding up one finger. She smiled at him, a bigger smile than the moment deserved, but she knew she had a great smile and was in the mood to use it.

She liked the look of the martinis, so when the waiter was done and had come over to her and asked her what she wanted, she ordered one.

"Vodka or gin?" he asked.

"Vodka."

"Any special kind?"

"Surprise me," she said, knowing that might mean she got cheaper vodka, but she didn't care, she wanted to flirt for a second, and a few ounces of Stoli were a small price to pay for seeing the handsome bartender wink again and tell her he'd do his best.

"You having dinner here?" he asked as he made her drink. The bottles were right behind him, so he could talk to her and pour at the same time, swiveling smoothly from the hips when he reached back to grab the things he needed.

"I don't know yet," she said, watching how he moved, his hands fast and assured as he poured the vermouth into the shaker, swished it around and poured it back out again. "Should I? Is it good?"

"That's what they tell me," he said, pouring the

vodka now. Grey Goose, so he hadn't stiffed her, after all. "I've never actually eaten here."

"They keep you too busy?"

"Something like that. Hold on now. You still want me to surprise you?"

"Definitely," Kathy said.

"Then close your eyes."

She covered her eyes with her hands, laughing through her palms, and when he told her to look again, there was a martini glass in front of her, and in it was a long toothpick with seven olives strung one after the other.

"Good?" he said.

"Fantastic." She didn't even like olives all that much, but she loved that he had tried to surprise her.

He poured the contents of the shaker into the glass and waited while she tasted it.

"Good?" he said again. His eyes were light blue, and his arms rippled with strong muscles under the white T-shirt that seemed to be part of a uniform, since the waiters at the restaurant wore them, too.

"Very good. Perfect." And it was. Everything was perfect at that moment.

"You want anything to eat with that? You can order from the menu here, you know. Everyone gets the crab cakes."

"I think I'll wait," she said.

He seemed to want to linger, but more people were walking up to the bar, and he took a reluctant step back. "Should I leave your tab open or do you want to settle it?"

"Open please," she said. "The night's young."

"Call me if you need anything," he said. "My name's Brad."

"Of course it is," she said, pleased. He smiled uncertainly, not knowing what amused her but willing to be a good sport about it, and, as he moved off, Kathy didn't even care that he was only being friendly because he wanted a big tip, or that she was at least ten years older than he was. She liked Brad. She was having a good night.

Right after Brad went off to take a drink order farther down the counter, a man came up next to Kathy. He didn't sit down, just squeezed in between the two empty stools on her left. She looked sideways at him and knew he wasn't the right guy but flashed him a friendly smile anyway.

"Hi," he said, nodding back at her. He was on the young side and a little fat, with a round baby face and a stomach that was squeezing over the top of his suit pants. "Just missed him, didn't I?"

"He'll be back," she said.

There was a pause and then he said, "How's your martini?"

"Excellent," she said. "You should get one."

"I'm more of a scotch man. Christ, it's hot in here, isn't it?" Sweat had slicked the hair on his forehead down along his temples.

"I guess," said Kathy who was perfectly comfortable.

"Women are lucky. They don't have to wear jackets."

"We get cold a lot, though."

"I guess that's probably true. That's a nice dress."

"Thanks."

Brad came up then. "What can I get for you?" he asked the man. Kathy noticed he was much more brusque with the man than he had been with her.

"Two scotches. Neat."

"Dewar's all right?"

"Fine."

Kathy was kind of relieved to hear him order two drinks. So someone was waiting back at the tables for him. It wasn't that Kathy was worried he might hit on her, not really. It just meant she didn't even have to think about the possibility. Plus it freed up the stool next to her, where he was currently leaning.

The guy paid for his drinks, said a pleasant goodbye to both of them, and moved away.

Brad said, "Man, he was sweating."

Kathy was thrilled that he trusted her enough to rag on another customer. "He said he was hot."

"I don't doubt it. You need anything?"

"I'm great," she said.

Someone else stepped up to the bar, on Kathy's right side, and Brad said, "How about you? Can I get you anything?"

The guy to her right said, "I'll have what she's having," and Kathy turned to look at him.

He was roughly her age and not bad looking. Not at all. Ten years ago, his hair had probably been thicker and his waist thinner, but he still had broad shoulders and the lines around his eyes were the good-humored kind. There was something about his face that was open and likeable, and this warmth made him more handsome than the quality of his features alone could have achieved. He was wearing a sports jacket over a white shirt that was open at the collar.

She realized he was watching her study him and smiled at him carefully.

"Hello," he said.

"Hi."

"This seat taken?"

"I don't know," she said. "I'll have to think about it."

He kept his hands on the back of the stool. "Give me a chance. I'm a good guy. You'll like me."

Brad the bartender plunked a shaker on the counter. "Grey Goose OK?" he asked.

"Fine."

Kathy said, "What makes you a good guy?"

"Well . . ." He thought for a moment. "I don't kill spiders."

"Oh," she said, then shrugged. "The only problem is that I don't really like spiders. I guess it's good that you don't kill them, but it doesn't really do anything for me."

"I also help old ladies cross the street."

"In hopes of a reward?"

"No," he said. "I just like old ladies."

"Like a grandson? Or in a perverted way?"

"I'm not perverted," he said. "Not in that way, at least."

"All right then," she said. "You can sit there."

They watched Brad mix the drink. It was mesmerizing, Kathy thought, to watch someone make a cocktail. Ritualistic and unpredictable at the same time.

She especially liked the way Brad did it, the muscles in his biceps moving gently under his tan skin, his speed and confidence making it look like the ice and the liquor and the shaker were coming together almost on their own and he just happened to be standing there. He poured the drink through the strainer, and the way he made the stream rise and fall left her almost giddy with delight.

Brad set the drink in front of him, and the guy who didn't kill spiders said, "And another for the lady. If she's ready for it."

"I'm not," she said. "Not yet. And I'll have to drive later."

"Maybe you won't," he said.

She considered him briefly. "Maybe not."

"You want to run a tab?" Brad asked, his eyes flickering back and forth between the two of them.

"Absolutely," he said.

Brad nodded and moved down the bar to another customer. Kathy ran the tip of her finger along the edge of her glass. "Do you usually drink martinis?"

"Never," the guy said. "It was time to try something new." He raised his glass to hers. They clinked. "Cheers," he said and drank.

She did, too. She had almost finished her drink and was starting to feel it. The edges of everything were softening. "What's your name?"

He grinned at her. Like it was funny. "Larry."

"Short for Laurence?"

"It's on my birth certificate, but I've never used it."

"That's like me," she said. "I'm Kathy. Born Katherine, but no one's ever called me that."

"We have something in common," he said.

"Maybe we'll find some other things."

"Sure," he said. "It's still early." He took a drink of his martini, then put the glass back down, carefully placing it right in the center of the paper coaster. Kathy liked his fingers. They were long and slender, and his wrists looked strong. There was a wedding band on the fourth finger of his left hand.

She looked away quickly. Then she picked up her glass and drained it. She said, "I'm ready for another now."

The guy—Larry—put his hand up to get Brad's attention, but then he stopped and turned back to her. "Or," he said, "we could just have some wine over dinner."

"Oh," Kathy said. "We're having dinner together?"

"I was hoping." She liked the way he was looking at her—admiring, tilting his head back a little to take in the whole thing, but not only looking at her tits. Noticing the tits, though. Prettily packaged in that awesome black dress, which held them up high and proud. "The food here is supposed to be good," Larry said. "And I'm liking the company. But if you had other plans—"

She hesitated—just to make him wait for it—then said, "No other plans. We can have dinner. But not yet. Let's have one more drink. There's no rush." And, "No rush," she said again because it suddenly seemed incredibly true to her. They had the whole evening ahead of them to talk and eat and drink, and even though it would all end with his hands on her body, it was nice to hold that moment off for a while and savor the anticipation which was, she had to admit, more often than not more delicious than its fulfillment.

She wondered, though, if she were coming across as too easy. Not for any moral reasons, of course. But was it what he wanted? Did he want to know this early in the evening that she was his, or was she ruining the game?

She decided she didn't care. And once she had that next drink, she suspected she'd care even less.

Larry had gone ahead and signaled to Brad, who came up to them now. "Ready for another round?" he asked. His tone was casual, but he was looking at her, his gorgeous blue eyes questioning, checking to make sure she was OK with all this, with the new guy sitting next to her and ordering drinks for her like he had a right to. Kathy loved Brad for being so protective, when he didn't even know her. She smiled at him, to let him know everything was fine. She wondered, though, how often he had to help women out of uncomfortable situations—tell a guy who wouldn't take no for an answer to take a hike. Did they teach bartenders how to do that? Was it slipped into Bartending 101, between mixing gimlets and salting the rims of margarita glasses?

"I'll settle the tab," Larry said when the drinks were in front of them. "For both of us."

"You don't have to," she said, reaching vaguely toward her purse.

"I want to," he said, and she let her arm drop back down.

When he had settled with Brad, he raised his glass to hers and they clinked again.

"Here's to not being in a rush," Larry said and they both drank to that.

★   ★   ★

Forty minutes later, they stood up to move to a table, and the room swiveled sharply around her. Kathy was reaching down for her purse, which she had slung against the bottom of the bar and almost fell right over, but Larry's hand was at her elbow, keeping her from falling. His fingers were warm on her arm and, as he helped her get righted, she could feel them digging gently into her skin.

"Sorry," she said. "The room's doing a one-eighty. How'd they get it to do that?"

"It's a special effect," he said. "They only have it at the best places." His hand lingered on her arm as they approached the hostess, who gave them a once-over then led them directly to a small dark table in the corner. She put their menus down and pulled out a chair for Kathy.

Larry released Kathy's arm, and she slid into the chair, tucking the short skirt of her dress under her mostly bared thigh. Larry sat down across from her, hitching his chair slightly closer.

The hostess wished them a good evening and, as she walked away, Larry said, "That dress you're wearing . . ."

"You like it?"

He shook his head, but not in disagreement. "If women always wore dresses like that, men wouldn't go off to war. Or play golf."

"You don't think that's a bit of an exaggeration?" she said. "Or that you're giving the dress too much of the credit and the wearer not enough?"

"You're right," he said. "The body makes the dress."

There was a pause. Kathy looked around. "I miss Brad," she said.

"And Brad would be—?"

"The bartender," she said. "He was looking after me."

"I'll look after you," Larry said. "What do you need done? I promise you I can outbrad Brad."

She started to answer and was interrupted by a loud wail from across the restaurant. They both turned. At a larger table in the middle of the room, a family was finishing up their dinner. The mother was desperately trying to get her toddler child to quiet down, but he was screaming uncontrollably, and the older sibling now raised her own voice in some kind of protest. Kathy looked at Larry and saw the expression on his face and laughed.

"What?" he said.

"Noisy, aren't they?"

"People shouldn't bring kids to nice restaurants on Saturday nights. Especially at this hour."

"To any restaurants ever," she said. "At any hour."

"McDonald's," he said. "Let them all go to McDonald's."

"Sure, they could go to McDonald's," Kathy said, "and we could spend our lives avoiding McDonald's, but is segregating them really the solution? The point is—"

The waiter came up to the table then. He was young and also wore a white T-shirt and black pants and was handsome enough, but not nearly so handsome as Brad, Kathy thought. "Can I bring you something to drink?" he said.

"Wine?" Larry asked, looking at Kathy.

"Sure," she said, even though she had already had too much to drink. The alcohol she'd already had was what was making her reckless about drinking more alcohol, and she knew it and also knew she'd regret it, but tomorrow's regret just didn't have a lot of power over her at that moment. "Red."

"You have a house red?" Larry asked the waiter.

"A chianti and a merlot."

He looked at her again and she said, "Surprise me." He didn't have to know she'd used the same line on Brad.

Larry ordered a bottle of the merlot and the waiter left.

"You were in the middle of saying something," Larry said. "When the waiter came. About kids and McDonald's—"

"Oh, right," Kathy said. "I was going to say that maybe it's not enough to ship them all off to McDonald's. There's a bigger issue at stake here. Why are people even having kids?"

"It's a basic biological drive, isn't it? Reproduction?"

"There are better biological drives," she said. "I can think of a few right now. But really, hasn't our culture, our civilization, moved beyond basic biological drives, anyway? I mean, I thought we'd reached a stage where our lives weren't only about reproduction, where we cared about things like art and music and literature, but everyone acts like it's still some kind of imperative."

"You're right," he said. "No one stops to question whether it's a good idea or not."

"Exactly. They walk blindly into it and then end up

regretting it. My God, the things you give up. I mean, I've seen this baby thing in action, and it's unbelievable. You lose all your free time, your sleep"—she started ticking things off on her fingers—"your privacy, your figure—"

"Your sex life."

"That, too. Especially that. And for what? Someone to take care of you when you're old? You can pay someone to do that—someone *reliable*—with all the money you've saved from all those years of not paying for private schools and big houses with grassy yards—"

"And soccer classes and swim lessons and piano lessons and doctors' appointments—"

"See?" she said. "You get it."

"Absolutely," he said. "They ruin your life."

"But people can't admit it," she said. "Especially once they have them. I mean, once you've given everything up to have kids, you *have* to believe it was a good idea, or you've ruined your life for nothing."

"Plus, who wants to be the only sucker, right? Once you've done it, you've got to talk it up. Otherwise, everyone else will be out having fun while you're stuck at home alone changing diapers."

She laughed out of sheer pleasure at the way he was keeping up with her. "Right! The emperor doesn't have any clothes, but all the other emperors won't tell him because they're naked, too."

The waiter came up with the wine, and, as he was opening it, Larry said, "So you don't think you'll ever want kids?"

"Me?" Kathy shook her head emphatically. "No. No babies in my future."

"That's harsh."

"I'm OK with it."

"You might still change your mind," he said. "People do, all the time." The waiter poured a splash of wine in one of the glasses and waited while Larry tasted it and nodded his approval. The waiter stepped forward again and poured two full glasses. He put the bottle on the table and left. Larry said, "I knew a woman who, at twenty, said she'd never have a kid. At thirty-five, she was giving herself fertility shots in the ass every single day."

"Unbelievable," Kathy said.

"I don't know," he said. "Maybe I should check back with you in a few years."

"Why would I want kids?" she asked, leaning forward. "This is fun right now, right? Being here, having drinks, having dinner . . . Why should I give that up for sticky hands and spit-up down my back?"

"Because everyone does."

"I know," Kathy said. "But what if you want something different? What if you want to be free to do other things? To . . . to—"

"Go to bars?" Larry suggested. "Meet new people?"

"Exactly."

He raised his glass to her. "To going to bars," he said.

"To meeting new people," she said and they clinked and drank.

They ate after that, but it wasn't about the food. Their fingers touched by accident reaching for things on the table and then on purpose.

The room buzzed and swam around them. The kids and their parents were long gone when Kathy and Larry shared a slice of flourless cake, pure chocolate really, the kind that clings to the tines of your fork so you can lick each and every one of them, slowly and deliberately, your eyes darting and playing with your dinner companion across the table . . .

"I think we should go now," Larry said.

He paid and she let him.

"But," she said as they stood up, "we shouldn't drive, either of us, it's not safe."

"This restaurant is attached to a hotel," he said. "Or didn't you know?"

Of course she knew and he knew she knew, but she didn't answer him, just let him lead her across the restaurant, not the way she had come in, through the bar, but the other way, toward the door that connected them to a hotel—and not the kind of a hotel where you went for a quickie after you met someone in a bar, but the kind of hotel where businessmen stayed on big expense accounts and couples spent anniversary weekends. A nice hotel where people didn't rent rooms by the hour.

She started to move toward the front desk, but he gently redirected her toward the elevator, where he punched the button for the seventh floor. So he already had a room.

"You stay here often?" she said.

"Never spent the night." The door closed and suddenly he had her up against the gold and green wall of the elevator and was making her open her mouth to his. Which was fine with her. Even better than fine.

They tumbled into the room together, and Kathy barely had time to take in the beach motif—two paintings of the coastline and a little dish of real seashells on the desk—and no time at all to wonder *why* a beach motif when they were miles from the ocean, before he had grabbed her by the tops of her arms and thrown her down hard on the bed, hard enough that she could feel the bed bounce under her. Then he was on top of her, both of them fully dressed, but practically having sex anyway, their bodies pushing and feeling and seeking and straining. It was almost painful how much they were both wanting it.

At some point they pulled apart long enough to tear off their clothes, stripping down separately, rolling back and forth as they undid zippers and shoved off shoes and tore at their underwear—and then he was back on top of her, only she could feel every inch of his body now, the muscles that bunched at his shoulders and biceps, the slight softness right above his waist, the sparse hairs on his lower back . . .

His skin felt lovely. She couldn't stop running her hands over his arms and back and ass, because it just felt so good how warm and smooth he was. And he was running his hands over her, too, only he was being a little more goal-oriented than she was, and his right hand was already slipping between her legs while his mouth was descending on her left breast. And that felt lovely, too.

The truth was it was all lovely, perfect really, just sweaty enough, just rough enough, just tender enough . . .

Absolutely lovely.

★   ★   ★

Still sprawled together, they fell silent and then dozed, both of them—not a real sleep, just the in-and-out drowse of being too drunk to stay awake. Kathy kept opening her eyes and thinking, "I've got to get out of here," but the alcohol kept pressing her eyelids closed again, and it was so easy not to move and to just let the bed gently rock and spin her into a soothing state of not-quite-consciousness.

Finally, though, she opened her eyes and they stayed open and the room stayed where it belonged, and she got herself up and out of the bed. Larry didn't move when she slipped out. He looked almost dead, the back of his right arm flung over his forehead, covering his eyes, his legs and other arm sprawling out from under the sheet. And the bed—they had made an awful mess of it. Sheets and blankets were torn away from the mattress and the pillows were mostly on the floor.

As was her dress. Kathy picked it up, and her underwear, and carried everything to the bathroom where she got dressed. She looked at her watch. Past one already. Late, but not awful.

When she came back to the bedroom, Larry stirred and lifted his arm from over his eyes. "Are you leaving?"

"I've got to. It's getting late." She slid her feet into her shoes.

"I should get up, too." But he didn't move, just watched her from under his raised arm.

"You don't have to," Kathy said. "It's all right. Take your time."

"Are you OK to drive?"

"Yeah. Fine."

"Are you sure?"

"Yeah. The alcohol's all worn off." She got her purse and went to the door. She stopped and looked back. "That was really nice."

"I thought so, too."

"Really nice," she said again.

"Maybe we could do it again sometime?"

"I'd like that," she said and left.

She drove home on Sunset, driving slowly and carefully. She didn't feel drunk anymore, but she had had a lot to drink, and even though a couple of hours had passed, she wasn't taking any chances. The streets were pretty deserted once she got to Beverly Hills, anyway. No one on the west side of Los Angeles ever went out after midnight. You had to go into Hollywood if you wanted some night life. Which she'd done.

In Brentwood, she turned north and went up into the hills, to the small, steep side street where she lived. She parked in the garage and went into the house.

She entered through the kitchen and continued on into the family room, where the TV was on—the end of *Conan*. Melissa was asleep on the sofa. Kathy kind of cleared her throat, and Melissa started and woke up.

"Oh, Kathy!" she said, swinging herself to an upright position. "Hi! I didn't hear you come in. I think I dozed off. What time is it?"

"Almost one-thirty," she said. "I'm sorry. It's even later than I said."

"It's fine," Melissa said, scrambling to her feet. "I don't usually go to bed much before now, anyway."

"You college kids," Kathy said. "I haven't been out this late in probably ten years. Here, I'll write you a check." She went back into the kitchen and got her checkbook out of the bill desk. Melissa had been there from six in the evening to one-thirty in the morning. Seven and a half hours at ten dollars an hour. Kathy sighed and wrote out the check, rounding it up to eighty. "The kids go to sleep OK?" she asked as she held out the check.

Melissa took it with one hand and pushed her hair out of her eyes with the other. She had great thick, springy hair and a long, lean twenty-year-old body. "Yeah. Pretty much. Caroline wanted to go to sleep in your bed. Hope that's OK."

"Fine. I'll move her."

"Oh, and Henry wants you to come say good night to him. He said to remind you that you promised to wake him up when you got home, no matter how late it was."

"Yeah, I did," Kathy said. "I don't know what I was thinking."

"You were thinking you wanted to get out that door without any more complaints," Melissa said. "Did you have a good time?"

"Wonderful." She wondered if Melissa could tell that she'd just rolled out of bed. Did she look noticeably rumpled? Not that it mattered—Melissa wasn't exactly the judgmental type. "Thank you so much, Melissa. I'm sorry again I was so late."

Melissa glanced at the check and smiled. "No problem. Any time."

They said good night and, as Melissa left, Kathy headed to the back of the house and the bedrooms.

She went to the master bedroom first. Caroline was curled up on the bed, sound asleep, covers thrown off, her tush sticking up in the air. It felt strange looking at her familiar little body, so sleep-sweaty and small on the king-sized bed, after such a wildly erotic evening.

Kathy changed out of her dress and into a pair of sweatpants and a T-shirt. She spotted her wedding band, which she'd left on top of the dresser. She slipped it on her ring finger and, barefoot now, scooped up the sleeping child and carried her into her own room. She dropped her gently onto the toddler-sized bed—gently but with a sigh of relief because Caroline was getting heavy—and tucked the sheets around her shoulders before kissing her on the forehead and whispering good night.

Henry's room was the next one over. Kathy entered. His bedside lamp was on, and the room was bright enough to read in. Kathy came over to the bed and, before she had even said his name, Henry was opening his eyes and sitting up.

"What time is it?" he asked, blinking.

"Late," she said. "But not morning yet."

"You said you'd wake me up."

"That's what I'm doing right now." She smoothed the hair back from his forehead.

"Did Melissa tell you?"

"Tell me what?"

"I told her not to. I wanted to."

"Tell me what? Is everything OK?"

"Look." He grabbed his lower lip and stretched it down and out, tilting his face up toward her.

Kathy peered in. "It came out!"

He released his lip and nodded. "Melissa said I should bite hard into an apple and it would come out and it did."

"Did it bleed?"

"Tons. It hurt, too. She said I could have a Popsicle but then we were all out of them. You should have been there."

"I'm sorry I missed it. Sorry about the Popsicles, too. I'll buy more tomorrow. This is number six, right?"

"Yep," he said. "Two on the top and four on the bottom."

"Did you put it under your pillow?"

He nodded. "And I wrote a letter for the tooth fairy."

"Good job," she said. "Hope she's not sick. I hear there's a bad flu going around in tooth fairyland."

He wriggled under the covers. "Come on, Mom."

"What?"

"I know you're the tooth fairy."

"Yeah? Says who?"

"I *know*. You are, right?"

"I'm not saying one way or the other."

"That's because you are."

"You'd better go back to sleep," she said, pushing his shoulders gently down onto the bed. "Whoever the tooth fairy is, she won't be able to leave you anything if you're awake all night."

"Melissa really didn't tell you?"

"It was a total surprise." She kissed him on the cheek and stood up. "Can I turn the light off?"

"No," he said. "Leave it on."

"It's awfully bright in here."

"I need it on," he said with a yawn. "For the tooth fairy. So she can find the bed."

"Tooth fairies can see in the dark."

"You don't know that."

"OK," she said. "I'll leave it on, if you promise to go back to sleep quickly."

She slipped her hand under his pillow, thinking she'd grab the tooth and his note while she was there, but he said, "What are you doing?" and she stopped.

"Nothing," she said. "Go back to sleep."

She left the room and gave a gasp when someone moved in the shadows of the hallway.

"Jesus!" she said. "You scared me."

Larry came forward into the light. "I'm sorry. I thought you'd hear the garage."

"I was talking to Henry. I didn't think you were going to come back tonight. You looked so sleepy lying there." She moved past him and into the master bedroom.

"You didn't?" he said, following her. "Why would I want to spend the night in a hotel by myself? Anyway, we're supposed to be at my mother's by ten tomorrow."

"By ten? God, that's in like eight hours. Can't we make it later?"

"*You* want to tell my mother we're changing plans at the last minute? She's probably already up cooking."

"I'm just so tired," Kathy said. "I was hoping we could take turns sleeping in tomorrow."

"You can sleep in. I'll get up with the kids."

"Really? That's a nice offer."

"I feel like being nice to you." He came over and put his arms around her. "I'm in a good mood. It's not every day I get to seduce a pretty girl and take her to a hotel room."

"I hope not." She leaned back against him and closed her eyes. She felt like she could fall asleep on her feet, with him there to lean against. "I had fun, too."

He kissed the top of her head. "My mystery woman."

"Next time, though, take off your ring. I could tell the bartender thought I was a total slut, letting a married guy pick me up."

"I tried," he said. "Couldn't get it off. Not without surgery. So are you saying there'll be a next time?"

"Only if you play your cards right."

"Happy anniversary," he said and released her with another kiss.

"Happy anniversary," she said. Then, "And by the way, tomorrow morning, if your mother starts attacking Henry about his lisp again—"

"She won't," Larry said. "And if she does, I'll make her stop."

"If she does, we're leaving." Kathy went over to the desk in the corner of the room and turned on the computer.

"What are you doing?" Larry asked, pulling his pajamas out of the dresser they shared. "It's two in the morning."

"I know," she said. "But I have to do a tooth fairy note. Henry's tooth came out tonight."

"You want me to do it?"

"No. I like doing it." She sat down at the desk. "You know what's funny though?"

He was heading into the bathroom, but he stopped and looked back. "What?"

"The way Henry is. I guess maybe it's his age, but he can't decide whether or not he believes in the tooth fairy. One second he's telling me he knows I'm the tooth fairy and the next minute he's worrying about whether she'll be able to find his pillow in the dark."

"He was like that about Santa, too," Larry said. "Remember? He kept saying he knew we bought all the gifts, but then he sat down and wrote a really serious note to Santa. And made us put cookies out, too."

"I love that about him," Kathy said.

"Yeah," Larry said. "Me, too. I don't want him to get old and jaded, ever."

He went into the bathroom and closed the door. Kathy sat there staring at the blank screen. She was so tired, she could barely think. "Dear Henry," she typed, then stopped.

The thing was, she thought, her fingers curled above the keys, everyone was like that in a way—you could believe in something and not believe in it at the same time. It was like the younger you and the older you were living together, side by side, right there inside your brain and the older one got to call all the shots, but that didn't mean the younger you was ever completely gone. You could know that the tooth fairy was your mom and also kind of believe that a little sprite flew into your room when you were asleep. You could have two kids and love them more than anything else in the world and still kind

of believe that only an idiot would sacrifice her freedom to have kids. You could be grown up and settled down and satisfied with the way things had
turned out and still sniff the air on a golden fall
night and feel like you're only just beginning the adventures that will come to define your life.

Sometimes, when you close your eyes in bed at
night, an old, forgotten dream will suddenly flash
around you, startlingly real for one brief moment before it's gone again.

Kathy went back to typing.

> *Dear Henry,*
>   *So you lost another tooth. Congratulations! I
> had some trouble finding your house, but then I
> met a nice lady in a black dress who told me how
> to get there. I think it was your mom, but then
> again, maybe it wasn't.*
>   *Please don't stop believing in me. I love you.*
>   *Yours truly,*
>   *The Tooth Fairy*

CLAIRE LaZEBNIK lives in Los Angeles with her TV
writer husband and four children. She is the author of
the hilarious comic novel, *Olivia's Sister* and co-author
of the recently published *Overcoming Autism: Finding
the Answers, Strategies and Hope That Can Transform a
Child's Life.*

Moving Day

CINDY CHUPACK

It was three days before her ten-year high school reunion when Madeline's husband told her he thought he might be gay. He wasn't sure if he was gay, having never been with a man, but he thought it was something he ought to figure out.

Matt chose that moment, Madeline decided, not simply to get out of going to her reunion, but because they'd spent the last six months looking at houses together, and that afternoon they'd finally found one in Pasadena that they both really liked. Apparently the "forever" of a wedding vow sounded vague and idealistic to Matt, whereas "thirty-year mortgage" was surprisingly specific. It sounded like a commitment—the kind of commitment one shouldn't make while one's sexuality is pending.

Madeline sat, stunned, in the living room of their Spanish art deco duplex apartment and thought about Mr. and Mrs. Rothman downstairs, who owned the building and were thrilled to rent to such a nice, young couple. They were probably just sitting down to dinner as they had for the past fifty-two years, discussing the brisket, their grandchildren, her garden. Meanwhile, it seemed Matt was still speaking. He said he'd been wanting to discuss this for some time now. It was ripping him apart. He didn't want to hurt her. He was hoping to find out he wasn't gay. Maybe he'd discover he was only, say, thirty percent gay and then, of course, he would rather be with her. He smiled. Apparently this was intended as some sort of compliment.

Madeline's head was spinning. How would they calculate his percentage of gayness? "I slept with ten men, and I enjoyed three of them"? Madeline never liked math. And would she still take him back when and if the experiment failed . . . or, should that be . . . succeeded? And what about the reunion? They were supposed to stay with her parents. Oh, God, her parents. How would she tell her parents? How would she tell her friends? How would she tell their real estate agent? Minutes went by. Maybe hours. Matt finally sighed and said he was so relieved to get that off his chest, he kind of wanted to have sex. Madeline looked at him incredulously. "With who?"

"With you," he said. Madeline wasn't in the mood. Madeline was tired. Madeline needed to cry, then sleep, then wake up when the bookstores were open.

The next day before work, she screeched into the

parking lot of B. Dalton Books and went directly to the self-help section, where all problems could be solved. However, there was no book for the wives of men who suspect they might be gay. There was a book called *Loving Someone Gay* for teachers and family members, but nothing for spouses. That's when she officially started to panic. She did not want to pioneer a problem. She wanted the validation of a book, the anecdotes of other women, the statistics of a study. It occurred to her that the whole point of the self-help section was simply the reassurance that your particular problem was at least widespread enough to merit a book. She was holding on to two tiny shreds of hope at that moment: (1) This is a bad dream, and (2) This is a small bookstore.

As she scanned the shelves for something, anything, that might make her feel less alone, her eyes landed on the title *How to Defend Yourself Against Alien Abduction*. A closer inspection revealed that this volume was not, in fact, a humor book, but an actual book with actual advice like: Block their mind control, Fight back, Guard your loved ones, Create a personal shield and finally, Get help from on high. This was the most upsetting thing since the last most upsetting thing. According to the laws of supply and demand, it would seem you are more likely to be abducted by aliens than to have your husband leave you for another man. Or men. Men in general. She pondered whether it was comforting that Matt was not leaving her for a person but, rather, a gender. It was not comforting, she decided. She started to cry. Actually, she didn't start to cry. She resumed crying.

A clerk, Patrick from Calabasas, asked if she needed help with anything, and Madeline wanted to say, "Yes, God yes!" then she would give him a three-page list that included: Find a therapist and Break the news to my parents. Short of that, she wanted to at least explain why she was holding a book about how to defend yourself against alien abduction, but Matt had asked her not to talk to anyone about any of this yet, and she assumed that gag order extended to strangers with nametags.

Matt wasn't ready to "come out" since he still wasn't sure if he was gay. If a tree falls in the forest and no one is there to hear it, Madeline thought. If a man has gay thoughts, but doesn't act on them? If a clerk asks a question and no one answers? She finally muttered, "This is the self-help section, Patrick. So clearly, I would like to help myself."

When she finally reached the sanctuary of her car, she saw that she had black smudges under her eyes and down one cheek. She made a mental note to buy waterproof mascara at lunch. Perhaps this was why waterproof mascara was invented. It's not for swimming. It's for break-ups. It lengthens, thickens and hides the fact that your world is crumbling like a stale cookie. As does your car. At least that's the common perception in Los Angeles. People spend so much time in their cars, it has become socially acceptable to behave as if nobody can see you in there, even though clearly they can. In the faux solitude of a vehicle you can sing, talk to yourself, apply makeup, pluck your eyebrows, practice a presentation, pick your nose or cry like a baby without feeling the least bit self-conscious.

Thus Madeline was reapplying makeup, crying and speeding through a red light when she remembered that her first impression of Matt was that he might be gay. He was altogether too easy to talk to, too animated, too charming, too good to be straight. Plus there was the matter of the tiger-print lining in Matt's too-orange leather jacket, but then he asked her out and they slept together and he asked her to marry him, so she figured he was straight, and the lining was simply lining, and the fact that he helped her pick her wedding dress was simply because they had just moved to Los Angeles and . . . yes, yes, hindsight is 20/20. And speaking of hindsight, why was a police car following her?

Madeline told the officer that she was just diagnosed with terminal cancer. She wasn't proud of her lie, but she could not face her husband coming out *and* an eight-hour defensive driving course taught at the Improv by a struggling stand-up comic. A girl has her limits.

She did, weeks before her wedding, confess one thing to one friend, Hannah, and this in and of itself probably should have been a red flag, because women talk (and Madeline was no exception), so anything a woman is reluctant to discuss with someone is probably the one thing she should be discussing with everyone. In any case, Madeline told Hannah that after she and Matt were already engaged, Matt had admitted one night over pad thai that he sometimes noticed men. He said he couldn't imagine sleeping with a man, but he did occasionally notice them. This had, at the very least, curbed Madeline's appetite, and she spent the rest of the meal wondering if Matt was "noticing" their waiter.

She casually floated this revelation out to Hannah as they were adjusting their stationary bikes at the gym, wondering if Matt's confession seemed like cause for concern. Hannah told Madeline her theory about the spectrum of sexuality, and how everyone lies somewhere along the spectrum. "Most of us appreciate looking at people of the same sex but would never do anything about it. Some of us have homosexual thoughts. And some of us are homosexual," Hannah said with complete and comforting conviction. It should be noted that four years later, Hannah realized she was a lesbian.

Matt got equally questionable advice at the time. He talked to a female therapist who said that he was probably just getting cold feet, which is perfectly natural before a wedding. (Madeline, in her darkest hours now, usually before a blind date, fantasizes about making an appointment with that therapist and bludgeoning her with her framed graduate degree.) Matt had also talked to a gay friend who said frankly, he couldn't even imagine sleeping with a woman, so if Matt could have sex with Madeline he was probably at least bisexual, and since he loved her, why not marry her? Two years later, Matt and Madeline were smack-dab in the middle of why not.

Madeline pulled into her parking space at work, thinking that if there were such a thing as alien abduction, she would very much like to be taken before her high school reunion.

★　　★　　★

Anyone who has tried to do a job during a personal crisis has discovered this frightening truth—you can get through a day doing very little work and very few people will notice. Madeline's job entailed sitting in a cubicle in front of a television wearing a headset and typing closed captions for the hearing impaired. You could do this almost without thinking even on a good day, so this particularly bad day was a good day to have this job. In fact, Madeline started to wonder what might happen if she typed whatever the hell she wanted. Maybe Chandler could admit to Monica that he dreams of doing Ross. Who would know, besides a handful of hearing-impaired *Friends* fans? They might actually enjoy Chandler's gay story line. Maybe Madeline could figure out how to write a happy ending, if not for herself, at least for Monica.

The downside of suddenly joining the ranks of the walking wounded (besides the obvious) is that you become aware how vast and stealthy an army it is. Millions of people in America are floating through red lights and job reviews every day, hearing only the deafening sound of their own heart breaking. This eventually gives way to the sound of more hearts breaking, because once you feel true pain, you realize how much more pain is all around you, and you soak up sorrow like a sponge. You can no longer function like you did before. Before, you could ask a colleague how his weekend was, and he might reply, "OK. I was in Chicago visiting my aunt," and you could nod and go on your merry way. You might never ask the question that would lead to the admission that his aunt is dying, that his weekend was spent dealing with his mother's grief because she doesn't want to lose her only sister, that maybe there are children—cousins—who are losing their mother, and an uncle who doesn't want to be alone. There is so much sadness in the world it is almost unbearable when you first encounter it head-on, like walking into sunlight after too many days in darkness, except you're walking into darkness after too many days in sunlight. And through it all we are expected to work, to be productive, to file it away or leave it at home. If America is sliding as a superpower, it very well might be due to grief.

Madeline spent most of her workday looking for a therapist, something she had managed to avoid for a blissful and unexamined thirty years. She found out that her insurance covered something called the Silver Group, which required only a ten-dollar co-payment each visit. It occurred to her that therapy is not an arena in which to be frugal, but it also occurred to her that she might be going once a week for the rest of her life, and that could add up.

The Silver Group was a trio of therapists who shared an office suite in the valley, and the valley is a depressing place to be even if your husband doesn't think he might be gay. Nevertheless, one member of the Silver Group had an opening, so the next day Madeline drove to the valley during her lunch hour. This turned out to be a very bad idea, because traffic was terrible in that annoying Los Angeles way, with no explanation, not an accident, not a blocked lane, not a sporting event, not rush hour, just traffic. In fact, there was so much fucking traffic that Madeline started to think the fucking stress of getting to her fucking appointment might be what she would have to fucking deal with in therapy. Maybe traffic is what keeps the Silver Group in business, Madeline thought, amused. Then she remembered why she was going, got sad and honked at some people.

When she arrived outside the waiting room, she realized she was not alone—not in a comforting way, in a literal way. A very random sampling of patients, all with issues possibly as pressing as Madeline's, were crowded around the buzzer wondering why they were locked out of the waiting room. "Could the members of the Silver Group have revolted," one man tried to joke, but it's a tough crowd (people who gave up lunch to go to therapy), so the disgruntled patients continued to deal with the problem individually. Finally a cell phone call resulted in the emergence of a very apologetic receptionist, something wrong with the buzzer, they'll get it fixed, sorry. Apparently you get what you co-pay for.

If she didn't already need a therapist, the paperwork sent Madeline over the top. She checked the married box, but noted that you could be divorced with a slip of the pen. Then she wrote down her last name (his last name), which led to a long inner-debate about whether she should go back to her maiden name if . . . no . . . when she divorced, change all her credit cards, her voicemail, her monogrammed luggage, what to do with the wedding photos, the gifts, the framed ketubah, whether to take a roommate, write a personal ad, move to a new city, become a nun. Finally, mercifully, the receptionist asked if she was finished, and led her from the Silver Group's tiny white waiting room into the tinier, whiter office of Dr. Joan Weissman, whom she was told would be with her in a minute. During that minute Madeline realized something significant: she was tired of being alone with her thoughts. She drove all the way to the valley just to be with someone else's thoughts. Where the hell was Dr. Weissman?

She looked around for a distraction and noticed that on the end table next to the clock was a book called *One Hundred and One Ways to Save the Earth*. This made Madeline instantly exhausted. She was having enough trouble getting through the day. The earth would have to be someone else's problem for a while. She averted her eyes and noticed two other disturbing things: (1) Dr. Weissman's plants had lost their will to live, not exactly a ringing endorsement for a therapist, and (2) Due to the extremely thin walls, she could hear someone else's session. It was a man, and he was sobbing. He wasn't happy with his job, but his wife . . . something. You couldn't hear everything, but it was enough to give you pause when it was your turn to talk. Dr. Weissman entered and turned on a small oscillating fan, which seemed to be the system the Silver Group had devised to deal with the soundproofing problem.

Dr. Weissman was a large Midwestern woman wearing red pants and a pink-and-white-striped shirt. Madeline worried that a woman who couldn't put together an outfit shouldn't be trying to put together people's lives, but as soon as Dr. Weissman said, "How are you?" (which might have simply been a greeting)

Madeline started talking and didn't stop until their time was up, and she didn't care who else was listening.

As she gave the receptionist her ten-dollar bill, Madeline decided the Silver Group was the bargain of the century. In fact, she was tempted to buy a session for everyone in the waiting room ("This round's on me!") when she was told there was more. There was a computer lab you could visit after your session to complement your therapy. Late for work, emotionally drained, but intrigued, Madeline entered the lab. It consisted of three computers, each accompanied by a box of Kleenex. The man who tried to make the joke earlier was sitting at one computer, looking a bit despondent. Madeline smiled at him, then sat down in front of another computer and saw what had presumably made him despondent. It was even more exhausting than *One Hundred and One Ways to Save the Earth,* the multiple choice list of things you were to scroll through and select from: Alcoholism, Anorexia, Anxiety, Bulimia, Depression, Divorce, Drug Dependencies, Fatigue, Financial Worries, Grief, Incest, Infertility, Infidelity, Job Dissatisfaction, Loss, Miscarriage, Mourning, Obesity, Post-Partum Depression, Separation Anxiety, Sexual Dysfunction, Sexual Identity, Sleeping Disorders, Suicidal Tendencies, Unexplained Weight Loss . . . It was overwhelming, all the things that could go wrong in a lifetime. Overwhelming and depressing, because whether you selected Divorce or Sexual Identity, "your husband thinks he might be gay" was never, ever an option.

★　　★　　★

The worst part of her ten-year high school reunion in Milwaukee, Wisconsin, was trying to pretend that everything was fine. This was her decision, to go with Matt as planned and pretend everything was fine. In her fragile state it seemed preferable to not going, or going alone and possibly melting into a weepy heap when asked what she'd been up to lately. No, it was a two-hander, the "Everything's OK" show, and she and Matt would be performing it all weekend. Of course Matt had experience acting. Not just acting like a straight man—but in college, he was in a group very much like Monty Python. Yes, they sang and danced. Yes, sometimes in dresses. Oh, the pink flags she had ignored.

Now, a high school reunion is traumatic for women no matter where you are in life. Single women feel self-conscious about not being married. Married women feel self-conscious about not being mothers. Mothers feel self-conscious about not working. Working mothers feel self-conscious about not staying home. And everyone feels fat.

Yet even in this sea of self-consciousness, Madeline was the most self-conscious of all. She didn't want people getting attached to her husband, she didn't want him getting attached to anyone else's husband, and when she won "Most Improved" (which she attributed to a bad perm in high school and laser eye surgery) she thought, "Yeah, yeah and I married a gay man."

To make matters worse (something Madeline kept thinking simply wasn't possible), staying with her parents meant she would have to make an effort to avoid her mother, because her mother was an eagle-eye for emotion. Her mother was the type of person who would leave you a message saying you didn't sound so happy on your outgoing message, which couldn't have been why she was calling. And even though you were just tired when you recorded your outgoing message, you could usually think of something you might be upset about when she pressed. It was almost a parlor trick. Madeline's mother could recognize emotions you didn't even know you had yet. She was an emotional clairvoyant. "You are about to become incredibly depressed." So for Madeline, being home with her mother while her marriage was falling apart was like being Eliza Doolittle at the Embassy Ball left to dance with that linguistics expert. Therefore Madeline had to plan her trips to the hall bathroom very carefully. She had to avoid eye contact. She had to exude the sense that life was better than ever.

This is why she was caught completely off-guard when her father looked up from ESPN to ask if everything was OK. "No," she screamed. "If everything was OK, Matt would be in here watching SportsCenter with you instead of in the kitchen flipping through back issues of *House Beautiful!*"

She never intended to talk to her father. She assumed that when and if she told her parents, she would follow the usual protocol: tell her mother and let her mother tell her father. But here she was telling her father. And once she started talking to him, she remembered why she never talked to him. His response to the whole situation was as if she was giving Matt permission to have an affair: "I'd like to sleep with Debbie Reynolds, but your mom's not going to let me," he said.

First of all, he must have been referring to a younger Debbie Reynolds, and second of all, "What if you wanted to sleep with Burt Reynolds?" Madeline asked. He didn't get it. You couldn't blame him. He didn't have much experience with homosexuality. There was one man in his college fraternity, Jerry Hobbleman, who everyone knew had left his wife and kids to pursue a "gay lifestyle," but no one had talked to him since.

Madeline and Matt somehow survived the weekend, but unfortunately their landlord, Mr. Rothman, did not.

Mr. Rothman's funeral was a relief to Madeline, not in the sense that she wanted him gone. She loved Mr. Rothman. He used to tell her stories about the early days of advertising, when spots were recorded live right in the television studio. No, his funeral was a relief only because a funeral is a place, Madeline discovered, where it is perfectly acceptable to cry, and she had been looking for a place like that ever since Matt told her his news. It might be odd, as a tenant, to cry harder than the immediate family, but death is death, and people don't really question your response in the face of it. The other comforting aspect of a funeral is that there is a body, a coffin, a grave, and a ritual that enables people to mourn. Someone is gone. There is a physical ending, not just an emotional one. There is a time of death. A burial. The end of a relationship is never so clearly marked.

Matt held Madeline's hand as the coffin was lowered into the ground. Then, it being a Jewish funeral, there was a need for a minion, and Matt was asked to leave with the men. Madeline really didn't want him to leave with the men. He would be leaving with the men soon enough. But this was a funeral and you need ten men for a minion so Madeline said, "Go," and she realized she meant it in the largest sense possible.

Mrs. Rothman was in the front yard gardening the morning the moving truck was coming for Matt's things. Matt was silently taping up the last of his boxes after their fight over *Love in the Time of Cholera*. Madeline had seen it in a box and asked if it was hers. He said it was his. She was pretty sure it wasn't. Matt yelled she could keep it, keep everything, she was already getting the television, stereo and washer/dryer. The previous week, as they drove away from the depressing 50s apartment Matt would be renting (probably to punish himself, because he certainly had good taste in architecture, another pink flag), he had told her he wanted her to have those things, wanted her to have it all. Apparently his guilt was wearing off.

"You have to tell Mrs. Rothman you're leaving," Madeline said, finally breaking the silence. "She's out front, and the truck will be here any minute." Matt continued packing. He refused to deal with Mrs. Rothman, just as he had refused to deal with everything else. That's why Madeline had gone with him to look for an apartment, why she had ventured into a gay bookstore to buy him a book about coming out, why she had been up late every night filling

out the forms in the *Do Your Own Divorce* work-
book she had ordered online. And that's why it was
Madeline who finally went downstairs to talk to
Mrs. Rothman.

She was starting to feel angry at Matt, which was
good, because up until that point only Dr. Weissman
had been angry with Matt. Dr. Weissman had been almost unprofessionally angry with Matt. She didn't buy
the whole "he thinks he might be gay" story, thought
Madeline should insist he take an AIDS test, thought
he might have been cheating all along. Dr. Weissman
clearly had some issues.

Thankfully, however, in the gay bookstore, Madeline
had found the help she needed. It was a book called *The
Other Side of the Closet*. There was not only a book for
people in this situation, she discovered, there was a
term. She and Matt were what is known as "a mixed-
orientation couple," which made her feel a tiny bit better, although she thought the book should be called *The
Closet Organizer*, because she was doing all the heavy
lifting.

"You know," her father had said the last time they
spoke on the phone, "homosexuality is like ninety-
nine percent genetic." She was impressed, and figured he'd been on the Internet doing some research.
She later found out that his new, enlightened self was
the result of a lunch date with Jerry Hobbleman. Her
dad had taken Jerry Hobbleman to Denny's. The
thought of it made her smile. She was certain there
had been many disclaimers, her father afraid it might
seem like a date, afraid the "married man" he was referring to might be thought to be himself. Of course,

Jerry would know that wasn't the case as soon as Madeline's father showed up in shorts, black socks and dress shoes, but still, he somehow managed to ask all the questions he needed answered, like: "Could you have stayed with your wife?" "Did you ever regret leaving?" "Are you happier now?" "Did your wife get over it?" It was possibly the nicest thing a father ever did for a daughter, taking Jerry Hobbleman to lunch.

Mrs. Rothman had always enjoyed gardening, but since her husband had died she seemed to be more devoted than ever to the flowers, to the living things, to seeing that nothing else slipped away. So it was particularly difficult to tell her that Matt was slipping away, and that Madeline was letting him.

"Matt's moving out," Madeline finally said. "We're having some problems, and we have to separate."

"But every couple has problems."

"I know," Madeline said, "but this is . . . tricky."

Mrs. Rothman didn't ask anything else. She didn't want to pry, and Madeline didn't want to offer. They sat quietly on the bench in front of the duplex. Mrs. Rothman was clearly disappointed in life and love and young couples and death and her wisteria. She and Mr. Rothman were married fifty-two years. Fifty-two years. Madeline and Mrs. Rothman sighed, and sat shoulder to shoulder, leaning on each other and not leaning on each other, two women newly alone and yet not alone, as the moving truck lumbered over to the curb.

CINDY CHUPACK wrote and executive produced HBO's Emmy and Golden Globe–winning series *Sex and the City*. She is also a magazine contributor and the author of *The Between Boyfriends Book: A Collection of Cautiously Hopeful Essays*.

Yoga Babe

LAUREN HENDERSON

"We're going to take a round of pumped breath now," Ivan, the teacher, says. "Let's take fifty, OK? Anyone who needs a tissue, just keep going, raise a hand, and I'll come round with the box. I'm going to keep count. Ready? One! Two! Three! Four!"

We start a series of short, pumped exhales in time with the count. Breath snorts out through my nose—hah, hah, hah—my diaphragm contracting nice and tight to push out each one. I always think we sound like dogs, or some kind of animal, anyway, huffing and puffing. I never know quite what this is for, but we start all the classes this way, so it must be doing us some good. Over the snorting I can hear Ivan's bare feet padding over the wooden floor. My eyes are closed, but I crack them open a fraction to see who needs a tissue. The girl next to me. *Really*. You'd think she'd know by now to blow her nose beforehand to open up the passages. This is the advanced class, after all.

We chant. I know it all by heart by now, the little stepped half-tune, all the proper pronunciation of the words. It's called the invocation to Patanjali, and no, I don't know what it means. I think it's about calling on the god of yoga to make your practice better. I skipped the orientation classes when I started. I'd already done some yoga at the gym and I was pretty fit anyway, after all those aerobics classes and the spinning. I didn't think I needed to start, you know, completely from the beginning, and I was right. I've been doing the advanced class for two years now. Most days. Brian says I'm addicted. But I love it. I couldn't do without it.

"OK, let's take dog pose," Ivan says, crossing the room to turn on the stereo. "Really stretch out those backs."

Music filters gently into the room, rising cadences, Indian sitars mixed with a trip-hop vibe. When you're deep into the sequences, you hardly notice it, but it pulls you along, almost like dancing, the music catching at your feet and keeping you going. It's very hypnotic.

I wish Ivan would come around and push down on my lower back. It feels so great. But that never happens in this class. Forty people in here at least and no teaching assistant today. I hope everyone knows what they're doing. Two weeks ago some idiot girl tried to do a handstand in the middle of the room and fell over backward. It was nasty. I think she cracked something in her neck. She should have known she wasn't ready. That's the thing about the big classes; the teacher can't possibly look out for all the morons trying to show off. I did go to another studio for a few weeks, where the classes were much smaller, only about twelve of us, and you did get all those nice adjustments from the teacher. But it was so scruffy. A walk-up just off 14th Street, paint cracking from the walls, the changing room about the size of the elevator here, and the people who went . . . well, they were so hippie. Dreadlocks and baggy T-shirts, and some of them pretty out of shape, too. Though sometimes that doesn't seem to matter with yoga. It's very unfair.

Anyway, I just didn't feel as comfortable there. Everyone who's anyone comes to this yoga studio. Supermodels, actors, hip-hop stars. It's been in two movies already, and hundreds of articles in all the New York magazines. Everyone's heard of it. And they have this lovely meditation room, like a little round egg with a thick gray wall-to-wall carpet inside. I sometimes go in there to zone out, come down from a long hard day. It's fabulous.

"OK, look forward between your hands to a spot in front of them and then step or jump your hands between your feet," Ivan says. His voice is always soft, but it carries effortlessly over the smooth flow of the music. I've wondered before whether he's an actor. Lots of resting actors and dancers teach yoga nowadays.

"And now we're going to do an adjustment on each other. Just briefly. I want you to pair up with the person next to you and take turns to do dog while the other one takes hold of your thighs and pulls them back. That's what we're always talking about. Take those thighbones right back into the hamstrings. Hold it for ten breaths."

Shit, I hate this. Touching strange people. Unless I got, I don't know, a supermodel or something. It would be cool to tell Brian I pulled Christy Turlington's thighbones back into her hamstrings.

The girl next to me is already looking at me and smiling. I sigh. I'm stuck with her. She's not exactly prepossessing. Short and stocky—I mean, isn't yoga supposed to lengthen you out?—and wearing lycra shorts, for God's sake. Everyone else is in little cami-vests and yoga pants. (Or capri leggings, like me, though you can only wear those if you're really slim.) Her skin's a sort of dull white, like thick matt paint, and her haircut is just not happening.

"Shall I go first?" she says.

"Sure."

I smile at her nicely and go around behind her as she goes into dog pose. I reach forward to grab her thighs and pull them back, bracing myself to take the weight.

Oh my God. She has hairs up the backs of her thighs. Her hair is really dark and her skin's so white that I can see every single one clearly. I guess she waxes or shaves them or something, because they're very short, hardly beyond the surface of the skin, and they look exactly like stubble. The hairs are thick and stubby. Jesus. Five o'clock shadow. She has five o'clock shadow on the backs of her legs. I can hardly bear to look, but at the same time I can't tear my eyes away. I'm gripped by a sort of horrible fascination. Why doesn't she laser them off, for God's sake? Or at least wear yoga pants to cover them up?

Her thighs are thick as tree trunks, really muscly. It's hard work pulling at her. I'm *so* relieved when Ivan tells us to switch over. She hauls on me like a tractor. No wonder. I must weigh half what she does. My hands are coming up from the mat, she's dragging on me so hard. I nearly fall backward. Ivan, walking by, tells me to push down harder with my index fingers and thumbs. Well, I'm trying, but I have a two-ton weight pulling at the back of my legs, OK? Finally she lets go. My back *does* feel longer, I have to admit. I tell her that, smiling politely.

Now it's my favorite bit. Long sequences. Half an hour at least of really working out. Ivan starts us slow, letting us rest in dog or uttanasana every now and then, but soon we're into the heart of it, a steady, heart-pounding series of movements, elegant, like dancers, but complete control, no wavering, nail that warrior pose and hold it like you were made of stone, plank pose to chattauranga again and again—that's actually my favorite, it's a kind of yoga push-up. Tough to do, no matter how much you worked out with weights before you started yoga, but it's the best thing ever for my upper arms. I never had so much definition before. My biceps almost pop. Great for all those little strappy tops.

The girl in front of me is sweating like a pig. I know it's hot in here, but *really*. She has a towel by the side of the mat, and she's wiping her face every few

minutes. Every time we take dog for five breaths she
sneaks one hand out for a surreptitious face smear. Ick.
I'm lucky, I suppose. I never go red in the face, or
sweat too much. I mean, you have to shower afterward, of course, it's a workout, but I've seen people
going out of here with faces like greased tomatoes. I
expect it's being slim, too. If you're fat, you sweat
more. The sweaty girl's in OK physical shape, but she
could stand to lose half a stone. Still, she looks well
put together, not one of those straggly hippies from
that other yoga studio. Nice drawstring pants and a
Gucci top in pale cream. I nearly bought that style.
Her pedicure is great, too. Chrome mauve. I make a
note to ask her where she gets it done.

I like Ivan's class because he always does sit-ups.
Yoga sit-ups, of course, but they still tone your stomach. I do regular sit-ups every morning, but there's no
such thing as too many. Arms stretched over our
heads, legs up to ninety degrees, down to sixty, down
to thirty, down to two inches off the floor—and sometimes then he doesn't let you drop them but makes
you swing them right up to ninety again. It's great.
You really hit all those lower abs, which are harder to
target.

After that, headstand. I hate headstand. I have to
use the wall, I just don't feel safe without it, and when
you're against the wall, you look out, so you see all
those smug bitches who can balance properly going up
in the center of the room. At least it doesn't last long.
Then we take shoulder stand and arch back down into
setubanda. I love that. Plopping my feet down on the
floor. It's supposed to be really good for your kidneys,

too. I think. The girl next to me is doing it, too. Not everyone can. I'm surprised at her; she seems to be doing it really easily. I would have thought she was a bit bulky to do it comfortably. You're not supposed to turn your head during shoulder stand, in case you strain your neck, but I flick my eyes around and turn my head just a fraction to see what she's doing.

"OK, we're going to take wheel from here," Ivan says. The music is slower now, more trance-like, now that we've finished the aerobic section of the class. Ivan's voice is so mellow it sounds like he's casting a spell, or hypnotizing us, rather than telling us we're going to do something as radical as turn our bodies all the way over into full backbend. "Those of you who don't go down into setubanda, come down from shoulder stand one leg at a time, lie flat for a moment, and then go up, OK? The rest of you, just go up in your own time."

I'm up already. So is the girl next to me. How competitive. I've always been flexible, I don't have problems with the wheel. It reminds me of school gym class. The Crab, we used to call it. I work on straightening my arms, and it's going well. I'm really pleased. Till I see the girl next to me is raising one of her legs. Correction: one of her stumps. I'm sorry, but they really are like tree trunks. She's straightening the leg right up, perpendicular to the floor, so she's balanced in a full backbend just on her hands and one foot. I've never seen anyone do that before. Then she lowers it and lifts the other one. I try to lift one of my feet but the other one slips, even though I'm on the mat, and I have to put it back down hurriedly. Then I'm all off-balance and I have to come down. Damn. Oh well, she's coming down too, and we'll do two more. I can try again.

But next time I can't get my foot off the mat at all. Meanwhile she's making it look like the easiest thing in the world. Those stubbly legs are raising to the ceiling, one after the other, all over again.

"This is about your own practice," Ivan says, "so everyone, at your own pace. But if anyone wants to stand up, or walk up the wall into handstand, off you go."

She puts her foot down, and I think she's coming down. But no. She arches her back even more and pushes her hands off the mat, and now she's lifted herself so much she's standing up. I've seen people do that before. It almost seems like an anticlimax after the foot-lifting. Then she bends right back again, with her hands in prayer pose behind her, and does a sort of backward dive down to the mat again with her upper body, her hands parting at the last minute to drop gently onto the mat, taking her weight. It looks really good. Or it would, if her body was better.

We do a third and last wheel, and there she goes again, standing up, diving down, like it's nothing. Other people are doing it too, of course, but she just looks so *unlikely*. That's what I don't get.

Anyway. Class is nearly over, Ivan's dimming the lights, we take fish pose for a few breaths and then it's relaxation. Corpse pose, that's what it's called, apparently. I'm glad I didn't know that at the beginning. I'd have found it creepy.

My body feels great. Really worked out. Every muscle connects to every other muscle, I'm all stretched and pumped up at the same time—that's the great thing about yoga—and my eyes are closed, darkness on my eyelids, my breath coming gently. I always feel like I could lie here forever. It's hard to roll over and sit up when Ivan tells us. He's sitting cross-legged. He raises his hands into prayer and bows his head, thanking us.

"Namaste," we all say softly. Or is it "Namaskar?" One of the teachers says that instead. I always mumble the end of the word so I don't get it wrong.

I roll up my mat. Stubble Girl smiles at me and says: "Great class."

"Yes, he's really good," I say.

"Yeah, it's my first one with him. But everyone's been recommending him to me, and it's true, he's great. I'll definitely be back."

"Good," I say at random, wondering if she's trying to pick me up. Oh God, that would be so awful. I wouldn't mind if she were really hot. I mean, I wouldn't do anything, my college days are way behind me now, but the thought of Stubble Girl thinking she might somehow be on my level . . . Jesus, how unflattering! And *unrealistic!*

I smile again and go over to the shelves to get my water and my bag before she can say anything else. She doesn't follow me, thank God. I drink some water. Across the room I see two women chattering away. One of them, making some point to the other, looks around, her bag in hand, and then puts it down so she can show her some sort of shoulder stretch. Only she puts it down on the altar. Whoops. Ivan has to come over and tell her to take it off. I did that once in the early days. God, it was so embarrassing. Ivan's being nice about it, but that teacher who told me it was the altar, God, she was a real bitch to me. It was an honest mistake. I mean, how was I supposed to know it was, like, a Buddhist altar to the yoga gods, or whatever they are? I thought all the studios just had display stands with some pretty statues on them, to brighten up the rooms a bit. I never took her class again. I didn't like her attitude at all.

I shower at home. They do have showers at the yoga center, but it gets pretty crowded. I check out the backs of my legs in the mirror as I exfoliate. Smooth as silk, and no nasty bulging hamstrings like that girl. I shudder, imagining having to wax the backs of my thighs. What a nightmare.

I'm having a late lunch with Brian, so I pull on a little orange cashmere sweater and my hipster jeans and sally over to Federico's, on Sixth. We love it there. Lots of celebrities hang out there. Federico, the owner, just put out a cookbook with all these black and white photos of movie stars eating there. Casual, sort of verité style, like the 1950s, twirling pasta around forks and clinking wineglasses and laughing. It looks great. I got the book for Brian for Christmas. We haven't cooked from it—we don't have time, we're much too busy, and besides, I don't spend all that money on manicures to ruin them chopping vegetables—but we couldn't believe how many famous people were in it.

"Baby!" Brian hugs me. He's wearing that black cashmere jacket I love, with a gray T-shirt under it. He looks great.

"Hi, honey!"

I kiss him, a long and lingering one. I've only got lip stain on, so I don't need to worry about smudges.

"How was yoga?"

"Great."

"You need to get your streaks done," he says as we sit down.

"I know. I'm overdue." I finger one long strand. "Pierre was all booked up. I finally managed to get an appointment for the day after tomorrow, but I had to beg. He was in *New York* magazine the week before last and he's got really popular. I hate when that happens."

I don't need to look at the menu; I know what I want already.

"Artichokes and then the carpaccio?" the waiter says, smiling at me.

"No dressing on the artichokes," I remind him.

He brings us a couple of glasses of spumante on the house. Well, he should. We're in here all the time and Brian is a great tipper.

Brian points out someone across the room he thinks might be Yoko Ono, and I swivel my head to look. It's not her, nothing like. But when I turn back, there's a ribboned box sitting in front of me. Small and sweet.

"Oh my God!"

Brian's smirking from ear to ear, waiting for me to open it. He's so great at giving presents. The last one he gave me were these diamond earrings. Two carats each, emerald cut. I wear them all the time.

I untie the ribbon and undo the paper, slowly, not

wanting to rush the moment. Inside the box, resting on a little pad of blue velvet, is a . . . necklace? Bracelet?

I lift it out.

"It's an ankle chain," Brian says smugly.

"Oh my God, honey, it's so *cute* . . ."

I trail it over my wrist. It's like a name bracelet, with a silver chain, only instead of the name are two words: YOGA BABE, in diamonds. It's just spectacular. And so me!

"I had to get it for you," Brian says. "I couldn't have lived with myself if I hadn't got it for you."

"You are such a *doll.*"

I lean across the table and kiss him again. I can see people at the next tables, including the fake Yoko, looking at us out of the corners of their eyes. I bet all the women are jealous.

I reach down and fasten the chain around my bare brown ankle (we were in St. Bart's last month and I'm topping up with St. Tropez). It looks fabulous. I hold it up for Brian to see.

"It's perfect," he says, satisfied.

I can't stop staring complacently at my anklet. It looks amazing against my skin. I think I'll wear it to class. Why not? Lots of people wear jewelry to yoga.

I bet that girl at class doesn't have a boyfriend who buys her diamonds. Well, even if she did, he wouldn't get this for her. It would be ridiculous. She is *so not* a babe.

New York–based **LAUREN HENDERSON** is the author of two wickedly funny novels of modern relationships, *My Lurid Past* and *Don't Even Think About It*. She has also written seven novels in the highly acclaimed Sam Jones series, which has now been optioned for a feature film: *Dead White Female, Too Many Blondes, The Black Rubber Dress, The Strawberry Tattoo, Freeze My Margarita, Chained!, Pretty Boy* and, with Stella Duffy, she has co-edited an anthology of female crime writers, *Tart Noir.*

The Truth About Nigel

JENNIFER WEINER

Sarah Compton started work at the First Bank of London on the third Monday of September, and Nigel Jones started two days later.

"Good morning," he said cheerfully, in an unplaceable accent, setting a cardboard box down on his desk and unpacking a coffee mug, a rubber-banded bundle of pens and a newspaper photograph of a woman's smiling face that he Sellotaped to his computer. "I'm Nigel Jones." He smiled and stuck out his hand.

Posh, was Sarah's first thought. His blue button-down shirt seemed to be woven of finer stuff than the shirts worn by most of the other entry-levels she'd seen at the First Bank of London, and more on a par with the shirts the directors and the managers wore—the ones that were usually made by hand and sported discreet monograms on the cuffs.

Close on the heels of posh followed a second thought: adorable. Nigel Jones was tall, with bright blue eyes and a smattering of freckles across the bridge of his nose. True, he was a bit on the gangly side, with knobby wrist bones and a too-short haircut exposing inches of pale, vulnerable unfreckled skin on the back of his neck, but still, his smile was lovely, and the haircut could be improved upon, and she could fatten him up a bit, invite him over for dinner, and . . .

"Um," said Nigel Jones tentatively. Sarah realized that a more-than-decent interval had passed and she'd failed to let go of his hand.

"Oh! Sorry!" she said, dropping his hand and blushing, and cursing herself for blushing, and cursing her mother for passing down her porcelain-fine skin that showed every single blush as vividly as if it had been projected on a movie screen.

"It's my third day," she blurted, by way of explanation, even though it being her third day didn't go far toward explaining why she hadn't let go of his hand.

Nigel Jones resumed his easy grin. "My first," he told her, and lifted his mug. "Hey, do you know where they keep the coffee? Or, um, tea?"

"Oh, sure!" she said, and led him toward the pantry, pointing out things he might need to know about along the way—the fax machine, the pile of for-public-consumption newspapers, the vending machine that sold Cadbury bars and packets of crisps.

"Thanks," he said, and smiled at her again, "Sarah." Her name, she thought, sounded delicious on his lips.

★　　★　　★

"College?" demanded her sister Charlotte the following Wednesday night. "Age? Status? Income? Location?"

"Um, Oxford," said Sarah, taking a sip of her pint. "In his twenties, I think, maybe early thirties. Single, as far as I know, although he's got a photo of some American movie star on his computer."

Charlotte flicked her manicured fingertips dismissively, as if shooing away a fly.

"Income. Erm, same as mine, I imagine."

"Good enough," said Charlotte, raising one finger. Instantly, a waiter appeared, as if his feet were attached to an invisible track that led directly to their table. Charlotte had that way about her—one finger, and the waiters appeared. Whereas Sarah could have been tap-dancing on the bar without ever being asked for her order. "Another round," Charlotte rapped.

"Actually, could I have a gin and tonic?" asked Sarah.

Her sister sighed. "Sarah," she began, "you can have whatever you want. You're paying for it, aren't you?"

The waiter wheeled away. Charlotte resumed her interrogation. "Location?"

"Notting Hill," said Sarah, savoring the sound. "But really, Char, it's too early to talk about any of this. I only just met him!" Which was true. But she liked him. There was something about him, something mysterious, in spite of his regular-guy good looks, and the easy way he spoke to everyone in the office, from the secretaries to the managing partners. He reminded her, somehow, of a cowboy; a cowboy from one of the books she'd read or the songs she'd sung as a little girl. It was the way he walked, she supposed, as if he were taller than he actually was, the rangy strides that suggested he was walking through the untamed wilderness as opposed to over the understated gray wall-to-wall carpeting of the First Bank of London. She could imagine him on horseback, in the hat, sleeping alone beside a campfire he'd built himself.

"It's never too early," Charlotte said. "You've got to have your strategy. Honestly, Sarah, have I taught you nothing?"

Sarah sighed into her drink, thinking that her sister was less a human being than a force of nature that just happened to wear girl's clothes. Charlotte had worked in public relations before moving home to tend to her twins, Henry and Ella, and handle the occasional freelance client, and it seemed she hadn't been the least bit disrupted by the transition from single-girl-about-town to stay-at-home-mum. She was always perfectly put together—her hair freshly cut and streaked, her clothes just so, the twins never scabby or sticky or poorly behaved. No piece of spinach would ever dare wedge itself between Charlotte's incisors, no smudge would dare darken her white linen pumps. Her sister, Sarah admitted with another small sigh, was formidable. Whereas she herself was something of a joke.

"We haven't talked much," she mumbled. In fact, she and Nigel had had a grand total of three conversations, the longest of which centered around the enthralling topic of how best to change the toner in the copying machine.

"You have to put yourself in his path," Charlotte instructed. "Make yourself obvious. Especially on Fridays. And then you can just casually mention that you're meeting your mates at the pub and would he like to join you?"

"I thought women weren't supposed to make the first move," said Sarah. Charlotte's last PR project had been representing the two lady authors of *Love Is a Battlefield: Using Time-Tested Military Strategies to Find a Husband*, and ever since then she'd gotten quite strident on the proper way to, as she put it, Wage the Campaign.

"That's not technically a move," said Charlotte. "Asking him to dinner is a move. Which you won't make, because once you've got him in the pub and you've had a few pints, he'll be the one asking you."

Sarah lifted her napkin and wiped away the lipstick she was certain had smeared on her upper lip. "And I thought," she continued, "that I wasn't supposed to shit where I lived."

Charlotte widened her eyes. "Sweetie," she said, "it's been two years. You've got to shit somewhere."

Sarah wished she had the courage to tell Charlotte to stuff it. But the truth was that her love life of late had been a bit of a disaster.

That summer, there'd been Edward. She'd had high hopes for him. She'd spent months smiling at him at the tube stop. It had taken her that time to work her way up from a smile to a tentative "Hello," but that time had given her a chance to observe him, and she'd liked what she'd seen. Edward always seemed so clean, his skin pink, as if it had been recently scrubbed, his cheeks faintly flushed with razor burn. They'd started talking, moving from the weather to their jobs (he was an assistant director's assistant on one of the morning chat shows—"but with grand ambitions," he'd told her with a smile) to their personal lives. Once Sarah had learned that Edward was single, she'd spent an entire week agonizing over whether he'd ask her out before deciding that she'd just ask him.

"On Friday next . . . if you're free . . . I'm having a small dinner party. Would you like to come?"

He told her he would like that very much. And she'd taken two days off from work, cleaning the apartment, shoving magazines and shoe boxes and plastic-wrapped drycleaning into the closet, buying cookbooks, buying exotic ingredients, making a curry from scratch even though her roommate, Siobhan, pointed out that there was a perfectly good takeaway shop not half a block away.

Looking back, she supposed that the way it had ended was predictable enough. Assistant director's assistant/aspiring playwright Edward had taken one look at part-time dancer/full-time waitress Siobhan—Siobhan, with her mop of russet curls and her brown eyes the color of strong tea—and you could practically hear the click. In the weeks and months to come, Sarah would have the occasion to hear a great deal more as Edward and Siobhan plighted their troth on the other side of the flimsy wall that separated the apartment's two bedrooms. Edward, she learned, tended to moan about Jesus during orgasm, even though he'd told her he was an agnostic. Just another lie, she thought, shoving wads of cotton into her ears and pressing a pillow against her head for good measure.

That night, she'd made herself a promise: no more men whose names started with vowels. She'd been burned by an Ian, shamed by an Oliver, dumped by Yves during her summer in Paris and now thrown over by Edward. It was a pattern she couldn't ignore. From now on, she was going to be strictly a consonant kind of girl. She'd date Davids and Fredericks and Georges, Harrys and Jacobs and Keiths and Liams and Matthews . . . and Nigels, she'd decided. There would definitely be a Nigel in her future.

Sarah had planned on following Charlotte's putting-yourself-in-his-path strategy—had even planned on relocating the picture of her parents on her desk to give Nigel an unimpeded sight line—but as it turned out, that hadn't been necessary. On Thursday, the day after her pub date with Charlotte, Nigel had wandered by her desk.

"Hey," he said, with his easy smile, "any chance you'd be free for a drink tomorrow night?"

"I. Erm." Her mind worked frantically. Did *Love Is a Battlefield* instruct against accepting a date at the last minute, or was that *The Rules?* Was it possible to follow both at the same time? She cursed herself for not paying closer attention and cleared her throat to buy more time.

"Please?" Nigel said, giving his extra-long eyelashes a special flutter. "I'm a little lost here, to tell you the truth."

"The toner again?" she asked.

"No. Well, that's part of it. It's just . . . everything, I suppose. I guess I'm not used to office work yet."

"Yet?" Sarah stared at him, puzzled, remembering that he'd told her he'd come from Credit Suisse, which, to the best of her knowledge, was an office much like this one.

He blushed and fluttered some more. "Well, you know, I had two weeks off—a fortnight—I guess I got out of the habit. Just lay around and watched the telly."

"Sounds like bliss," said Sarah.

"So I'll see you later, then?"

"All right," she said. He smiled at her—a smile, she thought, that could melt even the single brick of ice cream that remained frozen in the farthest reaches of Charlotte's freezer from one birthday to the next.

Sarah figured that she'd spend her night with Nigel playing another round of the familiar game known to single girls the world over as Are We Or Aren't We—as in, are we or aren't we on a date? The early signs were encouraging. Nigel let her walk into the lift first. He held the doors for her courteously, both at the bank, then at the pub, and once they'd gotten there he'd pulled out her seat, shaken his head at her offer of money, and walked to the bar to fetch them drinks. All good signs, Sarah thought, but a girl could never be sure. And she'd been burned before, assuming that an invitation for dinner or a movie or even dinner and a movie automatically spelled "date" when in fact, all the fellow had in mind was a little company (and, with embarrassing frequency, a chance to spill his guts about that latest woman who'd broken his heart in a way that made it clear that he wasn't even remotely considering Sarah as a replacement, but merely as a pal, a friend, an ear to bend, a shoulder to cry upon).

"So!" said Nigel, setting down her gin and tonic and his lager. "Tell me about yourself!"

Sarah laughed. "Which parts?" Then she blushed, worrying that he'd think she meant parts of her body instead of parts of her life, and gulped at her drink to hide her confusion, wishing she could dash into the loo for a quick consultation with the copy of *Love Is a Battlefield* that she'd tucked into her purse on her way out the door that morning.

But Nigel hadn't seemed to notice. "How'd you get into the glamorous world of international arbitrage?" he asked.

"Ah, now that's a long, boring story," she said.

"Tell me," he urged her. "I've got time."

So she did. She explained that she'd always been good at math, while her sister had always been good at English and drama and composition. So it was only natural that she'd gravitate toward the field of finance, while Charlotte would, of course, wind up in PR, wearing leather skirts to work and hobnobbing with models and race-car drivers and models who drove race-cars. "She's the glamorous one," Sarah explained, midway through her third drink. "I'm more the dogged one."

"Dogged," Nigel repeated thoughtfully. "Do you think most people in this field are dogged?"

"Well," said Sarah, "I've never thought about it much. But yes, I guess so. You have to be methodical," she said, lifting one finger. "You have to be organized," she said, lifting another. You have to be *kidding* me, shrieked a voice in her head that sounded suspiciously like Charlotte. You're sitting in a pub with a handsome man who's buying you drinks and you're talking about organization!

"Anyhow," she said, ducking her head and taking another slurp of her drink. "How about you? How did you wind up in the fascinating field of international finance?"

Nigel drummed his fingers against his glass. He was still nursing his first pint. "I'm not sure," he said. He gave her a half-smile. "It was the path of least resistance, I guess. My father's a banker, his father was a banker, my three brothers . . ."

"Let me guess. Bankers."

"Well, actually, they're lawyers—barristers—but you get the idea."

"If you could have been something else," asked Sarah, "what would you have been?"

He gave her a whole smile this time. "An actor, I think. I acted a little bit in college—a few Shakespeare things, nothing too much—but I really loved it. I think if things had been different—if I hadn't been so afraid of struggling and being poor—that's what I would have done."

"You can still do it," said Sarah. She wondered if it would be all right to put her hand on his forearm—just in a friendly, sympathetic fashion. She decided that it would.

"Do you think so?"

"Absolutely," she said. "There's community theater . . . and the BBC's always having auditions for extras. It'd be a foot in the door. And I bet you'd be good at it, too. I know someone who's an assistant director's assistant . . ." And she bit her lip, blushing. Trying too hard. *Love Is a Battlefield* had definitely advised against that.

He smiled at her. "Thanks," he said. "That's really nice to hear."

She thought then that there was a chance he might kiss her. She tilted her head at an advantageous angle and closed her eyes in case the brush of his lips against hers was imminent. But when she opened her eyes several seconds later, Nigel was still looking at her, smiling his pleased smile. "I should get going," he said. "But thank you. Really. Thanks for believing in me."

Over the next three weeks, Sarah and Nigel's Friday-night drinks turned into a ritual, along with semi-regular 3 p.m. snack breaks in which one or the other of them would head down to the stand at the corner and come back with crisps or a Cadbury bar. She told him about Charlotte, leaving out anything that would make her sister sound too terribly alluring, remembering the time when Charlotte had visited Sarah at university and Sarah had made the mistake of introducing her sister to her boyfriend of the moment, who'd blinked beerily at Charlotte—an inch or two taller than Sarah, a stone or so slimmer, her hair a shade blonder and her eyes a touch more blue—and proclaimed, "She's the digitally enhanced version of you!"

Nigel told Sarah about his brothers the barristers. "They do personal injury," he'd said, wrinkling his nose and telling her how once he'd had a wisdom tooth extracted and his face had bruised and his brothers had practically gotten into a wrestling match in their haste to find the family camera and record the potential evidence of his injury.

He told her about the pickup rugby game he joined in every Sunday and how the man in the flat next door would wake him up on Sundays blasting Broadway show tunes. She told him about Edward and Siobhan, leaving out the parts about how she'd liked Edward before her roommate had even met him, turning Edward's religious utterances during lovemaking into a funny story. She and Nigel even made a bet that if Edward ever invoked the Buddha, Nigel would have to take her to dinner in Paris. Slowly, Sarah let herself hope—and then believe—that things were progressing, that there would come a Friday night when their drinks would turn into dinner, and dinner would extend to a walk home along romantically rained-upon streets, and then, at her door, he'd take her in his arms and whisper something tender in her ear, and finally kiss her—preferably, just as Siobhan and Edward were rounding the corner and Charlotte just happened to be driving by.

On the fourth Friday, he'd held her elbow and gotten her into a cab, and she'd felt his breath, warm in her ear, and his lips against her cheek. "Thank you," he murmured, "for everything." She turned her head and for a brief flickering instant his lips had met hers. And it was perfect. Like something out of a movie. Completely perfect, except for the look on his face as the taxi had pulled away, which seemed to her equal parts pleasure and confusion—the face of a man, she thought, who'd bitten into an apple and found he was eating pizza instead, something good, delicious even, but not quite what he'd wanted, not quite the thing he'd had in mind. Then she decided she was being silly. He liked her. He'd kissed her. Things could only move forward from there.

The next Monday morning, Sarah walked into the office, smiling to herself, to find that Nigel's desk was empty. The coffee cup had vanished, the Bic pens had disappeared, the desktop calendar and haphazard stack of *Financial Times* were all gone. The only thing that remained was a newspaper picture—a little ratty around the edges—of Nicolette Nesbit, American singer and movie star—still taped to the right of his computer screen.

"Where's Nigel?" Sarah asked Nancy Rooney, the department's short, stout, fireplug-shaped secretary.

"Dunno, dear," Nancy called over her shoulder. "Quit, I suppose."

Quit, Sarah whispered. She sank into her chair. All day long, she'd look up at his desk, expecting to see him there, expecting him to be smiling at her, or sending her an instant message—a hello, or a request for aspirin or chocolate, or an inquiry as to whether Edward had started talking, mid-climax, to Mother Mary. But there was nothing. Nobody knew where Nigel had gone, and the office was full of rumors. Promoted. Transferred. Sick parents. Sacked. Sarah spent the whole day fruitlessly hitting Reload on her email, hoping she'd see something—anything—from Nigel. Nothing came. At five o'clock she sidled over to his desk, pulled the photograph of Nicolette Nesbit off his computer, and folded it into her pocket. She thought maybe by the end of the week someone would have figured out the truth about Nigel. And she was right . . . but not in the way she'd imagined.

"There she is!"

Sarah looked up, blinking. It was nine o'clock in the morning, three days after Nigel's as-yet-unexplained departure. And there, standing on the First Bank's marble steps, was Nancy Rooney, in a pair of truly unfortunate plaid-patterned pants, surrounded by half a dozen of Sarah's floormates and what looked like dozens of photographers and reporters.

"Here!"

"Miss! Sarah! Over here!"

"Did you know him?"

"Were you dating?"

"Sarah! Sarah Compton! This way, luv!"

"Did you really have no idea who he was?"

Sarah stared at the phalanx, then up at Nancy. "What's going on?" she called.

"Your Nigel pulled a fast one," Nancy said smugly.

"What do you mean?" Sarah asked. Possibilities were tumbling through her mind. Embezzlement, she thought numbly. Credit fraud, identity theft, or worse. There was all manner of mischief an unscrupulous bank employee could get up to . . . but Nigel? Her Nigel, with his guileless blue eyes and his funny stories of getting pummeled by his brothers during impromptu living-room rugby matches, and of how his father still insisted on wearing socks with his sandals?

She tucked her chin into her chest, squared her shoulders, and dredged up a term she remembered from a dozen movies. "No comment."

"So you had no idea, then?" This from a youngish man with his pen poised over his notebook.

"No idea," Sarah said curtly, thinking she'd figure out precisely what it was she had no idea about as soon as she was through the doors.

"Oh, I don't believe it," sneered one of the women standing beside a television camera, with a cakey layer of makeup on her face that Sarah figured had to look better on TV than it did in real life. "How could you not know?"

Sarah kept her mouth shut, but the youngish notebook man was clinging to her like a dryer sheet. "You never even guessed? I mean, he wasn't wearing disguises or anything, was he?"

She stopped. Disguises? For embezzlement? "I don't know what you're talking about," she said.

The man cleared his throat. "Well, Nigel Jones—that's what he was calling himself, right?—he's actually Adrian Stadt. The movie actor."

Sarah's jaw sagged open. Adrian Stadt? She'd heard his name, had probably caught bits and pieces of the movies he'd done. They'd mostly been teenybopper trash—one about junior high school, one about a man who inherits his father's whoopee cushion factory. Then Adrian Stadt surprised everyone by starring in a sensitive romantic comedy about a poor little rich girl who finds true love with the pool boy. He'd been the pool boy. Critics had raved. And Adrian Stadt had been hailed as the new millennium's new-age guy—sensitive without being smarmy, caring without being corny, good-looking without being unapproachably, otherworldly handsome. And he'd been here, Sarah thought. Posing as Nigel. Nigel, who'd been her friend.

"He was doing research for a role," said the man, shoving his glasses up on his nose and squinting from his little notebook up to Sarah's face. "And you really didn't recognize him?"

"I really didn't," Sarah admitted. "He was just Nigel."

The chorus of questions rose to a crescendo as a fusillade of flashbulbs went off, all but blinding her. Had they been dating? How well had they known each other? For how long? Was his English accent credible? What story did he use to gain employment? Did she ever see any of his famous friends hanging around? What about Nicolette Nesbit? Had she phoned? Stopped by? Did Sarah know that she'd been here too, living with him in a rented flat in Notting Hill?

She shook her head, said, "No comment" once more, and shoved her way into the building, into the lift and finally collapsed at her desk. A few minutes on the Internet were all it took to convince her—Nigel Jones, entry-level First Bank of London employee, and Adrian Stadt, world-famous Hollywood star, were one and the same.

"I am an idiot," Sarah whispered, just as Nancy Rooney rounded the corner, Burberry'd thighs swishing.

"Don't be too hard on yourself," she said, her voice oozing sympathy as phony as movie-theater butter-flavored topping. "It was an honest mistake."

Sarah kept her eyes shut until Nancy swished away, realizing two things—she had been a fool and, once again, in spite of her best efforts, she'd fallen for a vowel.

"Adrian Stadt?" Charlotte shrieked at 7 a.m. the next day. Sarah winced and pulled the telephone six inches away from her ear, realizing that the trio (well, quintet) of vodka martinis she'd consumed the night before might well have been a mistake.

"Don't scream at me," she whispered.

"Adrian Stadt?" Charlotte repeated, at a slightly diminished volume. "And you had no idea it was him?"

"I . . . well . . . no. No, I didn't. I mean, Charlotte, if you could have seen him, he looks just like a regular person."

"Except he's not," Charlotte pointed out. "He's Adrian Stadt."

"But that's not like being Jude Law or, or Tom Cruise or something like that!" Sarah said. "He was just a regular nice-looking guy."

"Did he wear a disguise?" her sister demanded. "Hats? Beards? Big fake prosthetic nose?"

"I don't think so," Sarah said. "Just glasses. That was all."

"And have you not seen *Saturday Night? Makin' Whoopee? Junior High Confidential?*"

"But he's so goofy in all of those," Sarah said helplessly. "He wasn't goofy with me. He wore nice shirts and, and his hair was always combed . . ."

"And he kept a picture of Nicolette Nesbit on his computer," Charlotte said. "Nicolette Nesbit, who he's been dating for the last six months."

"It was cut out of a newspaper!" Sarah protested.

"Any guy could have done that! Any guy with a crush!" She swallowed hard. Her head was throbbing in time with her heartbeat. "How do you know about the picture, anyhow?"

Charlotte's voice resumed its initial volume. "Have you not seen the papers?"

"Papers," Sarah whispered. She was remembering the day before, the parts that her vodka binge hadn't obliterated, the flashbulbs, the photographers, the young man with the notebook. "Oh, God." She set down the phone without bothering to hang it up, shoved her feet into the first two shoes she came across (judging from the way the right one pinched and the left one gaped, she figured she'd gotten one of Edward's and one of Siobhan's), grabbed her keys and staggered out to the news shop across the street, where she found her own face—wide-eyed, pale and bloated as the moon, with at least two more chins than she'd previously believed she possessed—staring back at her.

"STADT'S SCAM!" screamed the *Mirror*.

"HE WAS JUST NIGEL!" said the *Sun*. At least they quoted me right, Sarah thought.

The *Mail* kept it short and sweet. "DUPED" read the one-word headline. Sarah picked up the paper with shaking hands and flipped to page three.

American movie star Adrian Stadt got one over on the employees of the First Bank of London. For the past month the flashy actor and man-about-town has been living quietly in London, preparing for his role in the upcoming drama *Fast Money* by working as a trainee at the

First Bank of London under the name Nigel Jones . . . and none of his co-workers seemed to have a clue.

"A movie star?" asked Sarah Compton, twenty-seven, a colleague who shared office space and Friday-night drinks with the man she knew as Nigel. "He was just Nigel. We were friends."

More than friends, say some of Jones's/Stadt's colleagues. "She had a huge crush on him," confided Nancy Rooney, who worked closely with both Compton and Stadt. "I think he was leading her on. They had drinks at least three times a week, and he'd ask her all sorts of questions. Poor Sarah. He was probably just doing research. He wasn't interested in her a bit."

Meanwhile, men and women on the street are stunned that FB of L employees failed to recognize the movie star in their midst.

"If Adrian Stadt showed up at my office, you'd better believe I'd recognize him!" said Jemima Davies, a paralegal at Please Turn to Page 62.

Sarah decided not to. She refolded the paper, limped back to her flat in her mismatched shoes, passed by Edward and Siobhan, who were entwined on the couch, and started packing.

"Sarah?" her roommate called. Sarah ignored her. She started throwing random handfuls of clothing into her canvas overnight bag—underwear, sweatpants, a fistful of socks. She took her wallet, her keys, her mobile phone, two bottles of emergency vodka. And ten minutes later, she was gone.

★ ★ ★

"This is the worst thing that's ever happened to me," said Sarah. She'd spent the last two hours sitting at her sister's scrubbed-pine kitchen table with her head buried in her hands.

"No," said Charlotte, bustling from sink to stove and back again, "the worst thing was the time you were playing airplane with Henry and you threw him into the ceiling fan."

"That was an accident," said Sarah.

"Notwithstanding," said her sister.

"Agh," Sarah said. She was remembering, cringing with the shame of it, how she'd told Nigel—told Adrian, she reminded herself—how he should pursue his ambitions to be an actor, how the BBC was always hiring extras, how she knew someone who was an assistant director's assistant . . . "I have made," she announced, "a complete ass of myself."

"Sarah," said Charlotte. Sarah shoved her face into her forearms and groaned. "Sarah," Charlotte said again, and grabbed her sister by the chin. "A little perspective, please. You haven't committed a crime. You haven't hurt anyone. You were nice to a chap, which the last time I checked wasn't illegal."

Charlotte's telephone trilled. "Don't answer that!" Sarah begged. The reporters, she thought. They'd probably figured out where she was. Nancy Rooney had probably printed up all of her Emergency Contact information and faxed it to the newspapers.

Charlotte ignored her. "Yes?" Sarah heard her sister ask frostily. "And what is this regarding?"

No, Sarah begged in a stage whisper, shaking her

head for emphasis. Charlotte handed her the phone. "Adrian Stadt," she said.

Sarah took a deep breath, and did her best imitation of her sister's frosty, haughty, I'm-much-too-important-to-be-bothered-with-this voice. "Yes?"

"Sarah? It's, um, Adrian Stadt." There was a pause. "Also known as Nigel Jones."

Sarah said nothing.

"I'm calling to apologize," he blurted. "I saw the papers . . . my manager faxed them over . . . I feel just awful. I never meant to get you in trouble, or, or get you involved at all . . ."

Sarah said nothing. My heart is breaking, she thought. She felt as if she were in a spaceship, orbiting the earth, and the earth was her heart, and she could look down and almost see it crack and start to fall apart.

"I'm so sorry," he said. "I feel terrible. You were the only one there who was nice to me, and you didn't deserve any of this . . . Sarah, are you there? Say something!"

I fancied you, she wanted to say. *I liked you, and I thought you liked me, too. And I'm an idiot, and I should have known better. I should have known that hope is not my friend.*

"Sarah?"

"I'm sorry, too," she said softly, and pressed the End button before he could say anything else.

Her sister was listening. "Well," she drawled, "that went well, didn't it?"

The flowers came next. Gigantic, elaborate arrangements from London's top florist, each one bigger than the next. "Somebody die?" the delivery boy asked after the fifth vase in five days. Me, Sarah thought of saying, but she just shook her head and signed his form. The flowers were all different—roses, lilies, orchids, even, but the card was always the same. *I'm so sorry. I feel terrible. Please call me. Adrian Stadt.* On the sixth day there were slips of paper in the envelopes, two tickets to the London premiere of *Fast Money*. She thought about ripping them up, but in the end she slipped them in her wallet. A girl had to be practical. Her paid leave would be up in two weeks, at which point she could sell the tickets on eBay for some fast cash.

On the seventh day she signed the slip, took the card, tipped the delivery boy and told him that he had her permission to deliver any subsequent bouquets to the hospital, or the cemetery, whichever suited him best.

That Saturday night, Charlotte and her husband, Andrew, dragged Sarah out to dinner. "You have to leave the house at some point," Charlotte lectured, forcing Sarah to put on a skirt and heels and blusher, combing her hair the way she had when they were little girls. "One of Andrew's friends is coming."

"Oh, no," said Sarah, "no, I can't yet . . ."

"It's dinner. Food," Charlotte said. "It's not the end of the world."

But it was every bit as awful as Sarah thought it would be, because once they'd gotten through the cocktails and the pleasantries, all Andrew's friend wanted to talk about was the truth about Nigel. "You couldn't tell he was American?" he asked, as Sarah chewed the same mouthful of her rocket salad, over and over and over. "He must be quite an actor."

"All right," Charlotte acknowledged the next morning, "so that didn't go very well. But you can't just sulk around the house all day. It's not healthy."

Sarah had to concede the point. She hadn't breathed fresh air in the two weeks since the debacle that was Nigel, except for the minute between car and restaurant and car and house, and her pale skin was turning the color (and her flesh, the consistency) of a pot of paste. "Come on," she said to Ella and Henry. "Who's up for a walk?"

"Good. You can take them to nursery school!" Charlotte said, smiling her approval. "Wonderful. I'll have time to wax the floors."

"Your mum is obsessed," Sarah whispered, snapping the twins into their stroller.

"What's obsessed?" Henry hollered. Charlotte gave her sister an indulgent smile.

"Go," she said, and opened the door.

"Hello, there," said the man at the nursery school door. Sarah gave him what she hoped was a short, no-nonsense nod, swung the stroller around and kissed Henry and Ella goodbye. For a week now she'd been walking them the half hour to school every day—dropping off at nine, picking up at noon, sometimes stopping for sandwiches and soft drinks on their way home—and every morning and every afternoon, this man had been there. Sarah had noticed him even though she'd sworn off noticing men forever, because he was the only man there, and was impossible not to notice in the swirl of a dozen women and twice as many children.

"Miss. Miss!"

The man was calling after her. Here it comes, Sarah thought. She'd already gotten it from all of the mums, so now it was the single father's turn. The *Aren't you?* The *Didn't I read?* The *Tell me what he's really like!* She quickened her pace, but the man, with his long legs, matched it easily. "Excuse me," he said, "I was wondering if you have any friends who are available."

She blinked at him. Of all the impertinent questions she'd been asked, this came close to topping the list.

"It's just that I'm at my wit's end," said the man. "I thought I could handle him . . . I mean, what's one little boy? But he's running me ragged." He dragged his hands through his tousled hair for emphasis. "I'm thinking if I could find someone for maybe just a few hours a day . . ." He narrowed his eyes, taking in Sarah's confusion. "You're the nanny, right?" Sarah said nothing. The man muttered a curse under his breath. "Au pair?" he guessed. He raised his voice. "Do you speak English?"

Sarah started laughing. "Yes, I speak English, and no, I'm not the nanny. I'm their aunt."

The man's face reddened. "Oh. Oh, God. I'm terribly sorry . . ."

Sarah laughed even harder.

"I'm always doing that," said the man. "Just blurting things out, leaping first and looking later . . . I should have asked, but I just guessed . . ."

"Don't worry," Sarah said gravely. "There are worse

things than being mistaken for a nanny." She looked at him. He was maybe five years older than she was, long and lanky in jeans and trainers and a paint-splattered plaid shirt. He had a beaky nose and stubbly cheeks. No matinee idol, that was for sure. No wedding ring, either, but in this day and age that didn't necessarily mean anything.

"My wife died," said the man, and turned, if it was possible, even redder. "See, there I go, just blurting things out. I apologize again. I'm sorry."

"That's all right," Sarah said. Somehow they'd started walking, side by side, pushing their empty strollers ahead of them.

"I'm an artist," said the man. "My studio's at home, and I just figured, well, I can look after him while I'm working. I'd give him little bits of canvas, paints, he can play or take a nap, and I can work and it'll be all right. But it's not." The man shook his head, looking rueful and puzzled. "He hates to paint. And I don't think he's taken a nap since he was two."

Sarah found herself laughing again.

"Oh, sure," said the man. "You laugh. Go ahead. Meanwhile, I'm stuck raising Dennis the Menace. He hates painting, he hates puzzles, he hates all of his books. The only thing he wants to do is play Candyland. Endless games of Candyland. That, or destroy things. I'm getting a little desperate."

"I wish I could help," Sarah said. "Is his name really Dennis?"

"No, but it should be," said the man. "It's Sebastien. I call him Bash. That fits, too." They were standing in front of the coffee shop, the one she'd taken to frequenting, sitting in a tattered armchair while Henry and Ella were in school, with a book and a baseball cap pulled low over her forehead.

"Would you like . . ." she began.

"Do you want . . ." said the man.

Then they were both laughing, and the tall man stuck out his hand. "I'm Christopher," he said. "And you have a wonderful laugh. Will you have a cup of coffee with me? And dinner Friday night?"

Sarah stared up at him. Christopher, she thought. He had blue-gray eyes, thickly fringed eyelashes, and he smelled like turpentine.

"See, I did it again," Christopher said cheerfully. "Just blurted it out. You probably think I'm mad."

"No," said Sarah. "No, I don't."

He was still holding her hand. "So?" he asked. "Will you?"

"I'm sorry," she said. "I can't."

"Can't eat dinner?" Christopher asked. "How is that for you? Do you just have to fill up at lunchtime and hope for the best?"

Sarah laughed.

"You've probably got a boyfriend," he continued glumly. "Or a girlfriend?"

He looked at her sideways. Sarah shook her head.

"A husband, then," he said, and sighed. "And he's probably seven feet tall and eats blokes like me for breakfast."

"No," she said. "It's just that . . ." Her voice trailed off. He stared at her.

"Just that what?"

She opened her mouth, thinking that she'd try to

tell him, that she'd try to explain. But how could she? I was half in love with a man at work who turned out to be an American movie star only I didn't know and my picture was in the papers and I was a joke?

You were the only one who was nice to me, she could hear Nigel's—Adrian's—voice saying in her head. You deserve better than this. And maybe this was better; maybe this was her reward. "I'm busy on Friday," she heard herself say. "But Saturday's good."

JENNIFER WEINER lives in Philadelphia with her husband, Adam, and her rat terrier, Wendell. She is the author of three bestselling novels, *Little Earthquakes*, *In Her Shoes*, and *Good in Bed*.

Voodoo Dolls, C-Cups and Eminem

MELISSA SENATE

*B*efore brunch, I was engaged and happy. After brunch I was engaged and cursed—in more ways than one.

It was too bad; if I'd known at the restaurant that I'd lose my appetite for a few weeks, I would have eaten more of my omelet and the home fries my teenaged half sister kept stealing off my plate. At fourteen, Madison was perpetually on a diet and had ordered a plain turkey sandwich, but saw nothing wrong with poaching someone else's fries.

Let me start at the beginning.

Two days ago, my boyfriend, Michael, who I'd been dating for six months (almost six months, anyway), had proposed out of the clear blue sky, with a one-and-a-half-carat diamond ring. That same day, I'd gotten promoted at work from editorial assistant to assistant editor at Brazen Books, where I worked on romantic suspense novels, and Michael had taken me out to dinner to celebrate my whopping twelve-dollar-a-week raise (he was good that way). "I always knew you were excellent at romance, Rebecca," he'd said, blowing a kiss and clinking my champagne glass and making Groucho Marx eyebrows at me. That night, we'd made delicious love, then drifted off to sleep spooned together. In the middle of the night, I woke up to him whispering a proposal in my ear.

"I love you," he'd said, trailing a finger down my cheek. "You love me. Why wait? I know what I need to know now, which is that I want to spend the rest of my life with you."

Who was I to argue, especially because I loved him too and agreed with everything he'd said.

Not everyone did, though.

"Why wait?" repeated every friend and relative I had. "Because you've known him for six months!"

"Not even!" some added. "You're in love? You're in *lust.* You can't know someone in six months."

What I *knew* was that Michael made me happy. Made me feel good. Made me feel sane. Made me feel more me than I'd ever felt. Everything I did was either adorable, smart, funny or right.

"Yeah," the naysayers pooh-poohed with raised eyebrows. *"Now.* Six months from now, a year from now, when you're nagging him to pick up his dirty socks and underwear from the bedroom floor, when you're screaming your head off that he blew another fifty bucks on a Play Station game, you won't be so adorable. Trust us. We know what we're talking about."

Oh really? My mother, Queen Pooh-Pooher, her job on this earth, had been divorced twice. She'd known both her husbands over a year before she married them, and the marriages had still fallen apart. Marriage number one had lasted for ten years before my father went a bit nuts and bought a dude ranch (of sorts) in Montana, citing a need for wide-open spaces as far away from Barbara Simon as possible. Marriage number two, resulting in a surprise baby, had lasted for twelve years. Madison had taken her parents' divorce hard, as she did her dad's second marriage a year later to a very nice woman who fussed over her. That was when I really found out exactly what big sisters were for.

So, with all that time to know what you were getting and then all that time getting it, if you still got divorced, why did it matter if you knew your husbands for six months or six years before saying "I do"?

"Don't get fresh, Rebecca Simon," my mother had said to that. "It's not only the time—it's the fact that you're a baby. You're twenty-five, for God's sake!"

"You were twenty-five when you married Dad."

"In my day, twenty-five was a lot older than it is now," my mother said.

Perhaps—because my girlfriends, all in their midtwenties, had the same opinions on the subject of my engagement as my mother. Snippets of the telephone conversations when I called to let my friends know the big news:

Amy (good bud from work): "Are you crazy? You're *twenty-five!*"

Roxy (close friend from Forest Hills, Queens, where I grew up): "Are you kidding or serious?"

Me: "Serious. I'm so excited!"

Roxy: "Honey, you're not one of the heroines in the books you edit. Romance novels are *fantasy*. Life is reality! In real life, no one in New York City gets married at twenty-five—and not to anyone she's known for six months! You don't really *know* Michael!"

Roxy was a grad student studying English Education. She was writing her thesis on the effect of romance novels on the love lives of American women. According to her research, which mostly consisted of me, our relatives and our relatives' friends, all voracious romance readers, women expected men to act like heroes in romance novels, and they were perpetually disappointed when men were just men.

Deb (other close friend from Forest Hills): "Ohmigod! Congratulations! I'm so happy for you!"

Finally, I thought. A little congratulations!

Deb: "But are you sure? I mean, you've only known him for six months. Marriage is about partnership and compromise. I know Michael's cute and a great guy, but come on . . ."

Deep sigh.

Michael *was* cute and he *was* a great guy. And yes, I was sure.

Aunt Janet (my mother's sister): "Honey, I want to say *mazel tov,* I really do. But I'm nervous for you. You're just a baby! And what do you really know about this guy? He's a waiter? What man is a waiter at twenty-five?"

Actually, Michael was twenty-seven.

Cousin Joan (Aunt Janet's grumpy twenty-two-year-old daughter): "I'm not wearing some ugly-ass bridesmaid dress or leather shoes—I'm a vegan now."

My mother's best friend, Elizabeth-Jane (mother of my first boyfriend): "If my Stephen asked for the family heirloom engagement ring tomorrow, I'd tell him he was nuts. Twenty-five is too young to get married."

News flash: Stephen *was* nuts. And twenty-five was only too young to get married if the people getting married were too young to get married.

In other words, I trusted myself and I trusted Michael.

"You're twenty-five!" they all shouted for two days after the announcement as though I didn't know how old I was. "No one gets married at twenty-five! Twenty-five is the new eighteen!"

"What's the new thirty?" I asked my mother.

I could see I'd confused her. She'd lost track of her math. "Twenty-five," she said, her brows furrowing.

"So I'm really thirty," I pointed out. "Which is a perfectly good age to get married."

"Don't be a smart aleck, Rebecca," my mother said. "The reason we all waited two days before telling you how we really felt" (was she forgetting her reaction on the phone—dead silence?) "was because we figured you'd come to your senses, that you'd tell Michael he was sweet, but that you were both too young and had a lot of growing up to do before you made such a huge decision."

Even my father, my kind, soft-spoken, unassuming dad, got in on the action via telephone from the dude ranch. I could hear mooing in the background.

"Honey, you just got promoted," Bob Simon said.

"Enjoy it. There are going to be lots of promotions, lots of boyfriends in your future. Why rush into marriage with your first real boyfriend?"

Deep sigh.

The key word was *real.*

After my "celebration brunch," with my mother and sister, the three of us went back to my apartment for coffee and cake. My mother pulled out a bunch of dirty bridal magazines from her totebag and stacked them on the coffee table. "I found them stacked next to the recycling bins in the garbage chute in my building. What, you're too good to read old magazines?"

Madison snickered and refused a piece of the cake my mother bought at the bakery on my corner, then ate all the icing off the slice on my plate. "What's that?" Madison asked, gesturing at a big box on top of the television. She had frosting on her chin.

"Ooh, maybe it's an engagement present!" my mother said, taking a medium-sized box, wrapped in brown mailing paper, off the top of the television set where Michael must have put it. "It's addressed to you, dear." She gave the box a little shake. "Awfully light for crystal or silver."

Madison rolled her eyes and I winked at her. So, my mother wasn't happy that I was engaged, but she'd brought over twenty old bridal magazines with food stains and God knew what else and she was disappointed that my first engagement gift wasn't heavy enough to be expensive?

That was the thing about having a crazy family. If you were sane, you could block out their voices. Not much of the naysaying had gotten to me during the past two days.

I opened the box. Under all that plain brown wrapping was the familiar blue Tiffany's box.

My mother's eyes lit up. "Who's it from?"

"I don't know," I said. "I don't see a card and there's no return address."

Inside the box was a shrink-wrapped doll of some sort. I took it out. "What is this?"

"Ohmigod!" Madison said, grabbing it from me and tearing open the plastic wrap. "It's VooDoo Bride! I saw that at the mall last month when I was visiting Daddy. There's a VooDoo Groom too."

My mother picked up VooDoo Bride and grimaced at it. "What the hell kind of gift is this? Is this a gift?"

I hoped not.

"It's funny," Madison said, taking it back from our mom. "I really like her dress, well, except for the dagger sticking out of her chest and the dripping blood." She giggled. "Rebecca, I think you should consider this same gown—not!"

"Is this a gift?" my mother repeated. "Who sends something like this?"

Madison picked up the box the doll had been stuffed inside. "Pretty funny of someone to put it in a Tiffany's box."

Hysterical.

Yes, folks, step right up and laugh at my first engagement gift—a voodoo doll decked out in full bridal regalia. That's right—a voodoo doll with a dagger in her chest! Not a vase from Crate and Barrel. Not a top-of-the-line blender or talking scale that also blurted out your percentage of body fat. Not a crystal bowl. A voodoo doll. As in: envision someone you hate, think evil thoughts, such as *Get Fired! Get Dumped! Gain Ten Pounds!*, jab doll with stick pin and *voilà*, your victim will soon be penniless, loveless, and fat.

In college, when a guy I'd been crazy about (but who didn't count as a real boyfriend, according to my family), had broken my heart with the It's Not You, It's Me routine, Roxy and Deb had chipped in and bought me VooDoo Ex-Boyfriend: Get Him Back or Just Get Him Good! VooDoo Boyfriend was dressed in a white T-shirt and jeans and came with two sets of pins—red for poking in the heart region to get him back, and black for poking him in the semi-anatomically-correct groin area if it didn't work. I'd poked with red for a week, until I'd found out he'd fallen for someone else. Then I started poking with black. The happy couple had broken up a few months later, so VooDoo Ex-Boyfriend had been worth Roxy and Deb's nineteen bucks.

My new voodoo doll was also personalized. Voo-Doo Bride was indeed her name, according to the tiny instruction card around her neck. Her ropy yellow hair was twisted into a chignon under a lacy veil, and her ivory cotton body was clothed in a frilly wedding gown and painted-on shoes. With the exception of the little black dagger jammed into her chest, VooDoo Bride looked very happy.

My first thought was that a voodoo doll was a strange gift for someone who was supposed to be the definition of happiness. After all, wasn't a bride-to-be too busy blushing, glowing, and waving around her engagement ring to wish evil upon anyone? Perhaps I was supposed to use it on an overcharging photographer or an annoying mother.

Nope. The instruction card explained all: *Do you hate the bride-to-be? Are you a bridesmaid forced to buy a hideous royal blue dress? Or perhaps you just want the groom for yourself! Your every ill wish for the bride will be granted with every poke of the pin!*

Hey, wait a minute. *I* was the bride!

Handwritten below in red ink was: "Dear Rebecca, congratulations on your engagement. Too bad you're making a big mistake!"

Holy shit.

I dropped VooDoo Bride. She landed on the coffee table, staring up at me with her magic-markered blue eyes and red lips.

"What's wrong?" my mother asked. She grabbed the doll and read the card. "What is this nonsense?"

Madison grabbed it next. "Ohmigod!" She dropped it as though it were contaminated. We all stared at it, stock-still and holding our breaths as though it were about to come alive and attack us.

"Who's it from?" my mother asked.

I'd been so startled that I hadn't even thought to look for a real card saying "Gotcha! Just kidding! Love ya!" I searched the box and even inside VooDoo Bride's bloomers. Nothing. "I don't know. It seems to have been sent anonymously."

"Considering that *everyone* you know thinks you're making a big mistake, it could be anyone," Madison pointed out.

Thanks, little sis. I appreciate that.

"Do you recognize the handwriting?" my mom asked.

I shook my head. "Anyway, I'm sure it's just a joke. A stupid joke, but a joke."

"Oh, I don't know about that," my mother said. "You are now *supremely* hateable, Rebecca. You've joined the ranks of The Engaged. You're not the lonely single woman with only a cat for company like you used to be. Someone's clearly very jealous of you."

Did I mention my mother was crazy? I was too young to get married, ridiculous for getting engaged, but I was now Jealous Worthy *because* I was engaged.

"Honey," my mother said when I pointed this out, "this . . . *thing* isn't the work of someone who cares about you. Everyone's upset about the engagement because we *care*. Whoever sent this has some serious problems."

As Madison gleefully rattled off a list of who in the family thought I was making a big mistake, her finger dipping into my frosting with each suspect, I was pretty sure I was the one with the serious problems.

I spent the entire day looking over every inch of the wrapping paper, the instruction card, talking to the doorman who'd signed for it, calling UPS—anything that might give a clue as to who had sent it. Nothing. The postmark was New York, New York, which left eight million possible suspects.

"I'll bet it's from Michael's ex-girlfriend," Roxy said when I met her and Deb for show and tell that night at an Upper East Side bar a couple of blocks from my apartment. "Now that his family heirloom diamond ring is on someone else's hand, she probably wants him back."

I doubted that. I often saw Vanessa-the-ex gliding down Second or Third Avenue with shopping bags on one arm and a hot guy on the other. They liked to stick their tongues down each other's throats at red lights.

Deb pulled the dagger from the doll's chest and stuck it in its leg. "Hey, did you feel that?"

Roxy laughed.

"No, I'm serious," Deb said. "Did you?"

"I'm not superstitious," I muttered. But I pulled out the dagger and set it on a napkin anyway.

"So if it's not his ex, maybe it's some guy who has a wild crush on you," Roxy suggested. "Or some chick who has the hots for Michael."

That was more likely. Michael was indeed a waiter and met a lot of women. In fact, the fact that he was a waiter was how we'd met. Michael worked at a trendy restaurant in Chelsea, which meant he met more gay men than straight women, but beauties flocked there in droves as well and hit on him constantly. In response to "Are you ready to order?" he got a lot of "If *you're* on the menu, honey."

I wasn't kidding. Michael was very cute, and waiters in trendy restaurants were always Something Else, and women knew that. Michael was really a writer. He'd been working on his Novel (Jonathan Franzen and Philip Roth were his heroes) for almost three years. My mother, aunt, and Elizabeth-Jane insisted that Michael *was* a waiter, not a writer. "You are what you make money at," Aunt Janet had said.

"So you're not a *housewife?*" Madison had brilliantly retorted to Aunt Janet, who had never worked a day outside her home in her life. "What are you, then?"

My mother had slapped Madison across the face, and Madison had run from the room and locked herself in the bathroom.

Comedy. Drama. Comedra. Dramedy. You never knew what movie was showing in the Forest Hills apartments in which my relatives had their coffee klatches.

"The voodoo doll is just a joke," I repeated to my friends. "No one thinks I'm making a mistake. I'm sure whoever sent it will fess up with a phone call tomorrow."

Deb picked up the doll and dagger. "You're sure you don't feel this?" she asked, giving the doll a good poke in the stomach. "Where I come from, people believe in voodoo. Feel that?" She poked again.

"Deb, you come from *Queens,* not New Orleans," I reminded her.

"Did you tell Michael about the voodoo doll?" Roxy asked.

I nodded. Michael worked on Saturdays and Sundays, which saved him from the family brunch hell he would have been in for otherwise. He'd taken the voodoo doll and three-point shot it into the little wicker trash can by my desk in the bedroom. "It's a very immature someone's idea of a joke," he'd said. "It's not even worth an ounce of your time. Besides, if everyone thinks you're making a mistake, the doll is anticlimactic anyway."

He was right.

"Does it bother you?" he asked that night as we lay in bed admiring my engagement ring. It sparkled in the dim lighting. "That everyone thinks you're making a mistake?"

"Here's my answer." I slid on top of him and he smiled.

Michael's parents didn't think he was too young to get married or making a mistake. They lived in Ohio, where perhaps it was normal to get married at twenty-five. We were going for a visit soon.

"If you haven't met his parents before now," my mother said, "the relationship isn't serious. It's serious when you meet the family."

Unbelievable. "Mom, they live in Ohio. You live a thirty-five-minute subway ride from us."

"When it's serious, you make the effort," was my mother's response.

"That's why we're getting married," I pointed out.

The next day, my mother hoodwinked me. She told me she'd found the wedding dress of my dreams (I doubted she knew what that was) in a fancy bridal salon on Austin Street, a couple of blocks from her apartment. We were meeting at her apartment beforehand for coffee and my favorite chocolate croissants from the German bakery around the corner. She'd used the croissants to lure me into a trap. An intervention. Crowded around my mother's Laura Ashley living room, talking with their mouths full of my chocolate croissants, were my mother, Aunt Janet, cousin Joan, my mother's friend Elizabeth-Jane, and her son, Stephen, my first boyfriend (in a pre-teen sense). Every inch of the dining room table was covered with platters—bagels, tubs of cream cheese, pounds of smoked salmon, a half gallon of Tropicana, and a pot of coffee.

Hey, if you were going to stage an intervention, you needed to be fortified.

"We're here because we care about you."

"We don't want to see you make a mistake."

"You've only known him six months—not even!"

"He's a waiter!"

"Honey, you're only twenty-five."

Was I? I thought I was *five*.

"I'm surprised you didn't call Roxy and Deb," I said to my mother.

"I did, but they said they were supporting you," she responded with a shrug.

Score one for Roxy and Deb.

"You were always impulsive," my aunt Janet said, a bagel laden with lox and cream cheese midway to her mouth. "I remember when we all went to Hershey Park when you were how old—nine, ten?—and you hoarded all the chocolate and wouldn't share with Joaney because you were afraid you were never going to get more. Oh, how you cried. And what happened? You got more."

Was there a moral to this story? I'm afraid there was.

"You're marrying the first guy who asked," Aunt Janet continued. "Your first real boyfriend. It's the same thing."

"I was a real boyfriend," piped up Stephen.

"Now imagine if you'd married him," cousin Joan put in, laughing. "Just kidding, Steve."

"*Stephen,*" he grumbled. "Is there more vegetable cream cheese?"

Had they brought him to show me what I was missing? Were they kidding? Stephen had been a lot cuter at thirteen—with chin zits and braces—than he was at twenty-five.

"You don't see Stephen marrying the first girl to come along, do you?" his mother said, poppy seeds between her teeth. She took a sip of coffee and left a fuchsia mess on her mug.

Stephen was more interested in *Star Trek* and analyzing the *Matrix* movies than he ever would be in women.

"What is that *smell?*" Stephen asked, his nose high in the air as he sniffed. "It's like something's burning. Whoever's using the toaster, your bagel's burning!"

It wasn't the toaster.

"Mom!" Madison called from the bathroom doorway. "Help!"

Everyone ran into the bathroom. Madison had been straight-ironing a section of her hair and she'd managed to singe off a twelve-inch curl. She held it up, her face crumpling. The curl looked like a burned spiral French fry. "I burned my finger too," Madison complained, sucking the little blister on her pointer finger. "It hurts like hell."

"The mouth on this girl!" our mother snapped. I saw her mouth to Madison: *We have company!* Then she said, "And how are you going to write your report for English if your finger's blistered?"

"Who cares about stupid English!" Madison yelped. "I just burned off my hair!"

My mother rolled her eyes. "God gave you beautiful curly hair, like mine and Aunt Janet's and your sister's. I'm throwing out that straightening iron!"

"No!" Madison shrieked and locked herself in the bathroom.

I wrapped two chocolate croissants in a napkin, stuffed them into my purse and slipped out the front door, unnoticed. Saved by the curls. Who'd have guessed the family's kinky hair would be so useful?

The following Saturday afternoon, I cautiously agreed to go wedding band shopping with my mother. If I were serious about "this wedding business," she wanted me to put the rings I wanted on layaway so that she'd get a good price now instead of the mark-ups during the spring weddings deluge. My mother might have been crazy, but at least she was pre-dictable-crazy.

Madison threw a fit. She and I had a standing sisters-only meeting every Saturday afternoon; we usually went to the movies (she always tried to get me to take her to R-rated films and lie that she was seventeen despite the fact that she looked like the fourteen she was) and then we went to Serendipity and waited on line forever for worth-it waffles and amazing frozen hot-chocolates. It was our ritual. She was none too happy that she'd have to forgo both to go ring shopping—and with our mom tagging along.

They took the subway into Manhattan and met me at my apartment, where my mother had the chance to fake-hug-and-kiss her future son-in-law, fake-congratulate him on the engagement and *really* compliment him on the engagement ring. The one thing everyone agreed was the ring was great.

"He's so thin," my mother said when Michael disappeared into the bedroom to write. "You'd think they'd feed him for free at the restaurant."

As my mother did a little dusting and parted the shower curtain in the bathroom to inspect for mildew (feel free to clean the tub, Mom!), Madison sulked on the couch about her Saturday with me getting ruined. My mother relented and went to have her nails done so that Madison and I could have an hour and a half together before ring shopping. We were meeting at Fortunoff's on Fifth Avenue at noon.

Madison and I walked down Madison Avenue, my sister's favorite avenue because it was her namesake and there was great people-watching. Two weeks ago we saw P. Diddy. A month ago we saw Harrison Ford, but Madison had no idea who he was. She was always on the lookout for Hilary Duff and the cute lead singer of Coldplay, her favorite band, despite the fact that he probably lived in England.

Madison was telling me about a boy she liked at school. Gareth was his name.

"Gary?" I asked.

"Gar*eth*. Like Steph*en*."

I nodded. Apparently, Gareth didn't know she was alive. She had some competition for his affections in the form of a more developed fourteen-year-old.

"If I let him feel me up, he'll like me instead of her," Madison said, thrusting out her chest. "But there's nothing there anyway." She frowned. "When am I going to get tits?"

I stopped dead in my tracks and stared at her. Was this how fourteen-year-olds talked? I didn't remember throwing around words like *tits* when I was her age. I was probably too embarrassed to even use a word like that. "Madison, letting a boy touch you won't make him like you. Boys like girls for very complicated and very simple reasons. But making out or having sex isn't part of it."

"Then why do guys flock around Laura Geller, this girl in school?" she asked. "Rumor says she gives blow jobs in the bathroom between classes."

I almost choked. "Madison!"

"Rebecca, I'm *fourteen*, not twelve."

Oh God.

"See, if I looked like that"—she nodded her chin at a pack of teenaged girls—"I'd have everything I want." The girls all wore tiny tight shirts and tiny tight jeans and platform boots. They had tiny denim jackets too. They wore just a little makeup, sheer lip gloss, but they were way too sexy. "That's the hair I need," Madison said, staring wistfully at their retreating backs. "Straight and long and flippy. Instead I got stuck with this mess." She pulled at her wildly curly honey-colored hair and frowned again. "Now Mom won't even let me try to straighten it anymore. I'll never get Gareth with this frizzy mop head."

"I love your hair," I told her. "I *have* your hair. And didn't you tell me last week that you *liked* my hair? Plus, I had a boyfriend when I was fourteen."

She raised an eyebrow, rolled her eyes and crossed

her arms over her chest. "Stephen Guberman doesn't count. He's a total geekizoid. He has zits and he's, like, my teacher's age. Has he ever heard of Clearasil?"

I laughed. "Well, he was cute when he was fourteen."

"So what's the *objective?*" she asked. "That's what we're on in English. We have to write out the objectives of the novels we're reading."

"What would you say it was?"

"That you shouldn't marry Michael because even though he's cute now, ten years from now, he'll be a dork. He'll lose his hair and go totally bald and get a big fat stomach like both our fathers."

I smiled. "I assume you're getting A pluses in English."

She nodded and was soon captivated by a hot-pink leather motorcycle jacket with diamond studs in a store window. She was going to be all right. More than all right. As the cliché went, she was too smart for her own good; she thought too much, too thoughtfully. She was also too young to live.

"Do we *have* to go look at wedding rings?" Madison asked. "Let's just go to the movies or to Serendipity if we can't do both."

"We have to go," I said. "I *want* to go. But next weekend, we can hang out."

"Next weekend you're going out of town to visit Michael's family in Ohio," she reminded me. "And the weekend after, you're going gown shopping with Mommy and Aunt Janet. And the weekend after that you're going to caterers. You'll be doing wedding crap for the whole year it takes you to get married. And then you'll move to a house in the burbs."

I raised an eyebrow. "Where'd you hear that?"

"I don't know."

"I won't move to the burbs, I promise," I assured her. "I'd never move that far from you."

She glanced up at me for a moment, then sprang a wild curl around her finger and released it. "You say that *now.*"

I knew where she got *that* from—the You Say That Now committee otherwise known as my family and friends.

"Mad, do you think I'm too young to get married?"

"*Hello,* you're, like, my teacher's age too. You're not too young to do *anything.* Me, I'm too young to do anything. Mom won't even let me wear all black or shave my pits!"

Glad I asked.

Four days later, a self-help book on infidelity titled *Why He Cheats* arrived for me in another Tiffany's box. There was an inscription handwritten on the title page: *Now this is the masterpiece Michael should have been writing all along. I'm sure he'll stop cheating once you're married—if you're dumb enough to go through with the wedding. By the way, he's not too good in bed, is he?*

"Now you *know* it's a joke," Michael said that night. "I'm damned good in bed."

I hit him with the book. "Michael, this isn't funny. Who's sending this shit?" I dropped down on our bed, tears stinging the backs of my eyes. "The stupid voodoo doll, OK. But this is serious. This is someone telling me you're cheating on me."

He pulled me into his arms and lifted up my chin. "No, it's someone who has nothing better to do than try to make you think I'm cheating on you, which I'm not. And here's where this belongs." He took the book and the Tiffany's box outside into the hallway. I heard him open the garbage chute. "It's garbage," he said as he came back inside. "I have never and would never cheat on you, Bec."

You say that now, a little voice squeaked inside my head.

I shared that thought with Michael in the middle of the night. He wasn't pleased. He insisted I stop agreeing to wedding outings with my mother. Ring shopping had been another setup. A friend of my mother's worked behind the counter at Fortunoff's, but instead of being offered a discount, I got a story about her daughter who married "some schmuck" she'd been dating for seven months. Her newlywed daughter caught the guy having a *ménage à trois* in their bed two months later.

"If you still want to try on wedding rings after hearing a story like that," my mother said, "be my guest."

"I will," I said to spite her.

"What's a *ménage à trois?*" Madison asked.

My mother's mouth dropped open. "Madison, I thought I told you to go over to that counter and look at simple gold bracelets from your father!"

"If *I'm* picking it out, and *you're* buying it," Madison muttered, "it's not from *him,* is it?"

"That girl is going to be the end of me!" our mother said, waving her hands heavenward.

I winked at Madison and she laughed. We both knew who was going to be the end of who in this family.

Michael also insisted that we both take the next day off from work (he spent the mornings and afternoons writing and the evenings at the restaurant) and do something relaxing, just the two of us. We spent the day in Central Park, riding the carousel, petting billy goats in the children's zoo, staring at the rowboats on the lake.

We were sitting on a bench outside a playground, watching toddlers in the sandbox when Michael said, "I want two kids. Two girls, like you and Madison."

I mock-shivered. "I was no picnic and Madison knows what a blow job is. I'd rather have two boys."

He laughed. "How about I take you to dinner? I'm taking tonight off."

"But it's Thursday night," I said. "You'd be giving up a thousand bucks at least."

He kissed me on the cheek. "I'd give up anything for you, Rebecca."

Effectively reminding me of why I was marrying him.

"So you don't think we're too young?" I asked him. "Everyone's concern isn't getting to you? If everyone says we're too young, that we haven't known each other long enough, maybe they're onto something."

He shook his head. "You know that Eminem song, 'I Am Whatever You Say I Am'? Well, the point is that we're *not*. I'm not and you're not. We're what *we* say we are. And we say we're ready. I don't need another six months or two more years to *really* know that I want to spend the rest of my life with you. I really know now."

I agreed. But I didn't think I'd quote Eminem in my arguments to my mother.

Four days later, there was another "gift" waiting for me in another Tiffany's box. A Post-it note attached to a box of condoms that said, *Your fiancé is having sex with every hot waitress at the restaurant. I'd use these unless you want to catch something.*

Furious and shaking, I dropped the big blue box onto the floor, and something fluttered up, then fluttered back down inside.

A clue.

Desperation had made Anonymous sloppy. And not so anonymous anymore.

I took the local to Forest Hills. The longer it took, the better. This wasn't a confrontation I was looking forward to.

I found Madison in her bedroom, sitting on the floor on the far side of her bed, trying to stuff Bridal Barbie with a dagger in her chest into a Tiffany's box. My mother had a habit of saving everything, including gift boxes from her own engagement and wedding (both of them).

When Madison saw me standing in the doorway, she freaked and tried to slide everything under the bed. Then she burst into tears.

"Why?" I asked.

She continued to cry.

"Mad, I'll love you no matter what, OK?"

She sniffled and toyed with Bridal Barbie's veil.

Then she flung the doll hard across the room. It landed with a light thud on her desk, on her algebra textbook. "I don't want you to get married."

"*Duh,* as you would say. That much I figured out on my own."

She stared at her sneakered feet. "When Daddy got engaged to Suz-shit, I never saw him. Their stupid wedding plans were more important to him than anything. He blew me off a hundred times. And he didn't even come to visiting day at camp because Suz-shit The Great had a cow about losing a Saturday to visit caterers."

I let out a deep breath and sat down next to her.

"So you think I don't spend enough time with you?" I asked. "We see each other every Saturday."

"Not last Saturday, not really. And three weeks ago, you blew me off to do something with Michael's sister because she was in town—you weren't even engaged then. And you're going to miss *another* Saturday, because you're going to Ohio next weekend. You're going to spend the next year and then the rest of your life blowing me off because now you have someone else." She burst into tears again, hard tears, and I pulled her against me and hugged her.

"Madison, I love you like crazy. You know that, right?"

She sniffled and shrugged dramatically.

"I'll never blow you off," I promised. "If I can't make one of our weekends, we'll do something during the week. But I won't let the wedding stuff or Michael or anything take me away from you. I wouldn't want it to. I love hanging out with you."

"Even though I'm such a loser?"

"Madison, you really did hurt me by sending all that crap," I told her. "You made me feel awful when everyone was already making me feel awful. I really could have used your support."

She looked up at me and her face crumpled. "I'm sorry. I'm really sorry."

"The next time you're worried about something, Madison, tell me. Do we have a deal?"

She nodded. "I promise." She let out a deep breath. "How'd you figure out it was me, anyway?"

"You left a clue." I handed her a long spiral curl, half straightened.

"Gross!" she said, flinging it away. "Are you going to tell Mom?"

"That you've been using the straightening iron or that you're Nasty Gifts by Anonymous?"

She gnawed her lower lip. "Either?"

"I won't tell Mom."

She breathed a sigh of relief, real not exaggerated. "Do you still want me to be your maid of honor?"

"If we don't end up eloping, then I most certainly do."

"Hey, that's what you're gonna say to Michael. 'I do.' "

I sure was.

In the end, we didn't elope. We were tempted, many, many times. Las Vegas was just a plane ride away from the endless annoyances the next eight months brought. We let my mother plan the wedding to keep her too busy to bother us. She did a good job. We would have gone with a different band and without the swan ice sculpture, but we did say "I do" and that was the whole point.

Madison made a great maid of honor. She'd invited Gareth as her date and she was shocked that he accepted. When we were getting ready in our hotel room before the ceremony, she stuffed gym socks in her bra. Our mother stuck her hand down the front of Madison's dress and yanked the socks back out. "Jesus, I'm just experimenting," Madison muttered.

When Michael and I got our wedding pictures, Madison's chest was sock-size again. We'd all been too busy getting into place and checking our teeth for food that we hadn't noticed Madison's chest had gone up a few cup sizes. She was beaming in every picture.

"Michael says you are whatever you say you are," Madison explained when I showed her the pictures. "I say I'm a C cup instead of a double A."

My mother flipped when she saw the photos. She grounded Madison for a week. The good news was that Madison seemed so immature to my mother that my mother started seeing me as a wise married woman. She came to me often, dragging Madison by the ear, for advice about Madison's teenaged ways.

My sister thought she had it pretty good now.

MELISSA SENATE is the author of the bestselling novels *See Jane Date* (made into a television movie in 2003 starring Charisma Carpenter) and *The Solomon Sisters Wise Up*. Her third novel, *Whose Wedding Is It Any-*

way?, a spin-off of *See Jane Date*, was published in December 2004.

Melissa lives in New York City with her husband and son. Visit her website: www.melissasenate.com.

The Bamboo Confessions

LAUREN WEISBERGER

I knew the moment I'd arrived in the lobby of the oddly named Viet-Tang Hotel for our group's 6 p.m. meeting that I'd made the biggest mistake of my life. Actually, that's a lie: I really knew from the moment I impulsively added this "adventure trip" to my shopping cart online that it was a huge lapse in judgment, but I hadn't admitted it to myself until I'd laid eyes on everyone else. The nearly two full days of flying from Newark to Dubai to Kuala Lumpur to Hanoi had obviously sucked, as had the hottest, dirtiest cab ride from the airport to the center of town, but nothing compared to actually seeing my new travel mates. Gone were all my carefully cultivated fantasies of exotic, sophisticated foreigners who would want to dissect current events and politics late into the night.

Absent were all the beautiful-yet-sensitive men who would compete to charm and delight me and be crushed when they heard I was already taken. Missing was anyone who looked remotely appealing in any way, shape, or form.

My mother's voice rang in my ears. "Honey, I just don't think this little trip is a good idea. You *hate* to be alone. Why do you want to go halfway around the world to some godforsaken country all by yourself?" I'd tried to explain that it was just that—the fact that I'd never done anything *remotely* spontaneous before, that I hadn't so much as had lunch by myself in the six years since graduating from college, but she hadn't understood. Neither had anyone else.

"You're going *where?*" my father had asked when I announced my plan during one of my mandatory, bi-monthly visits to their house in Westchester, finally looking up from the *Wall Street Journal* for what must have been the first time in my adult life.

"Vietnam. For a backpacking trip. There will be a group of eight, people from all over the world, and we'll have a leader who will take us through the country. I think it'll be amazing," I said, not a little defensively, trying to convince myself as much as him.

"Humph," he exhaled, and buried his face back between the pages. "I spent some of the best years of my life trying to avoid that hellhole and now my kid's paying to go. Pretty damn ironic if you ask me." End of discussion.

Their doubts made it all the more appealing, of course. You don't have to be some angsty teenager to find enormous satisfaction in pissing off your parents, that much was sure. But I did have to admit, this was not what I had pictured when I'd carefully packed my cutest sundresses and shopped for weeks for hiking boots with the perfect combination of ruggedness and femininity. Staring back at me when I walked into the little lobby food area (calling it a restaurant would be like calling a kite Air Force One) were nine exhausted, weathered, and mostly unattractive faces, although I did notice one irritatingly beautiful couple massaging each other's necks right there at the table. I self-consciously adjusted the bandanna I'd tied just so over my hair—just enough to look bohemian and chic at the same time—and took the last remaining bamboo chair.

"Hi, all! Welcome to Hanoi! My name's Claire, but you can all just call me . . . Claire!" She howled. And, horrifyingly, so did everyone else. "I'll be your group leader for the next three weeks, so let's just get some of this here paperwork out of the way and then we can get to know each other." Her Australian accent irritated me immediately, but I dutifully filled in my passport number and signed my pledge that I wouldn't sue anyone if an early Vietnamese death found me in the next twenty-one days. Worthless little paper, I thought. Either my parents or my boyfriend would bankrupt this company if I came back with anything more than a scraped knee. The joy of having not one, not two, but three attorneys in my life was justification for suicide, but I took comfort in knowing that my death would not go unavenged. That is, if Matthew was still speaking to me when I got back.

"You're going *where?*" he'd asked in a frightening

parroting of my father, minus the *Journal* but plus the *Financial Times*.

"Matthew, this is something I need to do for me," I tried to explain, knowing already it was useless. Matt was a great talker—the best, actually. He could wheedle, persuade, explain, narrate, joke, teach, argue and debate, but what he hadn't quite learned yet was how to listen.

"I just don't understand. I thought you were happy with the way things are now," he said, as his eyes scanned the pink pages.

We'd finally moved in together after three years of dating when Matt "surprised" me with a new apartment and the announcement that he'd already notified my best friend and roommate, Isabelle, that I wouldn't be returning. And I had done what I always did: thanked him for the effort, ignored those nagging insecurities, and followed his lead. He decided, I agreed. This was just the way it worked.

"I am happy," I pseudo-lied. "It's just that I've never really done anything on my own before. I think it might be good for me."

He flipped the page and sipped some of the expensive red wine he bought by the case according to *Wine Spectator*'s recommendation each month. "But darling, you hate being alone and I'm just not sure you can handle a place like that yourself."

I had planned to truss that one out a bit more, but his cell phone rang with a call from the office and he carried it out of the room, most likely to berate an underling. He hadn't mentioned it again, just called a car to take me to the airport two weeks later and gave me a kiss on the cheek when I left. End of discussion.

Claire's screeching brought me back to reality, all one hundred and five degrees of it. Apparently, Intrepid Travel didn't believe in placing their intrepid travelers in air-conditioned hotels. "More of an authentic experience," Claire had grinned when I asked if this was going to be standard. We went around the table introducing ourselves and I was surprised to see that I was the only American. Another first. I'd never been anywhere in my entire life where I could make that claim before. Two girls from Dublin ("Best friends from birth," they giggled simultaneously), one gangly, awkward guy from British Columbia (but *not* Victoria, he rushed to assure us, as though this were equivalent to admitting you were from Baghdad), the gorgeous couple who turned out to be born-and-bred Romans and who'd made the poor, poor decision of sharing their honeymoon with all of us, and two middle-aged women from Melbourne who looked about as well suited for a rough-and-tumble backpacking trip as my great-grandmother Rose.

The good news was that I'd have my own room for the duration of our travels, since the self-loathing British Columbian was male and the leaders always had their own room and everyone else was paired up. Fine, I thought, unlocking my single and trying not to think about having to sleep on the piece of cloth-covered foam in the corner that was designated as a bed. This is going to be just fine. My positive attitude lasted precisely six minutes: just the amount of time it took to strip off the nasty clothes I'd been wearing for the past forty-eight hours, put on my flip-flops, and brave the darkened cave that sort of resembled a bathroom (broken tile floor, identifiable toilet, something that might be a showerhead stuck in the ceiling) and turned on what I guessed to be a faucet. Water flowed from the sink but not the overhead appliance. It sure as hell isn't a fire sprinkler, I thought, wrapping one of the short, itchy towels around myself and heading down the hall toward Claire's room. She followed me back to my cave—after commenting without any apparent sarcasm on how luxurious the rooms were here compared to other stops on our itinerary—and wrestled with the knob for a bit.

"There!" she cried out with obvious satisfaction when a rust-colored liquid began trickling out from the ceiling. "Enjoy your shower, Katie. I'll see you tomorrow, bright and early for our first day on the road!" And she was gone before I could tackle her.

As though the ice-cold water wasn't insulting enough after a two-day flight, it trickled so lightly that it was nearly impossible to wash the shampoo out of my hair. I struggled for a few more blue-lipped minutes before bagging the whole thing and collapsing on my foam. Alone. I would have killed for Matt's snoring, kicking body next to me and even could have overlooked his cover stealing, but there weren't any covers to share. It didn't matter much, though, because before I could start to feel too sorry for myself, there was incessant knocking at my door.

"Rise and shine!" Claire called through the paper-thin wood. "Everyone's already at breakfast and we're leaving in twenty minutes!"

I grunted something and she went away. I didn't remember sleeping for a single second, but there was a bit

of light coming in from the airshaft and my soapy hair
had dried into a hardened, dreadlocked tangle. My
watch read six o'clock, but it was impossible to tell if
that was a.m. or p.m., and it didn't much matter considering there was an eleven-hour time difference that I
hadn't yet accounted for. I threw on my most comfortable pair of shorts and a ratty old T-shirt, pushing all the
cute sundresses to the bottom of my brand-new backpack. No need to impress anyone here, I thought, as I
dragged everything to the lobby. The group was inhal-
ing milky tea and slurping at some sort of noodle dish,
and no one seemed the least bit concerned that there
was no coffee or bagels anywhere in sight. No one
seemed distraught that it was still mostly dark outside,
and all were talking and laughing animatedly, as though
they'd known each other forever.

This is why you don't go anywhere alone, I
thought, as I munched on a Snickers I'd bought in the
Dubai airport. Matt was right, my parents were right:
I obviously wasn't cut out for this. Everyone else finished up breakfast and piled into the minibus that was
taking us on a day trip to Halong Bay, a World Her-
itage Site a couple hours outside of Hanoi that was
supposed to be a stunning stretch of water interspersed
with mini islands. I immediately whipped out my iPod
to have something to do while they all talked to their
seatmates, but Stephen, the Canadian, started asking
lots of questions.

"So, what brings you to Vietnam?" he asked, plopping down in the little seat across from me.

"Oh, I don't know. Just needed a break, I guess.
What about you?"

"Same. Just broke up with my girlfriend, which was kind of tough. Thought I was going to marry her, and then she was just . . . gone. Of course, it's not like I hadn't seen it coming for ages—not like it wasn't the best thing for both of us anyway—but I guess I was just surprised when she actually did it. Kind of a shock, you know?" He twisted his hands and sort of stared out the window.

"I'm sorry." What was I supposed to say to a perfect stranger revealing the most intimate details of his life?

"Yeah, well, it happens. Nothing better than a solo adventure to get you back on track, right?" He smiled kindly and I decided that he wasn't quite as terrible as my initial assessment suggested.

"Sure. I'm having some trouble with my boyfriend now, too. Thought it might be good to get away for a few weeks and do some thinking." I was shocked to hear the words leave my mouth, since I hadn't acknowledged any of that to myself so far, never mind to someone I'd met five minutes earlier, but Stephen didn't seem at all surprised and looked ready to hear more. I blurted, "Cos, you know, no one thought I could come here on my own and I thought it was really important."

That wasn't all true. Isabelle had thought it was a fantastic idea, and was just upset that she couldn't get the time off work to join me. She shrieked when I told her I'd impulsively signed up for the trip online, but I knew that she'd never really liked Matt and would be thrilled to hear I'd be taking a break, however short.

"Well, I don't know you at all and I hope this

doesn't sound patronizing, but I think it's really cool for you to do this. My girlfriend sure wouldn't have done it. She can't function outside her little world of family and friends in our small town."

We chatted the rest of the way to Halong Bay, and by the time we arrived, we'd made fun of every single person on the trip. When it came time to pair off for the paddleboats we'd be using to explore the bay, Stephen looked furtively around at everyone else, and then glanced at me and mouthed, "Save me." I laughed and joined him in the boat, where we spent the rest of the afternoon trying to ditch the group and paddle well enough to move somewhere, anywhere, which wasn't easy. By the time we returned to the meeting place—Stephen and I had come back almost an hour late—the rest of the group was on the bus and most people were passed out. It was late afternoon, and the ride back to Hanoi was peaceful as I watched mile after mile of rice paddies go by. This isn't so bad, I thought, spying a family cook its supper over an open-air fire on the side of the road. This just isn't so bad.

Naturally, my feel-good attitude changed the second we hit Hanoi and the throngs of people descended upon us as we looked for a restaurant that served bottled water. The Italians hadn't yet stopped making out long enough to contribute to the conversation, and the two middle-aged Australian women looked so exhausted and miserable that they almost made me feel better about my own jet lag and the pain shooting through my arms and shoulders from the paddling. The heat had seemed to surge after sunset instead of wane, and the humidity had increased tenfold. All I wanted was a burger or a Caesar salad and a Diet Coke, but I'd been overruled in the voting process: the group had decided on a vegan noodle place and Claire was back to her hideously chipper and upbeat self. I tuned her out as she explained our itinerary for the coming days and began to dream about the hot showers and comfortable beds that did not await me. I'd had nothing but some bread and tea and a few Snickers since I'd arrived the day before, and wasn't quite sure how long I could last. But just as I was mentally preparing to survive night number two, Stephen announced to the table that he and I were going to have a cigarette.

"So I have a proposal," he announced with a mischievous look as he lit our Camel Lights. "Now, don't take this the wrong way—I'm not suggesting anything by it—but I thought we might check into a decent hotel, just for tonight."

"What? What do you mean?" Had I given him the wrong idea? He was funny and sweet and I was ecstatic to have a friend, but I had not one inkling of romantic feelings for him. And besides, I lived with my boyfriend. This just wasn't appropriate.

"No, no, nothing like that," he assured me, reading my mind. "It's just that it took three fucking days of flying for me to get here and I haven't slept more than three hours straight since I left, and I haven't had anything resembling a decent shower or a meal, either. I just figured it might be a good idea to get a nice room in a quality hotel, take as many hot showers as possible, get a good, real Western meal, and sleep for twelve hours. I think of it as an investment, you know? We spent serious coin on this trip, and if we're going to be so run-down and miserable from the very beginning, we're never going to enjoy it. Separate beds. Just friends. What do you think?"

Visions of carpeting and air-conditioning and possibly even a nice vodka tonic danced in my head. "I think that sounds fantastic. What do we tell them?"

He smiled. "I'll handle it. Wait here."

He returned within minutes and gleefully announced, "Told them that you were deathly ill and that I was taking you back to the Viet-Tang. We don't need to be at breakfast until eight tomorrow, so if we go now, we can sneak back there at 7:30 a.m. and no one will ever know we're gone. I checked the guidebook and there's a Marriott a few blocks away. C'mon." And before I knew what was happening, Stephen had negotiated with a cyclo driver and we were on our way.

It was blissful. Completely and utterly blissful. For the grand sum of $42 per person, we were quickly ensconced in a highly air-conditioned room with a marble bathroom, two queen-sized beds, TV with CNN, and a balcony overlooking all of Hanoi. We managed to stay awake for another hour and a half— just long enough for each of us to shower without flip-flops, order room service, and have a cocktail and cigarette on the terrace as the city settled in for the night beneath us. As I took my shorts off under the covers and leaned back into the down pillows, I remember thinking that life couldn't get much better than this.

We made it back to the group's ghetto hotel before

everyone else was up, except the indefatigable Claire, who eyed us both as we tried to sneak past her in the lobby.

"Well, well, aren't you two up early?" she crowed as we hit the stairs to pack up the stuff we'd left in our old rooms. "Were you both wearing those same clothes last night or is it my imagination?"

"We just took an early-morning walk is all," Stephen shot back without stopping. "See you in a few minutes."

"Katie, how are you feeling? Stephen said your diarrhea was pretty terrible!" A few tourists of indeterminate ethnicity eating breakfast in the corner started to laugh.

"Oh, yes, well, uh, I'm feeling much better today. Thanks!"

We both raced upstairs and managed not to break down until we were actually out of earshot.

"I feel like I'm fourteen again, sneaking in after curfew and thinking my mother doesn't realize," I choked through my tears of laughter. "And did you really have to say it was diarrhea? Great visual."

I was so well rested and revitalized that I'd forgotten all about Matt's email until now. I'd ducked into the Marriott's business center before we'd left that morning and quickly logged on to my Hotmail account. Among the usual junk mail and a few unimportant questions from my assistant at the PR firm where I worked, there was a single email from Matt. I'd printed it and tucked it in my backpack to read when I got a minute alone, and now seemed as good a time as ever. We didn't need to be downstairs for another fifteen minutes, and thanks to Stephen's brilliant idea, I had already showered and eaten a huge American breakfast at the Marriott.

I flopped down on the piece of foam, smashing my tailbone on the cement beneath it, and yanked the printout from my bag. I'd only been gone four days by now, but it was still going to be really nice to hear how much someone missed me.

K,

Did you manage to get upgraded to business class? I'm very much hoping that worked out . . . it's bad enough to fly to the other side of the earth, but to do it in economy would be unbearable. I went out for dinner last night with Daniel and Stephanie and guess what? They told me they'd gotten engaged the night before. She was sporting quite the rock—I always knew Daniel did better than he let on—but rest assured that yours will one day outshine it by a mile. Work is fine, nothing too interesting the past three days, but please keep your fingers crossed that the new client I'm courting will come on board. It'd be a huge coup right before the yearly reviews, you know? Oh, and your mother called to tell me to say hello to you and that she hopes you're wearing sunblock and please don't hesitate to change your flight and come home if it's actually as bad as it sounds. I agree with her entirely. There's nothing wrong in admitting you've made a mistake, so know that we're all here waiting for you.

XOXO, Matt

P.S. I just realized that you forgot to leave me the cleaning lady's number. Please write at your earliest convenience and let me know where to find it, because I'll need her more frequently now that you're away.

I read it twice more just to make sure I hadn't missed any implied "I love yous" or "I miss yous" or anything that would indicate that my absence provoked more in him than simply needing to schedule the maid more often. But nothing. Instinct dictated that crying was in order but, oddly, the tears didn't come. I sat on the foam and waited, even watched with interest as a large and somewhat menacing bug worked its way slowly up the wall, but I didn't cry. Instead, I calmly folded the paper, tore it into neat, even pieces and tossed them in the basket on my way out the door.

"Hey, you ready for more group loving?" Stephen asked when we bumped into each other in the hallway, saddled with our tremendous backpacks that didn't seem so heavy after nine hours of sleep. "Looks like Claire's all revved up for a full day and then an overnight train. I call bottom berth, by the way."

"Fair enough," I said with a not-too-forced smile. "But I call window on the bus."

The next week flew by. We covered Hue by bicycle, an historic city with a massive citadel and beautiful pagodas, and then headed south to my favorite city of all, Hoi An. More like a village than anywhere else we'd been, the main drag (which was just a dirt road lined on both sides with aging huts) was shopping heaven. Every little stand had expert tailors on staff, all ready with every imaginable fabric and patterns pulled straight from American and French fashion magazines. For a few dollars, they'd custom-make suits or dresses, capris or coats and everything would be stitched up and ready to go within twenty-four hours. I ordered an Asian-inspired jacket with pink silk buttons and spent some time choosing the perfect linen for the pants I was having made for Matt. I couldn't remember his exact inseam and thought it'd be a good time for my first call home. When the post office with the international phone line opened at 9 a.m., I calculated that it'd be 8 p.m. his time and he'd just be getting home from work. He picked up after five rings.

"Hello?" he called out, sounding very far away, but not because of any connection problem. U2 was playing in the background, and I could hear the clanging of silver to plates.

"Matt? It's me! I'm calling from Vietnam!"

"What? Who's calling? Hey, Barry, turn that down a minute. I can't hear a fucking thing. Hello?"

The music lessened slightly but the noise of the people increased.

"Matt! It's Katie. Can you hear me? How are you? I'm so excited we're actually talking from halfway around the world!"

"Katie? Hello?"

"Matt?"

"Hey, babe, how are you?"

Babe? He never called me babe. And who the hell were all those people at eight o'clock on a Tuesday night?

"Hi. I'm, uh, I'm great. Things were kind of tough in the beginning, what with the jet lag and the foreign food and some of the weirdest people in my group, but I have to say, it's really starting to—"

"That's my girl!" he interrupted enthusiastically, clearly putting on a show for everyone else. "Trekking all the way through Vietnam all by herself. I'm so proud of you, honey!"

I heard a girl's voice ask who was on the phone and another one remind him that it was rude to talk in the middle of dinner.

"Matt, who's there?"

"Oh, just some people from the office. We were going to all go out to eat, but they couldn't accommodate ten people at Gramercy Tavern tonight, so I decided it was time to pull out the old cooking skills."

"You cooked?" I asked, still not comprehending. In the three years we'd been dating he hadn't made me anything more romantic than an omelet. I asked him all the time, of course, to show me what he'd learned from the two years he spent as a chef-in-training before switching to finance, but he was always too busy, too tired.

"Yeah, well I figured what the hell. So listen, we're just getting started, but it's already morning there, right? Can I give you a call in a couple hours?"

"Matt, I'm standing in a post office that only sends or receives mail once a week, in a town so small it probably isn't even on the map, using the single international phone line—at eleven dollars a minute, mind you—within a hundred and fifty mile radius, and you want to *call me back?*"

"Oh, hey, I didn't realize it was that third-world there. How are you surviving? I bet the showers suck, don't they? And what about AC? You can't possibly be dealing without AC."

And even though I'd spent a good amount of time complaining about both such things, it really pissed me off that he was. I had, in fact, not showered in the past couple days, and I'd done it by choice. It felt good to get a little dirty once in a while, just like it felt good to sleep with a window open to the sounds of the night with nothing more than a mosquito net and a candle for company. There was something peaceful and sexy and exciting about it all at once, and besides, it was just a lot easier to accept it rather than fight it all the time. I would've tried to explain it to him before, but something had shifted, and I was quite certain he wouldn't understand.

"Yeah, well, I'm dealing. Listen, I'll let you get back to your dinner party. Just wanted to ask you a question: what's your inseam?"

"My inseam? Why? You buying me a pair of pants? In *Vietnam?* Isn't everything there midget-sized?" Gales of laughter followed in the background.

"I'm in this amazing little place where they make the most wonderful copies of all the latest styles, and they have fabulous fabrics. I was thinking that you might like linen ones with—"

"Honey, I totally appreciate the thought—really, I do—it's just that if I need a pair of pants custom made, I can get them in New York or London. Last time I checked, Asian countries were known for their sweatshops, not their couture. I'd rather you spend the money on showing yourself a good time, OK? Are you being safe? Feeling OK?" The questions were perfunctory and I could hear the urgency to hang up in his voice.

"Yep," I said numbly, wondering just briefly if he'd always been like this and I'd never seen it, or if he'd undergone some awful transformation within the last seven days. I pushed the obvious answer out of my mind. "Everything's great. Say hi to everyone for me and I'll talk to you later. Love you."

"You too, babe, you too. Call whenever you can, OK? Love you." And without a second's hesitation on his part, there was a click.

I paid my $77 in Vietnamese dong and stumbled back to the quaint (read: no running water or electricity) little hotel we were staying at that night. I'd only woken up two hours earlier, but already my head was pounding and I felt like I hadn't slept in years. I pulled on my headphones and angrily scrolled through the song list until I found Alanis Morrisette. And then, I slept.

"Katie! Katie! Are you in there? Open this goddamn door immediately!" It was Stephen's voice, and he sounded pissed.

I peeled the little earpieces from deep inside my ears and wiped the sweat from my brow on my pillowcase. What time was it? Where was I? Where was everyone else? I felt drunk and disoriented and even a little scared. But the knocking continued.

I pulled open the door to discover it was dark (where the hell had the whole day gone?) and that Stephen looked ready to pass out from anxiety.

"Have you been here the whole time?" he demanded angrily, pushing past me to look around the room. "Is anyone else here?"

"Oh, you mean my charming boyfriend who flew all the way over to visit because he couldn't bear to be without me? You just missed him."

"Katie, *you* missed two group meetings and lunch and dinner today, with no explanation to anyone. Claire is just about to call the police, but I told her to wait a few more minutes. What's going on with you?"

"Oh God, this group is like a fucking prison. I'm sorry. I had a really lousy talk with Matt this morning and I came back here to mope in private. I guess I fell asleep. For eight hours."

"I see." His brow furrowed.

"Really, I didn't mean to worry everyone, although I appreciate that you even noticed I was missing. My boyfriend apparently isn't even aware that I'm gone. Actually, I take that back: he's fully aware and absolutely delighted, by the sound of things."

Stephen stood up from his perch at the end of the bed and enveloped me in a bear hug. I was relieved to see that it felt warm and comfortable and not the least bit sexual, and I think he was, too.

"Well, if it makes you feel any better, I got an email from a friend saying that he saw my ex—of two weeks now—out with one of my coworkers last night." He looked miserable.

"I'm sure it was nothing. It could have been business, or they could've both been waiting for—"

"They were making out," he said flatly. "Apparently there's been some overlap. She broke up with me for him. And I really never had any idea . . ."

"Oh."

He walked toward the door again and stepped out into the space that was meant to be a courtyard but looked more like a landfill. "C'mon. Get dressed. Actually, do me a favor and get showered and then dressed. We're getting drunk tonight. I'll tell Claire you're alive so you don't have to deal with her and then we'll meet in front of the hotel in a half hour, OK?"

I wanted nothing more than to recharge my iPod and crawl back under the mosquito net, but he'd been so good to me and obviously needed a friend right now.

"OK, sounds great. I'll see you in a few."

We hitched a ride to Mr. Tam's, a bar that *Lonely Planet* described as "more Western than New York," and settled onto barstools to wait for all the cheesy love songs we'd picked on the jukebox. There wasn't much time to mock and belittle our significant others, however, because just as Springsteen's "Thunder Road" was getting started, two girls from our group showed up.

"Oh God, they found us," I muttered into my beer.

"They're not that bad. I spent all day with them, thanks to you, and they're actually kind of fun. Besides, it's not everyone." And before I could slap his hand down, he was motioning them over.

"Hey, guys!" squealed one of the two Irish girls. I

still couldn't tell them apart. "Katie, I'm so glad you're OK. Although, it was great fun seeing Claire all panicked."

"Yeah, I can't help but hate her," chimed in the other one, much to my surprise. "Do this, meet here, go there, be on time, wah, wah, wah. It's enough to make you want to slit your wrists!"

I couldn't help laughing and moved over so they could sit down.

"This round's on me," announced the first one who I think was named Shannon but may not have been.

"Easy to be a sport when the drinks cost thirty-five cents, huh?" the other one laughed.

The four of us had a few too many rounds and before I could say no, Stephen had dragged us all to the karaoke mic—the only technological item that the Viets seemed to have down pat. We belted out horrid, drunken songs from everyone to the Spice Girls and Marvin Gaye and even threw in a few Broadway show tunes. By the time we stumbled back to the hotel it was almost time for our flight to Saigon, and I had forgotten all about my "talk" with the *miserable* himself.

Saigon went by in one wonderful blur of French-Colonial buildings and night markets and a new-found—although still tentative—appreciation of Vietnamese food. Stephen and the Irish girls and myself had risen up in a sort of mutiny against the others, and I was delighted to hear Shannon (which is definitely her name, I can now confirm) inform Claire that the four of us would be doing our own thing. By the middle of the third week we had it all figured out: sleep in, have a leisurely breakfast outside somewhere, and then rent motorbikes to explore the city and outlying areas. Afternoons were spent by the pool at the five-star hotels we crashed with no problem simply because we were Westerners, and dinner was an adventure where we'd all force ourselves to try something new and usually unidentifiable. We went out at night, sometimes for a riverboat cruise and other nights just to have some drinks and dance, and we never, ever, ever followed a single "suggestion" of Claire's. When after four days the group was preparing to move on to the mosquito-infested jungles of the Mekong Delta for the trip's final segment, I lost the rock-paper-scissors and had to confront Claire myself.

"Um, we were just thinking that we're not quite ready to leave Saigon yet, so would you mind if we stayed behind for a few more days?" I asked the night before our scheduled departure.

She looked at me with decidedly un-chipper gray eyes and said through clenched teeth, "Do whatever you want. I'm sorry you're not all enjoying the trip, but we have an itinerary and we need to follow it. I'll drop off the release forms tonight for you to sign. You're officially on your own after that."

I thought about apologizing some more and telling her how much we'd adored everything, but I just thanked her and walked out. The girls and Stephen were waiting in the hostel's bar and we toasted our new-found freedom.

"So, we were thinking," said Shannon with a sly smile. "Do you guys necessarily need to be back at the end of the week, or could we interest you in coming with us to Cambodia?"

"You're going to Cambodia?" Stephen spluttered, his eyes widening more every second. He'd been reading a bootlegged copy of the *Lonely Planet Cambodia* the past few days and was dying to visit, but he always referred to it as a "someday trip."

"Yeah," said Marge, Shannon's counterpart. "We have no lives, that's for sure . . . nothing to rush home to for us. So if you guys are game, we could catch a flight to Phnom Penh, check that out for a little, and then go by boat to Siem Reap to see Angkor. I've been reading up, and it looks pretty easy to do."

Stephen was nodding furiously. "My girlfriend's sleeping with my coworker and my editor will be thrilled I'm going somewhere so exotic. He'll definitely assign me a piece on something inane and irrelevant, so I'm in. Ohmigod, I've been dying to go there. Katie? You in?"

They all stared at me.

I'd taken an official leave of absence from work before I left, figuring I would spend a few weeks shopping and catching up on stuff at home when I returned, so work wasn't the issue. My parents would freak, of course, but I rather enjoyed that idea, and Isabelle would be thrilled. As far as Matt was concerned, well, I couldn't decide what he would say. He'd either get really mad that I hadn't already returned, ashamed and homesick, or wouldn't even notice that I was still gone. Either way, not my problem.

"I'm in."

And after a few minutes of celebrating and planning the next segment of our trip, I found my way to an Internet café. I only had a little time before I was meeting the rest of the group for a midnight drink on the river, but I didn't have much to say anyway.

> Dear Mom and Dad,
> I'm not sure if either of you have figured out email yet, but you insist you have, so here goes . . . Just wanted to tell you that I'm having a wonderful time. I'm wearing sunblock and eating enough and haven't gotten sick once, so I decided to extend my trip for a few weeks. I'm with some great people and there's nothing for you to worry about. I was having some trouble with Matt's email, so could you just forward this to him? That's "File" and then "Forward," OK? Love you both. Don't panic. Love, Katie

I lit a cigarette right at my computer—one of the great joys of Third World countries—and opened a new window.

> Dear Is,
> Having the best time in Vietnam. Decided today to stay a bit longer and check out Cambodia. Have heard amazing things so I'm excited. If you can swing a week off from work, would love for you to join us . . . Anyway, sorry to be so short, but I have a quick favor to ask: will you start checking out studios and one-bedrooms for me and see what you find? I think it's time I tried living alone for a little. Miss you SO much. Xoxo, K

And with that I logged off, expertly peeled off the correct amount of dong, and went to join my friends for that drink.

New York–based **LAUREN WEISBERGER** is the author of the international bestseller *The Devil Wears Prada*.

Amore

LAURA WOLF

So why was everyone bent out of shape?

Linda didn't have a clue. In fact she found the whole thing incredibly disturbing. She had three sisters and one brother. Her eldest sister was married to a man who made chewing gum seem exciting. The next eldest was a lesbian whose long-term girlfriend looked and sounded disturbingly like their mother. Her brother was too busy failing out of a string of colleges to date. And after numerous relationships with men, as well as a battalion of battery-operated sexual appliances, her youngest sister had yet to achieve orgasm. Didn't this strike anyone as problematic? Weren't these situations that deserved close scrutiny?

Apparently not. Instead all the attention was focused on why Linda had spent the last decade dating foreign men. Her siblings acted like it was a mistake. Or worse, a *disorder*. "Your relationships are always so bizarre," they would complain. "Can't you find some American guy? Even a Canadian would do. At least you'd speak the same language."

As if that were a desirable thing. A common language just meant that Linda would inevitably find herself sitting in a restaurant with some bore, praying for the dessert course to be over so she could stop pretending to care about his stock portfolio or the outcome of a semifinals match of some sport that she didn't know how to play. That's right, sports and money bored her and beer gave her a headache so there was little chance of meeting "some American guy" she could relate to.

Which isn't to say that Linda thought all American men were the same. She was far too intelligent to think in such simplistic terms. But if dating was about finding a soulmate then you needed to date people with soul. And Lester, the really "interesting" accountant from her sister's storage company, didn't fit the bill. Linda needed more than a punctual guy with good organizational skills to share the rest of her life with.

It was a fact she'd been aware of since childhood. When her schoolmates were gushing over Brad Pitt or Tom Cruise, Linda was lusting for Tcheky Karyo and Patrick Bruel. Why Barbie found Ken—or worse, GI Joe—so appealing would forever elude her. So at fourteen she made herself a promise. Surrounded by foreign movie posters and clutching the latest issue of *International Vogue*, Linda swore never to settle when it came to love. If necessary, she would devote her entire life to finding a man who was cosmopolitan, fashionable, and exciting. He would educate her in the ways of the world and save her from a life of mediocrity.

He would be foreign.

But first she had to find an actual foreign man. It was a deceptively difficult task. There was only one Chinese restaurant in her small Ohio town—which oddly enough was run by a couple from Missouri. There were no French bakeries. And the only exchange student her high school had managed to woo was Tor, a senior from Slovakia who was standoffish and gruff and seemingly ambivalent about hygiene. Yet Linda remained determined. Scouring the student registry she found Andreas Leon. He was half-Cuban on his father's side and extremely handsome. Unfortunately he was still thirteen and even Linda knew that dating a younger man wasn't fashionable until a woman was middle-aged. So she set her sights on Johnny, a skinny sophomore from Kenya whose rich dark skin reminded her of the fancy chocolates that she'd once received in a Christmas stocking.

Initially surprised by Linda's interest, Johnny soon returned her affections. After a week spent pretending not to see each other they finally introduced themselves during a student assembly. Several days later their relationship reached its highpoint when Johnny unexpectedly kissed Linda outside the shopping mall. It was quick and clumsy but it was Linda's first kiss and it made her head spin. She completely forgot what she'd come to buy.

Though a flurry of kisses inevitably followed, their magic faded when Linda discovered that Johnny was an ardent baseball fan. She had expected far more exotic interests from an African man. Tales of spear hunting on the open range. Tribal rituals involving fire and dance. Instead Johnny seemed unable to stop discussing the minutiae of pitching styles and the strategies behind starting lineups. But Linda hung in there, struggling to keep the flames of love alive, until the day she learned that Kenyan Johnny had been born in Whiting, Indiana. The closest Johnny had been to Africa was the wild animal exhibit at the natural history museum.

It was a disappointing end to a short and mediocre relationship but far from souring Linda it served to strengthen her resolve—only a foreigner would do. When her girlfriends went to rock concerts and parties Linda stayed behind, locked in her room, determined to expand her horizons. With maps and travel magazines covering her rainbow-colored bedspread she quickly became an expert of world facts. She could tell you a country's capital city, primary language, major export, and current dance craze. She wanted to be fully prepared when the man of her dreams whisked her off to his native country, be it Burma or Belize.

Over time Linda did manage to have a number of foreign beaus despite her limited opportunities. Motivated and clever, if someone with a foreign passport arrived in town she would inevitably find him. She was so skilled at this art that when her nineteenth birthday arrived her siblings presented her with a globe. Eager to tease her they'd used a fluorescent yellow pen to color every country from which Linda had dated someone.

By age nineteen the globe glowed like the sun.

She'd dated Korean lawyers, Swedish mechanics, Israeli bus drivers, and Indian chefs. There was a two-day fling with a scruffy Australian drifter, and a three-month relationship with a Polish dockworker who spoke no English. They had twelve weeks of meaningful gesticulation until he was forced to leave her landlocked town in search of nautical employment. Her love life had become a series of men named Dieter, Hitomi, Pablo and Jhannj (pronounced *Yan*-ch). And despite her family's cynicism—"Can't you just find a nice guy named Joe?"—Linda forged on through the forest of foreigners searching for the one who would take root.

From her first kiss with skinny Kenyan Johnny to her first sexual experience with a visiting professor from Nepal during college, Linda steadfastly remained on her international dating quest. And though she purported to be offended by her bright yellow globe she secretly reveled in its glow.

When Linda graduated cum laude from a nearby college she received numerous job offers. Carefully assessing them she opted instead to return to her family's house in her small Ohio town. Dusting off her old rainbow bedspread, she boxed up her college term papers and found work at a local travel agency. Though she'd never been farther than a Canadian border town she was passionate about travel and extremely knowledgeable about geography. Her enthusiasm was infectious and touched every customer who walked through the door. She convinced elderly couples to cruise the fjords and college students to climb Machu Picchu. She explained in detail the joys of the Galapagos to young families and the beauty of Parisian nights to newlyweds. Her descriptions were breathy and full of longing. They made people want to go for her, not because of her.

Considered a rising star among her travel agency peers there were rumors that Linda would be fast-tracked to a managerial position. But her heart wasn't in it. She was there for a paycheck not a career. Determined to expand her horizons she was saving money to move abroad as soon as she found her true love.

With this in mind Linda continued to eschew the domestic dating pool in favor of foreign finds. That's when she found Raffaele.

Linda met Raffaele Vutto in a coffee shop on Thanksgiving night. After spending an obligatory afternoon of turkey and cranberry sauce with her family she'd gone to see a foreign film at a distant art house. The film was French and confusing and it had a surprise ending that she didn't completely understand. But she'd stayed because she liked looking at the French countryside and because she'd driven over forty minutes to get there.

Afterward, inspired by the film, she stopped in a coffee shop to have a café au lait. Without bothering to look up from his order pad the waiter grumbled that they served two types of coffee—regular or decaf. Linda chose decaf and drank it while watching the streetlights turn from green to red. She'd tried hard to convince her friends to join her that evening. She'd even invited her siblings. But they preferred televised football to foreign films. Linda drank her coffee in silence.

Few restaurants were open that evening and even fewer people were eating in them. So when a little bell rang as the coffee shop door opened Linda turned around, curious to see who else had ventured out on such a quiet night. It was a stocky man with thick brown hair, tanned skin, and eyes the color of maple syrup. He ordered an entire baked chicken. Linda smiled, not because his meal was obscene but because the singsong cadence of an Italian man struggling to speak English was filling her ears.

She'd always felt that English was more beautiful when spoken by a foreigner.

The man caught her eye and her smile. He introduced himself as Raffaele. *Raffaele.* Just the sound of his name gave Linda goosebumps. Her nose wrinkled in delight. When he asked if he could join her Linda was so busy listening to the sound of his voice that she could barely hear his words. She just kept smiling.

Linda continued to smile for the next six weeks during which time she and Raffaele dated regularly. He was Neapolitan, which Linda took pride in knowing meant that he was from Naples—a city famous for its volcano and tomatoes, and whose citizens were rumored to have created the first pizza. And he was handsome and rugged in a way that reminded Linda of a cultured Sylvester Stallone, except unlike Sylvester Stallone he was soft-spoken and elegant and always held the door open for her when they got into a car.

Unfortunately Raffaele's merits completely eluded her siblings.

"Naples? Isn't that where the Mafia started?" asked her brother.

"An Italian?" said her eldest sister while ironing a polyester/cotton–blend necktie for her husband. "I bet he's a hothead. Does he swing his hands around a lot when he talks?"

"You're crazy!" shrieked her younger sister. "Those Italians are notorious for mistreating women. Trust me, every man in Italy has at least five mistresses."

"Don't be ridiculous," insisted her sister the lesbian. "No one could juggle five women at once."

Linda shook her head. Her siblings were decent people but they were wildly unsophisticated and hopelessly ignorant. They'd never helped Croatian boyfriends apply for jobs, written political missives for Kurdish suitors, or assisted Filipino lovers with the purchase of new sheets. They didn't appreciate the world beyond their sightlines or crave the chance to grow. They'd live out the rest of their days shopping at Wal-Mart. They'd never use chopsticks.

Not so for Linda. Thanks to Raffaele she knew that tomatoes came in a variety of colors, tastes and sizes. That they were an historic food credited with sustaining entire cultures. And that when cooked under high heat they should be salted generously to preserve their flavor. Linda went from liking Raffaele to adoring him.

So when he asked her to marry him she immediately accepted. The car company he worked for was closing their American division and bringing him back to Naples. Raffaele wanted Linda to come with him. It was her dream come true.

"What the hell's wrong with you?" barked her siblings. "It's only been six weeks. You hardly know him. And you don't speak Italian. Can't you find some American guy?"

They acted as if she were joining a subversive group or giving herself a crew cut. Linda found the whole thing incredibly disturbing. For while she'd long ago abandoned all hope of expanding her siblings' horizons she felt the least they could do was show some enthusiasm for her happiness. And it was obvious to Linda that the past six weeks with Raffaele had been the happiest of her life. They'd gone hiking in the mountains, exchanged childhood memories, and eaten more food than seemed humanly possible. Yes, if there was one stereotype about Italians that Linda was discovering to be true, it was that they loved food. But not just any food, *good* food.

Food was so important to Raffaele that he'd gladly drive an hour for a superior steak and wait an entire week for fresh produce to arrive. Pies had to be home-made, juice freshly squeezed, and he refused to even look at a bowl of pasta until he returned home to Italy. Good food was at the top of Raffaele's priority list along with good sex—without it life was not worth living.

Motivated by Raffaele's passion for good food, along with her siblings' cynicism regarding her choice in men, Linda decided to invite them all to the family house for a home-cooked meal. It would be an educational opportunity for her naysaying brother and sisters to get to know her exciting and sophisticated fiancé. They would come to understand how wonderful he was—his knowledge of wine, his appreciation for opera, his fancy clothes with the European flair, and why she was ready to move across the world in order to be with him—his sparkling eyes, his gentle caresses, the respectful way he treated her like a lady every minute they were together. She would be vindicated and Raffaele would have a great meal.

Dinner was scheduled for Friday. Linda began the preparations on Monday.

First she planned the menu. It would include four courses of complex but tasty dishes. Each dish would perfectly complement the others and on the assumption that her siblings would be more likely to accept Raffaele if their bellies were full, Linda made certain to include only those foods that she knew they liked. On Tuesday she bought the wine and a CD of soothing dinner music to set the evening's mood. On Wednesday she went shopping, carefully choosing the freshest ingredients. On Thursday she began to prep the meal and selected an outfit with coordinating jewelry for the occasion. On Friday she called in sick to work, bought flowers, set the dinner table, and began to cook—all before 9 a.m.

By noon she was well ahead of schedule. Meats were marinating, vegetables were peeled, seasonings were measured, and her apple brown betty had already been baked. All it needed was a dash more bourbon just prior to being served. Assessing her work Linda felt a strong sense of pride. After years of enduring a never-ending stream of rude remarks from her siblings, she would finally be able to prove that her search had been worth the effort. The international quest had been a success. In a matter of weeks she was going to completely abandon her current life. With a chuckle she moved the television set from the sideboard and slipped a CD player in its place. Yes, she had dated enough foreigners to know that no one outside of America enjoyed watching television while eating a meal.

At precisely six o'clock Raffaele rang the doorbell. Had Linda not been up to her elbows in beef stock and roasted new potatoes she easily would have beaten her youngest sister to the door. But in the time it took her to wipe her hands on her apron Raffaele had been escorted into the living room to face a firing squad of her siblings. Linda gave Raffaele an apologetic nod and quickly receded into the kitchen where she had roasted the potatoes into charred little balls. Wielding a paring knife she quickly set about scraping away, one by one, the blackened exteriors in search of something salvageable.

At 6:20 Linda furtively peeked into the living room. She was anxious and had twice cut her finger with the paring knife while worrying that her siblings were scaring away the man of her dreams. She was surprised to see Raffaele seated between two of her sisters explaining the difference between farfalle and rigatoni. Good behavior was still prevailing.

She ducked back into the kitchen where she went to check on her lobster bisque. Unable to resist, she found a clean spoon and took just the tiniest taste. It was delicious. Probably the best lobster bisque Raffaele would ever have. He was certain to be impressed. Then it occurred to Linda that it would be even better with a pinch more salt. But when she tipped the salt shaker over the soup pot she accidentally knocked off the cap and watched in horror as the shaker's entire contents flew out. Her pinch of salt had become a punch and the soup was now completely ruined. Horrified, she tossed the soup into the garbage, briefly considered opening a can of Campbell's, but thought better of it when she glanced at the clock. It was already 6:45. Her pot roast would be ready in five minutes, dinner had been promised for 7:00, and she was completely uncertain how much time she had before her brother asked Raffaele if he was in the Mafia. Desperate, she sneaked into the dining room, removed the soup bowls from the table and decided to start the meal with the salad course. As she raced back into the kitchen, she heard a round of laughter coming from the living room. Unless her sisters were laughing at Raffaele's accent, then things must be going very well.

Mindful of the time and terrified that Raffaele would overvalue the genetic connection between herself and her painfully unsophisticated family, Linda was now moving at a frantic pace. She decided to splash a touch of bourbon on the apple brown betty instead of waiting until serving it. But as she reached for the bourbon bottle she accidentally knocked the dessert onto the ground. What only moments ago had been a golden and fragrant apple crumble now oozed from the baking dish onto the floor.

Taking a deep breath Linda reminded herself that none of this mattered. That in just a few weeks she'd be living her life's fantasy. She and Raffaele would be comfortably ensconced in Italy—which she remembered from her childhood studies was a country whose first inhabitants could be traced back to the Bronze Age, whose political system features a dual-chamber parliament, and whose artistic treasures include the Sistine Chapel.

At that moment her brother sailed into the kitchen to grab a beer. "This guy's great. Have you seen his Clinton imitation? It's hysterical." Her brother exited flashing her an enthusiastic thumbs-up. Still in shock, Linda's eyes went from the lost dessert to the beautiful honey-glazed walnuts that were mixed into the salad course. Something was wrong. Horribly wrong. Seconds later it occurred to her that Raffaele was allergic to nuts.

It was 7:10. From the living room she heard her second eldest sister declare that if all men were as fabulous as Raffaele she'd reconsider lesbianism. Raffaele cheerfully vowed to introduce her to his cousins. A round of laughter filled the room. Panicked, Linda's eyes fell on the bottle of bourbon. Soon she'd be in Italy. Gone would be the stifling way she'd led her life. Every day would be an adventure. Her eyes moved across the kitchen to the oven—she'd forgotten to remove the pot roast.

At 7:15 Linda's siblings were seated in the living room thoroughly enjoying Raffaele's company. Raffaele, in turn, was enjoying theirs. He found Linda's siblings charming and sincere, if not a bit naive. In fact he found them to be quite similar to Linda herself. And had the scent of something burning not been followed by plumes of smoke, neither he nor they would have noticed that dinner was late.

Later that night after Raffaele had gone, most likely forever, and Linda's sisters were helping her to sift through the charred remains of the kitchen, her brother stood outside with the firemen as they packed up their equipment. Thanking them for their rapid response to his emergency call he remarked, half-apologetically, that he didn't understand how the pot roast had caught fire. That his sister had always been such a conscientious cook. The firemen, in an effort to comfort the young man, encouraged him not to fault his sister's culinary skills and mentioned that the fire had originated not at the oven but across the kitchen at the other side of the room—just one of a thousand unfortunate mysteries in their line of work.

Back inside the kitchen Linda's eldest sister had plucked Linda's apron from a pile of ash and was brushing away the soot. Would a mix of lemon juice and water restore its original color? Perhaps a wire brush would do the trick. She continued to ponder this question even as the faint aroma of bourbon filled her nostrils and a book of matches tumbled from the apron to the floor.

So why was everyone bent out of shape?

_____

LAURA WOLF is the author of the bestselling comic novels *Diary of a Mad Bride* and *Diary of a Mad Mother-to-Be*.

Andromeda on the Street of Ducklings

JUDI HENDRICKS

*I*t's eleven o'clock on a Tuesday morning in May, and I'm standing on Boulevard St. Germain des Près in front of the beautiful old church of the same name. My suitcase sits next to me on the sidewalk and my daypack is slung over my back. I'm vaguely aware that tears are leaking out of my eyes and rolling down my face.

Parisians stream past me—students, office workers, shoppers, laborers—and if they notice me at all, they probably imagine that I'm moved to tears by the sublime proportions of the Romanesque bell tower, or that I'm just one more silly *Americaine*, enthralled at finally making it to Paris.

I don't much care what they think. After spending
the night with my knees under my chin, wedged between the tall kid in the aisle seat and the fat lady in
the window seat, my body is just beginning to un-
crimp. My short brown hair is dirty and flattened to
my skull. My eyes, which Evan once told me were exactly the color of Grade A maple syrup, are currently
so bloodshot they look like the street map of Paris I
picked up at the airport.

If I'd booked my flight months ago—January, say—
like the tall kid and the fat lady probably did, I might
have had better luck with seat selection. But in January, going to France was the farthest thing from my
mind. In January I was incapable of long-range planning. I was still trying to put one foot in front of the
other. Pour the cereal in the bowl. Remember how to
dress myself. Start the car. Preferably after opening the
garage door.

And anyway the date was the most important
thing. I decided I didn't want to be waking up in Los
Angeles on May 3, thinking of the same date one year
ago. Mornings are always the hardest. Just before you
open your eyes. That's when the memories come for
you, and you're too groggy to outrun them.

I couldn't bear the thought of going to work that
day, watching everyone tiptoe past my door. Seeing
them carefully avoid mentioning the Watkins account
in my presence. I didn't want to deal with the inevitable phone calls from my mother and Beth-Ann
Kennerlieber, my best friend from forever. And Evan's
mother. *We were just thinking of you today, Andy. We
know how much you miss him, honey. We do, too.*

By leaving on the evening of May 2, it was almost as if the third had passed me by in mid-Atlantic. As if I could erase it from the calendar, and thereby erase it from my brain. I hadn't thought of it at the time I booked the flight, but that's just how it worked out. Sort of an eerie coincidence. Of course, Evan didn't believe in coincidence. "It's all in the stars, Andy," he'd say. Then he'd ruffle my hair because he knew it annoyed me.

I have to say right up front, I don't believe in that star stuff. Oddly, I think Evan actually did. I say oddly because it didn't seem to fit with the rest of the package—finance major, soccer jock, corporate whiz kid, Trivial Pursuit addict. Oh, he'd joke around about Scorpio rising and moon in Libra, but more than once I caught him sussing out Sidney Omar's column in the *L.A. Times* while pretending to read the comics.

That was one of the things I loved most about him—the sense that all was not exactly as it appeared, his wonderfully loopy take on the world.

He could predict things sometimes. Nothing world shattering like wars or election outcomes, but things like the Long Beach Toyota Grand Prix getting rained out or the Diamondbacks losing the pennant or our favorite taqueria closing because Clarita's little girl had to be taken to the urgent care clinic. Weird stuff. And when I'd stare at him and demand to know how he knew, he'd just laugh and say, "I told you, it's in the stars. It's all there."

But of course it wasn't. Because if it had been, he would've seen it, and he would've known not to get on the bike that day.

★ ★ ★

I met him at a party, but not exactly the way you might suppose. It's not like our eyes locked across a crowded room. His hand didn't brush mine as we both reached for the same piece of California roll. Actually, I tripped over him.

It was my company's annual summer party. At the over-the-top (think Country French on steroids) home of Al Hoskins, president of Hoskins & Holthaus Advertising. One of those interminable, sleep-inducing affairs that makes you wish you could get seriously drunk and dance naked on top of the hors d'oeuvre buffet. You can't, of course, because it's difficult to face the art director in a Monday morning meeting and tell him the logos for the Watson account are boring rather than sleek and spare, when the last time he saw you, you were waving your lavender Miracle Bra overhead and singing "Chain of Fools."

It was August, and southern California was in the throes of a wicked heat wave. The air-conditioning was overwhelmed by the sheer number of people because, in addition to all the H & H employees, key people from our biggest accounts had been invited. Everyone kept going outside to see if it was any cooler out there, which it wasn't, and all the door opening made it even hotter in the house, and nobody wanted to be the first to suggest that we bag it and go run through the sprinklers on the golf course.

To make matters even more unbearable, I was dating Chris, my (married) boss, who'd been assuring me that he and his wife were discussing the details of the divorce, but ohmigod . . . he showed up at the party with her in tow. He and I were having this rapidly escalating "discussion" of the situation in the kitchen and the caterer was trying to get rid of us, and then Al came in and strongly suggested that we set aside our differences and get our butts out to the party. Chris was trying to pretend that Al had no idea what was going on, when, in truth, there was no one in the company, with the possible exception of the night cleaning crew, who didn't know Chris and I had been carrying on like bunnies for nearly six months.

Anyway, I stormed out, straight to the bar, and poured myself an eight-ounce tumbler of white wine. I continued out the French doors, across the patio, past the pool with its fake lava waterfall and rubber lily pads, across the perfectly manicured lawn. My destination was the white gingerbread Victorian gazebo on the far side.

I almost made it. But then my sandaled foot hit something warm—something rather like a body. The wineglass went flying, and I tumbled to the ground, somehow ending up half on top of this guy.

After the initial yelped expletive he smiled and said, "Hello." Quite calmly, considering the circumstances.

I was trying to collect myself, apologizing frantically, when it occurred to me to wonder what the hell he was doing sprawled on the grass. I pushed myself off him, and began rubbing my bruised shins and knee.

"Excuse me, but what exactly are you doing sprawled on the grass?"

"Watching the Perseids." He massaged his thigh. "Good thing your knee didn't travel any farther north.

It would have put a serious crimp in my ability to father an heir."

"What the hell are Perseids?"

"Meteor shower. Tonight's the peak." He held out
his hand. "Evan Watkins."

Uh-oh. "As in Watkins Enterprises?"

I still hadn't extended my hand so he reached over
and took it. It prodded me to say, "I'm Andy Harriman."

"As in our Account Manager?"

"Um . . . yes. Why haven't I met you before?"

"I've been working in sales for the last six months,
so I've been on the road." He laughed. "All this time
I've been thinking Andy Harriman was a guy. Been
meaning to buy you a beer and tell you how much I
like what you've done with our advertising."

"I don't drink beer." I winced when I tried to get to
my knees. "But I'm glad you like the campaign."

"Andy. Short for . . . ?"

"Andrea."

"Oh." He sounded vaguely disappointed. "Actually
I could see you more as Andromeda. She's kind of upside down, too."

"What?" I tried to take a closer look at him, but it
was dark in this little corner of the world. All I could
make out was a smile full of nice, even teeth. Black
frame glasses pushed up on top of his head.

"Andromeda, the constellation," he said, pointing,
and I tried to follow the general direction. "Of course
you can't see her right now. Too close to the northern
horizon and there's too much light in L.A. Can't see
Perseus either. Or Cetus. Just all these fabulous—"

I followed his gaze just fast enough to see a streak of light. "Oh my God. A shooting star."

He laughed, a pleasant, male sort of chuckle. "Lots of them. Except they're not stars, they're meteors. Look. Lie down here." He patted the grass next to him.

"Isn't it a bit . . . damp? Aren't there worms and things?"

"Nah. I promise. And even if it was a little damp, it would be worth it to see the Perseids at their peak." He put his hand on the grass, then touched my arm, and my stomach suddenly felt like a butterfly convention. "See?" he said. "It's dry."

I lowered myself gingerly. "What about the worms?"

"Watkins Enterprises at your service, ma'm. I'm heading up a new division. Earthworm and earwig protection services. Damsels in distress our specialty."

I couldn't help laughing, and I started to recline.

"No, point yourself this way. Now turn your head slowly."

It took a few minutes for my eyes to adjust. He called it "dark adapt." He said my retinas were being flooded with a fluid called visual purple, making them infinitely more sensitive than they are in the daylight. Meanwhile, my brain was being flooded with questions. *Who is this guy, really? What planet did he come from?*

While I waited for my eyes to adjust, he told me the story (which, I was embarrassed to say, I'd never heard) of Andromeda, the daughter of the King and Queen of Joppa, who somehow pissed off some sea nymphs. They in turn complained to Poseidon and he smote the waters—in mythology they were always smiting things—calling up Cetus, the way bad watersnake. The oracle told the king that in order to save his kingdom, he'd have to chain his daughter to the rocks by the ocean as a sacrifice to the monster. However, Perseus, who just happened to be in the neighborhood on his way home from slaying the Medusa, saw Andromeda and fell in love with her. So he killed Cetus and rescued her.

Even before he stopped talking, I began to see them—quicksilver streaks across the sky. You could do a lot of wishing on a night like this; so what if they weren't stars. It occurred to me that it was sort of a dicey situation—lying there in the grass next to a man I didn't even know—my client, for God's sake—watching stars fall out of heaven by the dozen and becoming ever more aware that his hand was less than an inch away from mine. But even the certain knowledge that I'd lost my mind and was probably going to lose my job wasn't enough to break the spell of the moment.

"So, why do they call them Perseids?" My voice was a bare whisper.

He turned just slightly toward me. "Because their radiant—that is, the apparent origin—is the constellation Perseus. I guess you'd call him the hero of our story."

We lay there for a few minutes without saying a word. But I could tell he'd moved a little closer. I could feel his breath on my face, I could hear my own heartbeat and see the tiny grains of dust becoming rockets in the blackness. The party seemed very far away. Suddenly I heard my name.

"Andy! Where are you? We need to talk. Andy!"

"Who's that?" Evan said.

"Andy, where are you?"

I watched another couple of fireballs shoot across my field of vision. He'd propped himself up on one elbow so he was looking down at me, not up at the sky.

"I think it's Cetus," I said.

Now with my dark-adapted eyes, I could see that he had a wonderful smile. We both started to laugh and when we stopped laughing, he kissed me, and his glasses slid down onto the bridge of his nose, and we laughed some more.

I shake myself back into the present, riffling through my daypack. Where the hell is the map of Paris? Did I leave it on the train? For an agonizing minute I'm pushing Cetus the panic monster back down into that scary cave where he lives inside me—invisible, but waiting. I have no idea what possessed me to come to Paris. What am I doing here? I had four years of French in high school and at the moment all I remember is the word for asshole. If I had to get away, why the hell didn't I just drive to San Francisco?

Maybe it had something to do with the campaign we put together for one of our clients in February— the photo of the woman drinking coffee in a sidewalk café. OK, and then there was the horoscope business. One bleak March morning in the *L.A. Times*, Sidney Omar had said "an unexpected trip" would bring healing. But an unexpected trip could just as easily have meant Cleveland. At least they speak English there.

I square my shoulders. I've made it this far just fine. Customs and immigration went pretty easily and I found the RER train into the city without much trouble. At the Gare du Nord I managed to locate the *Bureaux d'accuiel* where they find you a place to stay when you're stupid enough to come to Paris in May without hotel reservations. They booked me at a *pensione* called Chez Pauline on rue des Canettes, which I seem to remember means ducklings. Street of Ducklings. They gave me a slip of paper with the address, a Metro map and a hearty *bonne chance*. The Metro disgorged me at St. Germain and here I am.

Eventually I unearth the map. The street of ducklings looks to be close—only a few blocks, so I decide to save the cab fare and walk. Of course it ends up being more than just a few blocks, and I'm hauling fifty pounds of baggage, so by the time I find the place I'm sweating and out of breath. I drag myself and my daypack up the stone steps and ring the bell. Then I go back down for the suitcase.

While I'm struggling with it, the door opens and a fair-haired, smiling woman says, "Hello. You must be Andrea. Did you have any trouble finding me?" in a perfect British accent. I almost start crying again with relief.

The tiny room on the third floor is exactly the sort of place you'd hope to find in a house in Paris. The walls and sloping ceilings are painted a pale blue, bare except for one rather ugly small oil painting of a flower market done in full-tilt, overexuberant colors. White lace curtains flutter at the dormer window, and there's a white iron bed with a delicate crocheted coverlet, a chair, and a tall mahogany armoire with an ornate brass key.

Pauline shows me the WC down the hall and the *salle de bain,* with its pedestal sink and massive clawfoot tub. Then she gives me an appraising look and says, "You look as if you've had a rough trip. Why don't you freshen up and come down for some tea?"

Freshen as I might, I still look like I've been dragged backward through a knothole, and my eyes feel lined with fine-grade sandpaper. I open my suitcase on the luggage rack and stare dully at the contents for a minute, but everything looks as wrinkled as I feel, so I trot obediently down to the front parlor.

While Pauline fusses with the tea things out in the kitchen, I wander around the parlor looking at her books and knickknacks. There's a photo of her with a man. He isn't handsome. Tall and lanky with a beak of a nose, but he comes across with a certain *je ne sais quoi.*

When she reappears with a tray, I suddenly realize that I'm starving. I settle myself on a pretty green velvet chair and she serves me tea and croissants and cream scones with lemon curd.

Pauline LeCamp is a slim, elegant Brit who married a French pro tennis player—the guy in the picture. They had an amicable divorce five years ago and she ended up with not much other than this lovely old house and a big tax bill. To keep said lovely old house, she began, two years ago, taking in paying guests, mostly students and budget-minded tourists who didn't mind sharing a bath and eating breakfast at a common table.

"Are you a student?" she asks me.

"No," I say around a mouthful of feather-light scone.

"Just on holiday?"

"Yes."

"The *Bureaux* only booked you for one night. Do you know how long you'll be stopping here?"

"Not exactly." I can tell she's impressed with my sparkling conversation.

"Well, I generally like to have twenty-four hours' notice when you're leaving, but you can let me know this evening. Have you got plans for today? I can help you with day trips, shopping information, galleries and exhibits, lectures . . . There's quite a lot of interesting goings-on at the Sorbonne. I can give you the names of some good cafés and bars. And the quarter is full of dance clubs, although I don't frequent them." My exhausted mind is not digesting all this. "Are you meeting up with friends?"

I say nothing, but watch a look of comprehension replace her practiced, professional friendliness.

"Ah, I see. So this is a sort of I-couldn't-stand-another-bloody-minute-of-it holiday?"

I manage a weak laugh. "Something like that."

"Well, you're in the right place," she smiles. "I've never seen a muddle that couldn't be sorted out in Paris. But to start, why not try a little sleep? This neighborhood is lovely and quiet during the day."

"Thanks. I think I will."

I trudge gratefully up the two flights of carpeted stairs, turn the screaming colors of the flower market painting to the wall, and collapse on the iron bed.

★ ★ ★

When I open my eyes, the room is dim. I scan the walls while my brain flips through a list of possible locations where I might be waking up. My house. No. Not my mother's. Or Beth-Ann's. I have a terrific crick in my neck from sleeping facedown and there's a big wet spot of drool on the embroidered pillowcase. When I ease myself into a sitting position, my gaze comes to rest on the back of the painting. Ah. Now I recall. *Paris.* In a few minutes I feel strong enough to stand up and totter over to the window. A sea of slate-tiled rooftops in the pinky gray dusk greets me, and I feel a kind of wonder.

My eyes brim suddenly, and for a second the temptation is strong to crawl back under the covers and wallow. But there's this voice in my head. *Get a grip, Andy. You've already wasted a whole day in Paris sleeping.*

After a hot soak in the tub and a change of clothes, I feel somewhat more human. And hungry. The stairway is dark, but as I reach the top, a light comes on. As I come to the landing, that light goes out and the next flight is lit. Clever people, the French. Downstairs I literally bump into Pauline in a shabby chic trench coat.

"There you are. I was trying to decide whether to wake you before I left. Feeling better?"

"Yes, thanks. I was wondering if you could direct me to someplace not too expensive for dinner."

"Of course. How hungry are you?"

"Moderately ravenous."

"Well, there are plenty of student haunts up on

Boulevard St. Germain or BouleMiche. Or you can come with me. I was just going round to Drugstore St. Germain."

"That's really nice of you. I don't want to disrupt your evening, though."

"Not at all." She pronounces it "a-tall" and she smiles.

Drugstore St. Germain really is a drugstore. It's huge and the ambience is early Walgreen's, all bright lights and noise.

"I'm certain this isn't where you dreamed of eating on your first night in Paris," she says when we're seated at one of the tiny tables. "But I think you'll be surprised at the quality of the food. And the prices are quite fair."

"To be perfectly honest I hadn't thought much about where I'd be eating on my first night in Paris."

Suddenly the waiter appears with a plate of bread and that wonderful sweet cream butter. We order our dinners and a carafe of *vin blanc.*

"Do you like living here?"

"Very much. It was lots more fun when François was around, but you adjust. His family and friends like to pretend I don't exist, of course, but I've made some friends of my own—mostly expat Brits. And there's ever so much to do here. So I keep busy."

"Did you ever think about going back to England?"

"Good wine's cheaper here." She sips contentedly. "Actually my mum's passed on and my dad and sisters weren't keen on my marrying a Frog. I suppose I wasn't particularly interested in hearing the rousing chorus of *we told you so.*"

Her smile takes on a slightly wicked glimmer. "Besides, the French are much more appreciative of *une femme d'un certain age* than the English, so my social life is probably better here." With her pale hair falling softly around her face, and her gray eyes reflecting the glittering lights, she doesn't look even close to what I think of as *"un certain age."*

The waiter sets down our plates and I bend forward to inhale the warm fragrance of garlic and herbs rising from my *poulet roti.*

"What actually brought you to Paris, Andrea?"

"It was like you said. I just had to get away. And I—" I break off suddenly, realizing how woo-woo this is going to sound.

She raises one perfect eyebrow. "And you . . . ?"

"I was sitting at my desk looking at tear sheets of an ad for one of my clients. One was a picture of a café. I'm not even positive it was Paris, although at the time, I felt absolutely certain. And there was a woman sitting at a table with a cup of coffee. She was alone, but she was smiling . . . I guess it was stupid, but I suddenly wanted to be that woman." I decide to hold off on mentioning Sidney Omar.

"No, not stupid." She takes another sip of wine and says casually, "Married?"

"Almost." My eyes go automatically to the star sapphire ring on my left hand. I pretend to study the long rack of glossy magazines along the far wall and hope the tears that are pooling in my eyes don't spill over and dilute my wine.

"Sudden changes can be quite difficult, I know," she says gently. "But you can still have a lovely holiday here, if you'll allow yourself. Just begin slowly. Give yourself some time."

I smile carefully at her and begin to cut my chicken into perfectly square, bite-sized pieces. I want to tell her that's the easy part. Time. There seem to be vast quantities of the stuff spooling out around me in all directions, everywhere I look. Days and hours. Weeks and minutes. Years.

The hard part, I've discovered, is filling it.

I don't take breakfast with Pauline's other guests. On my floor there are two Aussie girls. They sound young. College age, maybe younger. Lots of whispering and giggling. They seem to bounce off the walls as they head down the stairs. I picture them in those dance clubs that Pauline doesn't frequent. Dancing with men who wear tight black pants and reek of Drakkar Noir.

On the second floor there are two couples—one American, one German. The men both have graying hair and large stomachs and the women look as if they get up before dawn to start applying their make-up. I've only seen them in passing once or twice, which is fine by me. Even at my best, I'm not big on polite conversation with strangers before my second cup of coffee. It's much nicer to drift in and out of consciousness under my comforter, listening to Paris come to life for another hour or so.

They're all usually gone by 9 a.m.—off on the Greyline City Tour or taking in the Baccarat Museum or the Rodin sculpture garden or Pompidou center, Notre Dame, la Tour Eiffel. When the house is quiet, I get up, dress and go downstairs. The dining room is empty, still and sunny. If Pauline's gone out, she leaves a thermal carafe of coffee and a basket of bread, a covered plate with butter and cheese. If she's around, she'll sometimes have a cup of tea and keep me company, ask about my plans, make suggestions.

At first I stay pretty much within the boundaries of conventional tourism. I visit the Louvre, which is overwhelmingly huge and full of Japanese tourists.

I do the Eiffel Tower and discover in myself a latent but fully functional vertigo. I make a quick pass through Au Printemps and Galeries Lafayette, the two major department stores. At Fauchon, I stare in awe at the window display of a leg of lamb that opens out like a cornucopia, filled with fresh vegetables sculpted into the shapes of fruit.

Out of the whole first week, the place that imprints itself indelibly on my mind is the Conciergerie, the forbidding prison of the French Revolution. The day I visited was warm and sunny, but the breeze around the walls seemed cold. The dark, airless cells and tiny courtyards seemed to exude sorrow, particularly the Cour des Femmes, where prisoners bound for the guillotine were allowed to say their final farewells.

The second week, I discover the Musée d'Orsay with its comforting and familiar paintings of the French Impressionists. I go jogging along the *quais*. I watch children floating their boats in the fountains of Luxembourg gardens and the old men playing *petanque* and sucking tired-looking cigarettes.

Paris begins to get inside me.

I take it up through the soles of my feet as I walk the tree-lined boulevards. I inhale it with the exhaust fumes, the steam off my *café au lait,* the bouquet of *vin rouge,* the sweet, roasted grain smell of the *boulangeries.* It seeps into my pores with the breezes, the puddles evaporating after brief, torrential showers. I feel myself unwinding in a long, slow spiral.

Versailles is disappointing. Formally stodgy and not particularly beautiful. The Hall of Mirrors is cavernous and weird, all that light and glitter and reflection and nothing there to reflect. No furniture except for a tiny, ornate desk upon which the Treaty of Versailles was signed. Just emptiness bouncing back and forth across the room from one mirror to the next. The *parc* is much nicer, but every flower and bush and tree is tortured into frozen perfection. Plus, it's expensive and I return exhausted. I think about skipping dinner in favor of a hot soak and a glass of wine, but Pauline talks me into going to a little bistro where the mellow sweet fumes of garlic soup loosen my tongue. OK, the bottle of Alsatian Riesling doesn't hurt, either.

I find myself telling her all about Evan. Well, except for the star thing. I don't know why. Maybe it's just too intimate, too quintessentially Evan. To share it with anyone else—anyone at all—might diminish it. It might make the picture of him in my mind seem a bit faded and trivial, like an old photograph of someone wearing amusingly out-of-style clothes.

I just tell her about how he loved movies, everything from the biggest Hollywood blockbuster to the most obscure art film from Yugoslavia. How we were both tired of expensive, pretentious restaurants, so we explored local dives in search of the juiciest hamburger, the smokiest barbecue, the most authentic Mexican, Thai, Moroccan, Persian—you name it. We frequented the House of Blues and the Jazz Bakery and some of the funky little clubs on Sunset Boulevard. We took long walks on the beach and drives into the desert.

I tell her how he made me feel, how some nights I lie awake wondering if I could ever feel anything like it again.

"So what happened?" Pauline's voice startles me.

I chew the inside of my cheek. "He was killed. A motorcycle accident. A month before our wedding."

She gasps audibly. "Oh, Andy. Dear God, I'm so sorry." She leans toward me, brows knit together in genuine distress.

Sometimes you just have to believe that people spend a lifetime stockpiling stupidity, so they can drag it out on special occasions. Like at funerals. Numb as I was, I still couldn't believe that people actually came up to me and said things like, *Don't worry, you'll find somebody else.* Things like, *At least you'll remember him as young and handsome and you'll never have to watch him get old.* And, *At least it was quick and he didn't suffer.*

I hope the flowers were all right. I used a new florist because he was having a special promotion.

Sorry I couldn't come to the funeral; I couldn't get off work on such short notice.

Too bad you were just living together. If you'd been legally married, you'd at least have his life insurance.

In the midst of regaling Pauline with tales of the funeral, I suddenly find all these misbegotten condolences oddly and excruciatingly hilarious, and I erupt into great shuddering spasms of uncontrollable laugh-ter—the first in a very long time.

"Oh, Andy, don't," she says, but after a few seconds she joins in. Every time one of us gets close to quieting down, our eyes meet and we start laughing again. I can't stop laughing. About the time I realize there's a kind of hysterical edge to it, the laughing has turned to crying. Which is equally uncontrollable.

She signals for *l'addition,* pays the waiter, and we stumble to the nearest Metro station. She holds my arm to steady me, brushing aside my soggy apologies. When we reach home, I'm ready for bed, but she in-sists that a proper cup of tea is needed to ensure a rest-ful night.

"Tisane, actually," she says. "Chamomile is very calming." As we sit in the parlor with our steaming cups, I feel her assessing the state of my mental health. "Are you all right?"

I sigh and nod and try to reassure her. "Just ex-hausted and embarrassed."

But there's also something else going on. I'd tell her, but I can't really explain the feeling yet, even to myself. It's almost a weightlessness, like an astronaut in deep space, and a loosening, as if something hard and heavy in my chest has shattered into thousands of tiny pieces.

Maybe it's that, or maybe it's just the tea, but I sleep deeply and dreamlessly that night.

Monday morning I head for the Metro stop early. Something almost like a smile forces its way to my face as I let myself be carried along by the river of people going about their daily business. Distinctive smells spike the morning air—coffee and garlic and baking bread, different perfumes and aftershaves. A woman carrying a bunch of intensely fragrant lilies seems unconcerned that they might get squashed against someone's coat or backpack. The ubiquitous accordion player is already at work in the tunnel, playing the love theme from *The Godfather.*

It's so different from driving to work in L.A., hermetically sealed into my VW Bug with my nonfat, nofoam double latté and my evergreen car deodorant. My only contact with other commuters is generally limited to a honk and a rude gesture if I unthinkingly cut someone off.

After a long ride north I exit at Porte de Clignancourt and follow the crowds along the avenue lined with tacky street vendors selling partially used phone cards and suspiciously rubbery-looking leather jackets. The sun is already warm, and water left on the sidewalks from the morning's scrubbing steams toward the blue sky. I turn left on the rue des Rosiers, into the heart of the beast—the Marché aux Puces de St. Ouen, which bills itself as the world's largest flea market.

And it is. It must be. It looks roughly the size of Santa Monica. The atmosphere pulses with color and motion, with noise—the traffic of moving bodies makes up the background, overlaid with sellers and buyers haggling over prices, kids with boomboxes. People walk by alone, engaged in animated conversation, displaying the full repertoire of Gallic facial expressions and gestures. I know they're talking on cell phones, but they still look like lunatics, talking to God or imaginary companions.

I have no idea what I'm looking for, but I told Pauline I want a souvenir of my trip, something other than the generic silk scarf from Au Printemps or bottle of perfume or framed watercolor of Notre Dame, and this is where she's sent me. I take a long breath and submerge myself in the crowd.

The market is actually divided into lots of separate markets, each one specializing in a different sort of goods—furniture, antiques, paintings, bronzes, clothes, china, phonograph records, books, vintage postcards, linens, jewelry—whatever you can imagine, you can buy here. I wander aimlessly among the stalls. Some of the dealers speak English, but most aren't interested in chatting unless you're a serious buyer. Their frank stares of appraisal—as if I'm just another kind of merchandise—are intimidating. And the mind-boggling array of stuff is overwhelming. My overstimulated brain wants to run up the white flag.

I love the antique buttons—handpainted porcelain, hammered silver, carved wood and bone, colored glass. But what would I do with them? Not only don't I sew, I lack the hand—eye coordination necessary for even the most basic crafty projects.

When the sharp-eyed dealer says, *"Vous desirez, Madame?"* I shake my head and murmur, *"Non, merci."*

Likewise, when I stop to admire the hand-spun, hand-dyed skeins of wool, it must be obvious to the young hippie-looking girl seated on a tall stool behind the metal cashbox that I'm just a grimy-fingered gawker. She barely looks up from her knitting.

I'm tempted to skip the book stalls altogether. I've already bought several things from the *bouquinistes* along the Seine, and a book really isn't what I had in mind today, but as I turn reluctantly away, one of the dealers catches my eye. He's short and stocky with a merry face. I can't tell his age, but he has a grand total of three hairs combed over the top of his head.

"*Bonjour, Madame.* How are you this lovely day?"

I swear I must have *Americaine* tattooed on my forehead. "Fine, thanks. And you?" I was planning to just keep moving, escape before I got sucked into a conversation, but he's beckoning to me, waving me over, and so I go. It's not like I have a hot date.

"You are looking for something." It's not a question, and he smiles, his dark eyes twinkling, like he's sharing some amusing secret with me.

"Well, I didn't really want a book," I explain apologetically.

He wipes his hands on a grimy rag lying on top of a book bin. "I have more. Not only books." My eyes settle on some cheesy figurines on a shelf—can-can girls and gendarmes and apache dancers. He follows my gaze and laughs. "*Non, pas comme ça.*" He turns around and pulls out a stack of prints from under a table. "You like stories, I can see this. These are the most old stories."

He shows me the series of black and white drawings, beautifully hand-tinted. Illustrations of characters from mythology. Venus and Adonis. Cupid and Psyche. Pomona and Vertumnus. All lovers. Ceyx and Halcyone. Orpheus and Eurydice. And the last one, at the bottom of the pile, is Andromeda. Alone. At first I don't recognize her because most pictures I've seen show her upside down, like her constellation. This one shows her upright against a diaphanous turquoise background. Her body faces forward, but her head is turned partially away, eyes closed. Even though she's obviously standing free, she still wears the shackles that bound her to the rocks as sea-snake snack. She wears a flowing lavender dress, and the stars of her constellation gleam from her auburn hair. I think it's the most wonderful picture of her I've ever seen. Evan would have loved it.

"Where can I get it framed?" When I look up at the dealer, he's smiling. Already counting his money.

"I'll be leaving on Wednesday," I tell Pauline that night as we wind through the narrow, cobblestone streets of the 18th *arrondissement*.

"Oh, dear. I shall miss your company, I'm afraid."

I smile at her. "Thank you for saying that, but I'm sure you'll be glad to get your life back to normal."

"I'd hardly call it normal." She gives a rueful laugh. "This time of year I feel like a glorified chambermaid-cum-secretarial service. Your visit has broken things up nicely."

"Do you ever get time off?"

"Oh, yes. I close down to guests from the end of November till the first of March. By then I need it desperately. But right now is just the start of the madness." Her stylish, high-heeled boots make a staccato tapping on the paving stones.

"Here we go, then." She reaches around me and pushes open a small wooden door, ushers me through into a dark, low-ceilinged, cheerfully tacky room. A roar greets us from a large round table in a far corner and Pauline waves.

"I hope you don't mind. We're meeting some friends of mine."

I try to hide my dismay. "Oh, you didn't have to drag me along. I'd have been fine. Look, maybe I should—"

"Don't be silly. I wanted you to come. See, they've kept two seats for us. Everybody, this is my friend Andy. Please go round and tell her who you are and warn her of any dangerous habits."

I try to pay attention as they smile at me around the table, three men, four women. They tell me names I can't hear through the ambient noise, and say things either to me or to each other, all punctuated with laughter. Most of them seem to be English, but one woman named Marie-Claire and the guy on her right, whose name I miss, are French.

Inside I'm shrinking. I'd give anything not to be here. I can't make conversation with these people. I want to slink back to the B & B to watch American cowboy movies with French subtitles on Pauline's tiny television.

Pauline is going around the table kissing and being kissed while a guy with a gray ponytail and a shapeless green sweater says in a perfect Inspector Clousseau accent, "Ah, *Madame*, how is it that a beautiful woman comes alone to Paris in the spring?"

"Bon question, n'est-ce pas?" says the Frenchman.

I smile awkwardly and say, "Just a quick vacation."

My reply is lost as they all begin talking at once in

Franglais, and it's dizzying. The waiter brings two bottles of wine and more glasses without being asked, so I figure this is a group of regulars. Someone else sets down three plates of different cheeses and a couple of loaves of bread wrapped in big white napkins.

After a few sips of my wine, I excuse myself to the bathroom. It's very small, just a urinal, a toilet and a minuscule sink fitted into one corner. I wash my hands and stare at my face in the mottled, grimy mirror. I look like a cardboard cutout of a woman—flat, gray, unappealing. No light, no spark.

The world keeps turning. Life keeps unfolding. People keep walking, talking, laughing, eating, drinking, smoking, going places, touching each other, sitting, reading. They get married, get divorced. Die. Yes, some of them die. My hands are trembling as I dry them on the coarse paper towel. I know I used to be a part of it, but I don't remember how it works. I can't do it. I don't have to. I'll just go out and tell Pauline that I'm not feeling well, and I'll go back to the house.

But when I come out of the john, I can't find Pauline. The whole place is packed, and the group has expanded, like an amoeba getting ready to divide. The chair where I left my jacket is occupied by a frizzed-out blonde deep in conversation with the guy in the gray ponytail. The table is covered with plates of food.

"*Mademoiselle. Andee.*" The Frenchman is waving my jacket and motioning me to the empty chair next to him. I bet his date is thrilled.

"I fix a plate for you," he says, smiling. "I am afraid it will all be eaten when you return."

I try to smile back at him. "That's very nice of you. Thanks."

"Let me tell you . . ." He turns the plate this way and that, pointing to various dishes. "These are *pin-chos*. Like hors d'oeuvres." There are thin shavings of ham, roasted red peppers, mushrooms, olives speared on toothpicks with anchovies and hot chilies. Hard-boiled eggs with flakes of tuna. Garlicky grilled shrimps and perfect silver dollar–sized potatoes, fried hot and golden, redolent of fruity olive oil.

He pours more wine in my glass.

"I must apologize." He puts down his fork and looks directly at me with luminous brown eyes. "I did not hear your family name."

"Harriman. Andy Harriman. And I didn't hear yours at all."

"Claude Massot." He turns to the woman on the other side. "My sister, Marie-Claire."

She smiles. "Always, it is noisy here."

So. His sister. OK, then, I forgive him.

"How do you know Pauline?" I ask.

"I know her for a long time. I am friends at school with her husband, François." He spreads some crumbly, blue-veined cheese on a piece of bread and eats it slowly. "I tell him when they divorce, a big mistake. Pauline is a wonderful woman."

"And what did he say?"

His grin broadens. "He said to me, 'You are not married to her.' "

We both laugh. I relax back in my chair.

"And you know Pauline from where?"

"I just met her. I'm staying at the house."

His thick eyebrows go up. *"C'est vrai?* I thought you were perhaps a friend from England."

I shake my head. "No, I'm American."

"Ah, that explains your accent."

I smile at the thought of a southern California accent. When he finds out I'm from L.A., he asks if I'm an actress, so I tell him yes, as a joke, and find it's not that far off the mark. What else would you call what I've been doing? He says he's a painter. A serious painter with a day job as a sign painter. Someone is tapping him on the shoulder, talking in his ear, so I concentrate on the food, which is simple and fabulous, and the wine, which is making me feel very cozy and warm.

"Do you like art?" He turns back to me suddenly.

"I suppose I do. It's not something I think about a lot."

"Because it's a *divertissement,* you know? When I paint or when I see paintings or think about paintings, I forget my problems." Without any comment or encouragement from me, he asks, "What art have you seen in Paris? What do you like?"

"Well, I went to the Louvre . . ."

"Bien sûr."

"And the Musée d'Orsay . . ."

"Ah, you like *l'Impressionisme?"*

"Yes."

"Do you like the new art?"

"Contemporary art?" I shrug. "Some of it."

"Sculpture?"

"Some of it."

"I can see you are very discerning."

I laugh. "I don't know anything about it."

"I could show you, if you desire to learn. I have many friends, artists . . ."

"I don't think so, Claude."

"*Et pourquoi pas?* You think I am a bad man?"

"No, really. It isn't that."

He tilts his head. "What then?"

"I'm going home on Wednesday."

"But tomorrow is Tuesday." He has the most beautiful eyelashes.

"This is just kind of a bad time for me."

"Yes." He nods gravely. "I can see. I am sorry."

"Me too."

The thing is that suddenly I am. Sorry to be leaving Paris. Sorry I can't spend time with this man and his pretty eyelashes. Sorry I won't be having any more mornings with Pauline in the Street of Ducklings.

He touches his glass to mine. "*À votre santé,*" he says.

Wednesday morning, I'm dragging my stuff down the stairs when Pauline comes bounding up, meeting me on the top landing.

"The taxi's here." She takes my daypack and precedes me down. "I really hate to see you leave."

"I hate to go," I say softly. "It's almost like I'm leaving home instead of going home."

At the bottom of the stairs, we stop and hug. "You'll come back, won't you?"

I nod. "Most definitely. Pauline, thanks so much. For everything."

A blast of the taxi horn makes her roll her eyes. "Parisian cab drivers."

The driver sits on his butt while we wrestle my bag into the trunk and hug again.

"Travel safe, Andy. Be happy."

I smile. "I plan to try."

As we career around the corner I look out the window at Pauline waving from the curb. There were things I wanted to tell her, but there wasn't time, and it was all sort of hard to explain. Anyway, I think she'll understand.

The taxi darts and weaves through the traffic, the driver alternately flooring the gas pedal and slamming on the brake, but I barely feel the movement. In the backseat I float, magically suspended, weightless. Thinking of my little blue room at Chez Pauline, the cozy iron bed, the dormer window with its view of Parisian rooftops. The mahogany armoire with its brass key. The ugly flower painting that adorned the wall is tucked neatly into my suitcase. And hanging in its place, my picture of Andromeda. Still wearing her shackles, but escaped from the rocks now. Right side up and standing on her own.

Andromeda on the Street of Ducklings.

JUDI HENDRICKS is the author of two bestselling novels, *Bread Alone* and *Isabel's Daughter*. She lives in Long Beach, California.

Bad Manners

CHRIS MANBY

*A*nd then one day my Prince did come along . . .
OK. So he wasn't quite a Prince. Or even a
Right Honorable. But he had been to the *right* school
and after that to the *right* university and he was definitely what Nancy Mitford would have called "U." He
told me so himself. After he did an impression of the
way I introduced myself to him that made me sound
like a farm girl who'd just celebrated a pig slaughtering
with a night on the cider.

"I don't talk like that," I said, reeling from the ugli-
ness of my voice as he relayed it back to me.

"I'm afraid you do," he said. "And you look like a
muppet when you're doing it. But it really doesn't
bother me."

Gee, thanks, is what I should have told him then. I

guess I'll see you around. But, at that time, I still thought he was just trying to be funny. British men are like that, my girlfriends back in the States had warned me. Particularly the upper-class ones. They're too uptight to come out with the compliments. You only know they like you when they say something nasty about the way you dress, or the style of your hair. Or mimic your voice. He had been smiling as he did it, so I took it to be the case that he was actually trying to tell me I was hot.

He, of course, had the kind of perfectly modulated voice that befitted someone of the officer class. Perfect for being heard above gunshot across bloody battle-fields. It carried equally well across the restaurant that evening.

"I don't know what that woman thinks she looks like in that blouse," he said. Moments later she knew exactly what *he* thought she looked like. As did everybody else within fifty, maybe even a hundred, feet.

I cringed when the poor girl blushed. I really did. But when I looked from her crushed little face back into his playful blue eyes beneath that floppy blond fringe, he had already moved the conversation on to music. And then he was talking about Sibelius and a lake on the Finnish border with Russia that had inspired some piece about a swan and already I had forgotten that he could use that beautiful voice to say some very ugly things indeed.

"Perhaps you would like to join me for tea one afternoon next week?" he said.

"That would be lovely," I told him.

"Christina," he said then, "when I say 'tea' I simply

mean the drink, not something to eat as well. You do know that, don't you? Or do you have your dinner at lunchtime too, in the United States?"

He laughed. And I laughed with him. But it took me the whole tube ride home to work out exactly what he meant.

We had tea in his apartment overlooking a garden square. We drank Earl Grey—hot water in the china cup first, I think, then the milk.

"We only drink it iced in California," I said.

He played me some opera and gave a running commentary on the libretto. It was Turandot. The humble maidservant defended her Prince to the death. The heartless Princess Turandot married him in the poor girl's memory. It would have been a better story if the Prince had ended up falling for the maidservant, I said. My own Prince laughed. Indulgently.

"I'll take you to Covent Garden next," he said.

"I've been to Covent Garden before. A client of the advertising agency I was working for took me to see *The Magic Flute*."

"Did you sleep with him?" my Prince asked suddenly.

"No. No, I didn't."

"But he wanted to sleep with you."

"No. I don't think so," I said.

"Opera tickets are expensive, Christina. I wouldn't waste time taking someone to the opera unless I wanted them to be around for a while. To understand the things that interest me."

The thing that interests me is modern art. We saw a

lot of opera in the next couple of months. We didn't see the Rothko room at the new Tate Modern.

But arguing about art became the Prince's favorite new hobby. Whenever he introduced me to someone—never his female friends, I noticed in retrospect—he would say, "Christina likes modern art," as though he was telling them I had a communicable disease. And that would segue into "all modern art is rubbish," illustrated by examples from the exhibition of young British artists Giuliani wanted to ban from New York back in 1997. Or any piece that had ever been nominated for the Tate Britain's Turner Prize.

"An unmade bed. How can you tell me that an unmade bed is art?" he would open in exasperation.

At first, I couldn't find an argument in favor. I knew I thought Tracy Emin's unmade bed wasn't a total waste of space and time but I couldn't quite verbalize why. Until one evening when we were having the "modern art is rubbish" debate for the hundredth time in front of a man he particularly admired. A man who was sympathetic to *my* side of the row.

"The thing is," I started hesitantly, "what you're seeing in the gallery might not make sense because it isn't actually the *whole* work of art. Tracy Emin is part of her artwork. There is art in the way the bed came to be unmade."

"Good point," said the other man. The mediator.

"*There is art in the way the bed came to be unmade . . .*" parroted my Prince in a new, more accurate parody of my accent. "You'll have to excuse her," he added. "She's from the colonies."

★   ★   ★

Never a more true word than spoken in jest. You don't have to look too closely to realize that those little things he jokes about at the start of your passionate romance are going to be the big things that tear you apart later on. Your funny laugh is going to become a witch's cackle. That cute mole on your neck is the beginnings of a wart.

We went from the private members' club to dinner in an intimate Italian on the Strand.

But I had already lost my appetite. Or rather, I had lost my nerve.

I didn't dare order the soup because I couldn't see a soup spoon and even if I had found the soup spoon, where would I have put it when I was done? On the side plate or in the bowl? Handle toward me or facing away? I couldn't order the fish for exactly the same reason. Where was the fish knife? Did smart people even use a "fish knife" these days? How would I get the skin off? What was one supposed to do with the bones? How about the asparagus? *How about the asparagus?* With the cutlery or with my fingers? I was sure I'd heard you are supposed to eat it with your fingers but that simply didn't seem possible since I also remembered that you are supposed to eat a banana with a knife and fork.

All this worry was making my throat dry. But which of the glasses should I reach for? To the left or to the right of me? Was that even a glass right there? What if it was the fingerbowl? It had a piece of lemon in it but no ice.

I reached for a bread roll in desperation.

My charming Prince Charming slapped my hand away from the bread basket. Reader, he . . . slapped . . . my . . . hand.

The waiter arrived.

I went for the tagliatelle.

"Tag-lia-telly," I said to the waiter. He nodded quickly and wrote my order down.

"*Tag-lia-telly?*" mimicked my Prince as the waiter walked away. "*Tag*-lia-telly? What is that stuff you ordered? Please tell me one more time."

"Tag-lia-telly." My voice came out like a mouse-squeak.

"Are you saying it like that to upset me?" he asked. "*Tag*-lia-telly!"

"What's wrong with that?"

"You are pronouncing the 'g,' Christina. Everybody knows you don't pronounce the 'g.' It's *ta-lia-telle,*" he purred, bringing out his best Italian. "Ta-lia-telle. Say it after me. And again. And again. And again."

The couple sitting opposite, with a program from *My Fair Lady* on the table between them, stared and stared and stared.

"Ow!" The Prince covered his ears as I repeated my poorly ordered pasta. "Ow! You're hurting me," he said. "Stop torturing me. Speak *properly,* for God's sake."

"This is my proper voice."

He gave a little sniff as though he didn't quite believe me. The *ta-lia-telle* arrived.

"Is it al *den*-tay?" he teased.

"It's al *don*-tay, yes," I replied.

It looked perfect but I didn't put a single piece into

my mouth. I simply pushed the strands around my plate, terrified that the coil I so carefully raveled around my fork would unravel again before I could get it into my mouth, forcing me to suck in a stray string like those dogs in *Lady and the Tramp*. No prizes for guessing who *wasn't* the Lady.

I don't think he noticed that I didn't eat a bite. The waiter took my plate away with a disappointed shrug. We had coffee. I could just about manage coffee. There is only one way to drink coffee right. Right? Though at one point I managed to clatter the fragile white cup back down onto the saucer and a single black drop leaped out onto the perfect white tablecloth. It was the only mark on the tablecloth. On my side. His eyes were immediately drawn to it and stayed there while he told me that he didn't think we should see each other anymore.

"We're very different kinds of people," he sighed. "We don't even share a common language."

He saw me to a taxi and looked suitably downcast as it ferried me away from him. I watched him from the back window for a while, clutching the ten-pound note he had given me toward my fare as though it was the rope that kept me from falling over the precipice into despair.

But suddenly, I didn't feel like crying. I didn't feel like a woodcutter's daughter who had lost her chance to marry into the palace. I felt like a troublesome rescue dog being sent back to the pound. He had tried to train me but it just wasn't taking. I was untrainable. An old dog who definitely couldn't be taught a new trick. That was how he saw me, wasn't it? I felt a sudden urge to give somebody a bite.

"Stop here, please," I said to the taxi driver.

"What? Here?" he asked.

"That's what I said."

We pulled up at the curb alongside Ed's Diner. It was still open, though there was no one inside but a single waiter, mopping the counter with a dirty old rag.

"Do you want me to wait for you?" asked the cabbie.

"Nope," I told him. "I think I'm going to eat in. Keep the change." I gave him the ten-pound note to cover a three-pound fare.

The waiter looked surprised to see me.

"Can I help you?" he asked, probably expecting me to ask to use the bathroom or a phone.

"I want everything on the menu," I said. "Everything. I want burgers and milkshakes and fries and a big bowl of melted cheese to dip them in. I want a fried egg on top of a salad. I want tomato ketchup on top of the egg. And I won't be needing any cutlery. Or napkins. I mean, *serviettes.*" I let a word the Prince would never utter drip off my tongue like a curse.

"You got it!" said the waiter.

Within minutes my feast was laid out in front of me. My appetite was back like a small starving street dog as I crammed a handful of fries into my mouth. Then a slurp of my milkshake, before I even finished chewing. Then a bite of my burger and another bite and another bite until my gob was so full I could *only* eat with my mouth open.

"That good?" asked the waiter.

"Oh, yeah," I said, through a muffler of sesame bun. I stabbed the fried egg with a plastic straw and watched the golden yolk ooze out like the blood from my poor broken heart.

"Can you put on some music?" I asked.

"What do you fancy?"

"How about some rap? Have you got something with cursing in it?"

"I've got the compilation CD I'm not supposed to play until we're shut."

"Play it now," I said. "There's no one here to report you. Up yours, Sibelius," I shouted as the Asian Dub Foundation started up.

"Who's Sibelius?" asked the waiter.

"Some Finnish bloke," I said.

"Yeah. I heard the Finns were weird," the waiter sympathized. "Do you want me to beat the crap out of him for you?"

"He's already dead," I replied. "But thanks. Want a slurp?" I offered him a suck on my milkshake. He took it from me and I couldn't help smiling as his nice big mouth puckered around the straw.

He was no handsome Prince as the storybooks describe them. His golden locks had been shaved to a millimeter of scary stubble so that you could see the dragon tattooed on his skull. His regal nose was adorned with not one but three silver rings. He had a peculiar sort of piercing in his bottom lip too. A futuristic tribal adornment, like a small bullet that must have clicked against his teeth when he talked. He talked in a mumble.

I had a sudden urge to find out what it would be like to kiss him with that strange thing in his mouth. I tore another bite from my burger and his eyes crinkled upward at the corners as he saw the new kind of hunger in mine.

"I'd like to go somewhere quiet and get really rude with you," I told him before I even finished chewing.

That one sentence was two fingers to every rule I'd ever lived by. Nice girls don't speak with their mouth full. Nice girls wait to be asked. Nice girls don't . . . Don't. Don't. Don't.

But the Prince had already established that I wasn't a nice sort of girl.

He closed the shop. His name was Marc, he said. Marc with a "c." Definitely "non-U."

"I'm Christine," I replied. "Not *Christina*. Christina might have gone to a convent school. Christine kissed boys behind the bike sheds, lost her virginity at fifteen and talks about it in front of strangers."

"What are you talking about?" Marc asked me.

"Nothing," I said. This wasn't the right time for words.

We took the tube back to his place. He shared a flat in south London with four other guys. One of them was snoring on the sofa as we tiptoed into Marc's damp-smelling bedroom. A sculpture made of beer bottles adorned the windowsill. The green glass turned the orange glow of the streetlight outside alien yellow.

"Close the door," I whispered as Marc pushed me down onto his unmade single bed.

"There is no door," he said.

Who cared anyway? The bloke on the sofa snored more loudly than I squealed when Marc made me come.

Marc was still asleep when I woke up in the morning. His friend was still on the sofa as I tiptoed out of the flat again. I didn't leave my number. I just closed the door behind me and sashayed to the tube station. A pretty mongrel dog wagging my tail.

Perhaps I should have left a thank-you note on the kitchen table. Thanks for the burger, Marc. (He hadn't made me pay for it.) Thanks for the hardcore rap. Thanks for the shag. But I didn't.

Do you think that was bad manners on my part?

In 1995, **CHRIS MANBY** met a New York psychic who told her she would write seven novels. She has just finished her eighth. Which means she probably won't marry that millionaire either! Raised in Gloucestershire, Chris now divides her time between London and Los Angeles. Her hobbies include reading in-flight magazines.

Chris is the author of eight bestsellers: *Flatmates, Second Prize, Deep Heat, Lizzie Jordan's Secret Life, Running Away from Richard, Getting Personal, Seven Sunny Days,* and *Girl Meets Ape*.

The Two-Month Itch

SARAH MLYNOWSKI

You're having an urge to kiss the boy sitting next to you on the plane.

You get a lot of urges you know are dumb. Like detaching the keys on your laptop to see if you can clip them back on. Or galloping through your apartment butt-naked even though you and your roommate Moon never got around to putting up blinds. Or using shampoo in the dishwasher when you've run out of detergent.

Or cheating on your boyfriend.

Not to worry, said Dr. Clark, the shrink your parents forced you to see eight years ago for six entire months after they got divorced for the *second* time. From each other. They're now remarried. To each other. Till death do them part or until they start throwing china.

Clark reassured you that your urges didn't classify you as a psycho. They don't define you, she said definitively. They're perfectly normal as long as you don't act on all of them, and especially not all at once. She told you that as long as you tried to be rational and weigh the pros and cons of each urge, you'd be OK. Try to understand why you're having these urges, she urged. She even suggested that the urge you had to drive your mother's car without a license had been a cry for attention. And here you thought you'd just needed a ride to the mall. Not that it had made a difference.

You definitely didn't mutilate your laptop for attention. After clicking the S off the keyboard, you realized that you were unable to snap it back on. You were forced to call a computer repairman who charged eighty dollars for a new keyboard and ninety-five for labor. Urges can get costly.

You don't always give in.

You haven't yet washed your dishes with shampoo. You almost did, once; but then you imagined the potential flooding and the cranky, whiny man who lives below you and complains to the landlord about every infinitesimal thing. How exactly are you supposed to become a famous saxophone player if you can't practice at home, anyway?

"You boast more than an average person's share of crazy," Moon, your roommate of two years, said yesterday during one of your many naked post-shower apartment sprints. And you were—*hah!*—delighted to observe that the shades in the apartment facing you were drawn.

And no, her parents were not on LSD when they

named her. They were into LDS. As in Latter Day Saints. Mormons. So definitely no hallucinatory drugs since Mormons won't even do coffee.

"If you're naked in a room full of people and you can only cover one body part, what do you cover?" you asked in mid-sprint.

Moon shook her head. "I'm not often naked in a room full of people. What would you cover?"

"My face. So no one would know it was me! Get it?"

Laughing at your oh-so-wicked humor, you ran to your closet, unfortunately located outside your bedroom because of space issues, and put on panties and a tank top. Then you decide to organize your remaining clothes by color.

Moon was still shaking her head when you returned to the living room. "Uh-oh. I know what the naked sprints, the bad jokes and the closet re-org mean: You're getting antsy. You always get antsy before you break up with a boyfriend. Gavin is about to be history, isn't he?"

What? Breaking up with Gavin? LSD, LDS, whatever; this girl was delusional.

"I am not."

"Yes, you are. You have the two-month itch. You always get it. You're a friggin' commitment-phobe."

The one Mormon teaching that Moon hasn't been able to shake is her parents' no-swearing rule. Luckily she's had no problems with the abstain-from-stimulants rule. You two have decorated your apartment in empty Absolut bottles.

Anyway, she didn't know what she was talking

about. You've never been afraid of commitment. "First of all, I'm not breaking up with Gavin. Second of all, what's a two-month itch?" It sounded like one of those unmentionable social diseases.

"You always dump the guy you're dating two months into the relationship. You're afraid of it turning into anything real."

"I do not. What about Matth—" You stopped in midsentence. OK, so it happened once.

Moon laughed. "Matthew? You were supposedly madly in love with him until you dumped him on your two-month anniversary. Dumped him because he didn't acknowledge the dating milestone."

What kind of a guy doesn't remember how long you'd been dating? "There, you see? Gavin remembered. He even sent me a card. Why would I break up with him?"

"I don't know. But you'll come up with some flaw, I'm sure."

How could someone live with you for so long and know you so little? "Why would I break up with someone who makes my bed when I'm in the shower?" Really. He does. Isn't that sweet? He even makes hospital corners.

"You broke up with Evan after seven weeks, and he swept your floor."

"But he was missing one of his toes. That was too weird. I couldn't be in a relationship with someone who had nine toes."

"Who cares how many toes he had? This is New York. He would have only worn sandals for three months a year."

She shook her head. Then you shook your head. The mutual head shaking continued until she told you to put on some pants.

So. Back to the airplane. You're on your way to the bathroom, and have a brief urge to kick open the exit latch Charlie's Angel–style to see if it would suck you out like a vacuum cleaner, but instead you open the *unoccupied* door. You brush your teeth, scrunch your lazy brown hair with tap-watered hands in a futile attempt to create volume, add a coat of mascara and eyeliner to make your eyes pop or at the very least snap and crackle, and spray a spritz of perfume to your armpits to mask the stale smell that sprouted from sitting on the tarmac because a snowstorm held you grounded for three hours. At least you're finally in the air.

You are attempting to transform into a delicious specimen because, for the first time ever, you have been seated next to a godlike creature of Times-Square/Calvin Klein Underwear advertising proportions. No bullshit. He's stunning, and he smells like a mixture of clean laundry and roasted marshmallows.

Because of the three hours spent taxiing around Chicago O'Hare's airport, you've had some time to get to know each other. So far you've discussed leg room (his legs must be at least six feet), *People* magazine (you wish you had brought a copy of *War and Peace,* but what's done is done), what you do for a living (he's in PR, you're in marketing), your ages (he's twenty-six, you're twenty-four), where you're from (he lives in Chicago, you're from Arizona but live in

Brooklyn), why you're going to Arizona (he has a bachelor party, you're overdue for a parental visit), and your respective significant others (he has a girl-friend named Janey, you immediately counter by mentioning Gavin). He's also spent an awful lot of time smiling, and you've reciprocated by batting your eyelashes. You've decided that your fingers are getting a manicure as a reward for having the magical insight to route you to Phoenix via Chicago and not St. Louis.

All done. You slide open the lock, and head back to your seat, checking out the herds of people the airline could have seated you next to along the way: three single girls, one man taking up two seats, one greaseball who looks like the bad guy in *Grease*—the one they call Crater Face—and two mothers holding screaming, drooling babies on their laps.

You slide back into your jackpot of a seat. He smiles. You bat.

Your prize has wavy, sandy hair, wide blue eyes, and a Disney-hero cleft in his proud, square chin. Bobby, he said his name was.

Gavin, Gavin, Gavin.

A pit of guilt begins to swell in the recesses of your stomach. But that could be the hamburger you had at O'Hare.

You're just flirting. You met an interesting guy and you're engaging in innocent conversation. That's not *wrong*. And it's not the two-month itch. Exercising your inner coquette doesn't mean that you no longer want Gary. You mean Gavin. You mentally review your why-you-like Gavin checklist:

1. He opens the car door for you. Even when you're the driver.

2. He gives amazing back massages. Without making you beg for them.

3. He doesn't get mad when you tell him you don't feel like coming over, and that you'd rather just hang out at your place and watch *Sister Act II* again with Moon.

4. The sex is good. He's always pulling you on top of him, which *Cosmo* claims will give you better orgasms. Which has yet to be proven. The truth is, it gets a bit boring being on top, every single time. Sometimes you wonder if he's sensitive or just lazy.

"Do you have any tattoos?" Bobby asks, leaning closer. The cabin lights are off and the passengers' reading lamps flicker like candlelight.

"No. I have a belly ring."

"Let's see."

You suck in your stomach and lift the tip of your shirt. He gently touches the blue stone, detonating the pit in your stomach and replacing it with intense heat.

"Cool," he says.

Gavin who?

Your turn. "Do *you* have tattoos?"

He rolls back his left sleeve, exposing thick black letters across his glorious bicep.

B-O-B-B-Y.

Interesting.

His face has magnetically pulled close to yours, his lips a creamy mix of brown, red and juicy peach.

"Have you ever cheated on your boyfriend?" the lips ask.

You shake your head no. Your philosophy has always been that if you want to be with another guy, first you have to break up with your boyfriend. You once told a date you would rather a boyfriend call you to end the relationship four seconds before he slept with another woman than have him cheat on you. Obviously a misguided notion. Whipping out your cell phone at this moment would definitely be inappropriate, and would possibly cause a miscommunication of air signals to be sent to the pilot, resulting in an airplane nose dive. Potential to cause multiple deaths definitely nullifies the philosophy.

"Have you?" You purse your lips into your most kissable pose on the final vowel. If he moves in even closer, you won't pull away.

He shakes his head no.

"Ladies and gentlemen," the pilot says, "thank you for flying with us. We hope your experience was enjoyable. We are now beginning our descent. Please—"

Damn, time is running out. His lips are only a centimeter away from yours. Come on . . . come on . . .

How often does the airline put you next to a drop-dead gorgeous stranger during a snowstorm? This could very well be the most romantic moment of your life. *Carpe Diem!* You're young! You have to take advantage! Live, love and learn!

An opportunity like this might never come again. What if the plane crashes?

It's not like Gary and you are engaged.

Gavin, Gavin, Gavin.

This will surely break his sensitive un-domineering heart.

If you tell him.

You don't have to tell him. You're not joining the mile-high club. It's just a kiss.

A millimeter away. Why doesn't he bridge the damn gap? Maybe you should.

Should you?

The pilot is still talking in the background, but all you can think about is that it's now or never.

To do it or not to do it? What do you do . . . what do you . . . what do . . . what . . .

Option A: You Cheat

"—please turn off and stow all electrical devices."

You kiss him. Ohmigod, you can't believe you're doing this. You're cheating. Not past tense, not conditional, but in the present. It's really happening; you're kissing a stranger on an airplane. This is the highlight of your romantic life. What a fantastic story. Something to tell the grandchildren. Fine, maybe not the grandchildren. You don't want them thinking Nana's a slut.

Ah. Oh. Ew. That was a little too much saliva. Yuck. Does he think he's a water fountain?

You pull yourself backward in an attempt to avoid choking on his flabby tongue, but he doesn't let go. He's obviously trying to drown you. Holy shit, did he just bite your tongue?

You shove him away. "What are you doing?"

"*Sor-ry,*" he says, breaking the word into two obnoxious syllables, not sounding sorry at all. "But you're a weird kisser."

Weird kisser? You kiss conventionally, thank you very much. From age nine to twelve you read every available teenybopper magazine article that instructed you on how to perform the perfect French kiss, and then proceeded to practice on your pillow. Plus, off the top of your head you can think of at least four guys, Matthew, Mike A., Mike D. and Gavin—yes, sweet Gavin—who've called you an exceptional kisser. *Exceptional*, Bobby. Do you understand that? Exceptional. The polar opposite of weird.

Bobby presses the button beside his seat, returning it upright. He looks away and stares vacantly out the window. Loser. You don't need Bobby. You have Gavin, who adores you.

You twist the other way and watch as the lights of Phoenix approach over the shoulders of the people in the aisle on the right. You continue to watch until you feel the plane rumble against the tarmac.

Option B: You Don't Cheat

"—please turn off and stow all electrical devices."

You pull back, snapping your elbow against the armrest. Ouch.

You have a boyfriend. Kissing another guy is not nice. You don't want to be The Girl Who Cheats. You wouldn't want Gavin getting it on with someone else, and you won't do it to him.

Bobby smiles wistfully. You feel overwhelmingly sad. Your throat tightens and your eyes fill with tears.

You're not sure if this is because your elbow is stinging, or because of the situation's unbearable futility.

You sigh. You could have had something amazing, something magical, the most romantic moment of your life, but you're so good. You and Bobby, star-crossed lovers. Think *Romeo and Juliet*. Think *Titanic*. Think *An Affair to Remember*.

You lean closer together and watch the lights of Phoenix rush up to greet you. The landing of the plane on the tarmac is bitter and sweet like dark chocolate.

You'd offer to meet him in one year on the top of the Empire State Building but you saw *An Affair to Remember* and you don't want to get hit by a taxi.

Back to Option A, Not Long After You Cheated and Were Bitterly Disappointed

Who does he think he is, exactly? Don Juan? You'd rather kiss someone blistering with cold sores than him again.

You're both standing on the curb, waiting to be picked up, ignoring each other. Your parents are late, as usual. And both your feet are cramping because of the mile hike from the landing gate to the baggage claim. Why did you put on these two-inch-heeled boots for a plane ride? Are you a moron? What if there had been an emergency landing and your life depended on your running skills? You can barely stand in these things, never mind sprint. Even though you're in serious foot pain, you make click-click tapping sounds against the sidewalk in an attempt to appear busy.

Weird kisser.

Loser. You don't need him. You have a boyfriend. Gavin. Sweet Gavin.

Bobby and you are the only ones left. Where are your lazy-ass parents? They should realize it's hot out here and you're wearing full-on New York winter gear.

Maybe you *are* a weird kisser. How do you know? Your ego feels like an egg that's been smashed against a brick wall. Thankfully you've found someone who adores you, in spite of your deficiency. You will not end up alone with just your deviant lips for company, because you have Gavin. You love Gavin. Gavin and you will probably get married—one day. So what if he only likes to be on the bottom? There are worse fates. He could only like doggy style.

The brown clunky Suburban that is your parents' car passes you and stops up ahead. Your parents furtively look around. How can they not see you? Only two people are still standing here, you and the giant-legged freak. You drag your bag to the car, passing and ignoring him on the way.

Who tattoos his own name on his arm, anyway? Is he afraid he'll forget?

Back to Option B, Not Long After You Didn't Cheat, and Now You Are Feeling Martyrish

Surely there will be some karmic reward for not hooking up with this hunk of manhood. Like bumping into David E. Kelly on the street and being asked to appear as the hot new career woman in whatever new show he's producing.

You and Bobby are standing on the curb, casting furtive, sexy glances at each other.

You feel warm and fuzzy, like a bath towel on a heated bar at a pricey hotel. You're proud of yourself, dammit. It's like you just gave a homeless guy a twenty. You are moral. Who knew? You could have cheated, but you didn't. You're not the type. Though you could have been *his* type. You've stared temptation in the face and remained Teflon strong. Crumbling is for crackers.

Your parents drive by, stop, then reverse. Why did they have to get here so quickly? You turn to your Romeo, the love you left behind, and poignant emotions swell up in your chest like air bags.

You step away from the edge of the curb. He moves closer to you. He's less than a foot away. So close. Almost touching. People rolling suitcases stream by in front and behind, oblivious to your despair. You are a tragic pylon in the middle of their route. The meat in the sandwich of heartbreak.

You take a deep breath. "It was nice to—"

"So I guess this is—"

You both laugh, swallowing your pain.

"You first," he says.

"Honey!" your mother calls. "Yoohoo! We're right here!"

You ignore her. Can't she see the sorrow? The love? She's killing the mood.

"It was nice to meet you," you say.

He nods. His muscles press against his shirt. "You too. I guess this is it."

"Honey! Yoohoo!"

You nod. You could keep this going, exchange numbers, email addresses, anything, but what's the point? You live in different cities. You have significant others. This is the end. It must be accepted so you can have closure and return to your respective meaningless existences. If only fate had dealt you a different hand.

"Goodbye," you say.

"Goodbye." The sadness hangs heavy in the air, smothering you like excessive aerosol deodorant. You don't lean toward each other for a hug goodbye. The touch would be too much to bear.

Eyes locked, you go your separate ways.

Back to Option A, The One Where You Cheated, but Now It's the Next Day and the Seed of Guilt Is Beginning to Blossom Deep in Your Abdomen

"I can't sleep," you say to the phone, from your bed in your old room.

"But I can," Moon says, sounding mildly grumpy. "It's three-fifteen. I thought that the one weekend you weren't stomping around the apartment getting water and then going to the bathroom in the middle of the night would be the one weekend I would get some rest."

"I did something bad."

She sighs. "You didn't try to pluck your own eyebrows again, did you?"

You are not very good at plucking your eyebrows. You make yourself look too surprised.

"I kissed someone on the plane."

She inhales sharply. "No! What about Gavin?"

You've been feeling guilty since yesterday. Ashamed. Gavin has left two messages on your parents' answering machine, wondering how you are. He saw online that your flight was delayed because of the snowstorm and wanted to make sure you arrived safely.

You feel sick at the idea of talking to him. You've told your parents to say that you're at the store/washing your hair/joining a cult whenever he calls.

"I'm the worst girlfriend ever."

"Why would you kiss a stranger on a plane?" she screeches into the phone.

Because you didn't meet a stranger anywhere else? "I don't know. I thought he was hot. But he wasn't. He was totally revolting."

"Don't you see? I told you—it's your two-month itch. You purposefully sabotaged something good."

Doesn't sabotage mean destroy? That sounds a wee bit harsh. But it also means damage. Damage as in it can be repaired? "This had nothing to do with Gavin. It was just one of my stupid urges. And I went for it. I didn't think it through."

Back to Option B, The One Where You Don't Cheat, You Virgin Mary You, but Now It's the Next Day and You're Kicking Yourself for Letting the Probable Love of Your Life Slip Through Your French-Manicured Fingers

"—the one weekend you weren't stomping around the apartment getting water and then going to the bathroom in the middle of the night would be the one weekend I would get some rest."

"I know," you say, "but this is big."

"How big? Bigger than the time you finally figured out how to work the call forwarding and opened the bottle of champagne I was saving to celebrate something a little more significant? Like finishing my thesis?"

"Bigger. I'm in love."

Moon groans. "This is what you called to tell me? Freak. You've been dating for two months—that's not big news."

"No, with someone else. A mysterious, handsome stranger I met on the plane." You recount the events and then let out a tiny sniffle.

She laughs in that annoying, knowing way. "I knew it. You're breaking up with Gavin."

"I'm not breaking up with Gavin. What would be the point? It's not like I can find this guy. I'll never know if he's the love of my life."

Your sniffle explodes into a sob. Fate threw you one ball of chance and instead of you catching it, it bounced off your glove and dropped into the mud.

Back to Option A, The One Where You Cheated, You Whorebag

You're back on the phone, the receiver cradled against your shoulder, a sick feeling in your stomach.

"Finally! I've been trying to get in touch with you the entire weekend," Gavin says cheerfully. Poor, sweet boy. Poor, sweet, clueless, cuckolded boy.

"Sorry. I've been really busy with my family." Doesn't he know from your voice? Can't he tell something's wrong?

"I know, I know. But I can't wait to see you tomorrow. I'll pick you up at the airport. I hope your plane ride home isn't as eventful as your trip down."

Your stomach jumps into your throat. He knows. He must know. Why else would he make such a leading statement? He's giving you a chance to come clean. You should take it, you should tell him—

Downstairs, the front door opens and closes. "Pizza!" your mother hollers. "Come and get it while it's hot."

Another time then.

Back to Option B, The One Where You Didn't Kiss Him, You Pathetic Coward

You offer to pick up the pizza.

As you drive over, you imagine that Bobby will be standing at Mamma's Pizza counter, picking up a large, all-dressed pie for his friends. Don't they eat pizza at bachelor parties? You'll gawk at each other, laughing, and realize that fate gave both of you the pepperoni urge for this very reason, so that the two of you could meet up again, and your lips will be drawn magnetically to each other and you'll live happily ever after.

He's not at Mamma's.

You should have ordered ribs.

You get back into the car and drive turtle-paced through downtown. Wouldn't it be amazing if you passed him on your way home? If you were minding your own business, la-la-la, and he was crossing the street, and you'd spot him in your rearview mirror, slam on the brakes, reverse back to him and then slam on your brakes again. He'd be standing there, in the rain—OK, so it hardly ever rains in Phoenix, but this is obviously a fantasy, OK?—and his hands would be spread, palms open, and through the rain-streaked windshield, beyond the furiously sweeping wipers, you'd see that look of angst on his face—oops, that's *Bridges of Madison County*. OK, how's this? He'd be standing next to a street lamp looking very James Dean.

Thirty minutes later the pizza box is no longer steaming and Bobby is still nowhere to be found. Where is he? Why isn't he outside? Doesn't he feel the cosmic pull?

You give up and drive home.

Your parents are watching TV in their room. "Did you get lost?" your mother asks.

You shrug. "Pizza took forever."

"Gavin called again," she says. "He wanted to know what time you're coming in tomorrow so he can pick you up at the airport."

Crap. You are so not calling him back.

The next day, you slide your ticket to the check-in woman and ask, "Is there a twenty-something male named Bobby on this plane?"

She raises an eyebrow. "I can't release that information, ma'am."

You are scheduled to be on the three o'clock flight to Chicago, but if they've overbooked and Bobby's on the four-thirty, you're willing to let them bump you, and you'll even take miles instead of cash.

"We don't release the names of our passengers, ma'am."

You contemplate slipping her a twenty, but you don't want to freak her out. You give her your best smile. She isn't wearing a wedding ring, so you try the single-girl card.

"Look, I met a star of a guy on my flight over here and I would love to see him again. Can you please, please check for me?" You think of your dead grandfather so your eyes fill with tears.

She looks like she's about to break but then shakes her head. "The best I can do is put you next to a male traveling alone."

You shrug. It's better than nothing.

The man in the seat beside you is in his sixties, smells like cottage cheese and is wearing a wedding band. He falls asleep right after takeoff so at least you don't have to make small talk.

Damn that Gavin. This is all his fault. If it weren't for him, you would at least have asked Bobby for his email address. You're too young to blow off opportunities. You should never have agreed to be exclusive. He ruined everything.

You try to take a nap, but the married geezer is snoring loudly in your ear. You reluctantly accept the pretzels from the flight attendant and chew loudly, hoping to wake him up.

Back to Option A, The One Where You Cheated, and Now You (Sigh) Must Come Clean

You are a horrible person. A tramp. Who kisses a stranger on a plane? You have a perfectly good relationship at home, and you threw it all away for a moment of nothing. What's wrong with you? Are you destined to ruin everything you have? To jinx yourself? To sabotage—destroy, not just damage—your own good fortune? Do you secretly want to be miserable? You can't even blame this on the boy. Gavin's been a sweetheart. It's all you. You are evil. You may as well have warts on your nose and a dozen black cats and take pleasure in scaring small children. You are an evil, slutty woman who is destined to live the rest of your life alone.

At least you have your own two-seater on the plane. You take your shoes off, lift the armrest and stretch out your legs. The entire cheating situation is making your back tense. You could use one of Gavin's back massages.

Maybe you won't tell him. What's the point? He'll never know. It's not like you slept with the jackass. You can bury the secret deep within your soul, only to be pulled out on lonely nights for self-inflicted torture.

When the flight attendant offers you pretzels, you accept. You hate pretzels. They represent all that is twisted in this sorry life. You munch away. Let this mark the beginning of your self-induced punishment.

No. You have to tell him. What if it turns into *Fatal Attraction?* What if someone saw? What if Bobby tells his girlfriend? What if he tells her that you initiated it, and she freaks out and finds you and confronts you at a restaurant where you're having dinner with Gavin? No, Gavin and his parents. Ohmigod, what if it's the big Meet-the-Parents

Night and Bobby's psychopathic girlfriend shows up and blames it all on you?

You have to come clean. He'll probably never speak to you again, but it's the right thing to do.

Back to Option B, The One Where You Didn't Cheat, but Now You Hate Your Boyfriend

You spot Gavin waving at you in the arrival zone. Could he be any more smothering? Does he think you're a complete invalid, incapable of making your way home?

"You're here," you say and then let out a long, pained sigh.

"I thought I'd meet you so you wouldn't have to take a cab."

That's just like him. He doesn't consider what you want. Maybe you like taking cabs. You are totally suffocating in this relationship.

You should end it right here while you're waiting for your luggage. But what would be the point of that? Then you'd have to pay for the taxi, and Gavin has already sprung for parking. Face it, you know you're procrastinating. But really, no one likes getting dumped at an airport. Too *Casablanca*.

Your bag lands on the belt. You go to pick it up, he tries to intercept and you grab it away from him. "I have it," you snarl.

When he pulls into a parking space in front of your apartment and then turns off the ignition, you know you have to end it, now, otherwise he's going to expect to have tiresome him-on-the-bottom sex and you're so not in the mood. "Gavin, we have to talk."

"What's wrong?" he asks, concern coating his face like a clear pink polish.

You hate being the dumper. Granted, it's preferable to being the dumpee. What to say? *Gavin, I'm sorry but you don't excite me sexually and I'm in love with someone else?* Might be a tad harsh.

"I don't think we can see each other anymore. I'm really sorry. It's not you, it's me. We want different things." Jeez, you hate reciting the liturgy. To your credit, you don't say, "I hope we can be friends."

He freezes mid-seatbelt-unsnapping. "I came on a bit strong by surprising you at the airport, didn't I?"

"It's not just that. I don't want to be in a relationship right now."

He opens the trunk. You take out your bag and head up to your apartment.

Back to Option A, The One Where You Cheated, and Now You REALLY Must Come Clean

When you spot Gavin waiting for you when you get off the plane, your eyes instantly fill with tears. You are evil. He is fantastic. He is the nicest, most considerate boyfriend you have ever had.

How can you tell the sweet boy in front of you what you've done? You will destroy his soul.

You hug him tightly, possibly for the last time. Once he knows, he won't ever want to see you again. He picks your bag off the conveyor belt. What a sweetheart.

You have to tell him. He will hate you, but alas, you must.

He opens the car door for you.

Your intestines wrestle with each other.

Gavin, there's something I have to tell you . . .

Gavin, this is the hardest thing I have ever had to say . . .

He pulls into a parking space on your street.

You take a fat breath and blurt it all out. "Gavin, I don't know how to tell you this, but I kissed another man over . . . New Mexico, I guess. I'm really sorry. I know what I've done is horrible and that you won't ever want to speak to me again, but I had to tell you."

His hand freezes mid-seatbelt-unsnapping. "Are you going to see him again?"

As if. He was the worst kisser ever. "No. Definitely not."

He sighs. "These things happen. I can't say I'm not disappointed, but I'm happy you were honest with me. I trust you."

The balloon inside you withers. Huh? "But I'm a terrible person. Don't you want to break up with me?"

"I don't have to."

The front seat starts to shrink, reminding you of a trash compactor. Well, um . . . you can't be with someone this good. You don't deserve him. Really. It'll never work. "Gavin," you sob, "you're too good to me. I can't be in a relationship in which I'll always feel guilty. It's not you, it's me."

You apologize quickly, try not to look at his flabbergasted expression and then exit the car. You pick up your bag from the trunk and scurry home.

How It Ends Either Way

Moon is eating popcorn and sitting on the couch in your Snoopy pajamas. You're not sure how they ended up in her wardrobe, but you think it had something to do with the time you borrowed her Juicy Couture sweatshirt and then went to play paintball.

"How was your trip?" she asks, stuffing a handful of kernels into her mouth. She eats them unpopped.

"I just broke up with Gavin."

Her eyes don't move from the *Friends* rerun she's watching on TV. "Told you."

"How'd you know?"

"The two-month itch."

"There's no two-month itch." There's a hunger-itch, though. Those pretzels just didn't do the trick. You take out the jar of peanut butter and a spoon, and then curl up beside her on the couch. "I swear, Moon, this time it wasn't my fault. Not really. It just wasn't working."

When the show's over, she yawns and rises. "Run the dishwasher before you go to sleep?"

"No prob," you answer.

You watch another rerun. Then you stretch, get up and put the spoon in the dishwasher. You reach under the counter, but can't find the detergent. You're out. Moon must have finished it.

Giddy, you run into the bathroom, pick up the shampoo bottle and return to the kitchen. You fill the hole, close the door, hit the latch and turn the dial.

Some things are inevitable.

Based in Manhattan, **SARAH MLYNOWSKI** is the author of four wickedly funny novels, *Milkrun, Fishbowl, As Seen on TV,* and *Monkey Business.*

Visit her website at www.sarahmlynowski.com.

I Know a Woman

QUINN DALTON

*L*et's call her Judy. I like the simple names that sound as if they could belong to your next-door neighbor or the mother of your best friend in second grade. So Judy works for this janitorial company, not doing the jobs, but sales, corporate contracts. This is in a medium-sized town in the southeast, the kind of place where if you live there ten years, as I have, you get to know everybody, or at least the connections between them. Anyway, it gets around that Judy strips on the side. This guy she works with, a guy named José, is telling it; says he gives her half his paycheck every week in tips.

The boss, Dennis, doesn't believe it. Upstanding Christian type—loves God, pays *illegales* cash under the table, that sort of thing. Then one night when

Dennis is working late, only one left in the office, Judy's twelve-year-old daughter calls, asking for her mother. Dennis says she isn't there. "Must be on her way home," he says, though she left hours ago. The girl says, "I know she's there because she just called me and said she was working late." Dennis says he'll try to find her. He calls Judy's cell phone. No answer. He locks up and gets an idea. He drives past the Dockside Dolls out near the interstate where she's supposedly stripping. He sees her car. He decides he'll call the daughter back and tell her that her mother is working late, and, yes, he'd forgotten that he'd asked her to run some errands or something—he's going to give her some cover, see, because that's a good Christian thing to do, though he's already imagining the solemn confrontation in his office, how he'll tell Judy what he knows. But then he realizes he doesn't have her home number with him so he can't call her daughter back.

The next night he drives by again, and again he sees Judy's car. He doesn't have kids himself, doesn't even want them, but he thinks about Judy's daughter, sitting at home alone, waiting for her mother. He wants to go in and drag Judy off the stage. He's enraged, really. And he's scared to go in there. Not because he's never been. He went once on the night before he was married, a bachelor party, of course, and his friends bought him a lap dance, stuffed the money in his pants so the girl had to fish it out. This was before he was saved, understand. She reaches in there and he's hard as a rock and she says, "I love the small ones, honey." So he's nervous. 'Course, he figures that same woman couldn't still be there after four years, and even then she couldn't recognize him in the blur of men who line the stage every night, red-faced, meaty necks rolling over their collars or sweat still glistening on their arms, regulars after their shifts, or, like him, men who come in once before sacrificing themselves to marriage, giddy with some kind of last meal mentality.

On the third night he pulls into the parking lot at Dockside Dolls and sits there for a while, looking at Judy's car, but can't go in. Another man would've left this alone, wouldn't have even gone to the place. So why Dennis? He wants to *save* her, see. He talks his wife into going with him—he explains he's worried about this employee. The wife decides to bring her sister and her husband because who knows what might happen and they wouldn't want anyone to think that this is what the wife and Dennis do for fun, in secret, when they're not planning pig pickings to pay for new robes for the women's choir. The next night, the four of them walk in the door and find a table. Judy's up there stripping, and pretty soon she's topless, with a little thong panty, shaking her money maker, as they say. She looks good—definitely hasn't had her breasts done like the other girls, who are a little younger and have implants the size of softballs glued to their chests—but she has long legs and slim hips and she knows how to move. Dennis and his wife and her sister and her sister's husband sit there, not sure what to do. Dennis waits for Judy to see them. Eventually she does. She loses the twitch in her hips for a beat. Her face becomes real again—she's looking at them, reacting to them, fighting to get back that blank Barbie doll smile. She dances to the other side of the stage—

it's a four-leaf clover, the catwalk a stem, and she stays on the other leaves until the men on their side of the place start complaining, howling and beating the slick stage. Then the music changes and Judy dances back behind the curtain, and another woman comes out.

After that, Dennis and company don't have any reason to stay. There's a two-drink minimum, but Dennis refuses to buy even a ginger ale, and the waitress is getting pissed. So they leave.

Of course, Judy quits pretty much right away. She does it really well. She calls in sick for a week, and Dennis bides his time, thinking she'll eventually come around and confess everything. But what she does instead is tell Dennis she needs to take more sick leave to care for her widowed mother, who's fallen and broken her hip. Doesn't even mention the other night at Dockside Dolls, and Dennis figures he can't bring it up under the circumstances, what with Judy's injured mother in the picture now. Later, after the sick leave checks run out, he learns she's skipped town. No trace. The daughter is left with the grandmother, who, it turns out, is perfectly healthy and, when Dennis calls, is still miffed about a bank account Judy cleaned out. Dennis talks to Judy's landlady, who's been relieved of a microwave, area rug and small freezer that came with the place.

You'd think that would be all. But there's this weird twist: Dennis's wife files for divorce a year to the day after the Dockside Dolls excursion. She puts her half of the janitorial company up for sale, and Dennis is out of a job since he can't buy her out.

Things turn out OK for Judy's daughter, by the

way. It's not easy to be abandoned, to be sure, but her grandmother brought her up well, and she's going to start college in the fall—that gives you a sense of where we are now.

And where am I, in this story? I'm the wife. Ex-wife. Usually when I tell about Judy I leave out the more personal details because it only begs the question as to how I know. The way I tell it, I was just working with Judy in the cleaning business at the time, and José, the guy who stuffed half his paycheck in Judy's g-string every week, saw the whole thing.

And I didn't divorce Dennis because of Judy. Not specifically. See, there are some details you'd have to smooth over if you decided to tell this story while sitting, say, at a ten-top in the City Club for a Dinner for Qualified Investors, ". . . with investable assets of $1,000,000 or more," to discuss Comprehensive Wealth Management. Let me note here that I have nowhere near a million dollars, even if I sold everything I owned, which isn't much. I think I look the part in my sage green silk suit cut loose like a man's, but the fabric unmistakably female. I like that about it—the form being one thing and the details being something else.

Anyway, in this dining scenario, should I find myself telling this story, Judy would be an employee of mine in a business I once owned and have since sold, not that far from the truth, and it would be a story about the secret, desperate lives of the middle class. Something to get the table warmed up. It would be that rather than the story of a twenty-six-year-old woman married fresh out of college to an older man who found God while building his business on the backs of migrant farm workers. But yes, it would still be a story of escape.

I am from a small town where people dropped out of high school in their rush to gain employment in the mills. I hadn't done anything in life except sell cleaning contracts with Judy. Dennis explained to me we'd never have time for kids; we worked too much. When we went to Dockside Dolls to see Judy that night, I knew I'd never forget it.

At the City Club, I'm sitting next to John, who owns Poseidon, a national business-to-business supplier of tropical fish, tanks, pumps, and maintenance services. He hands me his card, which is, predictably, light blue with a sparkling angelfish on the left side, next to his name. John tells me that exotic fish are getting big. "Doctors' offices buy them to keep the patients in the waiting room calm. Bigwigs buy them for the executive offices. Nightclubs and hotels love 'em. There's one of mine over there." Flat blue eyes, shiny skin, soft white fingers sweeping to direct my attention to the far wall next to the hostess stand. A small shark swims sluggishly in the lit purple water. He seems perfectly at home in his circumstances, or maybe just resigned.

The seat to my left is empty. Next to John sits Karen, CEO of the Center for Business and Behavioral Research, where executives go to spend three days to two weeks flinging themselves backward off platforms into each other's arms and taking seminars on how to treat their employees like human beings or appear as if they are doing so. Karen comes over with her card. She is blond, neatly wedged into an ivory sheath dress with gold buttons, a knuckle-sized knot of gold in each earlobe. She's about to ask me what my deal is when a man slips quietly into the seat on my left. I don't even notice him until I feel the wool of his suit sleeve brush my arm. He introduces himself as Neil. It just so happens that Neil works for the brokerage firm that is sponsoring this dinner for High Net Worth clients, as the invitation noted. Neil hands me his card. "And you are—?" he asks, with deep and gentle interest, like a doctor inquiring as to how much pain I am in.

I had chosen the table in the back, the seat nearest the door. I have no idea how I got on the mailing list, but I thought this would be fun. I have a little money, yes, from the sale of my half of the business. I have a nice apartment in one of those older buildings where you pay for the architectural details and you get used to your neighbors pacing over the floorboards, phones ringing quietly up and down the hall, muffled as if under water.

I offer my hand to Neil and he shakes it softly. Almost just holding it, really. "Neil," I tell him, "I need to make a quick phone call."

I step out of the room, flipping open my cell. I decide to call my sister. Usually I tell her when I'm doing something like this, going to a support group for a condition I don't have, slipping into pink, hushed funeral parlors and saying goodbye to people I never knew, or hobnobbing with this town's eager elite. She doesn't necessarily discourage me. She married an older man, too. He is away often on business, just like our father was before he retired, a traveling salesman. So maybe we both married our father. Except her husband Ed is a lot nicer than Dennis or my father.

Sasha picks up on the first ring. "What are you doing?" I say.

"Reading an article about this guy who married a woman his friends picked out for him in the Mall of America."

"They picked her out in the Mall of America? Do they sell women there?"

"No, they got married there. His friends took applications from women and chose the bride."

It's six o'clock, and I figure she's just gotten home from work. "Sasha, I'm at the City Club at a millionaires' dinner."

"Really?" I hear the catch in her voice; she's sitting forward in her chair.

"Seriously. You have to have a million in investable assets to come."

"A million?"

"Investable. Cash." Everyone agrees that I take after my father and my sister takes after our mother, who is athletic, efficient and shy. Like my father, I can sell almost anyone on anything, and so I can make friends with anybody, even the dying, the grieving and the rich. "What do you think I should be?" I ask.

Sasha's thinking. I can hear her breathing into the phone. We've done this dozens of times. She gives me a story, and I make people believe it. When I told her I wanted to divorce Dennis and make it cost him, she helped me think up hiring an auditor to value the company—the story was to see how we could save in taxes. I got all the numbers I needed right under his nose. "How about a matchmaker?" she says.

"A matchmaker."

"Yeah, one of those really expensive ones. I saw a full-page ad in a magazine one time. This woman with bleached hair and a pink suit talking about her discreet services, success rates."

"Sasha, that's not the same thing," I say. Sasha's one of those satisfied people, so sometimes she misses details. She's happy with her office job and her working man and a house with little window boxes. She likes going out to eat and renting movies. I might be all the excitement she needs. "Were you looking at some kind of skin magazine?" I ask her, and I think of Judy, I can't help it. I wonder what she did after she disappeared. I keep expecting her to turn up in a new generation of the forbidden—Internet babe, reality TV show queen—but maybe she got rich! Maybe she founded a colony on some lush island. I want to know what she did next, so then maybe I'll know what to do.

In the dining room someone's tapping the microphone, and there's the shuffling of slick-bottomed shoes on low-pile carpet as people turn their attention to the podium. I could leave now, but I know that I won't. It's too attractive, this sea of dark suits and bright dresses flitting across the room as people find their seats. The walls are practically all glass up here, and through the open door I can see the late-spring sky shifting to a liquid purple, and the light seems thick enough to float in.

Sasha laughs. She loves me. I don't deserve so much love. "Listen," she says. "She's a matchmaker, not the other. She charges ten thousand a pop!"

"OK. Ten thousand a pop. I'm on it."

Back in the dining room, no one's taken my seat, probably because Neil has draped my swan-folded napkin, which I hadn't even moved from my plate, over the back of my chair. When Neil sees me, he stands and pulls my chair back from the table with his right hand and lifts my napkin. As he turns to face me, I see that he has no left hand. At first I think his suit jacket is too long on that side, but another glance makes it clear.

Now there, I think, is a story.

When I look up to meet his eyes, Neil smiles at me, professional, yet intimate, as if we've been doing business for years. He's tall and good-looking, but not in an aggressive sort of way, really. He has lovely brown eyes. I can't tell what his smile means, though. Is he waiting for me to ask about his hand so we can get it over with? Is he on the lookout for imposters?

I sit and he moves my chair smoothly to the table, then settles himself beside me. "Cocktail?" he asks me.

"Sure," I say. "How nice of you to save my seat."

Everyone around me is ordering scotch rocks or martinis with a twist, so I order a margarita. "Tell me," I ask the waiter. "Are your margaritas premixed?"

He nods regretfully. He's a college kid and nervous; maybe he's new on the job. I'm nervous, too, but it's a good kind of nervous, different from the kind that hit me when I realized my husband had acquired me like cleaning equipment, that he expected to get his use out of me. *Depreciation* is the word that comes to mind. "I want a top shelf, then," I say.

The kid looks at me blankly.

"One shot of Cuervo, one of Grand Marnier, and one of lime juice, shaken on rocks, salt," I tell him. He stands there writing for a while, and I wait until he looks up. "You're a sweetie," I say, and he smiles, and I love to see a young man smile.

This little comment makes Neil's head snap up from the pad he's been making notes on during my exchange with the waiter. He cradles the pad in his left arm. I have no idea what he could be writing; the first speaker is just now introducing himself. Then Neil nudges the pad in my direction. GUEST LIST, he's written at the top. And, on the next line: NAME, COMPANY, PHONE/EMAIL.

I know then that Neil's onto me. He already has everyone's business cards, a neat stack by his dessert plate. It's a thrill. I've never been caught before. I take his pen, still warm from his hand, and make up a name. I write "Matchmaker" under COMPANY. Under PHONE/EMAIL I add: "I notice you don't wear a wedding ring, Neil. Would you be interested in a consultation? Discreet, only the best people."

I realize this is a little cruel. In any case, it's possible he's married, but of course there's no way to tell. I tear the paper off the pad. Everyone at the table glances at me, and I smile, and just then the drinks come, which distracts them as I fold the paper twice and hand it back to Neil with his pad and heavy fountain pen.

Neil lays the paper on his plate, anchors it with his

arm, unfolds it slowly. He reads it, leans over to me, whispers in my ear, "I think you should go."

I never really quit drinking after Dennis got saved. I just had these notions about growing with the marriage and being sensitive to one's partner's needs, etcetera, and so I tried my best. I'd sneak a drink at Sasha's house when I could. A sip of wine became almost erotic, the warmth spreading on the tongue. I carried a toothbrush everywhere.

How it started—Dennis told me one day that he'd dreamed of a wall of water standing over our house, and that the wall of water had spoken to him. It had said, "Go forth."

"Go forth?" I remember asking. I said, "Have you been watching Charlton Heston movies or something? Moses and so on?"

Dennis looked at me the way I imagine a wall of water would look at you if it had narrowed eyes and rather bushy brown hair dusted with gray. He towered. He quivered with anger about to spill over. "I'm telling you about God speaking to me and you ask me about movies?"

I decided to try. I decided that once the waters had parted, and the new path was revealed, it was better to take your chances. Dennis told me the dream meant service. He picked out a church, and we started going to hear people play rock and roll hymns with guitars and synthesizers and waving arms. They didn't drink, so Dennis stopped, and I pretended. He joined the choir and started nailing houses together on weekends. It was noble work, but walking around with a hammer in my hand and no clue of what to do with it made me feel heavy and exhausted. I hadn't gone to church as a child. I wasn't prepared for the fellowship, the hugging. I made only one friend in that whole church, a woman who later died, but not before she told me that there was, in fact, no path.

I sit in the lobby bar for a while. I haven't eaten anything but ancient peanuts and cheese crackers from the snack bowl since getting kicked out of the City Club (and, thinking fast, taking the margarita with me). It's too depressing to call Sasha; I'm putting it off, not answering when she calls me. At about eight Neil steps through the brushed steel elevator doors with a pack of men in dark suits. He's the youngest one in the group. He carries the projector screen, a satchel strapped diagonally across his chest. His hair is nearly black, cut close, and as he looks up at the ceiling, laughing at something, I can see the pale cords of his neck. I decide to focus my energy on him as if I had just spoken to him. I decide that's as close as I'll ever get to praying.

He looks at me. I don't raise my eyebrows or wiggle a little greeting with my fingers. I look back at him, and wait to see if he walks over.

He does. He's very smooth about it, waving off his suit friends with his handless arm; maybe he's telling them he's forgotten something upstairs and he'll see them in the morning.

Neil takes his time getting over to me, threading the projection screen through the cluster of low tables. He sets the screen down, slides his bag off his shoulder and stands in front of me with his good hand—his *present* hand—in his pocket. His other arm hangs relaxed at his side. "So, did you sign anyone up tonight?" I ask him. "Get some juicy commissions?"

He leans against the bar and looks at me. He smiles, not the professional, solicitous smile from the City Club, but still friendly, amused. I amuse him. That's fine with me. Generally, I don't amuse anyone except Sasha. "You know, it's usually men who try to sneak into these things," he says.

"Why so top secret?" I ask, swiveling on the stool. "What are you really doing up there, anyway?"

Neil signals the bartender by lifting one finger, points to the tap for a beer. His hand is quite graceful. "You didn't miss anything," he says. "I got cornered by the fish guy who started raving about piranhas. Did you know a school can clean the meat off a human in less than a minute? And Karen invited me to try out their sensory deprivation tank." Neil flips the napkin the bartender set out with his drink. "The last guy who snuck in was a Vespa salesman. You know those little scooters that sound like a distressed mouse?"

"I wonder why it's always men," I muse. I also wonder why Neil is talking to me at all. I'm making myself a little dizzy, swiveling back and forth on the stool, but it's probably also hunger, and my curiosity.

"That is a good question," Neil says, sipping his draft. "This guy just wanted some customers, I think."

"That's all I wanted."

Neil looks at me, eyebrow raised.

I chomp down on a disintegrating peanut. "I'm a matchmaker, remember?"

"Give me a break," Neil says. And then he does something that surprises me, and I haven't been surprised in a while, about two years, to be exact. He leans forward as if he's about to kiss me, but he doesn't. His eyes are inches from mine. "What do you really do?" he asks me, staying close.

I'm not sure if he's asking about my work life, but I answer that way. "I have some investments," I say. "Nothing specific, really. A little consulting here and there." That's all I feel I need to tell him, or anyone. I think we're rather obsessed with this career stuff. Who cares, if I'm paying the bills? I touch Neil's arm, the one closest to me, the one that ends too soon. "Listen," I say. "I know this woman."

I don't tell him about Judy. I tell him the other important story, about this woman from all the way up in Caribou, Maine, who joined a church down here with a huge singles Bible study group. Who knows what made her come all this way. Well, she proceeds to sleep with all the men in the group. Nobody tells, it's too good a thing; they don't want the women to find out.

The women love her. They've adopted her because when she came to town she was living out of her van. She becomes their project. They find her an apartment, they perm her hair, they take her shopping and teach her beauty tips they've collected over the years, like dabbing a touch of frosted gloss in the center of the lip over matte lipstick to make the mouth look fuller, or putting a light swipe of shadow in the inner corners of the eyes to make them look wider apart. It all helps her campaign with the men in the group. She gets an office job and goes to every church function. She doesn't drink, she always looks great. When she wants to go to bed with a man, she comes up to him during social hour with, say, a cup of Kool-Aid in her hand, her lips shiny and red with it, and she talks to him for a few minutes. Then she waits until she's sure no one is looking and touches him in a way that makes him know he's chosen—brushes his hip or squeezes his wrist, and asks him to come over to her brand-new apartment later.

After a while, she runs through the singles group and moves on to the men's choir, starts with the tenors. Takes up with a married guy. The tenor falls in love with her. He gets a night with her and he's hooked. He begins calling her all the time; he buys her things, but she isn't interested. She moves on to other men. He threatens her one night and she leaves town all in a hurry in her van. Apparently, she's been threatened before and does not think it's a joke. He hears she's gone back up to Caribou. He hires a private investigator up there. The PI tracks her down; he's parked on a street in Caribou one morning, watching her walk to work. PI's somehow gotten her cell phone number. He calls the tenor from his own cell, gives him the number and tells him to call. He does. The woman answers, hears the tenor's voice, drops her phone and runs away. The detective says, "She moved to another state, man, to get away from you. You need to leave her alone."

When I finish telling this to Neil, he takes it in for a little while, tapping his glass with his one thumb. He says, "I don't even think you've told me your real name." He smiles at me as if he's just bet me on whether I can stand on my head. He isn't going to ask me any questions about this story of mine.

I say, "That guy with the detective, that was my husband."

Neil, still gazing at his beer, does not move a muscle. I can see he must be good at what he does, advising millionaires.

I say, "I want you to know, I don't really hold a grudge."

There's another related part of the story that for now I'll leave out. That night when Dennis took me and Sasha and Ed with him to see Judy, that was the beginning of my new life. Some people go to church or AA to start over; I did it at a strip club. I didn't know it at the time, or if I did, I couldn't admit it to myself right then. When Dennis told me he wanted to save Judy, my mind rattled back and forth between imagining him climbing on the stage and striking her on the forehead with the heel of his hand like a revival preacher and me climbing on the stage to dance, just for him, in a way that would save us both.

I invited Sasha and Ed to come with us so I could sneak sips from their drinks. I figured a little alcohol might be nice—it didn't take much for me to get a buzz anymore. I actually wondered if I'd enjoy myself. But the fact was, the place was depressing. I guess I wasn't prepared for the number of overfed men in gray suits, road warriors who looked not all that different from my father at the end of one of his trips, that traveler's stare, disoriented and bored at the same time. Or the businesslike way Judy and that other woman worked the stage. Except for that one moment when she saw us and we saw her. She looked straight at me. We went on sales calls together every day, but right then she could have been anyone. Her nakedness was like a cloak. She looked at Dennis, and he leaned forward in his chair, as if ready to grab her. Then she looked back at me and turned hard on her spike heels, and I knew I wouldn't see her again; she would get away clean.

Neil pulls up a stool next to me. He leans to tuck his projector screen against the foot of the bar, to keep it out of the way so no one trips over it. He's a thoughtful man. He says, "I went to high school with a girl who had been missing for fifteen years. Her babysitter stole her. She walked into a sheriff's office outside of Phoenix and turned herself in. They found her mother in Milwaukee—ex-drug addict, never reported it. The girl, Cass, was seventeen, and they gave her a test and put her in tenth grade." He folds his fingers around his beer. "We had a class together. Algebra. I failed it."

"So you failed algebra and you're from Milwaukee?" I ask.

"Yes, that was exactly my point," Neil says. He taps one finger against his lips, smiling at me. He pushes his glass toward the bartender for another draft. "Actually," he says, "she was the only one who would date after my brother cut off my hand."

Obviously, the version I'm getting of this story is intended to jolt. It works. I look at him with my eyebrows raised, my mouth in a little "o."

"Of course, it was an accident," Neil says. He's in

no hurry; it's his turn now. "We were hiking Lake Peak outside of Santa Fe. It was early in the season, chilly, but no big deal. There's some amazing views . . ." His voice trails off. He sits with both elbows on the bar now, a secret up his sleeve. "There's some drop-offs, and we decided to climb down one a ways, then back up, for fun. Well, I went first, stumbled, started a little avalanche. I remember thinking I would get through it. I don't believe what people say about their lives flashing. All I saw was the rocks falling. Then I was on my back, my shoulder up against the mountain, my hand under a rock. On my other side, I could see the rest of the way down. My brother climbed down, tried to get me free. He couldn't get leverage in such a tight spot, and anyway there was the danger of making more rocks fall if he moved that one. I don't remember much. I was bleeding a lot. We spent the night there together, no cell phones back then. Nobody on the trail; it was too cold. My brother tied off my arm with his sweatshirt. In the morning, he cut me free. We talked about it for a while, whether we should do it, but it was hard, because I kept blacking out. The cutting woke me up, though. He hauled me back up. I held onto his neck. Good thing it happened to me instead of him. He's the bigger one. We both would have died, maybe."

"He saved you," I say. I whisper it, really, but Neil hears me.

"He wrote me a letter about it while I was in the hospital. He wanted me to know about every moment. He wanted to know if he should go back and get my hand."

"What did you say?" I ask. My stomach is solid in my belly.

"He felt guilty, you know," Neil says. He doesn't flinch when I put my hand on his arm. I can feel where the warmth ends. "I told him I had everything I needed, and that he shouldn't worry."

You can never predict the cost of escape. Not too long after Judy disappeared, the woman from Caribou, Maine, whose name is too pretty to mention, showed my husband what she thought of a good tenor. She was already in town the night we paid our visit to Judy. She was probably getting her eyebrows plucked and her hair highlighted by the huggy, well-meaning women in our church. Maybe Dennis would have fallen for her anyway, naked Judy or not. Maybe everything was going along just as his God intended. But I like to think that the night at Dockside Dolls was pivotal. I like to think my story has shape.

"It wasn't all bad for me at Dennis's church," I say. "There was this woman I really liked. Her name was Amelia. She was older, with really short white hair and gray eyes that changed color depending on what she wore. One day she started to notice little metallic flakes in her fingernails. At first, just one or two, but then they became streaks of silver. She goes to her doctor, her herbalist; no one knows what to do. So she decides not to worry about it. When I found out about Dennis and the woman from Caribou, and my sister was helping me with a story so I could get my cut of the business once I divorced him, I went to Amelia. At that point I wasn't sure if I really wanted to give up. I was hoping for a sign. When I asked her if there was some way I could understand what path God wanted me to take, she shook her head. She said, 'You're asking for something that doesn't exist.'"

I stop to catch my breath; I've been talking fast. Neil opens his mouth to interrupt me but I keep going. "By then," I continue, "her nails were almost completely silver—I mean, you could see the skin beneath the nails, but the silver was cloudy; it looked like metal shining up from the bottom of a lake."

Neil says, "And so that was it? She said she didn't have an answer for you and you took it?" He shakes his head. "I don't believe you, whoever you are." He pulls his arm away from me but I reach for it again.

"Don't give up on me yet," I say. "You're right, I begged her. I cried and told her I couldn't take the hard answers right then; I needed something specific. She said whatever I needed, I had it in me. Something like that; anyway, it wasn't what I wanted to hear," I tell him. But that isn't really all: after she told me what I had in me, she showed me the backs of her hands, fingers spread wide, nails flashing, as if to offer evidence.

"Hers was the first funeral I ever crashed," I say. "Her family didn't like the church since she'd willed everything to it instead of them, and I guess I can't blame them. So it was a family-only affair. I slipped right in there, though."

"And were you happy you did?" Neil turns his arm under my hand, so that the part where it ends, right above the wrist, is facing up. He lets me slide my fingers inside his shirtsleeve and I can feel where the flesh has scarred over the bone, protecting it. I think we could both be naked, and I wouldn't be any more scared than I am now. I think of that night when I saw Judy's pale breasts colored pink and purple in the circling lights, how she revealed us.

"At the time, no, I wasn't very happy about it," I say. Neil is sitting very still, my fingers on him, reading him. "I was sad. I was there because I loved her. The family had requested a closed casket, you know," I say. This was for me the saddest part. I had walked in there expecting to see those beautiful hands crossed over her chest. I wanted to see them one more time, because—and I'm going to try to explain this as accurately as I can—when she'd showed me her nails the last time I saw her, the fingers fanned out like that, I saw how the future comes out of you, mysterious and shining, and there's nothing for you to do except move into it, naked and willing to leave everything you once knew.

QUINN DALTON is the author of the short story collection *Bullet-Proof Girl*, shortlisted for the Iowa Short Fiction Award, and the hilarious novel *High-Strung*. She lives in Greensboro, North Carolina, with her husband and daughter.

Just Visiting

NANCY SPARLING

"You didn't," I say, gripping the phone so tightly my knuckles turn white. I must have misheard her. My mother wouldn't have told those two they could stay at my place. She wouldn't do that to me.

"Michelle and Kim are lovely girls and you have plenty of room. It'll do you good to see some people from home."

"But Kim is Tom's sister," I say, the full horror of what's happening slowly sinking in. "I don't want her here."

"Now, Danni," says my mother, in a voice that's sympathetic but firm at the same time, "it's not her fault. And, besides, it's settled, we can't tell them they're not welcome."

"Why not?" It comes out more shrilly than I intended, but I'm getting jittery. They can't come here. They just can't. This is my new life and I don't want any reminders of the past. I'm done with all that. It's finished. Over. Gone.

My mother sighs. "I've already invited them and you're the only person they know in London. We can't turn them away now. What would people say?"

"I don't care what people say," I snap, but we both know that's a lie. If I hadn't cared, I wouldn't have run away. I left my job, my hometown, my state and even my country in my haste to put some distance behind me. I hadn't felt safe until I'd crossed an ocean, leaving Tom and his pathetic I'm-sorry-Danni-I-couldn't-help-it excuses on the other side. Of course, he should have been the one to pack up and go, that would have been the decent thing to do, but decency is obviously a concept with which he's unfamiliar.

The curse of a small town is that everyone knows everything. No secret is sacred. Gossip is the kryptonite that brings down even the most independent. Whispers turn out to be crucifying when they go on long enough. I didn't do anything wrong; Tom was the guilty one, not me, but because of him I was part of the story. When the empathy inevitably turned to pity, I had to leave. There are only so many plenty-more-fish-in-the-sea comments you can take before you start snarling at people who tell you they're sorry the wedding's off.

"Sweetheart," says my mother, after a pause, "I know you're nervous about seeing them, but I worry about you all alone over there."

"I'm fine, Mom. I told you everything's great. I love it here. And I don't need visitors to check up on me."

"They're not checking up on you. I just thought it would be nice to let them start off at your place and get used to things before they start traveling around the rest of Europe. You know they've never been abroad before."

Like I care that they've finally decided to have a big adventure. It's nothing to do with me. "Next you'll be telling me that I inspired them to do it," I say.

"But you did. Everyone's talking about how well you're doing. I've been forwarding on all those digital photos you've been sending, so the whole street knows about your exciting new life."

I bite back a hysterical laugh. "They do?"

"Of course." My mother's voice softens, taking on that persuasive tone I know so well. "And, honey, I know it's not like you, but this is a great opportunity to rub Tom's nose in it. You can show off how well you're doing. Kim and Michelle will be able to report back firsthand about your gorgeous boyfriend, fantastic apartment and great new job. That boy needs to realize what he missed out on."

I'm silent, desperately wondering how I can get out of this. Time to panic, I think. Time to panic. Sinking down onto my lumpy single bed, I glance around the small bedsit I call home. It's in central London and it's clean, but those are the only two good things I can honestly say about it. The traffic roars past my window day and night, the walls are damp and it's so tiny I have to turn sideways to squeeze between the dresser and the bed, and there's absolutely no chance of opening those bottom drawers. I won't let Kim and Michelle see me here. I can't.

Needless to say, I didn't send digital photos of this place. My mother thinks I'm living somewhere else. Everyone does. And it's not as if I've been generous with the truth, either; there's been no exaggeration—I've simply made it all up.

The first lie just popped out. There was nothing intentional, no plotting, no foresight, no long-term plan, I merely couldn't bear to admit that I'd failed at something else. When you're jilted two weeks before your wedding, you deserve a little slack. After my first month over here, when I'd been turned down for every job I'd applied for, I stopped accurately reporting my life. On the one hand I didn't want to worry my family, but mainly I did it because I couldn't stand the thought of Tom or anyone else feeling sorry for me. I knew my mother would pass on the news of how I was doing, and I wanted everyone to know what a success I was, how *lucky* I was that Tom dumped me so I had the chance to strike out on my own.

I try to argue my way out of accepting visitors, but with a combination of logic and guilt my mother defeats me. Without admitting what I've done there's no escape. Kim and Michelle are coming to stay. I hang up the phone in a daze. I'd start to scream if I thought it would help, but it won't. Nothing will. I scream anyway.

Two weeks later, I'm standing in the arrivals area at Gatwick. I can't believe I agreed to meet them at the airport. I was going to send them on the Gatwick Express to Victoria and let them catch a cab from there, but my mother pointed out that that wasn't very hospitable, so here I am. Little Miss Hospitality, that's me.

Kim comes through first, looking sickeningly put-together even after a nine-hour flight. She's a picture of health and vitality: her long blond hair bounces as she walks, her skin glows with a light sun-kissed tan and her eyes are bright without a hint of tiredness. Michelle, equally blond but not quite as pretty, follows just behind. For an instant, I'm thrilled to see them, I can't wait to show them around, but then everything that's happened comes back to me.

Plastering a sunny smile on my face, I wave wildly, trying to mimic the actions of someone who's excited rather than terrified. I can do this, I tell myself. I will do this. I only have to survive ten days. In 243 hours they will be on their way to Paris and I'll be free. Impoverished maybe, but free.

"Danni," cries Kim, as she wheels her luggage cart toward me, "I can't believe we're here."

Neither can I, but my smile doesn't flicker.

When they reach my side, we all hug and laugh, and then Kim steps back to take in my appearance. "You look fantastic," she says encouragingly, cocking her head to one side like a spaniel, her eyes huge and wounded, speaking to me as if I'm an invalid.

"You certainly do," agrees Michelle, head bobbing in agreement, her expression matching Kim's. "And you're so thin."

"Thanks," I say. I'd have to be in a coma not to recognize pity when I see it. I bite the inside of my cheek. I will not make a bitter comment. I will not make a bitter comment about Tom. I'm above all that. And, anyway, I should look good: I certainly made the ef-

fort. This is exactly why I spent three hours this morning making myself look perfect, in a casual, carefree
way, of course.

I help them with their luggage and we take the train
in to London. I don't have a car, and even if I could af-
ford it I wouldn't want one. Give me ten years, then
maybe I'll consider driving over here. And it's not even
that they drive on the left—if it was just that I could
get used to it—most roads are simply too narrow.
When I'm behind the wheel, I like to know that once
I'm in a lane I'll get to keep that lane, and I won't suddenly have to share it with oncoming traffic because
someone's parked in the road. It's a good thing I didn't
tell my mother I'd bought a fancy car. If I had, I'd have
been forced to make up some convoluted excuse as to
why it was being repaired for Kim and Michelle's
whole visit. That or rent one at astronomical expense.

"It was so nice of you to take the day off work," says
Michelle.

"Yeah, we really appreciate it. Especially," says Kim,
sharing a quick look with Michelle before turning
back to me, "after, well, you know."

I let the pause continue until it's just getting uncomfortable, then I cross my ankles. "So how is Tom?"
I ask casually. Take it back, take it back, take it back. I
should bite my tongue and spit it out. I wasn't going
to ask about *him*. I don't care what's been happening
in his life. I don't care how he is. The slimy toad
doesn't deserve space in my mind.

Kim glances at Michelle again. I don't miss the sig-
nificance of their exchange. They've clearly expected
this, but I refuse to give in to the urge to badmouth

him. Let them see it doesn't bother me. Let them tell the big fat pig that I am so over him.

"Oh, he's great," says Kim.

Fabulous, I think. Just what I want to hear. Not.

"He ended up buying that house on Elm Street," continues Kim.

My face freezes. "Really?" I ask, concentrating on keeping my eyes blank, trying to show no emotion. "Good for him." I found the house on Elm Street. I was the one who wanted to buy it. Tom didn't even like it until I convinced him it was perfect. I hate him. I hate him. I hate him.

"But you should see what Susie's done with it," says Michelle quickly, shuddering. "She found this magazine article that said that orange and green were this year's in colors, and now the living room looks as if it belongs in some psychedelic frat house. It's awful."

Kim nods. "And you know what's even worse? Susie giggles. She's so immature. I mean, she acts like a teenager, for heaven's sake, what can he see in her?"

What does Kim want me to say? Susie's only after his money? Tom's having an early midlife crisis? Any comment I could make would come across as jealousy.

"Word on the street," says Michelle with a wicked smile, "is that when she was in high school she serviced half the football team at homecoming."

"You said it, I didn't." I start to chuckle, laughing from tension and not because anything's funny or even slightly amusing. I feel like smashing my head against the side of the train, anything to try to knock some sense into myself. What have I done? What was I thinking? Why did I say they could come? I don't want to relive all this. It was bad enough the first time. I'd managed to blot most of it from my mind, but seeing them, especially Kim who was going to be my sister-in-law, makes it seem as if it happened a few days ago.

Tom, lovely, handsome, wonderful, perfect Tom, to whom I'd been engaged for ten months and been inseparable from for the two years before that, decided he didn't want to spend his life with me after all. Of course, I didn't find out about it right away. Tom had the foresight to tell me he was going to a real estate convention so I wouldn't wonder why he was out of town when, in actuality, he flew to Las Vegas to marry someone else. He was kind enough, however, to catch a flight back the next day to break the news to me.

"It's not that I don't love you," said Tom. "I just can't live without Susie."

At first I thought he was joking. I didn't believe him. I couldn't; it was only two weeks before our wedding. We'd been planning it for months. He's the one who insisted on a big church event; I'd have been happy with something simple. While he was away, I'd had my last-but-one dress fitting, the final numbers had been given for the reception and I'd double-checked the menu to make sure there was plenty of food.

"I don't understand," I said, as what he'd done slowly started to sink in.

"I'm sorry, Danni." Tom had the grace to look me in the eye as he apologized. He even took my hands in his, as if I wanted support from him when I knew where his hands had been. When I snatched mine away and stood up, he sighed and said, "I was hoping we could be friends, but I'll understand if you need some time."

I stared at him as if I'd never seen him before. And maybe I hadn't. Maybe my wonderful Tom didn't exist outside my head. Perhaps he'd been like this all along, filled with the potential to do this to me, and I'd never seen it. No, that's not true. He'd been perfect. He'd always treated me well: he'd been romantic and kind, strong and sexy, all that a fiancé could be.

"And don't worry," said Tom, filling the silence when I didn't say anything, "I'll have my mother break the news to my side of the family so you won't have to do all the work."

My eyes widened. Did he expect me to be grateful that he was being thoughtful about something? "At least your family won't have to return their presents," I said snidely. "They'll only have to buy new nametags. Susie obviously has the same taste as I do, so it should work out OK for you."

"Oh, honey—"

"Don't call me that," I snapped. "Don't you ever call me that again."

He had the gall to look disappointed at my anger. "This was never supposed to happen," said Tom. "It was meant to be a fling. That's all. I didn't want to hurt you. I thought you'd never find out, but she's just so—" He broke off, hesitating, then he smiled and said dreamily, "She's just so perky."

Perky. To this day I don't know if he was talking about her personality or her breasts.

After that I didn't want to hear any more and I kicked him out. I locked myself in and stared at the wall, but word spread quickly and before long my mother showed up at the door and enfolded me in her arms.

That's the problem with small towns. When you're happy and things are going well, they're great, but when something happens and you'd give anything for some anonymity, all those knowing sympathetic looks start to drive you crazy. They should put up warning signs on the highway at the edge of town. *Beware: you are now entering a high-gossip area. Before taking any action, you should first stop and think, What will people say?* Or, even better, WWPS bracelets should be handed out at birth and worn at all times. Maybe I'll have one commissioned and send it to Tom on what would have been our anniversary. He, of all people, should think WWPS before taking any major decisions.

No, forget it, I'd rather not have any contact with Tom. He'd take it all wrong. He'd think I wanted to be friends. He'd think I wasn't over him.

"So, how's Matt?" asks Kim, breaking into my thoughts. "I'm dying to meet him."

"Matt?" For a second, I'm confused. My head is filled with images of Tom looking so cheerful and happy when he told me he was married to Susie instead of me. I force the memories aside, not wanting to think about them anymore. What's done is done. There's no point rehashing old ground; what I need to do is concentrate on getting through the next ten days. I refocus on Kim and Michelle, thinking, Matt who? Then it all comes back to me. Ah, yes, Matt my fake boyfriend. That Matt. "He's great," I say, smiling broadly. "He had to fly to Zurich this morning for some meetings, but Matt's hoping they won't take more than three or four days."

"Hopefully not," says Kim. "I promised Mom a full report on what he's like. She wants a word-for-word replay."

My smile slips. That's exactly what I've been expecting.

Kim catches sight of my face and laughs. "Don't look at me like that, Danni. You know what she's like. She's been worried about you. We all have."

"And we were so glad when we heard about Matt," says Michelle. "Everyone's happy for you. Even Tom. He's thrilled you've found someone new."

Suddenly, all my lies seem worthwhile, and the guilt I've been harboring is gone. As the stories have become more convoluted, I was starting to have second thoughts, but now I'm delighted that I stuck it out. I'd rather pretend everything's wonderful than admit the truth. I may be lonely, homesick, broke and celibate, but I've managed to prevent my whole town pitying me. That's certainly something, and I don't even care that Tom's probably feeling let off the hook for what he did to me. Allowing his conscience to rest in peace is ten thousand times better than having Tom and his Susie feeling sorry for me. That's one thing I couldn't stand.

I shudder at the thought of my true state of affairs getting out. I have to keep Kim and Michelle believing that my life is as great as I've claimed, regardless of the difficulties ahead. Not only do they think I live in a stunning two-bedroom flat in Covent Garden and that I have a prestigious job in charge of exhibits at the

British Museum, they've also heard all about how I'm madly in love with and loved by a hunky British guy named Matt.

The truth is not so glamorous. Based in my tiny bedsit on Euston Road, I have a couple of jobs to keep me in food and not enough for luxuries like clothes. I'm a part-time tour guide, giving two ninety-minute walks every week, specializing in the gory, macabre facets of London's past. What a fine use of my history degree. It makes those years of study and all that expense seem so worthwhile. To my surprise, I enjoy my talks, but when you've left a research position at one of the best universities in the Midwest, it can never have the same cachet. In order to supplement the fortune I don't earn for my hour and a half's lecturing, I'm a dog walker. Every afternoon and most evenings I go into rich people's homes and take care of their dogs while they're at work or away on business trips. The dogs I look after eat better than I do. They're certainly more loved.

The photos I sent home of "my" apartment were taken in one of the dog owners' flats. I fell in love with the lighting and layout and saw nothing wrong in snapping a few digital pictures so my mother wouldn't worry. As I was creating my dream space with carefully selected shots, I had no problem with moving the location from the reality of Docklands to my desire for Covent Garden.

Matt, he of the dark good looks, is the owner of Benjy, an adorable black lab that I walk three times a week in Hyde Park, then feed, water and groom. I've never met Matt. I was merely inspired to invent a boyfriend with dark hair so he'd be the opposite of Tom. When my mother asked for a photograph, it was easy for me to remove a couple of Matt's photos from his frames, take some digital snaps, crop them so they appeared to be genuine photographs and not just photos of photos, and email them through. For Kim and Michelle's visit, I thought I'd go for an added touch, so I've had some of my digital pictures printed onto photographic paper and then framed.

As we reach Victoria Station and head for the taxi rank, Michelle asks, "How long does it take to get to your apartment? I can't wait to have a shower and freshen up."

"Didn't my mother tell you?" I ask casually, as if it hadn't occurred to me that they might not know.

"Tell us what?" asks Kim.

"My flat's been flooded," I say. "My upstairs neighbors left their bath running a few mornings ago and the ceiling sagged. Plaster started dropping down and everything. It's not safe so I've had to move out for a few weeks while they fix it."

"Really?" Michelle flicks her hair over her shoulder and readjusts her handbag so it's hanging safely across her stomach. "That's terrible."

So far so good. They appear to believe me. And why shouldn't they? I'm good old Danni, the girl next door. I'm one of them: wholesome, honest and caring.

"But where are we going to stay?" asks Kim. "We didn't bring any camping gear and everyone says London's real expensive."

"Don't worry," I say soothingly. "It's all under control."

"You've found us a cheap hotel?"

I smile, trying to give off an impression of happy-go-lucky good fortune rather than poverty-inducing trauma. "My insurance covers something better than a cheap hotel. We've got a fully furnished executive apartment to play around in until my place is fixed." Adding this to the price of my bedsit—I couldn't risk letting it go for a few days or I'd lose it—and we're talking break-the-bank costs here. I don't earn enough to cover one night, let alone ten, so I've had to raid my not-to-be-touched-except-in-an-emergency savings account. Originally, the money was intended for a house deposit, but it's not as if I'm going to be moving to Elm Street now. I had to do something to keep the story going. One look at where I really live and Kim and Michelle would know the truth of my debacle. Better to be poor than pitiful, that's my saying. Pride should be cherished when it's the only thing you have left.

For the first five days they're easy guests. They go out early and hit the tourist spots, and I'm careful to quiz them over breakfast so I know their plans. It wouldn't do to bump into them. It's unfortunate that I have to dress up each morning, as if I'm going to a fancy job, but it's not too great a hardship. I simply take my tour guide uniform and dog-walking clothes with me in my backpack and change when I can. I work only partial days, so what I'd really like to do is hang out at the apartment and use the Jacuzzi—I'm paying for it, after all—but I can't risk the girls coming back early and catching me when I'm supposed to be at the museum.

On day six I tell them Matt phoned and that he's been held up in Zurich, but he's not sure for how long. I feel it's important to keep Kim and Michelle hanging on, to let them think they're still going to meet him in the end. Kim keeps nagging me about my flat; she says she fell in love with it from the photos and really wants to see it, so I tell her it's been declared structurally unsound and we can't go inside. Eventually I give in enough to point out "my" building, picking a pretty blue converted Georgian mansion that has always caught my eye.

Just as I'm starting to relax and thinking that maybe I will get through these ten days, Kim says, "I wanted to surprise you and turn up at the British Museum this afternoon, but Michelle said we should warn you so you can try to clear your schedule."

"We'd like you to show us around," says Michelle. "Maybe in your lunch hour or during a break?"

My heart is racing, but I try to make my voice sound normal. "Today's not a good day," I say regretfully. "I've got three meetings plus my weekly budgeting session. Sorry."

"Then what about tomorrow?" asks Kim, with her usual persistence.

I'm not going to get out of this one. She's not going to take no for an answer. If I don't arrange a time, they'll just show up at the museum and ask for me, and I know exactly where that would lead: exposure. My apartment is off-limits, my boyfriend is out of town, I can't deny them a chance to see my place of employment as well. If I do, they *will* start getting suspicious. Kim and Michelle have seen no real evidence of my new life. I'd better give them some proof—and soon. While they're not really here to spy on me, it certainly feels that way, and I know that whatever they say will be heard, digested and discussed back home. I'm not about to let all my hard work and money go to waste. Not now. Everyone has to continue thinking I'm having a wonderful time. They have to.

My decision's made; there's nothing else I can do. "Friday's my day off," I lie, knowing I can arrange for someone else to look after the two dogs that I'm supposed to be walking. "Let's spend the whole day together. I can show you around and we'll include the BM as part of our tour."

I hardly sleep for the next couple of nights, terrified that Kim will change her mind and decide to surprise me at work, but when Friday does arrive it's still too soon. My future happiness depends on today's success. I have to pull this off. If I don't, I'll be an object of scorn and pity, a laughingstock, for decades to come. I'll never be able to go home again.

It's nearly noon when we head down Museum Street and I try to remain calm and composed. I can do this. I will do this. "I hope you don't mind," I say to Kim and Michelle, "but I don't want to stay too long, or someone's bound to accost me with some work questions that could easily wait until Monday."

"Hey," says Michelle, "you don't need to explain. You won't catch me going anywhere near my office when I'm not scheduled in."

"And I try to avoid mine even on the days I don't have off," laughs Kim.

As we pass through the gates, I beam at the security

guard and say, as if I know him, "Wow, it's really crowded today, isn't it?"

"It's the weather," he says pleasantly, "whenever there's a spot of rain in the forecast our numbers double."

I carry on walking, not giving the girls time to try to engage him in conversation, letting them assume we're on my turf now. We head across the courtyard, up the steps and then we're in. "I'll show you the Great Court and the Rosetta Stone first, then I'll take you upstairs to see my exhibits." I make a point of saying hello to every security guard we pass, and they all smile and respond, unknowingly contributing to my deception.

Kim's sidetracked by the Egyptian pieces. "This place is amazing," she says, turning to me. "I can't believe you get to see all this every day. I know how you love history and everything. It really suits you here." She smiles. "I'll be sure to tell Tom exactly how much fun you're having."

I blink. "Oh, thanks."

"He's my brother and I love him, but he's still a jerk. He deserves to suffer." Kim squeezes my shoulder. "I'm just sorry I lost such a great sister-in-law."

A flush sweeps up my neck and across my cheeks. She's being nice and I've been deceiving her.

"Everyone says you'd have made him a better wife," adds Michelle.

I don't know what to say to that. My face turns redder and Kim laughs. "OK," she says, "now that we've said what we wanted to say, let's change the subject. I don't want any depressing thoughts interfering with our vacation again. Deal?" As Michelle and I nod, Kim glances to the left and right and her voice drops. "Could you take us into one of the storage areas, Danni? You guys must have so many things that aren't on display. I'd love to see something that regular tourists can't view."

"I'm not allowed," I say, my mind whirring, hating to come up with yet another excuse, but not having any choice under these circumstances.

"You're not?" She looks really disappointed.

"It's the insurance," I say regretfully. "They won't cover us if nonemployees are granted access. But I can show you one of my displays." I'm tempted to claim the mummies as my own, but they're too high profile. "I've been working on redesigning the Anglo-Saxon section."

As I lead them toward the front stairs, I spot a woman up ahead with a museum pass around her neck, gathering people for a gallery tour. Quickly, I turn to the right, cutting through the crowd.

"Hubba bubba," says Kim in admiration. "Who's that?"

I glance around. "Who?"

"Him." She nods at a tall, dark-haired man in an expensive suit who's chatting to one of the security guards. As I watch, the man laughs and I catch sight of his face for the first time. Hubba bubba is right. His eyes are bright blue and they crinkle at the corners in the cutest way when he smiles. And his face, wow. I have to stop myself from staring. He's gorgeous.

"Oh, him," I say. "That's Julian." Ha. So there, Tom. I know lots of attractive men. Your sister will be able to vouch for that.

"You know him?" asks Kim, her eyes lighting up. "He's hot."

"Julian's one of the museum's corporate sponsors." I start to have a bad feeling about this, so I point to the left. "The stairs are that way."

Michelle is still studying the man, and her steps are getting slower and slower. "Is he British?"

"Yes," I say aloud, but inside all I'm thinking is keep walking. Keep walking.

"Can we meet him?" asks Kim, stopping. "I love men with accents. Especially him."

I hesitate. "Julian must be here for a meeting. He won't have time to socialize."

"Come on, Danni, please," pleads Michelle. "Are you embarrassed of us or something? We haven't met any of your friends. We're not that grotesque, are we?"

What can I say? I haven't introduced you to anyone because they know the truth about my present circumstances and you don't? I don't think so.

"Hey, Julian," calls Kim loudly.

Both the man and the security guard glance toward us, then away as a tourist approaches the guard with a map. Kim opens her mouth to call again, but I cut in before she can. "Shh, Kim, let me do this the British way. I'll go over and see if he has time to chat. You two wait here."

Kim gives me a huge grin. "As long as you bring him back."

I try not to think about what I'm doing as I approach the man. This is going to be so humiliating. "Please, please, please, you must help me," I beg him. "Please smile and pretend you know me."

"OK," he says slowly, smiling, "but how is this helping?"

Oh, it's helping, I think, as the impact of his smile hits me. I feel butterflies in my stomach at being so close to him, but after a moment I pull myself together. This is no time to enjoy the view. "You see those two women over there?" I ask, pointing out Kim and Michelle. "They think I know you. It's a long story, but basically Kim's brother dumped me, and I moved over here and lied about how great my life is. You just need to shake your head, wave at the girls, then leave." I don't care how desperate I'm coming across, surely he couldn't be so grumpy as to refuse, could he? "Please, please do this for me. I'll be forever in your debt."

He grins. "You'll owe me," he says.

I glance at Kim and Michelle, and they take that as a signal to head this way. "What was that?" I ask, panicking, his words not registering.

"You expect me to do a favor for a beautiful woman for nothing?"

Blinking, looking between him and the girls, I whisper desperately, "Please, just wave and leave. That's all you have to do." Wave and leave. Wave and leave.

"At the very least I expect you to join me for dinner," he says. "Maybe dinner and a drink, depending on how well I do."

"Please," I beg again. "Just wave and leave. Wave and—" It's too late. They're here. Forcing my mouth to smile, I say to him, praying that he'll play along, "Julian, I'd like you to meet Kim and Michelle. They're visiting me from the States."

"It's a pleasure," he says smoothly.

Kim shakes his hand, holding on a fraction too long. "So how long have you known Danni?"

He glances at me. "It feels like ages, doesn't it, Danni?"

"Julian and I met a few weeks ago at a fund-raising ball," I say, directing my words to Kim and Michelle, but trying to let him know what he needs to pretend. "Goldman Sachs is sponsoring a few of our restoration projects and Julian's one of their financial gurus."

"We're just going out for lunch," says Kim, as soon as I pause for breath. "Would you care to join us, Julian?"

Before he can answer, I blurt, "I thought you wanted to see some of my exhibits."

"I do, but I'm starving." Kim tucks a long strand of blond hair behind her ear. "Let's do lunch first, then we can come back. Unless, of course, Julian's meeting isn't finished, then a snack would tide me over until he's ready."

"You're in luck, ladies," he says, glancing at his watch. "I have an hour and a half before I'm due back at the office."

"That's great." Michelle laughs. "I could listen to you speak all day long. I just love your accent."

"We wouldn't want to impose, Julian," I say. "I know how busy you are."

He winks at me, then gives me one of his devastating smiles. "I told you I wanted to get to know you better." Then, to Kim, he says, "All she does is work, work, work, but I keep telling her she has to let someone sweep her off her feet."

"But she has," says Kim, a bit too eagerly for my liking. "Hasn't Danni told you about Matt?"

"Matt?" He looks quizzically at me.

"Her boyfriend," says Michelle.

Just barely I shake my head no, the gesture so subtle I think he's missed it until he smiles. "Ah, yes, the boyfriend," he says. "I'm working on changing her mind about him. It's just a matter of time."

"So what restaurant would you recommend?" Kim asks him, her voice a soft purr, ignoring what he's just said.

I feel a pang of jealousy that Kim's coming on to him. I saw him first. Well, no, actually, they saw him first, but I spoke to him first. I'm the one who's living here. I'm the one with the broken heart that needs mending. Wait, no, what am I thinking? He knows I'm a basket case. But, then again, he is helping me. And he called me beautiful. I may be rusty and out of practice, but that certainly seemed like flirting to me. I start to smile, but then the panic starts again. He can't join us for lunch, he just can't. It would get too complicated with two of us lying. I can't risk messing it all up now. Not when I'm so close.

He's about to respond to Kim's question when his mobile rings. "Excuse me for a moment," he says, taking out his phone and stepping away.

While he's carrying on a quiet conversation, Michelle and Kim grin at me. "He's gorgeous," whispers Michelle. "So sexy."

"He's mine," says Kim. "I let you go after that man on the plane."

"Not fair," Michelle protests. "I didn't know we

were going to meet Julian, did I? And besides, that guy was flying home to propose to his girlfriend. He doesn't count."

I'm watching out of the corner of my eye, so the second "Julian" hangs up, I shush the girls.

"Bad news, I'm afraid," he says. "Something's come up and I can't make lunch."

"Oh, no," says Kim. "That's terrible. Well, how about dinner, then?"

"I'm afraid I already have plans." He looks genuinely regretful. "But it was lovely meeting you. Friends of Danni's are friends of mine." He turns to me and says, "May I have a word, please? We had some thoughts about the peat bog exhibit."

"Of course." I follow him across the room. When we're a safe distance away and can't be overheard, we stop. I roll my eyes and quote, " 'Friends of Danni's are friends of mine.' "

"Sorry, was that coming on too strong?"

I grin. "No. It was absolutely perfect."

"Excellent." His grin matches mine. "I thought it was a good touch to play Julian as besotted with you."

"I can't thank you enough," I say. "You have no idea what you've done. You've saved my life."

"But you didn't want me to join you for lunch." He sounds hurt, his face reproachful.

My smile drops. "It was nothing personal—"

"Gotcha," he cuts in. "And don't worry, I've been expecting a call. I knew I wouldn't be able to dine with you, as pleasant as it would have been."

I start to laugh. "Sneaky, but I like it."

"So how long are the girls in town?" he asks.

"Fifty-two more hours," I say, not needing to check the time.

"Well," he says, "do you think in fifty-two more hours you could start calling me Christopher? My cousin's name is Julian, and it just doesn't sit right on me."

"Christopher." I savor the name. "I could do you an extra special favor and call you that."

"And I wasn't kidding about dinner," says Christopher. He takes out his wallet, withdraws two of his cards and hands me one. "Hide that, or tell your friends that Christopher is a top lawyer I'm recommending to sort out your affairs." From the inner pocket of his suit jacket he extracts a pen. "Now," he says, flipping the other card over to write on the back, "you'd better give me your number. It's not that I don't trust you, Danni, it's just how these things are done." He gives me a searching look. "And Danni is your name, isn't it?"

Smiling, fighting the urge to giggle like a fool, I tell him my phone number. As he leaves, kissing me on the cheek and waving goodbye to Kim and Michelle, I feel more cheerful than I've felt in months. My mother was right. Having visitors from home did do me good. And maybe once they've gone I'll have to ditch Matt, lose my job at the museum in an annual round of layoffs and, as a consequence, have to move out of my designer flat. Maybe. Or maybe not until the next visitors from home have bought their plane tickets. Perhaps I'll think about it then.

NANCY SPARLING is the author of two hilarious romantic comedies, *Being Alexander* and *Free Lunch*. Born and brought up in the USA, she now lives in Hertfordshire with her husband and family.

Forty Days

JILL SMOLINSKI

I didn't think it was any big deal. Turning forty. In fact, when a friend mentioned, "Gee, your big 4–0 is right around the corner, isn't it?" I hardly gave it a thought. That was, until that same night, when I woke in a cold sweat with the sudden realization: *I can never get my belly pierced! I've had my chance! The time for belly piercing has come and gone and I've missed it!* Never mind that I have no interest in inserting jewelry anywhere near my midsection. Or that when I'm sitting I can hardly find my belly button anyway.

Point was, it set my mind racing. I began compiling a mental list of the things I'd never done.

It was a long list.

Granted, I'd been busy. There was getting married, and having a baby, and working a job, and getting a divorce, and running errands and wiping around the kitchen and picking up and putting away and on and on.

But I began to wonder if someday, lying on my deathbed, none of that would matter.

What would matter was that I'd never worn thong underwear.

And, trust me, no one wants to see some old lady on her deathbed trying to wrestle herself into a thong.

Something needed to be done. Soon.

"You should take off for an exotic island," my best friend, Ellen, suggested after I confessed my worries to her. "Have yourself an affair with a young stud. Get your groove back."

I laughed and tossed a towel at her head. We were at the gym for our regular Saturday morning workout— me, speedwalking on the treadmill while Ellen jogged next to me. "Don't I need to have had a groove first in order to get it back?" I quipped.

"I'm serious."

No doubt she was. Ever since we met in college, I've been in awe of Ellen. Naturally athletic, tall, she's one of those people who just gulps life. Ellen isn't afraid of anything.

"Believe me, I wish I could go somewhere," I said, "but the timing's terrible. I'm broke, and I'm swamped right now at work. Plus, Jeannie has homework, and gymnastics, and—"

"And, and, and," Ellen interrupted.

"Hey! All I'm saying is—"

Ellen ignored my protests. "So, fine, you can't go away. That doesn't mean you can't shake things up. We live in Los Angeles, for crying out loud—there are plenty of ways to get into trouble right here at home."

I pushed up the speed on my treadmill, the idea of getting into trouble sounding strangely appealing. "Maybe I could squeeze a few things in . . ."

Ellen saw an opening (and perhaps a chance for a partner in crime) and interjected, "Sure! It's perfect! And I don't think you need to worry about Jeannie. She's thirteen—she's hardly ever around now anyway." Then she shot me a look, adding, "Besides, if you need help, it's not as if that deadbeat of an ex of yours couldn't pitch in more."

Please—as if Frank could possibly think about anyone but Frank? I couldn't help but sigh, "I'd just like to find out what I've been missing. Maybe finally feel better about myself."

Ellen nodded. "You know what would help raise your self-esteem?"

"You think I have low self-esteem?"

"A young stud," she continued, as if she hadn't heard me. "That's what would help."

It was a few days later, having woken in the night—tearful that it was too late for me to be a groupie, even haggard old rock stars would find me decrepit now—that the idea struck me.

Sure, I may have missed out on some things.

But not everything.

There was still time to squeeze more life into my life. Make up for all the years that I'd been too cautious, too scared, too stuck in the same routine.

So right then and there I issued myself a challenge.

A personal exodus, as it were, across the valley of me. Because, with forty days and nights left before my fortieth birthday, I, Donna Dawson, made a vow to do one thing—however small—each day that

1) I'd never done before,
2) I'd been afraid to do,
3) was just for *me*.

It wasn't going to be easy. I've practically made a career out of taking the safe route. God knows I didn't know where I'd find the time. Yet somehow I knew I had to make this happen. It felt like more than just forty days.

It felt like my last chance.

I decided to jump right in, feet first.

Day 1: Go skinny dipping.

Even though I lived less than a mile from the beach, I drove the hour to the Valley to use the pool at my parents' condo—more privacy that way. I'd hoped Ellen would join me for moral support, but she had to work late.

It was my mother who kept me company while I sat at the edge of her pool, waiting for night to fall. Toes in the water, I wore nothing but a towel, which I clung to like a life raft.

"How is it possible," my mom asked after I'd outlined my plan to her, "that you've never skinny-dipped?"

Her tone suggested this omission was an affront to her mothering skills. That at some future date, she feared I may appear on the *Jenny Jones* show and say—

to the gasps of the audience—Well, I wouldn't have murdered all those people, except *my mother never let me swim naked*.

"You know how cruel kids can be," I said. "What if someone saw?"

"Lots of people get caught; it's part of the fun!"

"Yeah, well, the whale jokes wouldn't have been so fun."

My mother, bless her innocent heart and fuzzy memory, was genuinely perplexed. "Why would anyone do that?"

"Mom," I said, "I *was* a whale."

"You were no such thing. You were a healthy girl."

Seeing me roll my eyes she added, "Well, you *were*. You're pretty now, too. But you were darling then."

Whatever my mom's got, I wish I could bottle it. Take a swig and look back at my life through kinder eyes.

Fact is, since I can remember I've fought my weight (and weight usually won). Still, I'd managed to marry a man who didn't mind some extra pudge on his woman—probably because he liked eating as much as I did. Then Frank and I went on Weight Watchers together when Jeannie started kindergarten. I lost forty pounds, he lost sixty. As he got smaller, however, his ego got bigger. Even though I was feeling better about myself than I ever had—wearing size fives and getting second glances from men—suddenly I wasn't good enough for my husband anymore.

I pulled the towel more tightly around me, as if a chill had set in.

My mom patted my shoulder and then stood to

leave. "Well, honey, I'd join you on your little adventure, but you don't need to see your mother's saggy old bottom. You have fun. I'm going to fold the laundry."

OK, I scolded myself, pulling up to my feet after she disappeared inside. *Enough stalling.* Glancing around for passersby, I took a deep breath and let the towel drop. Then I plugged my nose and jumped, feet first.

As soon as I made the plunge, I couldn't believe it! This was nothing like swimming in a bathing suit! The water wrapped itself around me. Cool hands seemed to touch me all over. I felt fizzy . . . floaty . . .

Squealing a laugh, I turned over and did a slow backstroke across the pool. I felt transformed already. I was a mermaid . . . my hair curling gently around my face . . . my breasts buoyed . . . my hips gently curving into . . .

"Well, sweetie!" my dad's voice rang out. "I thought you might like some lemona—"

I ducked down into the water.

Too late.

I could hear the clatter of plastic cups and a platter hitting concrete, and my mother hollering, "Marv! Make sure you don't go outside! Marv!?"

And there you had it.

One down.

Thirty-nine to go.

My work-buddy, Martin, assured me I didn't have low self-esteem. I was simply too nice. I needed to discover my inner bitch.

"Quick"—and he turned to me as we strolled back

to the office with coffees—"don't think about it. Give
me the first thing that pops into your head. Name
something so bad you'd never do it."

I knew exactly what to say: "Litter."

He looked disappointed. "Litter?"

"You asked."

"OK then." He handed me his empty Starbucks
cup. "Litter it is. Your task for today. Go on. Do it."

I gawked at him. Litter?!! Was he kidding? Couldn't
I do something easy, like drown baby kittens or set a
building on fire?

"All right. Fine," I snapped. "Give me that." I'd already managed in the past few days to take a yoga
class, try a new restaurant for lunch, finally see *The
Godfather,* and wear thong underwear (which I
promptly took off when I got home and tossed in the
trash). To be honest, I was happy not to have to think
of something to do for the day. People litter all the
time. How hard could it be?

I held the cup in my hand and started to open my
fingers. They wouldn't let go. I couldn't do it. Not after
a lifetime of conditioning—of seeing that commercial
with the Indian crying on the garbage-filled front lawn.
I gave a hoot, I couldn't pollute.

Finally, in slow motion it seemed, the cup floated to
the ground.

"Excellent," Martin said.

A woman came up from behind. "Excuse me, you
dropped something," and handed me the cup.

Day 8.

"Quit staring at my tits," I scolded Ellen in a
whisper.

"I can't help it! They're just so . . . so *buoyant.*"

Ellen had signed us up for one of those Speed Dating workshops—the ones where you essentially have a dozen or so blind dates in a row, each lasting a matter of minutes. For the occasion, I'd worn the water bra I'd purchased the day before. Each of its cups (designed for lifelike look and feel!) held enough water to take me from my usual B to a very buxom D—or, as Ellen had pointed out when I first walked into the conference room, enough to float half of the U.S. Navy fleet and still have some left over for splashing about.

OK, so maybe it was a bit much, especially on someone with as small a frame as I have. I just thought it might help with my self-esteem problem.

There were thirty of us in the room, divided evenly between women and men. By seven o'clock we were still at the "meet-n-greet" stage of the event, which involved standing around, pretending to read the information packet and stealing furtive glances at who you were about to be forced to bond with.

"I hope they're rocket scientists," Ellen groused, "because nobody here is much to look at, much less—" She stopped mid-sentence and elbowed me so hard it nearly caused a tidal wave. "Over there, at the registration table! Girlfriend, I am in luuuuuuurve."

I turned to look and . . . *woah!* She wasn't kidding. He was that startling kind of handsome. Tall, dark, cheekbones you could hurt yourself on—looking luscious in a black shirt and jeans. "He can't possibly be coming for this," I whispered. "He must think it's a—"

I was interrupted by a frighteningly chipper woman clapping her hands. "Everyone! Everyone! I'm Brenda," but she said it like Bren*dah*. "Welcome to Speed Dating! Let's get started!"

With the efficiency of a Nazi soldier, Bren*dah* soon had the men sitting at individual tables in a circle around the room. "Here's how it works: you've been given a card with the names of the men, or women, you're going to meet tonight. Each of you ladies will be assigned a table at which to start. You'll have precisely seven minutes to get to know that person, then I'll say 'Switch,' and you'll move on to the next table!

"Now don't worry, ladies," she added, "you'll get a chance to meet each and every one of the fellows here tonight!" and—did I imagine it—or did all the women's heads swivel as a unit in the direction of one fellow in particular?

"Ready?" Bren*dah* chirped. "Let's go!"

I'd come prepared with an ice-breaker question to get the conversation flowing: *What do you want to be when you grow up?* First on my list: Scott. I sat across from him as he opened with, "What do you want to be when you grow up?"

Good thing I hadn't asked it first. What a stupid fucking question.

I hesitated before replying, unsure of how truthful to be. I decided to go with a straight answer. "A painter."

"You'd make one sexy painter. I can just see you wearing a big tool belt."

Thrown by his salacious remark, I didn't get a chance to clarify that I meant painter as in pictures, not houses.

Besides, I'd moved on to Peter . . . Patrick? . . . whatever—who wanted to know my life's dream. I confided that I hoped some day to sell some of my paintings, to become a professional artist.

He shared his dream, too.

A threesome.

As I rotated around the room, the men clearly split into two distinct categories: those before the gorgeous guy in the black shirt, and those after him. I swore I could *smell* his sex appeal from tables away—from where I was talking to . . . Greg, was it? . . . telling him, yes, my job as a publications manager for an insurance agency was, indeed, every bit as rewarding as it sounded.

And before I knew it, there I was, about to be one-on-one with a god. That flipping in my belly should have been desire. It was, in fact, dread.

Men like him are never interested in me. He'd probably stare at his watch the entire time. *God, please let me not make a fool of myself.*

I walked up and said a casual hello, as if I have the opportunity to gab with Calvin Klein model look-alikes every day of the week.

"Ah, my beautiful lady at last," he said, his voice dripping in a French accent.

Beautiful lady? I looked around—no supermodel standing behind me. He must mean me. Huh.

He introduced himself as Jean Pierre, and situated our chairs so that we sat nearly knee to knee. I could feel the warmth of his leg where it brushed against my own.

"So," I opened, growing jittery when he didn't say

anything else right away, "what do you want to be when you grow up?"

Ugh. Please. Kill me now.

He shrugged, one of those Frenchy shrugs that's usually accompanied by a cigarette in one hand and a drink in the other (which, come to think of it, was sounding awfully good about now). "Who says I'm going to grow up?"

Jean Pierre, I learned, had recently moved to the States. That's why he was at Speed Dating. He hadn't had much time to meet anyone. Especially, he added, leaning closer, anyone nearly as exquisite as myself.

He touched the edge of my neck, and a sudden flush shot from my face down to my heaving—and I do mean heaving—breasts. "You have such lovely . . ." he breathed, trailing a finger down my collarbone, ". . . skeen."

I gulped, and before I could blurt what I was thinking (which was *Take me! Take me right here, right now!*) Bren*dah*'s voice bellowed, "Switch!"

Then it was on to Tad . . . poor Tad . . . a nice enough guy who had the grave misfortune of following Jean Pierre with the ladies. A handshake after you'd just been given a mind-splitting orgasm.

At last, we were instructed to mark on our papers who we liked well enough to exchange phone numbers with. Out of pity, I circled poor Tad's name. Everyone else, to be honest, blended together. Except for, of course, Jean Pierre. They should have put a check by his name right on the form—saved all us ladies the trouble of filling it in ourselves.

I was exhausted by the time I met back up with

Ellen, having depleted my store of small talk for the next decade. Plus, I couldn't wait to take the bra off. That water weighed a ton.

Bren*dah* returned to give us our tally sheets—the men we chose who chose us in return. Although Ellen had several names on her list, her voice quavered as she said simply, "We're not a match. He didn't pick me."

There was one name on mine.

Tad, the cheeky little loser—didn't he realize he was only a mercy pick?—hadn't selected me.

Jean Pierre had.

When I showed it to Ellen, she snipped, in very un-Ellen-like fashion, "He only wants you because of your boobs."

Nevertheless, I woke the next day feeling buoyant. Faux bosom or not, the evening had been the ego boost I needed.

Just for fun, instead of the oldies station I usually listened to while I got ready for work, I thought, hey, why not try some new music? *Day 9: Listen to something other than the Monkees.* I cranked one of Jeannie's Eminem CDs on the stereo. Hmm, not bad, really. Quite peppy!

I was dancing around the living room when Jeannie—dubbed Recessive Jean by her dad because she's so trim and lovely and perfect we can't figure out how she could possibly be a child of ours—emerged from her bedroom. Her hair was in six tiny buns on her head. She'd probably copied the style from a magazine and, unlike my attempts at that sort of thing at her age, had pulled it off. She looked like a cupcake.

"Mother," she said primly, "that is so disgusting."

"What?"

"That!" and flailed her arms in my direction.

Oh. That. *Me.*

I responded by playing air guitar and giving my best Mick Jagger pout.

After she stomped off, however, mumbling about mothers refusing to grow old gracefully, I turned the volume down and went back to ironing my pants.

I'd just gotten home from a charity race-walk on Saturday when Jean Pierre called to ask me out. A date already and only day ten! I couldn't believe my good luck. Until he said he wanted to meet for drinks that same night.

So close and yet . . .

Despite my vows to be more spontaneous, it wasn't going to work. I'd promised Jeannie I'd come watch the rehearsal for the play she was in. Plus, I was snack mom.

Of course I didn't tell Jean Pierre any of that. Only that I couldn't make it.

I sure wished I could make it, I clarified. Drinks would be nice, mmm, I love drinking, yes I do! I'm one of the thirstiest women I know! In fact, here, let me get my appointment book because, if not tonight, then perhaps . . . let's see . . .

"No problem. Another time," he said cheerfully as he hung up.

Scrawled in my journal is a list of what I accomplished over the next week:

Sing karaoke
My first pedicure
Invest $100 in stock market
Treat myself to fresh flowers
Learn to drive a stick shift
Rock-wall climbing at the Y

And, in a moment of supreme bravery:

Post one of my paintings for auction on eBay

It's amazing I managed to squeeze all that in, what with the time I devoted to my other new activity. Obsessing about Jean Pierre. Nonstop.

He hadn't called back, and I couldn't help but fret—was that it? Did I miss my one chance? Was I a slightly used, thirty-nine-year-old Cinderella and no one could bear to tell me that my charms had expired?

It occurred to me I could call him. We'd exchanged numbers. I did have his. That could've been one of my adventures, in fact: *Today, for the first time in my life, I call a boy for a date.*

But it wasn't. Instead, I scowled at the phone, which, in the ultimate treachery, insisted on only allowing telemarketers through.

Checking my email Saturday morning, I found one from Ellen.

Sorry I was such a bitch the other night . . . just

being a jealous cow. Of course he wants you. You
looked amazing. You ARE amazing.

P.S. Went out with Tad last night . . . Remember
Tad? Girlfriend, I think I'm in luuuuuuurve!

I emailed her back:

Invite me to the wedding!!! And nothing to be jealous of on this end. My love life is . . . as usual . . .
not.

Day 18. I was painting highlights in my hair with one
of those do-it-yourself kits—praying to the Lord above
in the way one does when one is administering home
beauty treatments—when I heard Jean Pierre's unmistakable voice on my answering machine.

I leaped for the phone.

Before he could even so much as get another word
out I was insisting yes, yes—*oui!*—tonight would be
perfect. I'd love to meet for a drink.

Perfect wasn't exactly the right word.

More like a big-fat-pain-in-the-ass. If that's a word—
and if it isn't, it should be. I'd already promised Frank
I'd shuttle Jeannie and some of her teammates to a gymnastics finals over in . . . oh, I couldn't remember where,
precisely . . . but somewhere so far he'd suckered me
into covering for him again. Now I was going to have to
beg someone to cover for me. But it'd be worth it.

I needed this.

I deserved this.

And in order to get to this, I was trying to hurry off

the phone—cripes, how long had these highlights been in? Had I even set a timer?—when Jean Pierre asked, "Tell me, what are you wearing now?"

"Wearing?"

"I want to peecture you."

"Um, shorts and a T-shirt," I answered, and immediately wanted to die from shame. A *T-shirt*—sexy lady! Couldn't I have made something up?

At least I'd left out the part about the foil cap on my head.

"Mmm," was all he said, leaving me to wonder if he'd even heard me.

Drinks were at Nate's, a restaurant up the street from my house that I'd been wanting to check out for ages. Jean Pierre kissed me hello on each cheek.

"Ah, *belle,*" he purred, giving me a lingering once-over. I'd tried to redeem myself from the T-shirt comment by wearing a strappy top and skirt. The highlights had turned out more subtle than I'd hoped—the water bra, however, more than made up for it. You couldn't miss my breasts for a mile. They nearly grazed my chin.

But enough about me because, if it was even possible, Jean Pierre had grown more broodingly handsome than since I'd seen him last. Not that that sort of thing matters, but . . .

Hoo, boy, he's a looker.

We cozied into a corner booth and ordered wine, which was joyously received (remember that thirst I boasted about?). When the waiter set down a basket of bread along with bowls of garlic oil, it was waved away. "No garlic. We will be keesing," Jean Pierre explained.

Pretty nervy, when you think about it—did the *bread* really need to go? Except that moments later we were, as it turned out, kissing. Right at the table. I couldn't even say why, other than to say, why not?

Besides, it's not as if there was a lot to talk about. The majority of our conversation, it seemed, involved my assuring Jean Pierre that the music wasn't too loud, that we needn't go to his apartment to hear each other better.

OK, so he's a man on the make, I thought. I'm not so naive. I was having a great time anyway—at a hot club, kissing an even hotter guy. It's the type of thing that never happens to me.

Before I could do something I might regret—and since we'd plowed through a couple of bottles of wine there was an increasing chance of that occurring—I murmured an excuse and grabbed a taxi home. Jean Pierre didn't let me stumble out, however, without first extracting a promise that I'd stay longer next time.

Next time. I leaned back in the cab and smiled. Mere weeks since I'd set a goal to rev up my life, and look how far I'd come already. Doing the sort of things I'd never do. Dating the sort of man I'd never date. Taking the sort of chances that . . . well, who knows?

I wasn't expecting to find love in forty days. To be honest, I was more interested in finding *me*.

Still, I sighed, it might be nice to add "get laid" to my list of accomplishments. It wouldn't qualify as something I'd never done before. But it sure would be fun.

I tell you, coming up with this forty-day idea was nothing short of *brilliant*.

"I tell you, this forty-day idea is nothing short of a *disaster*," I cried to Martin the next day as I stared numbly at the computer screen.

The painting I put up for eBay auction? It was about to end in an hour. With zero bids. *Zero.*

"Don't worry, you'll sell another," he assured me.

I struggled to hold back tears. "It's not just a lost sale. It's a lost dream."

"Well then," and he patted my knee, "as long as we're not being overly dramatic."

How could I explain it, the courage it took to post *Dog?* The painting snarled at me in its on-screen digitized form. *Dog,* a rottweiler in oils, was my exploration of dog being God spelled backward. I hadn't even given it a proper name after I painted it, as if somehow I knew it was never truly mine to keep.

"Just one bid, just one teensy bid," I sniffed. I'd set the minimum at $9 to get things rolling. All I wanted was for someone to buy it. With the exchange of cash for art, it would elevate me from the level of hobbiest to pro. It'd prove that I wasn't crazy for thinking I could be an artist—and, maybe, also that Frank was wrong for saying I *was* crazy. Just. One. Teensy. Bid.

Leaning back in resignation, I hit the Refresh button.

And there it was.

Cowboy 100—whoever he was—had come through.

Nine big ones.

I leaped to my feet. Martin threw his arms around me, and we started jumping up and down and screaming like we'd just scored on *The Price is Right*.

Then he looked at me, wild-eyed, and uttered the words that I suspected immediately I would come to regret: "I have an idea!" He fired up the computer in the next cubicle and logged onto eBay. "I'll pretend to be the competition!" he shouted over the wall.

The next thing I knew, a bidding war was underway. Martin (user name Hot&Sexy, which I could have lived without ever knowing) vs. Cowboy 100.

The clock was ticking.

My heart positively clattered in my chest.

The price kept climbing, dollar by dollar. Martin and I were drawing a crowd. One of the agents brought microwaved popcorn. An office pool started up to guess the final price.

With seconds left, *Dog*'s price had reached a whopping $301.50.

"This is it—stop!" I shouted to Martin. "Ohmygosh, I can't believe it!" I blubbered, high-fiving the people packed in my tiny workspace.

Then I heard Martin whoop, "Yee-*hah!* Let's take this cowboy for a riiiiiide!" Followed by the unmistakable clacking of fingers on computer keys.

My heart froze in place.

The auction ended.

I became the lucky buyer of my own painting.

"Gosh, Donna," Martin said, sheepish. "I sure didn't see that coming."

I limped out of the office, stopping by Miss Grace's

on my way home to pick up a tin of lemon muffins—a treat for Day 19 that I haven't dared allow myself since . . . well, I suppose since I was the type of person to eat them all in one sitting.

I ate them all in one sitting.

Martin felt terrible, he really did.

That's why—when I got an email from Cowboy 100 saying he liked my work, asking if I had any other paintings for sale—I made a point not to mention it until hours later. Let the boy stew for a while.

"He emailed?" Martin exclaimed when I finally told him.

"He wants to come to my studio. Apparently, he's local."

"Terrific!"

"Sure, except I don't have a studio."

"Humph." After much deliberation, it was decided that Martin would take digital photos and help me compile a portfolio. I'd meet the cowboy on neutral territory.

"Can we do it today?" I pleaded. "I can count it toward my forty days."

Day 20. My first-ever portfolio.

It felt as exciting as my first-ever box of crayons.

Cowboy 100—real name, Bill—and I arranged to meet Wednesday at a coffee shop not far from my house.

I'll be there at 9. How will we find each other?
Donna

I was aiming for professional with a touch of friendly,
yet I couldn't shake the feeling I was setting up a blind
date.

> Looking forward to meeting the artist! As for me,
> I'm about 6', brown hair, medium build. I'll proba-
> bly be wearing jeans and a T-shirt.
> Bill
> P.S. Oh, and I have just the one arm.

I wasn't sure what to make of his message—was that a
piece of real information or an odd sense of humor? I
sent back:

> Great. I'll be holding a rose in my teeth.

He replied only with one of those smiley-face emoti-
cons. :-) I cringed. If he likes those, what does that say
about his taste in art?

When I walked into the coffee shop, it was packed.
This cowboy had better really be one-armed, I
thought, or I won't stand a chance of finding him. The
place was positively rife with brown-haired guys in
jeans and T-shirts. Take for example that one standing
over there . . . with the ice-blue eyes and the sweet
curve of a jawline and the shoulders and the . . .

One arm. And another that stopped just above the
elbow.

OK. I'd say that's my man.

My first client.

Taking a breath for courage, I marched over, clutching my portfolio. *I don't want to blow this. Please let me not blow this.*

"Bill?"

"Hey, you found me," he said, his easy Texas drawl answering any questions I might have had about the cowboy moniker.

Blame the nerves—or that strange phenomenon that makes people say the very thing they're trying hardest not to—but I quipped, "Yeah, well, no thanks to your description! Technically, you've got at least an arm and a half there."

There was a pause.

A waitress turned away, averting her eyes from the car crash before her.

He opened his mouth . . .

Then burst into a laugh so robust I swore I could feel it reverberating inside me.

"Well, so I do," he said. "Now let's grab us a table."

I figured it shouldn't take long to go through my portfolio. I only had a couple dozen paintings. Yet I was on my second cup of coffee and we still hadn't finished. Neither of us seemed to be in any hurry—me, in particular, since I'd only be heading back to work. Plus, he was so easy to talk to.

He studied each painting, asking when I did it, what was the inspiration, and so on. I was thrilled to learn he worked as a graphic artist. It seemed an endorsement of my own work to have a professional interested.

By cup of coffee number three, I happened to mention my forty-day experiment.

Bill nearly knocked over his chair to go rifling through his briefcase. "I have the perfect thing for you to do," he insisted. I stifled a groan. Since I started all this, I'd been plagued by well-meaning friends trying to fulfill their fantasies through me. Trust me, there are a lot of people out there who for some reason want to see me leap from a plane.

He handed me a flyer. "It's for a performance art piece I'm in Friday night. An interactive sort of thing. You should stop by."

"I'll try," I said. The Art of Therapy, it was called. Well, maybe. I tucked it in my purse.

He flipped to the last page of my portfolio.

"Is this you?" he asked, smiling.

It was an abstract—an image of a nude woman, curvy along the hips, with wide eyes and a heart-shaped face . . . and an expression that seemed almost hopeful. I'd done it in the days and weeks after my husband said he was leaving.

I didn't answer but drained the last of my coffee.

He paid me $301.50 for it.

Apparently that's the going rate for fine art these days.

Just as I was starting to wonder if I'd ever hear from Jean Pierre, he called to ask if I'd care to join him on a road trip to Vegas.

Las Vegas—Sin City? With a fabulous Frenchman? You *bet* I would. "When?" I asked, already mentally packing my bags, dropping my thirteen-year-old un-ceremoniously at the curb in front of her father's house. Being free, free . . .

"Now," he said, breezily.

"Now?" As in, *now?*

"You need a few meenut to get ready? Eet's OK. I can wait."

Minutes to get ready . . . that's a good one, ha ha. I could hardly be ready for a trip to the front porch in *minutes*. The clothes that my mind packed were already being tucked neatly back in their drawers.

It occurred to me as I said thanks-but-no-thanks to Jean Pierre—catching a glimpse of my daughter at the kitchen table, bent intently over a science project due the next day—that there's a whole other world out there.

It's filled with the type of people who don't think twice about going away last-minute. Who as a matter of habit drop everything and *do* the sort of things I was trying desperately to cram into forty days. Making up for forty years.

This other world is stranger than Vegas. It may as well be Mars.

Jeannie must have sensed my gaze on her because she lifted her head. "I can't get the paper to stick right," she scowled. There was a worry knot between her brows.

I recognized that worry knot.

I saw one like it in the mirror every morning.

"Why don't you set that aside?" I said. "I'm going to try roller blading. I'd love it if you'd join me."

Even when I promised to fall and look incredibly stupid, she insisted she couldn't. She had a ton to do.

Day 23: Today I am staying in the moment. My experiment in Zen. No thoughts of the past or of the future. No regrets. No worries. I was simply to let myself *be*.

As I made breakfast, I experienced the buttering of the toast, the pouring of the juice. Chewing. Swallowing. I stayed focused as I drove to work, participated in meetings. I allowed my feet to walk and my eyes to see. While I washed the dishes—concentrating on the suds and the movement of the rag around the plate—my mind never wandered from the task at hand.

Which was good, I suppose. My thoughts would have just been about how boring I'd let my day-to-day life become.

"You realize," my mom said, leaning against her car as we waited for Jeannie to get ready, "you have to stop letting that man walk all over you."

"That Man" had become her pet name for Frank since we'd split. *Has That Man picked up Jeannie yet? Do you think That Man would be so kind as to let us come to our own granddaughter's party?*

"That Man, unfortunately, is the father of my child." Although, I had to admit, this was bold even for him. He'd called saying it was his turn to have Jeannie and, since he was vacationing in Palm Springs, I was required—*required!*—to bring her to him. My mom, bless her heart, offered to do it. I'd had plans to check out that art event Bill had mentioned—I thought I'd use it as my opportunity to hand-deliver his painting.

"I just don't understand why he thinks he can make such ridiculous demands," my mom grumbled.

"Trust me, it's easier to let him think he's getting his way."

"He *is* getting his way! He has you driving for him,

and rearranging your schedule for him, and constantly apologizing for—"

I heard the bang of the front door and Jeannie ran up holding her overnight bag, "Hi, Grams!"

Eager to change the subject, I chirped, "Hey, you know what I'm going to do tomorrow for my forty days? I'm going to open the dictionary to a random page, pick the first unfamiliar word I see and learn it—expand my vocabulary by one!"

My mom tossed Jeannie's bag into the car. "Try to open it to the letter N," she said, her eyes fixed on me. "You could stand to learn the word 'no.'"

An hour later, Ellen and I waited in the lobby of an art studio in Venice for the first of our fifteen-minute sessions with the "therapists" we'd signed up for. "I wish we could see what's going on," I said, squinting as though that would help me see better through the solid doors into the other room.

The sign-in sheet had warned that this was not real therapy. It was for fun. It was "art." As it was explained to us, we should just make up a "problem" and our therapist would help cure us.

All I knew was that—if sharing your fake problems with an artist posing as a therapist qualified as "art"—I was grateful I'd wrapped the painting I'd left for Bill at the front desk. Suddenly it seemed so pedestrian. As much as I longed to be part of an art community, it was becoming clear that I'd never really be cool enough. (Like the time I'd brought a nice bottle of Chardonnay to a book club? When I got there everyone was sitting on the floor drinking whiskey. How do people keep up?)

Ellen and I agreed to have our first therapy session together. I'd also signed up for a "Dr. Cowboy," assuming that was Bill.

The doors burst open and a woman began calling names for the next appointments. "Donna and Ellen . . . for Madam Love!"

We followed her inside a large, dimly lit room where stationed about were a dozen or so "therapists." I spotted Bill, dressed in full cowboy regalia, and gave a little wave as I passed by. He tipped his hat.

"Is that the guy who bought your painting?" Ellen whispered. When I nodded, she said, "Hmm. Cute."

Madam Love conducted our session inside a tent pitched in the room's center. Before Ellen and I could tell her about the problem we'd concocted (we thought it'd be fun to be quarreling lesbians), the good madam let us know there would be no talking.

Only screaming.

Ellen without hesitation let loose a piercing wail, as if there was nothing in the world she'd rather be doing than scream therapy with a crazy madam in a tent in a room full of people.

I, alas, was not cured so easily.

Sure, I screamed—again and again, as instructed—but Madam Love was never fully satisfied that I really *meant* it.

It was nearing the end of the night by the time I had my therapy session with Bill.

"Howdy, Miss Donna. Have a seat." When I did, he added, "Now, what brings you in here today?"

I felt silly making up a problem with him. "I've already tackled the big issues," I said. "My klepto-mania . . . my fear of the word moist."

"Ah, that moist word trips a lot of people up."

"So . . ." I hesitated.

"No problems, huh?" He reached inside his desk drawer and pulled out a bottle of tequila and two shot glasses, pouring one for me, then one for himself. "How about, then, we just have a visit?"

"Interesting . . . is this how you treat all your patients?"

We clinked glasses and drank them down. He poured another round. "I've been dying for a drink all night. I don't know how real therapists handle this. Some of these folks need *serious* help. I've only got one person after you"—and he paused to down his second shot—"they'll have to take me in whatever state they find me."

"My friend Ellen is next. Trust me, you might need a third one of those."

So we just talked, and I was feeling loose from the tequila and relieved that it was finally a normal conversation. We talked about our jobs and our kids (he's got a son in college) and our ex's, and the new things I've tried in the past few weeks, and how I should try mountain climbing, and how he often goes and it's not a problem because they have these special ropes that accommodate his arm—"Or, as you so delicately pointed out," he said, "my arm and a *half.*"

I found myself blushing, grateful he was such a good sport. "I hope it's not tacky to ask," I ventured, "but how did it happen . . . losing your arm?"

"Boating accident. I was eighteen," he said simply.

"And, no, it's not tacky. I like the fact that you're not afraid to mention it."

"Do you ever feel it? I've read that—how people who lose an arm say that it still hurts or itches."

"Sometimes," he nodded. "They call that a ghost limb. Drives me crazy. I can look straight at myself and see it's not there, but I'd swear it is."

It was after Ellen joined us and the last session was the three of us, hanging out and drinking tequila, that it occurred to me.

The reason I was so messed up.

The reason I'd made so many changes in my life and yet couldn't seem to recognize that I was no longer that overweight girl, scared she's going to be made fun of, or left out, or left altogether.

I didn't suffer from low self-esteem.

I had ghost fat.

Day 30. The buzz of the alarm clock demanded that I get up.

And it could just piss off for all I cared. I rolled over and buried myself farther under the blankets. I couldn't do it. I couldn't face another day. In the final stretch of my forty days, I was so exhausted even my follicles ached.

The past week's activities, scrawled wearily in my journal:

> *Day trip to a mud bath*
> *Take a cooking class*
> *Slot car racing*
> *Swing dancing*

*Get a massage by a man—preferably one named
Sven*

I'd even gotten Jean Pierre to commit, at least for the
next night, but, tired as I was, I couldn't drum up enthusiasm.

The energy it was taking to decide on new things to
do each day, much less execute them, was cutting into
every aspect of my life. I was low on sleep, constantly
late for work, and winning no popularity awards with
my daughter.

Ah, yes, my daughter, who I could hear bellowing
outside my bedroom door. "Mooooom! I've got
praaaaactice. I need a riiiiiiide."

I tried to ignore her, but she barged in. "Get up."

*Hello? Who is the mother here, and who is the daugh-
ter?*

"I'm too tired."

"Oh wonderful," she snapped, "you're sick!"

"Your empathy is touching. And I'm not sick. I'm
simply not getting up."

She narrowed her eyes at me. "Ha! Yes you will, I
know you will, because you have to do one of your
new, *important* things." She nearly spat the word important.

It didn't offend me as much as one might think.
Fact was, for thirteen years—the entirety of her life—
the world had revolved around her. For the past thirty
days, it had shifted on its axis to accommodate me as
well. I gave her a bleary smile, my bright, beautiful
daughter, my stunning Recessive Jeannie who, like it
or not, was simply going to have to deal with it.

"Staying in bed for me is a special treat. I've decided to play hooky."

"But I need a ride!"

"Sweetie, just go down to the Kramers; you know you can catch a ride with them."

"But I want *you* to drive me!"

"Well," I sighed, and fluffed my pillow before sinking more deeply into it, "people in hell want ice water."

As I dressed for my date with Jean Pierre—strapping on the water bra like armor before battle—it occurred to me I was eventually going to have to come clean.

Eventually.

Maybe when he was drunk.

Or so overcome with lust that he wouldn't care one way or another.

And, who knew? Maybe he *wouldn't* care. Who's to say he wasn't interested in *me*? My rapier wit? My supreme intellect?

Sigh . . . or my bodacious ta tas.

It was later, when I was slow dancing with Jean Pierre—at Klub Kat, one of those cavernous clubs with a dance floor so dark, packed and offset by strobes that you're nearly blinded—that I realized the time was upon me.

"Ah, cherie," he said, pressed up against me, nuzzling along my ear. As we danced, his hand slid along my waist, then, slowly . . . upward . . . under my shirt.

I started to pull away, "Jean Pierre . . ."

"Relax," he said, tugging me back, "no one can see."

And no one could, really, so lost were we in the cloak of the bodies around us.

The hand found my bra, and rubbed slowly along the curve of my breast.

Far from aroused, I was stiff with terror—would he be able to tell? Apparently not, because as he ran his hands over the bra, he murmured, "You are so soft . . . but firm . . . so soft . . . but firm . . ."

He gave my breast a gentle squeeze—who am I kidding? The *bra* a squeeze—and then, growing more passionate, a firmer squeeze, rubbing me, caressing me. "I want to make love to you," he moaned, and as he said it, I could feel it—a trickle of wetness, running down my belly. Oh shit! I'd sprung a leak!

I yanked his hands from under my shirt. "Me, too," I said, breathlessly. "Just not tonight. I'm sorry, but I have to go."

And off I ran, leaving my prince charming behind on the dance floor.

When I walked into the house, deflated in more ways than one, Jeannie was on the couch with her best friend, Celia, watching a *Buffy* rerun.

"Hey, Mrs. D," Celia said excitedly, "Jeannie and I were just talking—she said she helped you put on one of those henna tattoos today. You know what'd be fun? You guys should get real tattoos! Matching ones!"

"Yeah!" Jeannie piped in.

"That'd be a sight," I said absently, and stole some popcorn from them before heading for my room. "Don't stay up all night, OK?"

"OK. Oh yeah, I almost forgot," Jeannie said.

"That guy who bought your painting called. He said to tell you he hung it up and it looks great."

I smiled. Bill rang just to tell me that? I found myself imagining it—his cool, intelligent eyes taking in the strokes of my painting—and it did something funny to my insides. "Did you tell him I'd call him back?"

"Nah," she said, turning back to the TV. "I said you were at your boyfriend's and you'd be gone all night."

"You said it like that? That I was at my boy-friend's?"

"That's what you said!" she shot back defensively. "That you were off on a date and you'd be out late!"

"That's fine, honey. Good night," and I went to bed, not knowing how to tell my daughter I'd rather she'd said that I was off on my meaningless fling.

Speaking of calls . . .

Frank phoned to say he'd prefer I didn't show up to Jeannie's gymnastics event the next night. He'd be there with his new girlfriend, and she didn't like the idea of his ex showing up. It would make her uncom-fortable.

I didn't have any fight in me. I was spent from the kickboxing, the driving range, riding my bike to work, and pulling out my old clarinet. Anyway, I said fine, *whatever*, there were other meets. I told myself that I could use the free evening for the big tête-à-tête with Jean Pierre.

But all the justifying in the world couldn't cover up the other voice in my head. The one saying my mother was right. The one saying that I needed to stop letting That Man walk all over me.

★   ★   ★

Day 37.

I had feared disappointment, perhaps even anger.

Hoped for happy acceptance.

More than anything, though, Jean Pierre appeared confused when I showed up on his doorstep for our date.

"Where are your . . . your *bosom?*" he asked. His hands made rounded shapes over his own chest, as if to indicate where the correct placement of breasts should occur, the proper elevation they should be achieving.

I stood proud. They stood proud. "This is me. This is how I really am."

"They're so leetle."

Shrug.

"OK," he sighed, and I could see him peeking around me, checking if I might be hiding them anywhere. "Eet's not so bad," and he perked up. "What the hell," he said benevolently, "we can still fuck . . . no?"

He started unbuttoning his shirt as he leaned against the door, propping it wider so I could come in.

And, then, just like that, I learned it.

It was easier than I thought.

Hard to believe it took me all these years.

"No," I said, my voice soft but firm. *"No,* we cannot still fuck."

To keep the evening from being a total waste, I stopped by Jeannie's gymnastics meet—sat right next to Frank and his new girlfriend, Lisa. Frank glared, whereas she didn't seem to mind my being there. In fact, she was nice. A bit young, a tad thin, but nice.

As the evening wore on—and Lisa and I did that chick thing where we felt compelled to compliment each other's shirts and hair and shoes—I started to suspect that Frank was trying to keep us apart not by her directive, but more in fear I'd tell her how he used to be fat.

Who knows, I thought. Maybe I will. I glanced down the bench and gave Frank a smile so kind, so knowing, that he immediately paled and offered to get up and grab us some sodas.

I said, thank you, a Diet Coke would be lovely.

Perhaps I'd grown more in touch with my inner bitch than I'd realized.

And so, with days left to go, it was time.

I'd put it off long enough. Forty years, in fact, give or take.

The only full-length mirror in the house was in Jeannie's room. I waited until she was downstairs, let myself into her room, then secured the lock.

Standing before the mirror, I let my robe fall to the ground.

And just looked.

Of course, I'd seen myself naked before. A million times. This time, however, I was determined to really see myself. Not up-close scrutiny—the kind you do, say, in brightly lit bathrooms, where suddenly every flaw leaps to attention. Just eyes open. Looking.

What I saw surprised me.

After all, I'd made so many changes recently. I'd

tried new things, spoken up more, let myself make mistakes. I had to laugh, thinking how important it had seemed to have Jean Pierre want me, never stopping to wonder whether I really wanted *him*. Surely, I thought, the wisdom and experience of the past thirty-eight days would be reflected in the mirror.

Yet standing before me was a woman who could best be described as curvy along the hips, with wide eyes and a heart-shaped face . . . and an expression that seemed almost hopeful.

In other words,

And I'll be darned,

Me.

Day 39: For the first time in my life I called a boy for a date.

He said yes.

Well, and here it is. Finally. *Day 40.* I made it! Happy birthday to me.

I don't look any older and, remarkably, I feel younger than I have in ages. Go figure.

Jeannie brought me breakfast in bed this morning—lemon muffins, my favorite. Then Frank actually showed up with a gift. A shirt. His girlfriend picked it out.

Maybe I'll wear it tomorrow, when my cowboy and I go to the movies.

Anyway, you'll never guess the special thing I'm doing today.

Nothing.

Absolutely nothing.

I can't wait.

JILL SMOLINSKI has written for women's beauty, health and fitness magazines, and is the author of the best-selling romantic comedy *Flip-Flopped*. She lives in Los Angeles with her son, Daniel.

The Uncertainty Principle

LYNDA CURNYN

*I*t's the computer I notice first. Not the computer really, but the sight of my words disappearing into a pinprick of light on the screen.

It isn't world annihilation I think of first. And it's usually world annihilation I think of first. At least, ever since I'd watched those twin juts in the Manhattan skyline disappear into a heap of dust that beat at my windows for weeks. Nowadays anything from a discarded suitcase on a subway platform to a pungent chemical smell drifting through the window from the street below could signify the beginning of the end.

Today it just seems like the beginning of my end. Tomorrow at three o'clock, I'm supposed to send an email to the copy director at Two Rivers clothing company containing the text to go along with their spring catalog. A full forty-eight pages of fashion. Well, fashion for the kind of people who don't seem to do anything else but swim in lakes, lounge before roaring fires and hike mountains in rugged yet handsome shoes. People who don't have to deal with subway platforms containing suspicious artifacts or pungent chemical smells drifting through their windows. People who only exist within the pages of the Two Rivers catalog.

I can't even tell you where the Two Rivers are. I can't tell you anything right now because my computer is down.

My mind is already conjuring up excuses. "I was on the final layout when the computer just *crashed*," I imagine myself telling the copy director, injecting the last word with the kind of surprised horror I'm feeling right now. "Didn't you save to disk?" she'll ask next. Did I save to disk? I always save to disk. Well, usually before I shut down. But I hadn't shut down. I'd been shut down on.

I'm undone. Destroyed. She'll never believe me. There's no excuse large enough to cover the fact that I received this assignment two months ago and really only started it today. I wasn't procrastinating. Not exactly. I had shit going on, you know? Two months ago my roommate decided to move to Oregon with her boyfriend. He was going to work for a software company; she was going to make homemade soaps. I found it somewhat hilarious that a woman who couldn't bring herself to wield a bottle of antiseptic in our bathroom was now devoting her life to making soap. Even joked about it to Jess when I told him, until I realized the fact that I was now the sole lease-holder on a West Village two-bedroom was not exactly funny. "You don't need her," Jess said and for a brief shining moment, I believed him. I had, after all, just landed my first major freelance gig since quitting my day job in advertising to pursue what everyone from my boss to my best friend Shauna told me was my real job, writing. And since I'd gotten the Two Rivers gig not two days after her announcement, I took it as some sort of sign. I was ready to move to the next level. The next roommate. And the next logical room-mate was Jess. We'd been together two years. I always imagined we would be together for forty more. In fact, I was a sledgehammer's throw away from converting my cozy two-bedroom back to one when I broached the subject with Jess while lying in bed one night. We had laughed, giddy with the glittering possibility of it. But when his eyes met mine in the dark, when he saw that I was no longer laughing, the smile faded from his eyes.

"I don't know, Trace," he said. "Things are good be-tween us the way they are." But from that moment on, they were never good again. I could no longer share my dreams with him, now that he no longer seemed a real part of them. At least he'd helped me move into this rent-stabilized studio I'd found through the mira-cle of a friend-of-a-friend-of-a-friend whose grand-mother had died.

I suppose I should have been grateful. Though I haven't spoken to him since. "Let's take some time," he said, in answer to the sad silence I fell into the morn-ing after he moved me in and I was faced with all that hadn't been said, all that needed to be done. That was two weeks ago.

Two weeks of staring at this computer screen, knowing I should start again, yet somehow not knowing where to begin.

I glare at my surge protector. Wasn't this supposed to protect me from my poorly wired building? Where was the justice? More importantly, where was the steady little red indicator light designed to assure me that no surge, electrical or otherwise, would keep me from meeting my deadline?

I check the plugs. I flip the reset switch. Nothing.

A fuse. I have blown a fuse. Yes, I'm living in a building with fuses, though from the number of times I've blown them in the short time I've been living here, I suspect it's a malnourished hamster on a wheel that's supplying the power to all twelve apartments. Now I'll have to call the super. This, however, will require me to put on a bra. I can't let a strange man in my apartment while I'm bra-less and though I'm just barely on a first-name basis with my super, I'm familiar enough to know that he is strange. I also know that strange man will likely take no less than two hours to return my cry for help (this having nothing to do with the twelve apartments under his supervision and everything to do with his taste for loitering in the basement doing God knows what). I pick up the phone.

Dead.

Dead?

I've blown more than a fuse. Maybe even two, though I can't imagine that an apartment this size requires more than one. I head for the kitchen, which is really a closet that has been turned into a kitchen, and judging from the amount of meals I've cooked in it thus far, I would rather have the extra storage.

I flick the switch. Nothing. I turn on a gas jet. Nothing. Though I'm not technically sure whether the gas jets have ever worked, I sense that something's happening and it's not good.

I pick up my cell phone, locate Super Hank in the phone book, wondering again why I've named this latest entry this way since my super is the only Hank I know and he's far from, well, super. I wonder at the silence, pull the phone from my ear to look at the screen. Dialing. Redialing. Connecting . . .

Signal faded! Call lost!

OK, so maybe the world is coming to an end. Either that or I'm paying too much for this cell phone service. Which is probably likely, since I seem to be paying too much for everything these days now that I have a limited amount of funds to pay for everything. Which only makes the thought of world annihilation comforting. If the world is coming to an end, I won't have to hand my copy in by 3 p.m. tomorrow. Won't have to face the fact that quitting my job last year to become a freelance writer was Mistake #374 of my life.

"Well, how could I get my text in? The *world* was coming to an end for chrissakes!" I'll explain to the copy director.

Unless, of course, I'm about to be killed by a serial killer. Which is entirely possible. The power goes out. The phone goes dead. The guileless (read: stupid) protagonist (usually female and usually a virgin) sets out alone for the basement in search of answers, only to come face-to-face with the grinning instrument of her demise. Which, in the end, will likely turn out to be the basement-lurking super.

Fortunately I'm not a virgin, nor the kind of woman who goes creeping down dark staircases in search of answers. In fact, I'm considering crawling under the covers and pretending to sleep (so as not to bear witness to my own demise) when I hear a pounding on the door.

Do serial killers knock?

I jump from the chair and, a bit like a stupid virgin, head for the door. Peep through the peephole (I'm not that stupid). The super. And right now, with his face misshapen by the little glass I'm viewing him through, he looks like a serial killer.

"Yes?"

"Power is out."

"In the whole building?" I ask.

"All of Manhattan!" he declares, in a tone that smacks of the satisfaction of a man who knows that he can't, at least, be blamed for this.

All of Manhattan?

"You need anything?" he asks.

The super-cum-serial killer cares. I go a little warm inside. Not that I open the door. "I'm OK," I say, causing him to move on.

Am I OK?

I glance about my apartment. Candles. I have candles everywhere. In fact, they're one of the few things I've unpacked since I moved into this place. That, and the chandelier, which is the only decor I've given in to thus far. From the moment the super (who didn't look so strange at the time) showed me this place, I could picture the chandelier hanging from the center of the room. Jess had helped me hang it up. His last act of love (or was it guilt?). Everything else I own (aside from some flatware, a dish, a few glasses and some wardrobe) is still in boxes stacked by the window. Including the flashlights.

It won't last that long. It can't last that long. This is, after all, New York City. I have a deadline of 3 p.m. tomorrow. Less than twenty-four hours away. I glance toward the window, where the late-afternoon sun is streaming in. I still have daylight. And if I still have daylight . . . I still have work.

My eye falls on my darkened computer screen. How can I work?

Well, I could work, seeing as I wasted a full twenty minutes of "work time" this morning by printing out twenty-four of the jpegs I was to add text to, believing that seeing the photos on paper would somehow inspire me to get started.

I sit down at my desk and pick up the photo of a couple sitting on a dock at sunset that I'd been working on when my words had disappeared into the void. "Create the fantasy," the copy director had urged. A fantasy designed to convince the unwitting consumer that she, too, could have this kind of hazy, sunlit life with purchase.

I study the sweater on the woman and though this printout is black and white, I know from staring half the day at the jpeg version on my screen it is really a soft yellow. "Chamomile" the color was described as, I think. The man wore a sweater in "lettuce." Lettuce and chamomile? I mean, really, is it any wonder I'm having trouble with this? What kind of people are these? I study their faces, which are turned to one another, their smiles soft, eyes clinging, and I know I'm no closer to coming up with the three little words required for this photo than I was before the power went out. Three little words. That's all I need. All I'm allowed, really, according to the rules of design. "For balance," the copy director said.

Three little words I spent a full forty-five minutes trying to conjure up until, in a fit of frustration (or procrastination), I zipped the jpeg off in an email to Shauna with the words: This is happiness?

Which only caused an avalanche of email from Shauna, who added her own phrases in a thought bubble above the woman's head. Though unlike me, she didn't have an obligatory fantasy, or word count, for that matter.

"Was he this cute before the tequila?"

"If I knew things were going to go this way, I wouldn't have had the brussels sprouts for lunch."

Shauna liked to engage in this kind of daily repartee, though it was usually she who was sending the jpegs. She was a photographer by vocation; by day she maintained the archives for *Natural World* magazine. Every morning when I opened up my box, I was bound to find some short-snouted weevil or spindly arachnid, usually accompanied by some attribution of Shauna's making. "Has he been in your underwear drawer?" This morning I logged on to a white-faced monkey clinging to a limb, teeth bared above the words, "Why don't you come up and see me some time?" When Jess had called our relationship to an end (or a standstill, I wasn't quite clear on this point), you should have seen what creatures she reduced him to.

I stare at my dark screen. Where is Jess during all this?

Home. He's home. At least, I believe he's home. Not only because, like me, he works from home—he designs web pages for a living—but because, not five minutes before my screen went black, I clicked on to my instant message service and saw his screen name on my buddy list, indicating he was online and available to receive messages. Not that we message one another anymore. It was as if some silent agreement not to communicate in any way, shape or form had sprung up between us. Yet neither one of us has removed the other from our buddy lists. I'm not sure why he hasn't. I hope it was because he found my comings and go-ings just as soothing as I did his. Somehow the fact that we could message one another meant we were there for one another on some level, that there was something still connecting us.

Now there's nothing connecting us.

I grab my cell phone, not to call Jess. I can't call Jess. And not just because my cell phone signal is dead. I dial Shauna instead.

Dialing. Redialing. Connecting . . .

Signal faded! Call lost!

Where is Shauna?

Voices rise up from the street and I head for the window, negotiating the line of boxes beneath and blinking against the slant of sun coming through. I look down, watch as buildings open and bodies pour out, some walking with the steady stride of a destination in mind, others looking a bit bewildered. On the corner, someone has thrown open a car door, radio blaring onto the street. A small crowd has stopped before it to listen.

I listen, too, trying to make some sense out of the strident monotone. The only words I can make out of the crackle are "surge," "outtage," "coast."

Coast?

Maybe the world is coming to an end. My part of the world anyway. I've never lived anywhere but the east coast.

I feel a sudden need for information.

I sit down at my desk, mostly because it's the only place to sit in my apartment, other than the bed, which floats at one end of the room, looking a little lost among the boxes. I turn to my screen, the usual source for information, and feel the first spear of despair. I can't even email Shauna. Then it occurs to me that Shauna isn't likely to be on the other end of this terminal, fruitlessly waiting for information. Shauna is more likely one of those bodies currently pouring out onto the street, heading home, which is only three blocks from me, on Perry. Work is about forty blocks north. She's probably on the subway by now.

Is the subway even running? I grab my cell, head to the window again, but since I can't see the subway station from my corner, this yields nothing. I hit the speed dial for Shauna and stare down at the street. There are more people now, walking, walking, walking. I can only assume the subway isn't running. An image fills my mind of Shauna, walking home. In heels. No, that wouldn't be Shauna, that would be me. I'd gone to work on 9/11, just moments after watching the second plane hit. It seemed like the thing to do. Of course, it wasn't. I walked home in heels, wondering if I would die of blistered feet or biological attack. Shauna had spent the day at St. Vincent's giving blood. That's the kind of person Shauna is. Reliable. Informed. Prepared. She's also the kind of person who probably keeps a pair of sneakers at the office.

Dialing. Redialing. Connecting . . .

Signal faded! Call lost!

What is going on out there? I peer out the window again, as if I can divine what's happening digitally by simply looking at the sky. But the sky is just as bright and blue as it has been all day. As it had been that day two years ago. I shudder. Maybe this is some act of terrorism. I look down at the crowds on the street, suddenly aware that some faceless, nameless faction could have rigged this blackout, knowing everyone would rush out onto the streets as a shower of some life-threatening gas or germ, odorless, debilitating, fell upon them.

I think of Shauna pounding the pavement in her sneakers. Shauna, probably leading a crowd of co-workers through the streets to safety. Someone should warn her (because unlike me, Shauna isn't prone to worry about the unseen elements that could kill us). I pick up the phone, dial her again.

Dialing. Redialing. Connecting . . .

Signal faded! Call lost!

I feel a fresh ping of anxiety.

"You need to calm down," Shauna would say. Which always unravels me, of course.

I move away from the window, just in case. Feel an almost painful urge to talk to Jess, who'll laugh at my anxiety, then tell me everything is OK. I look at my cell phone. I have a signal, though I know this is no guarantee of anything. Which is probably what gives me the courage to dial Jess's number. I feel strange as I do, as if I'm crossing some line neither one of us has even dared to toe in the weeks since we ended. But it seems even stranger not to talk to him now. I mean, there have to be extenuating circumstances. I remember how we sat immobilized by the sight of the towers, which tumbled down on my television screen all day long. Though Jess railed against the way the media kept replaying it, neither one of us could seem to tear our eyes away. By the time we had duct taped our windows against the fumes, we were numb.

Dialing. Redialing. Connecting . . .

Signal faded. Call lost!

I'm cut off.

Profoundly cut off.

How long can this last?

My gaze falls on the radio, resting on top of the box I'd yanked it out of. I need batteries.

I look at the stack of boxes, lining one wall. I know there are batteries in there. Somewhere. Probably with the flashlights.

It's easier to go out and buy new I realize, jumping up to look out the window again. A crowd is forming outside the bodega across the street. People are already lining up for supplies.

Should I be lining up for supplies? I do a mental inventory of my refrigerator. I don't have to open it to know that it contains half a container of cottage cheese (from a dieting attempt already abandoned); two beers left over from the six-pack Shauna brought over the day I moved in and a jar of salsa, salsa being one of the few condiments I keep.

I have canned goods. A shelf full of tuna, peas, pineapple slices and a can of coffee I picked up while traveling through Guatemala last summer with Jess. We lugged home three cans of the stuff and, within weeks, Jess gave up coffee. I should have taken it as a sign. Like the way he took up jogging and going to the gym just as our relationship started falling apart. I remember feeling resentful of his sudden pursuit of a healthy lifestyle. Just who was he staying healthy for? Soon even the sight of his running shoes, abandoned on the bedroom floor, filled me with sorrow. I didn't know this man, this jogger, didn't understand his sudden disdain for all carbohydrates, his quest for a good piece of pavement beneath his feet.

I, on the other hand, had taken up smoking.

Cigarettes . . .

I open my desk drawer and feel a shot of reassurance at the sight of two unopened packs. I purchased four packs on my credit card just a week before, either because I had no cash and was too embarrassed to charge only one, or because I'd finally given in to the notion that I wasn't quitting, at least not this week.

I open one of the packs and, after locating a fresh

book of matches, I light up, drag deep. At least I'm prepared in this regard. Prepared to die anyway.

I puff silently for a few moments and realize I don't want to go outside. And not just because this will require putting on a bra. I stare at my dark screen, knowing I need something but that something won't be found in the bodega downstairs. I need to talk to Shauna. If only to know if she's all right. And Jess . . .

Dialing. Redialing. Connecting . . .

Signal faded. Call lost!

Cut off.

I light another cigarette, though I know I should do something else. Like get dressed. Get batteries.

I finally hit the closet and give in to undergarments. And clothes, though I'll admit there have been some days when, out of sheer laziness, I've headed to the bodega in my sweatpants. But today there's a veritable party on the streets and maybe it's the thought of encountering people, so many people at one time, that has me foregoing my usual uniform of sweats and flip-flops and reaching for my jeans and a baby blue tank top. You never know, after all, who you might run into in the midst of a blackout. A vision forms of me, the seductress in baby blue, reaching for the last package of Duracells at the same time as some dark-eyed stranger, who looks oddly like Jess though I've allegedly never seen this man before. Shy smiles are exchanged; a flirting banter ensues about wrestling each other for the batteries, until we decide to pool our resources and spend the night guiding each other along dark streets and up dark stairwells. Years later we'll laugh as we relay the story to our grandkids.

But as I slide my jeans over my body, I feel whole-heartedly unready for this encounter, my body shapeless and soft, curved to fit a relationship—a life—I no longer have.

I put on lipstick anyway.

After I step into my flip-flops I remember something else.

I have no money. Well, yes, I have money. I have a mountain of money. A small mountain but more of a mountain than I've ever had. A year's salary stored up. A pocket of time I've bought myself to do something, something more than just conjuring up bits of words to sell sweaters and monogamy. But since I can't even conjure up bits of words, you can imagine how much progress I've made otherwise.

Now, I have no access to that mountain. I drew out forty dollars two days ago, but this was spent on the take-out meals I resorted to, believing that by holing myself up in my apartment, I would make my deadline. You know, the deadline I'm about to miss.

I dig through my wallet and pull out my remaining three dollars.

I realize I can stay in the house. There's no need to emerge, despite the fact that the rest of the world seems to have deemed this necessary. I have batteries. I have flashlights. Somewhere. I won't starve, though depending on how long this lasts, I may die of scurvy due to the lack of vitamin C–drenched items in my canned-food collection.

I look at my dark screen and think of Jess.

I need to go out. If only because I can't bear the thought of staying in. Without him.

I grab my keys, stuff my meager funds in my jeans, and open the front door.

To darkness. I'm amazed at how complete the darkness is. And just as I'm contemplating clinging to the banister and making my way down the three flights to the street, a vision of myself, broken-necked and twitching at the bottom of the first flight, fills my mind.

I close the door, turn to the boxes stacked by the window and realize I'll be forced to do what I've been avoiding doing ever since I moved into this space. Unpack.

At least until I find the batteries and the flashlights.

I stare at the line of boxes by the window, the weight of this task making me understand why I haven't, during these last two weeks, pulled out more than the bare necessities. And the chandelier.

It was my grandmother's chandelier and when she died last fall, I rescued it from the garage sale oblivion my mother was ready to relegate it to. I didn't hang it up in my last apartment, probably because I always sensed that I would move on. I mean, I knew I wouldn't live with a roommate forever and this chandelier is one of those golden-winged, crystal-hung clusters that takes root in your ceiling. I wanted the place where I hung it to be the place I would be for a long, long time. "You should just put it up," Jess insisted after he lugged it up three flights. "What are you waiting for?"

I was waiting for him, I realized, as I watched him drill the holes, knowing with every anchor he stuck in the ceiling that I was waiting for nothing.

My cell phone is ringing. My cell phone is ringing!

I make a mad scramble for the phone, hit the Talk button. "Hello?"

"Tracy!"

My mother. I wonder briefly why I can't get through to anyone, why no one (apparently) can get through to me, yet my mother has persevered. It's the first thing I ask her (in a nicer way).

"Your father and I keep a regular phone in the garage for emergencies. You can't get anything out of those computerized doo-hickeys when the power is out. Don't you keep a regular phone around for emergencies?"

This question has a tinge of accusation, as if the fact that I don't keep a regular phone on hand explains why I'm still single at thirty-one, still shuffling my things from one rented space to another, despite the fact that my (younger) sister has a husband, a house on Long Island and a garage-full of spare telephones, batteries and flashlights.

"Are you OK?" she asks.

Her question does me in. I'm not OK. Despite the fact that I've spent the last two weeks in this apartment alone, I've never felt more lonely than I do right now. But I don't tell her this. This isn't the answer she's looking for. In fact, she has already moved on and is asking about the temperature in my apartment.

"It's hot," I say and I realize I'm sweating. Which I've been doing for the last two weeks, since the air conditioner is still in one of these boxes. Not that I tell her that either.

"Well, at least you're home," she says. "Kinda makes

you glad you're not going to the office anymore, huh?"

I have no answer for this. "Are the subways running?"

My mother gleans from this question that I have no answers for anything and proceeds to tell me about some power surge in some town I've never heard of. "Do you have candles?" she asks.

I have candles, I tell her. Now she's going into a story about the blackout of 1977, how my sister was conceived during it. I'm thinking about the candles, how I took them out to add a little mood lighting to the take-out dinner Jess and I shared on that first night in this new place. I remember how we made love on the mattress on the floor afterward. Had I known it would be the last time, I would have at least put the sheets on first. Why hasn't he come by? Would he come by tonight? He wouldn't. He would see it as regression. We're taking a break and during a break people don't light candles and make love, even in a blackout. I feel an urge to cry, knowing this is more than a break. Knowing that he could be making love to someone new right now. Making love with someone new in the midst of a blackout would feel like some fortuitous, romantic beginning. I feel a sob rolling up, certain he's one orgasm away from what he thinks is true love, but is really just some crazy case of lust transformed by a crisis situation.

I light a cigarette.

"Are you smoking?" my mother asks.

I hold back the breath of smoke I was about to let loose, but it's too late.

"Tracy, you know how bad that is for you. I was

just watching a special report on the news the other night. Do you know that cigarette smoking can damage your fertility?"

My mother is a font of information like this. And now that I've been assured that I will never marry and never bear children, I decide to hang up. "I have to go. I need to get batteries . . ."

"You have no batteries? Oh, Tracy . . ." She sighs and the sound is filled with all the regret of a woman who wonders where she went wrong with my upbringing.

I assure her I have batteries; they just need to be found. This is enough information to allow her to hang up, apparently assured that I'll at least get through the next few hours, if not the next forty years.

I look at the line of boxes, a jumbled history of the last thirty-one years.

I don't know where to begin, because although I've labeled the boxes, the contents are as murky as the words I've scrawled on them.

I reach for the first, dubbed "living." I can only assume this means "living room" though what I have technically, or what I'll have once I unpack the rest of these boxes, is a living space; that is, the space between where I work at the desk, and where I sleep. I realize that batteries and flashlights are just as likely to be in here as they are in the box labeled "kitchen." Flashlights and batteries have had no real place in my life up until now; they're like some floating artifact that someone told me I would need someday though I can't remember who and I can't remember why. I'm confronted with a mass of newspaper, which I've used to pack and I wonder if while packing, I'd deemed the flashlights and batteries precious enough to wrap in paper. Since I have no idea, I begin to unwrap. A crystal doorknob falls into my hand. It's one of seven I've culled from antique shops I liked to hunt through, usually during Saturday afternoon strolls with Jess, or Shauna. Seven crystal doorknobs I always imagined on the doors of some home I would one day live in; a home that never seems to be the one I am currently living in. I was collecting them, knowing that one day I would want a home with crystal doorknobs and not knowing if I would have the money to buy them all at once (they were expensive, after all). I look around my apartment, study the crown moldings, the moldings that convinced me that this was the place for the chandelier and realize that these knobs would look lovely in this apartment if this apartment were a home where I could see myself living for the next forty years. But it's too small to live in for the next forty years. Unless, of course, I'm planning on living alone for the next forty years. I gaze up at the chandelier and see that it's already growing dusty, that it's already taking root, that I'm already growing older in this place I'm not planning to live in for the rest of my life.

I stare at the knob a moment before I begin to shine it against the shirt I'm wearing, leaving a black smudge on the baby blue tank that I was going to seduce the boy in the bodega with, then get up and place the knob on the windowsill, watching it sparkle in the fading light.

I head for the desk and the cigarettes, light one up, imagining my ovaries shriveling in my body as I do, my eye falling on the photo of the couple on the dock.

A memory fills me of Jess, his body seeking mine in the darkness, curling around me. We were so good together. Now that we're apart, I don't know what we are.

A sound pierces the stillness. Startled, I think of alarms, body lifts, calls to action. Then I realize it's my cell phone, telling me I have a message.

A message? The phone hasn't even rung.

I pick it up, hit voicemail.

Dialing. Redialing. Connecting . . .

Signal faded! Call lost!

Who was it?

Jess? I want to think it's Jess, but I feel certain that it isn't. Jess wouldn't see this blackout as some crisis worthy of a phone call. I know Jess. Know him well enough to realize that despite my earlier worries, he's not making love with someone else, not seeing this as some romantic happenstance transformed into love in the fading light. Know that he's likely lying alone on his bed, or his couch, likely reading one of those philosophers he loves so much. Philosophy is what he studied in college. Web design is what a philosophy major does when he realizes theories of being won't pay the rent. Now that there's no computer to stare at, no baseball game to amuse him, no girlfriend to drag him to an antique market, he has probably returned to what he once was. Before me.

I also know Shauna well enough to realize it's likely her message on my voicemail. Telling me she's home. Or telling me she's somewhere. Somewhere safe.

OK, I need to get out of this apartment. But between me and the outdoors is a set of batteries, buried deep in one of these boxes.

I sigh, drop my head back and stare up at the chandelier dangling in the center of the room, a glittering fossil.

Then I remember I have neighbors. Neighbors I've never met. Well, only one on this floor. Mrs. Meyerson, who is eighty-six and living on social security, but might have a flashlight.

I open the door again and am startled once again by how dark the hall is. I wait for my eyes to adjust, then step out, edging my way toward her door, using the banister as my guide. I can't decide which is worse. The darkness or the silence. I wonder if Mrs. Meyerson is even home, then remember she's always home. She has no place else to go.

Once outside her door, I feel embarrassed. Here I am coming to ask an eighty-six-year-old woman for help when I should be the one offering help. Shauna would have thought of Mrs. Meyerson, alone in the dark. Alone and in need of supplies. I'm an awful, awful human being. An awful human being whose ovaries are shriveling in her body, not from nicotine, but because some higher being understands that she's not capable of caring for children, not capable of caring for anyone, not even herself.

I knock anyway, either because I've resolved to be a better person or because my ovaries can still be saved or because I still need a flashlight and I have nowhere else to turn.

A woman answers almost immediately and I'm shocked at Mrs. Meyerson's sudden spryness until I realize it's not Mrs. Meyerson, but the aide who visits Mrs. Meyerson every day, her coffee-colored skin bathed in perspiration, her eyes expectant.

"Hi," I venture forth. "I just came by to see if you . . . if you need anything."

She smiles at me, apparently unaware of my shriveling ovaries. "No, we're fine."

"OK, 'cause I'm going down." I don't say this with much conviction, considering I'm standing in a pool of darkness.

Fortunately she catches on quick. "You need a flashlight."

"Yes. I mean, if you have one."

"Of course," she says, disappearing into the apartment and returning with one.

"Don't you need it?" I ask.

"No, no," she says, shaking her head. "We have another one. Besides, in a little while I'll be putting Mrs. Meyerson in to sleep."

Sleep. This sounds like a good idea. The minute she closes the door, I realize it's the best idea I've heard all day. It is, in fact, the only idea I've heard all day. And seeing as I no longer have a need for information (thanks to my mother) and light (thanks to Mrs. Meyerson), I return to my apartment, stack the boxes against the little light that remains and lie down on the bed, placing Mrs. Meyerson's flashlight on the floor beside me.

But I don't sleep. I can't sleep. Instead, I stare at the chandelier looming above my head, and think of Jess. I remember lying with him in this apartment, after the chandelier had been hung and the bed assembled, after we had shared a carton of takeout and a lovemaking session that caused all those questions I could no longer hold in to bubble to the surface. "Why can't you just let it be?" he said. "Let us be?"

"What is the good in that?" I replied.

"What's the good in analyzing everything?" he countered. "The more we talk about the relationship, the worse things get." Then, when he saw he couldn't reach me on this level, he moved to the subatomic one. "It's like Heisenberg's uncertainty principle. You can't observe the position of an electron, without altering its momentum. In a similar way, the more you try to figure out where we are, the more you alter who we are."

And while he was marveling over the brilliance of his metaphor, I was wondering how I always managed to fall in love with men who fell in love with metaphors.

Maybe it was me. Maybe I listened too much to words and disregarded facts. When he first said, "I love you," I thought, *This is it.* But then, Jess also said the towers would never collapse. I believed him then, too.

Sleep. I need to sleep. But I don't sleep. I'm thinking about the fact that the world isn't ending; this is just some human error, some bit of frailty in the system that will only temporarily keep me from what I must do. I'll still have to wake up tomorrow, will still have to write my copy, will still have to call my super the next time the fuse goes out, will still have to unpack my boxes, will still have to quit smoking, will still have to call my mother and assure her I'm OK, will still unravel every time Shauna tells me to calm down, will still have to believe "this is it" the next time someone says "I love you."

God, I don't want to hear it again. I don't want to live it again.

That thought sends me back to the desk, where I light a cigarette, and begin to work.

Not on the couple. I can't suffer any more defeat. Instead, I pick up a photo of a boot, a wellie they call it, knee-high and rubber with soles thick enough to slog through a lake. And though I've never slogged through a lake, a word for this boot comes as easily as the smoke rolling down my throat: *Indestructible*.

I feel suddenly fragile in the face of this . . . boot. I stub out the cigarette and notice the plant on the corner of my desk, the plant I had moved with me, the plant I'd all but forgotten, is nearly dead. Which seems like a perfectly good reason to abandon my work again. So I get up, water my plant and while I am at it, I light every candle in the room. And maybe because the sight is so pretty, or maybe because I know I'll never finish my work today, I decide to return to bed.

As I watch the shadows move along the wall, I think of Shauna, who I'm sure has opted for a bar instead of home, who's likely laughing among strangers and making the kind of friends she'll have for years. I think of Jess and for a moment I feel certain he's in the same place that I am, lying in the dark. I'm bewildered that we're not together on this night. A moment in history I am participating in alone.

I blow out a breath and with it every anxiety, every doubt I have burdened myself with over the past few hours.

I think: I want to be the girl who knows where the batteries are kept. Who remembers to check on the neighbors and water the plants.

Then I remember that I am the girl who knows not to fall asleep to burning candles and I get up and blow out every one.

I lie down again, remember Jess, curling against me in the night.

I think: I want to be the one whose body you seek out in the darkness.

It's dark when I awake, disoriented. I'm not even sure what has pulled me from sleep until I hear my name being shouted.

"Spence!"

A memory cuts through of being on the softball field when I was twelve. Because the only people who ever called me Spence—short for Spencer, my last name—were the girls on my junior high school softball team. And Shauna.

I sit up, taking in the shape of the desk, the boxes, and remember I'm home. Remember I'm alone.

"Spence!"

I lean over to the window, look down and realize Shauna is, in fact, calling up to me from the street.

"What are you doing? Come down!" she insists. Though I can't see her face, I know her expression is incredulous, judging by the ring of disbelief in her tone. She probably doesn't understand how I could be in on such a night.

Suddenly I don't understand how I could be in on such a night. I grab Mrs. Meyerson's flashlight, raking fingers through my hair and contemplating lipstick until I remember no one can see me anyway. Still, because it seems strange to descend onto the street without some sort of preparation, I brush my teeth.

"What have you been doing?" Shauna asks when I finally make my way down.

"Sleeping."

"How can you sleep on a night like this?"

How could I? I wonder now, watching the crowds move along the streets, feeling the restless tremble of anticipation in the air.

"We haven't had a blackout in New York City in twenty-six years!" she says, as if this is something worth celebrating.

And maybe it's the sight of her, jean clad, flashlight wielding, resilient in the dark, that makes the weight of every lonely moment I've spent begin to dissipate.

"The lights are on in New Jersey," she says. Then, lured by the prospect of such a spectacle amid all this darkness, we head west, toward the river.

I want to make the argument that the riverfront is dangerous and probably desolate on a night like this. But the words die in my mouth at the sight of Shauna striding along, snapping pictures with the digital camera she carries everywhere.

Once we're at the river I'm surprised to see there are people everywhere. Then I remember this is New York City; of course there are people everywhere. And light, I realize, amazed at the sight of New Jersey shining at us across the Hudson.

"You see?" Shauna says, as if she had lit up the waterfront herself.

When we come across two abandoned chairs, I decide not to ask myself why no one else has claimed them as we drag them up to the rail and sit down, watching the lights play over the river.

"Isn't it beautiful?" Shauna says, leaning forward to snap a picture. She sits back and shows me the screen, which is filled with an image of New Jersey like I've never seen it before. Sparkling. Statuesque. Durable. "The promised land," she says. Then she laughs. "And New Jersey, of all places. Who would have thought?"

"Who would have thought," I say and I almost laugh myself.

As I study the glowing skyline, Shauna tells me about her night, a story I'll hear for years to come. How she climbed down the twenty-three flights from her office to the street, how she met a guy on the seventeenth. "Check him out," she says, leaning close and flipping through the images on her camera until she comes across one of a tall, lanky guy standing next to her at a bar on 14th Street, smiling against a candle-strewn background. She will tell me his name is Bill or Bob or Brad and in the years to come, neither of us will remember which is right.

"He's adorable," I say hopefully. "Did you get his number?"

She shrugs. "He knows where I work." This is the kind of person Shauna is, too. Eschewing something as mundane as exchanged phone numbers in the hope of the next romantic gesture. If she does believe that love begun in crisis can bloom into something more, she'll never let you know it.

"Jess and I are over," I say. The words feel odd in my mouth.

I see her looking at me in the darkness, know that she knows this just as well as I've known it for weeks, though she graciously does not remark on this fact.

Instead, she picks up her digital camera, takes a picture of me, then hands me the camera.

I study the image there, myself a minute younger, my mouth open as if I'm about to say something and though I don't remember what it was, I'm certain I don't want to hear it now.

"You're going to be OK," she says and though the thought of what this will entail wearies me, I know that it is true.

Tomorrow, when the lights go on again, I'll call the copy director, who will assure me that an extra week, in light of the circumstances, will be OK. Tomorrow, when my cell signal is able to touch that invisible cord that ties it to the rest of world, I'll find a message from Jess in my voicemail, asking if I'm OK. I'll feel a little foolish for not understanding that we're still friends, and a little sad to realize that's all we'll ever be.

But for now I'm content to see the Hudson bathed in soft light, to imagine that at any moment, the power will come back on and I could be sitting right here when it does; to live in this moment before it becomes a memory told. Before my words strike the page, defining it, destroying it. Before vows of love are whispered and meanings misconstrued.

When everything is still possible.

LYNDA CURNYN is a native New Yorker and the author of the bestselling novels *Confessions of an Ex-Girlfriend, Engaging Men,* and *Bombshell.* She has been published in over fourteen countries and is currently at work on her fourth book. Say hello at www.lyndacurnyn.com.

Small Worlds

GRETCHEN LASKAS

Marnie Haselton is going to Florida to have an affair with a man she met on the Internet.

"It's the only way to save my marriage," she tells the three women who are sitting with her in the kitchen of the Methodist parsonage. After she's announced this, Marnie peers at the women through the steam of her teacup. She is surprised to see that only Janice looks shocked.

"How will that save it?" Lois asks. She is the minister's wife, and she is the one serving the tea, which she mixes and blends together and filters out with a spoon she bought in England during her honeymoon. Lois doesn't look shocked at all, Marnie is sorry to see.

"It will give me something to look back on, you know, this moment of intense passion where I couldn't help myself."

"But you can help yourself." Janice finally manages to swallow the cookies she has been chewing and say something. "You don't have to go."

"I want to go," Marnie says, putting her cup firmly down in the saucer, and listening to the clink. She doesn't want to break the china, just make everyone aware that she can.

"Why?" Lois asks.

"It's silly," Janice points out.

"You've never been out of West Virginia," Marnie tells Janice, whom she has known for more than twenty-five years—since they were in kindergarten. "Don't you ever feel this overwhelming need to just escape?"

"No," Janice tells her.

"Do you have to go so far away?" It is Glenna speaking, in that trebly little voice that makes her sound scared even when she isn't. She's a bit older than the rest of them, but for some reason Lois likes her. Marnie thinks Lois treats Glenna like a pet. "Or find someone closer? Surely you could find someone suitable around here."

Marnie cannot help but look shocked at this herself, and she's embarrassed when Lois laughs.

"You don't understand," she tells the table, for really, none of the women do. None of them can. Lois is married to the preacher, for heaven's sake. Janice wouldn't know about passion if it bit her on the butt and Glenna, well, what man could stand to hear that wobbly treble calling out for him in the night?

"I'm talking about passion. I'm talking about giving in to something greater than myself."

"You're talking about cheating on your husband," Janice says, her own teacup cracking into the saucer. Lois is starting to look concerned, no longer looking at her guests, but at the china, which had been her grandmother's.

Marnie stands up and puts her hands on the table. Her fingers grip into the snowy white cloth. She wonders if she will leave dents in the wood when she leaves. "I'm going," she announces.

"So go," Lois says, whisking the cup and saucer out of harm's way.

"Have a good time, dear," Glenna says.

Janice says nothing, although Marnie waits and hopes just an extra second before stomping out.

When she arrives back home, Marnie listens before she puts the key into the lock. She doesn't think that Guy is home—she doesn't expect him back until suppertime—but lately he's been popping up at the strangest times. Last week, when she was in the chat room with Chad, she didn't even hear Guy until he was standing right behind her.

"What are you typing?" Guy asks, squinting at the screen.

Marnie's hands shake so hard she can hardly type. "I've got to go," she writes to Chad. She clicks and posts, "Talk to you later." More clicks. "See you soon." The conversation darts up the screen, farther and farther away as she types.

"What are you doing home?" she asks Guy, who has given up trying to make out the rapidly moving screen. She'd told him once that she did the bills here.

"Ricky had to take his car in, so I gave him a lift home." Ricky is Guy's boss—if you can call the person who checks things off on a clipboard a boss. At least he isn't moving and stacking them, which is what Guy does.

Chad owns a computer store. Marnie can just picture it, filled with white machines, screens glowing and flickering like white candles.

"I wish I'd known you would be early," she tells Guy, logging off. The screen flashes and turns dark.

"I thought you'd be pleased," Guy says, knowing now that she isn't, but not knowing what to do. That's the whole crux of the matter, Marnie thinks. Guy never knows what to do.

"Oh I am," Marnie says, and looks up at him and smiles. Guy smiles back, but they know that everything is all wrong, has been wrong for a long time.

After that, Marnie always checks to make sure she is really, truly, alone in her own house. Standing there on the porch, she sees Mrs. Fowler across the street, who is waving frantically, no doubt puzzled as to why her neighbor is peering into her own windows. Marnie waves back, shouting something about streaky glass. Mrs. Fowler nods, but still keeps watching until Marnie turns the key in the lock and heads inside.

When she closes the door, she knows there is no one there but herself. The room is dim and cool, the curtains closed. The house smells a bit dusty. The computer stands in the corner. This morning, Marnie placed a vase of flowers on the desk and they are pretty and brightly colored.

Marnie checks her answering machine and picks up the mail. There is nothing unusual. There is nothing that Guy might find. She is very careful. Chad called earlier that morning—Marnie can tell it is his voice—but he only says that it is the library calling, with a book that Marnie had requested. Marnie has always gotten calls like this. She used to read all the time. Guy might have been suspicious if the calls from the library had stopped, which they have, except for the ones that Chad makes. After all, Marnie has no time to read.

She sits down at the computer and turns it on. The air around her smells sweet from the flowers. The hum from the computer sounds like the wind blowing.

The phone lines click and then there is the voice saying that there is mail—real mail—not like the pile of papers stacked in the kitchen. One by one she opens them, hearing Chad's voice speaking inside her head as she reads them. Suddenly, from out of nowhere, from the very depths of space and time and eternity, there is a hum of music and the flash of a box wrapped in bright blue like a present. It's Chad, speaking from the box, all within an instant, a split second, a moment of time. "Are you on?" it reads.

"I'm on," she types back. They have just discovered the instant message boxes. Now there are no more chat rooms. There is no chance that anyone will interrupt them.

"Are you alone?" reads the box.

Marnie smiles and writes <giggle> in her box and clicks it away. She knows all the tech symbols now, from LOL for "laughing out loud" to "NAWY" which

means "naked and wanting you." She offers him a cup
of coffee:-/> as if he was right here with her.

"I miss you," pops up on the screen.

Marnie sighs. "I can't wait to see you," she writes. "I
have never looked forward to anything as much as I
have this."

"I love you," Chad flashes back.

Tears come into Marnie's eyes. This is not the first
time he has said this, but it isn't often. Chad isn't like
that. He doesn't wear his heart on his sleeve for everyone to see.

"I love you too," she types, her hands looking for
each and every key.

She looks at the clock. It is nearly four o'clock. Guy
will be back in an hour, but she doesn't want to take a
chance. So she sets the kitchen timer for forty-five
minutes, the sound of its ticking blending with the
tapping of the keys.

A few days later, Marnie is talking to Chad on the
phone when she hears a knock at the door. She knows
it isn't Guy—he wouldn't knock at his own door—and
she tiptoes over and peers through a side window,
hoping to tell who it is by the car. When she doesn't
see a car and the knock comes again, Marnie tells
Chad, "I have to go."

When Marnie opens the door, she is surprised to see
Lois standing there, standing alone on the front porch.
Lois is hardly ever alone. There is always someone who
wants to be with her, usually at the parsonage.

"Come in," she says, holding the door open.
Marnie knows the house is clean, but she can't re-

member if it is tidy or not. She can't remember the
last time she vacuumed the rugs, or swept the
kitchen. She knows the dining room windows are
filmed from a gritty rain that flew in all the way from
the west coast, across the Great Plains, the weather-
man said.

"It's nice to see you," Marnie tells Lois. Already she
is running through the things in the refrigerator, the
cupboards, the shelves. There doesn't seem to be much
of anything worth offering. If Marnie had known Lois
was coming, she would have gone to the store. There
is iced tea that is fresh, but it came from a mix.
Marnie doesn't think that Lois will want to drink powdered tea. It isn't English enough.

"I wanted to talk to you," Lois says, and sits down
on the couch. Now Marnie realizes that Lois hasn't
come to see her—not in a good way, the way friends
do. Lois isn't here just as Lois; she represents the
church. She represents her husband. She represents
God.

Marnie sits down in a chair. "You're going to tell me
not to go," she says. It is not a question.

To her surprise, Lois blushes. She turns bright red,
and her sandy blond hair that curls around her ears
but nowhere else, looks almost white against her face.
"I don't know what to tell you," Lois mumbles.

Marnie wishes she could think of something to say,
something witty, something that would make Lois feel
better without making Marnie feel bad. It would mean
a lot, Marnie thinks, if Lois were on her side. Because
this is important. She isn't going to back down. It's too
late, anyway. The airline tickets are already bought—

they are sitting in her purse right now, in a dark blue folder with silver letters on the front.

"I wish you wouldn't," Lois finally says. "Let's leave it at that."

"I know what I'm getting myself into," Marnie starts.

"No, you don't," Lois says. "How can you know anything about him? He could be anybody. He could be the next serial killer. Like Ted Bundy. They say he sounded nice too."

"Chad is nice," Marnie insists. She knows this. It isn't as though she hasn't thought about things. About different things that could happen, although they probably won't.

"I just don't understand why you're doing this," Lois says. She twists a piece of hair around her finger. "I know that things between you and Guy haven't been very good, but . . ." Lois breaks off, and looks away. "Look, I don't want to tell you what to do . . ."

"Then don't," Marnie tells her.

". . . but I'm worried about you. This isn't like you."

Now Marnie understands, even if Lois doesn't. What she likes about this, about this whole thing, is that it isn't like her. No one suspected it. No one saw this coming, not even she. In a small town like Fair Springs, that means a lot. Marnie smiles.

"I'm not like you," she tells Lois. This is true. There's no pretty china in the cupboards, no college degree hanging on her wall. Her husband doesn't wear a suit to work and silk ties that a wife has chosen for him, one by one, just for him because she likes them. "I didn't come from someplace exciting like you did."

"Johnstown isn't exciting," Lois says, looking a little surprised.

"You had the flood," Marnie points out.

"That was over a hundred years ago! You're jealous over a flood?" Lois asks. Her voice rises a little.

"I'm not jealous at all," Marnie says, although she gets a twist in her stomach because she knows this isn't true. "But when you tell people that you're from Johnstown, people know where that is. They have a picture in mind."

Lois opens her mouth but Marnie keeps talking.

"But when I say I'm from Fair Springs, West Virginia, it's like a big blank. A big space filled with nothing. When I tell people I'm Guy's wife, they don't know who he is. He doesn't mean anything to them. I don't mean anything to them." She stops talking when she realizes that she's starting to cry. Lois is just looking at her. Looking at her as though she can peer right through her, as though Marnie is made of glass. "You don't understand," Marnie says, crying for real now. "You don't know what it's like."

Marnie cries for a few minutes, then Lois comes over and hugs her. "I wish I knew how to help," Lois says. She hands Marnie a Kleenex from her purse.

"You can take me to the airport," Marnie tells her. This has worried her all day. "I'm flying out of Pittsburgh on the twentieth. At ten o'clock," she adds, blowing her nose, "in the morning."

"I can't . . ." Lois starts. Marnie feels her eyes tearing up again. She's going to start to cry again, any moment now. Lois sighs. "OK," she says.

Marnie smiles.

★　　★　　★

Two days later, Glenna and Janice stop by. When Marnie sees them coming down the street, she knows that they are coming to see her. They can't even come one at a time, she thinks, they are too afraid. At least Lois managed to do that. But as she watches Janice talk and talk and talk and Glenna just nodding, Marnie is suddenly glad that they are together. She couldn't stand to deal with someone on another day. She is getting tired of this, of everything, of everyone.

Guy is angry with her. Marnie can't understand why, as the credit card bill with the airline tickets hasn't arrived yet. She buys phone cards at the Rite-Aid, so he can't trace the calls. But even so, he's suspicious. He knows. Marnie wonders if she looks different. If she smells different. If she smells like a woman that wants to have sex. Maybe this scent turns on Guy without his knowing why. Without him remembering what it is.

She and Guy haven't had sex for a long time. It hasn't been a year, surely not, but Marnie can't quite remember the last time. Not since the miscarriage, the second one, when Marnie carried the baby for four months before losing it. After that she had some tests, which were all just fine. She made Guy take some tests too, even though she was surprised that he agreed. He had a daughter, a girl about twelve, gangling, with braces on her teeth, from his first marriage. Having a baby didn't matter to him the way it did to her.

"There's something wrong with your sperm," the doctor told them, looking down at a chart as he spoke. Marnie wondered why he wouldn't look up.

"I have a daughter," Guy told him.

The doctor shook his head. "It's probably more recent. You work with chemicals, don't you?"

Guy didn't say anything. The doctor sighed. "There is no way to be sure," he said, turning in his chair and looking out the window. "But this is something you both need to know." Marnie wondered how they can know something that they can't be sure about.

"I'd like to talk to your wife a minute," the doctor continued, and Guy nodded his head and got up from the chair. Marnie could hear him breathing, the air going in and out of his lungs so hard it sounded like a pant. His face was pale and sweaty and Marnie forgot all about the doctor and stood up to go with him.

"Please have a seat, Mrs. Haselton," the doctor said. Guy didn't turn around to stop her, so Marnie sat back down. The doctor had finally looked up. Sitting behind his desk he stared straight at her. "This will be hard for Mr. Haselton," he said.

Marnie nodded.

"He's going to need you to be strong. To help him shoulder this." Marnie nodded again. "He's going to blame himself." The doctor peered into her eyes as though he could make her read his mind.

And suddenly she could. She knew what he was saying.

"I'm the one who miscarried," she said. "People think there is something wrong with me."

This time the doctor nodded. He even smiled a little.

"But there isn't," she made a point of telling him.

The doctor shook his head. "With these things it is impossible to tell."

★   ★   ★

Marnie is thinking all this when she hears the knock.
She has forgotten all about Janice and Glenna. Remembering all this has made her tired, and the visit
hasn't even started yet. Maybe, she thinks, if she
doesn't answer, they will go away. There is another
knock. And another. "I know you're home," Janice
calls out, shaking the doorknob. Of course she does.
Marnie would know where Janice is, if she were the
one out looking. That is all part of everything, a piece
of the larger whole.

"Come in," she says, opening the door. Janice steps
in right away, almost shoving her aside. Glenna pauses
and after looking up at Marnie a second, hugs her.

"Do you want something to drink?" Marnie asks.
Suddenly, she doesn't mind the company, even if it is
only Janice and Glenna. Yesterday, when Chad was
working, she cleaned the house and went to the store.
The refrigerator is bursting with things to eat.

"No," says Janice.

"Yes," says Glenna, at the same time.

Marnie goes into the kitchen and cracks ice from
the trays. She can hear them in there, talking about
her. The sounds of whispers hush with the fizzle of
ginger ale, which Marnie pours into three glasses. Janice will want one, even if she said no.

Back in the living room, Glenna and Janice are sitting
together on the couch. They are so close that they look
like children, or a couple on a date. Not a married couple, Marnie thinks. She never sits that closely to Guy.

"Thank you," Janice says, taking the glass. Glenna
just smiles.

"You're here to try to talk me out of going," Marnie says. She sits in a chair and props her feet up on the ottoman. She painted her toenails this morning, so they might as well see. It's a new purple color.

"I'm here to keep you from being stupid," Janice says. Marnie rolls her eyes.

"I think it's exciting," Glenna announces. "I went to Florida once myself."

Janice turns and looks at Glenna, who takes a gulp of ginger ale and shuts up.

"You know how worried Lois is about this," Janice starts to say.

"Lois is taking me to the airport," Marnie tells her. The glass hides her smile, but nothing can keep the smugness out of her voice, and Marnie is pleased to see by the way Janice sits back that this is news to her. News that Lois didn't share. It occurs to Marnie that maybe Lois is ashamed, and she doesn't like this one bit.

"She offered to help me," she continues. Lois did, and Marnie intends to make her keep her word. Lois is always talking about helping people and keeping secrets and sticking to promises—all the things a preacher's wife is supposed to do. All of those things that Lois does. Only this time it's going to help Marnie get what she wants.

"I don't believe it," Janice finally says.

"Oh, it's true," Glenna says. "Lois told me yesterday."

The skin around Janice's mouth puckers. So Lois wasn't ashamed after all, Marnie thinks. She suddenly feels sorry for Janice. No one likes to be the last to know.

"You can pick me up at the airport," she offers.

Janice's mouth stops moving. "No way," she says, looking away from Marnie and taking a drink of ginger ale so big that it makes her cough.

"I'll pick you up," Glenna offers.

Marnie laughs, but she's wishing that Janice had said yes. She can't, after all, ask Guy to do it. "You can't drive all the way to Pittsburgh, Glenna," she says.

"I can so," Glenna answers. She sits up straight on the couch and puts the empty glass down on the coffee table. "I drove myself home from the airport years ago, and I can do it again."

"When did you go to Florida?" Marnie asks. She can't remember it, so it must have been a long time ago. She wonders why Glenna has never told them before.

"Back in 1978," Glenna says. "In August. It was hurricane season."

"Oh," Marnie says. She is watching Janice, who is pretending not to be paying attention to either of them.

"I went with Bud Dyer," Glenna talks on and on and on. "He was having trouble with his wife then and needed to get away."

Marnie is playing with her glass when she finally hears what Glenna is saying. "Bud Dyer?" she repeats. "Isn't he the druggist that was busted for selling pills?"

Glenna nods. "He had problems even then. Reason I was driving home was he was passed out in the backseat of the car, drunk as a skunk." Glenna sighs. "They used to hand out little bottles of booze on the planes back then," she says, as though she flies all the time—a frequent flyer. "It was scarier."

"Why did you go to Florida?" Marnie asks. She can't believe this. She looks at Glenna and wonders if she isn't making it all up. Marnie remembers Buddy Dyer. He flirted with everyone—girls aged four to women at eighty. Marnie remembers putting on a new dress once—she must have been about seven—and walking to the drugstore, just to see if Bud would notice. Of course he did. You could always count on Bud to notice.

"We couldn't very well, you know . . ." Glenna laughs nervously. "Well . . ." She takes a deep breath. "We couldn't have sex here. Bud was too uptight about it."

Marnie's mouth falls open and she drops her glass. The ice rolls on the carpet and Marnie jumps to clean it up. Janice gets up and goes into the kitchen. Marnie can hear more ice cracking.

"You had an affair with Buddy Dyer," Marnie says.

Glenna picks up her drink and tries to drink, but there is only ice left and it hasn't melted yet. "It wasn't an affair. We weren't really cheating on Helen. Buddy wasn't having sex with anybody just then. We thought going to Florida might help."

"Did it?" Marnie has to ask.

Janice comes back into the living room, holding a dishtowel. Marnie can tell that she's upset because she's pressed her hands close together, as if she's about to start clapping. Marnie also knows that the hands are sweaty; they are always damp when Janice gets worked up. Wet isn't the right word, but drip-dry is pretty close.

"I have to go," she says, but her voice, normally so

bossy, is thin and high. She hands the towel to Marnie.

But Marnie won't be distracted. "Did it help?" she repeats.

Glenna doesn't answer. Marnie gets up and starts walking toward the couch, where Glenna is just sitting, watching her.

"I said," Janice raises her voice, "that I have to go."

Glenna stands up and follows Janice. "You call me when you know what time the flight is," she tells Marnie. "And I'll be there." She is almost out the door. "It did make it better, well, a little better. At least I guess it did." Her voice is very low. "I hope it works out for you." Then she smiles. "It had its moments."

Marnie barely gets the door closed before she starts to feel all undone, all loose inside as though she is made of string and someone has untied her. She picks up her glass from the end table and holds it in her hand. The glass is cold and damp, just like Janice's hands are, right now, right this second.

Marnie pitches the glass at the wall and listens to the crash, the tinkle of ice and breaking glass.

From behind the foggy window of the airplane, Marnie tries to act as though she flies all the time. That this is just another trip. A business trip. A place to go. From up here, the land is flat. Rivers are gray, smooth and marked like a pencil line. Above her, the sky is brilliant blue.

She tries not to think about Chad, getting on his airplane out in Houston and flying to Orlando, where he will meet her at the Marriott. It's a nice hotel, three stars, with a pool—she checked, even though he is going to pay for it, since Marnie paid for the tickets. Put them on her credit card, anyway.

Marnie looked up Orlando in all the books she picked up at the Morgantown AAA. She got maps too, although they decided against renting a car. "It isn't like we'll be driving," Chad said once, and Marnie, she's embarrassed to admit, didn't realize what he meant until after they had hung up. She loves looking at the maps, though. They are filled with color—blue for lakes, green for open space, red lines for roads, which are straight and narrow. From Orlando, they spin out like a web, like open fingers, like the veins of leaves.

Marnie looks at her watch. Chad should have been on his airplane an hour ago, but she never can remember because of the time difference. Is Houston an hour behind West Virginia, or two? Once she called him in the morning and it was still dark there.

At least she is away. No one, not Guy or Janice or Lois can stop her now. She is in the air, where they are not, and even if they were to get into cars, if Guy gets into his truck and drives as hard and as fast as he can, he will not find her in time. By the time he got to Florida, it will be all over.

Guy knows that something is going on, although she's been very careful. Last night, when he saw her take her suitcase over to Lois's, he called her horrible names. She told him that she's doing a women's retreat, with some people from the church, but he knows she doesn't like those women. He knows that it's another man, but he just can't figure out who it is. He went into her room, and started accusing her of dressing like a slut.

"It's a church retreat," Marnie yells. "I'm not going to dress like that." But she is. She knows that every piece of clothing in her suitcase, from the bathing suit to the halter tops, to the underwear is brand new. Guy has never seen them. He'll never know the Marnie that she is when she's wearing them. "Call Lois if you don't believe me."

Guy stands up and picks up the phone. Marnie watches him, her arms folded across her chest to keep her hands from shaking. Lois could ruin the whole thing. Lois could tell the truth, the whole truth and nothing but the truth and that won't help Marnie at all.

Guy dials the phone. He stares at her. When someone answers, his face smoothes out. "Reverend Smythe," Guy says, and Marnie tries to remind herself to breathe. Guy looks at her again, and then his entire body wilts. He turns away from her, still talking. "Marnie's over here wondering if she might have forgotten her purse over at your place this evening." With his back turned to her he keeps talking. "Yes." A pause. "Thank you for looking."

He hangs up the phone and, without facing her, he walks into the living room and turns on the TV, as though nothing has ever happened.

The hotel is right on the strip of highway by the airport, at least, this is what the AAA book says, but Marnie can't find the right bus to take her there. She has never traveled alone before, never traveled much at all before, and everyone around her seems in an incredible hurry. Everyone around her knows exactly where to go.

Finally, she calls the hotel and asks for Chad. "He's not checked in," the desk clerk says. His voice is bored, and Marnie wonders if he has tried or looked.

"He must have," she says. "His plane got in over two hours ago."

"He's not here," the clerk says. And he hangs up. Marnie is furious. When she sees Chad, she will tell him that they should find another hotel.

Because she doesn't know what else to do, Marnie wanders around the airport. She checks at the information counter to make sure Chad's flight has arrived, and it has, but maybe he's lost in the airport just as she is. The thought makes her feel better, more like an adult, a person in control. From the information counter she calls the hotel again and finds out where the shuttle bus is. Within ten minutes, she is standing at the hotel counter.

"I'm with Chad Winters," she says. "He should have checked in by now."

The clerk types slowly, using one finger. "He's not here," he finally says, his voice accented and as careful as his typing.

"He will be," Marnie says, not knowing what else to do, she is almost on the verge of tears. She hands the clerk a credit card. After the plane tickets, it is almost full, but surely it will pay for this. Chad can pay her back.

"Room 507," the clerk says, not even looking at the names. For all Marnie knows, Chad has checked in and no one even knows. He could be in room 508 and who could tell? Who could remember? The lobby is filled with people. Orlando is the most crowded place Marnie has ever been.

Marnie lugs her suitcase to the elevator and presses herself into the mass of bodies. She can smell everyone's breath. She looks at all the faces, trying to see the face from a photograph in her purse, looking for Chad, for his smile, for his chin, which looks like a model's. None of them are exactly right, although she stares at one man so long that the woman next to him mouths the word "bitch."

The room is small, but it feels clean enough. The window looks out onto a parking lot. Every space is filled and several cars line the outer curbs. The highway is bright red with lights as the sun is going down. When the room is completely dark, Marnie turns from the window. She turns on the television so she doesn't feel so much alone.

By morning, Marnie has not slept. She has stopped crying. There isn't any point to crying because no one is there to hear her. Even if Chad is in the next room, sitting on his bed with the bright blue flowers and the pillows that are too soft and smell of antiseptic, there is no way that she would know.

She goes into the bathroom and looks at her face, wondering if this is why Chad never came. She had sent him a picture, a really good one, right after a haircut and a new perm. She was wearing her sister's earrings and a necklace that Guy had bought for her when they were dating. It's funny, she didn't think about Guy buying her the necklace when she put it on for the picture, but she's thinking about it now, and she isn't even wearing it. The necklace is sitting on her dresser back at home, next to a picture of Guy's daughter and one of Marnie's nieces.

This morning, she looks awful. Her hair is frizzy from the humidity and her eyes are bagging like dirty clothes. She runs her hands over her skin, noticing how scaled and wrinkled it seems. She is over thirty now. It is time for fine lines, but surely, not this, not yet.

After a shower, Marnie puts on her new clothes, tearing off the tags. She wanted Chad to know how much the trip meant to her, that she would buy new clothes. Only her shoes were old, because everyone knows wearing new shoes will give you blisters. For a long time, she sits there, trying to make up her mind, to decide what to do. She thinks about calling Chad, but chickens out. What if he answers the phone? Is that really going to make her feel any better?

Yes, it would.

Marnie reaches for the phone and starts pushing buttons, but the operator breaks in and she realizes that this phone isn't like the one she has at home. This phone is foreign, with blinking lights and codes.

"I wanted to know if there have been any calls," she asks, trying to sound like she stays in hotels all the time, as if there are dozens, hundreds, thousands of people who might want to call her, instead of Chad who is the only one who knows where she is. She knows that the operator knows she is lying, but she doesn't care.

"Is the red light on your phone blinking?" the operator asks. Her voice is flat and dry. Marnie wonders how many times she is asked about this every day. Knowing that everyone asks makes her feel less stupid.

"No," she answers.

"Then no one's called," the operator says, and hangs up.

Marnie hangs up too. There isn't any point in calling Chad. He isn't here, and that is all that matters. She hasn't come here to have a relationship, to get married, to make a friend. Marnie came to Orlando for one thing, and it looks as though she isn't going to get it.

Two tickets to Disney World came with the room. Marnie wonders where she put them—when she checked in, she really didn't care. She hadn't come to Orlando to see Mickey Mouse, but now that she's here, now that she has nothing else to do, she might as well go. People will ask her when she gets home what she did, and it will be good to have something real to say.

She takes the shuttle bus from the hotel, and stands in the ticket line for half an hour before she realizes that she can go right inside, that she doesn't have to wait. The entrance is crowded with people, all dressed in nice pretty clothes, just as new as the ones Marnie is wearing. The buildings of Main Street are bright and colorful. Everyone looks like birds; everyone seems to be happy.

A few steps in and Marnie sees Cinderella. At least she thinks it is Cinderella, although it might be Sleeping Beauty—she can't quite remember which one is which. The woman is tall and blond and beautiful. "Take my picture," she hears people say. Little girls surround Cinderella, and flashbulbs are popping around her but the woman's eyes never blink. Chil-

dren come up and hug her, although Marnie notices
that more than one hangs back, grasping a mother's
skirt, which may be new, but can't compete with Cinderella's dress.

"Can I see the glass slipper?" a little girl asks in an
accent that makes Marnie think of Scarlett O'Hara, or
maybe it isn't the voice at all, but the belled skirts.
Cinderella pulls back the dress to show her foot, which
is bare and tanned, encased in clear plastic. Jellies, just
like the ones Marnie used to wear back in high school.

A few feet away is Mickey Mouse, and here there
are as many boys as girls. Mickey doesn't really have a
face, just that big heavy mask that bobs up and down
as the children talk. Most of the children are wearing
Mickey Mouse ears, like the ones they wore on
Mickey Mouse Club. Everyone here seems to know
everybody else, to belong to someone. Marnie decides
to buy some ears.

For more than an hour, Marnie wanders around the
park, not going in and doing anything, but looking.
She has spotted Goofy and Tigger and Dumbo, but
the other women characters from the more recent
movies are ones that she doesn't know. She's looking
for Snow White—at least she knows what to look
for—but hasn't found her yet.

There are long lines everywhere. The sun is beating
down on everyone, but no one seems to care. Babies in
strollers look like they are melting, and most of the
adults are wearing sunglasses. When Marnie runs into
Cinderella again (at least she thinks it is the same one)
the woman's hair looks as hard as glue. She heads back
into a dressing area and Marnie follows far enough to

watch Cinderella throw back her head and guzzle down a jug of water before wiping her mouth with the back of her hand.

"You can't be in here," someone tells her—a woman dressed like Rabbit, from Winnie-the-Pooh.

"I'm sorry," Marnie says. "I was just hot."

"Sorry," the woman says, not sounding for a moment as though she means it. Marnie can't really blame her—she must be broiling in the plush yellow suit. Marnie is sure that Rabbit, at least the Rabbit in the story, is a boy rabbit, a male. She wonders who is under all the other costumes. She wonders if Mickey is really a Minnie in disguise.

During a parade, when the line is a bit shorter, she waits to get on the boat for "It's A Small World." Even all the way out here, she can hear the song, chanting through the lyrics like a children's choir at Christmastime. Still, even with the parade, the line is long and people are starting to lose patience. "How much longer?" the woman ahead of her mutters, juggling a toddler from one hip to the other. Her husband is pushing a stroller filled with toys and bags.

When she is halfway in the line, when it would not be easy to get out, Marnie realizes that she has made a terrible mistake. As long as she kept moving, kept walking, kept looking, she didn't have to think about why she was here. But now, after standing in line for twenty minutes, she has nothing else to do. She has already noticed the ketchup stains on the girl's shoes and the rip down the sleeve of the woman two groups in front of her. Marnie knows most of the children's names, which are ordinary enough, except for one that is called Isaiah and a little girl with a frilly dress and more jewelry than Marnie owns, who is called, at least by her parents, Jason. She keeps seeing children. They are all around her.

Marnie doesn't want to think about Chad, but suddenly, she can't think about anything else. She wonders if Chad is here, standing in line with another woman—with a wife, with a family of children all of whom look like her. The other woman. The real one. He said he wasn't married, but he also said he would come and he didn't, so how is she to know? How is she to believe in anything?

The music is giving her a headache. All those happy, happy little voices that never, never stop. She can see the boats up ahead, and watches the people get on and off. That man, that one right there, with the dark hair, could be Chad. Or the red-haired man behind him. He had sent a picture, but who can say? After all, Marnie had sent him a picture but it didn't look much like her, not the way she looks on any given day. But it wasn't someone else; it wasn't Cinderella. She did not pretend.

For a moment, Marnie realizes that Chad could be a woman, like the woman dressed as Rabbit. No, that can't be right. She's talked to him, heard his voice. But now, standing in this heat, standing in this line pressed against all these people she does not know, the happy happy song playing over and over and over, Marnie can't remember what the voice sounded like. Was it deep, like Guy's? Or was it high and soft, like Reverend Smythe's? Her daddy had a girlish voice—not that you would mistake him for a woman—but what if Chad was only pretending? What if it was all a joke?

Marnie feels her stomach turn over. She hasn't eaten all day, but that isn't going to stop her from throwing up. Instead, a little girl steps on her toe and she bursts out, "Ow!" without thinking. The little girl just stares at her, and reaches for her grandmother's hand. The grandmother looks like Glenna—Glenna who came to Florida with her lover, with a man, and came home a woman. But maybe it isn't true. Maybe Glenna just made the whole thing up. Maybe it isn't the little girl's grandmother after all.

Standing right there in the line, Marnie bursts into tears. The women and men about her look at her with fear and gather their children around them. "Stand by Mommy," one of the women says to her son.

"But the lady's crying," the boy says.

"It's not our business," the woman tells him.

Marnie knows it is their business. Not this woman's perhaps, but it is the business of many, many people. Lois's business, and Glenna's and even Janice's. It will be the business of everyone that she knows, because they will know. They will know that she came to Florida to have an affair with a man she met on the Internet. She has done something that none of them has ever done. That none of them would ever do. Right now they think that they know what she is doing, and whom she is doing it with.

But she isn't doing that. She's here.

"It's your turn," the young woman running the ride tells Marnie.

"I don't want to go," Marnie tells her, still crying, although not as hard.

"The exit is to your left," the woman says, already turning to the next person in line.

"I'm going, I'm going," Marnie tells her, jumping into the boat so quickly that the boat rocks back and forth as though it is in the high sea. She sits on the seat and looks at the dolls that move and sing. She knows the ride is only a ride. That it will end and she will have to get up and leave the boat. That she will have to leave Disney World, leave Orlando, leave Florida, and take the plane home. Marnie knows that, even as she wonders what it means, to go back to West Virginia. Sitting here in the boat, she looks at her watch and puts every person that she knows into their proper place. Lois will be at the Ladies luncheon today, because it is Tuesday. Glenna will be there too. Janice will be at home, frying bacon or slicing tomatoes. Guy will be at work, lifting boxes, moving them from here to there. At every moment, on any given day, Marnie knows exactly where they are.

But she is here. She is in her boat, and she is sailing away.

GRETCHEN LASKAS is the author of the highly acclaimed novel *The Midwife's Tale*. An eighth generation West Virginian, she now lives outside Washington, D.C.